THE TIME OF
MUTE SWANS

Also by Ece Temelkuran

Deep Mountain: Across the Turkish-Armenian Divide
Turkey: The Insane and the Melancholy

THE TIME OF MUTE SWANS

a novel

ECE TEMELKURAN

Translated from the Turkish by
Kenneth Dakan

Arcade Publishing • New York

First English-language Edition

First published in Turkish in 2015 by Can Publishing under the title *Devir*

This is a work of fiction. Names, places, characters, and incidents are either the products of the author's imagination or are used fictitiously.

Arcade Publishing books may be purchased in bulk at special discounts for sales promotion, corporate gifts, fund-raising, or educational purposes. Special editions can also be created to specifications. For details, contact the Special Sales Department, Arcade Publishing, 307 West 36th Street, 11th Floor, New York, NY 10018 or arcade@skyhorsepublishing.com.

Arcade Publishing® is a registered trademark of Skyhorse Publishing, Inc.®, a Delaware corporation.

Visit our website at www.arcadepub.com.
Visit the author's site at www.ecetemelkuran.com

10 9 8 7 6 5 4 3 2 1

Library of Congress Cataloging-in-Publication Data is available on file.
Library of Congress Control Number: 2017952974

Cover design by Erin Seaward-Hiatt
Cover photo credit: iStockphoto

ISBN: 978-1-62872-814-9
Ebook ISBN: 978-1-62872-816-3

Printed in the United States of America

To my nephews, Max Ali and Can Luka,
who lived through
the July 16, 2016 coup attempt
at the same age I lived through
the September 12, 1980 coup.

I wonder what you will not forget
and what you will remember.

The swan sighed, stretched his neck and, with a wave of his wings, rose and flew off, touching the water with his wings. He rose higher and higher and flew alone over the mysteriously rocking waves.

—Leo Tolstoy, "Swans"

Contents

Author's Note

To the uninitiated, Turks across the socioeconomic strata appear to be not only on a first-name basis but one enormous family. Surnames were not widely adopted until 1934, and even today they are rarely used in social settings. Instead, appended to first names are respectful terms of address such as *bey* (for men) and *hanım* (for women). Less formally, one's elders can be addressed as uncle, aunt, elder brother (*abi*), or elder sister (*abla*), among others, depending on their gender and age. Finally, it is not unusual to refer to someone by combining their occupation with their first name. In this novel, we have retained the honorifics *bey*, *hanım*, *abi*, and *abla*.

Some of the characters' names include letters with diacritical marks used in Turkish. The following is a simple guide to pronouncing the letters with those marks:

Ayşe	eye-sheh
Önder	urn-dair
Hüseyin	hoo-sayn
İlyas	illy-ahs

THE TIME OF
MUTE SWANS

Prologue

Straddling the continents of Europe and Asia, the Republic of Turkey is the realization of a centuries-old dream, for better or worse. In the middle of secular Turkey is its modern capital, Ankara, and in the middle of that city, a park. Mute swans swim in circles in a small pond in the park. They never leave. Every day, at least a few of the people strolling through the park stop and stare at the swans, as though the swans might know something they themselves cannot remember having forgotten.

In the summer of 1980, Turkey was a hot spot in the Cold War. The restless spring of '68 had bequeathed to our country armed revolutionaries on university campuses, and far-right militias clandestinely supported by the state. Just like today, Turkey was going through a period in which the lines between good and bad, between beautiful and ugly, and between right and wrong were blurred with blood. As civil unrest raged in the cities, everyone did their best to cope. The country had become ungovernable, but life went on, as though the coup everyone expected would continue to march closer yet somehow never arrive. This story, which starts at the beginning of the summer and ends with the September 12, 1980 coup, describes Ankara, the heart of Turkey, during that summer so many have tried to forget.

A strange coincidence . . . Swans began migrating from Siberia to the Turkish coast of the Black Sea for the first time in 1980, the year of September 12 coup, one the bloodiest in modern history. The swans continued to visit Turkey every year after that. Then, in the summer of 2013, a summer in which the people rose up against an authoritarian regime for the first time since 1980, the swans suddenly stopped coming.

UNIT 1

This Is My Family

The Bakar Family
LIBERATION NEIGHBORHOOD, ANKARA

If I were dead, would they love me more?

That's what I said inside. I was hanging in the air between our balcony and the one next door. All the lights in the neighborhood came in through my eyes and went down to my belly, filling me up. A song was playing in Jale Hanım's apartment on the floor below: *"This can't be! Am I dreaming?"* Somewhere, potatoes were frying golden. Down in the darkness, the big brothers raced through the streets, *bang bang!* The mulberry tree in front of the police station whispered *whoosh whoosh.* A car horn went *a-hooga!* over on the avenue. It was all perfect, just perfect. Everyone was so happy. But there was something in their voices. Something like fear. And they were shouting:

Mom said, "Aydın, be careful! We'd better not do this, Aydın!"

Dad said, "Sevgi, they might start shooting again . . . Don't make me talk about it in front of her!"

Grandma said, "Son, don't talk while you're holding her. You'll end up dropping her, God forbid!"

Samim Abi said, "I've got her. You can let go now. I've got her. Tonight, Ayşe's going to watch the Olympics! You're going to see

Mischa the Bear too, aren't you, Ayşeyevich? We're bringing Moscow right to your feet tonight! We're having a movie night and a vodka night, too. You've turned eight, haven't you, little miss? I think you're old enough now. Ha-hah!"

Ayla Abla said, "Samim, put down that cigarette at least! And stop shouting, or they'll hear you!"

And it was right then, with everything so perfect—and the song from Jale Hanım's apartment asking, "*If I die of misery, will your heart not ache, even a little?*"—that the power went off. No one said a word. The mulberry tree kept whispering. I closed my eyes and said to myself:

If I were dead, would they love me more?

With my eyes shut tight, everything came to a stop. And I felt like I could keep it all inside me forever, a picture.

My Name Is Ayşe Bakar

So, noontime came today and it was hot. It's summer, the hottest summer ever, Grandma says. And there's no water again. At naptime, like always, Grandma falls asleep reading to me. When she starts going *tsss tsss*—the book, *1001 Peaches*, rising and falling on her belly—I know I can finally get up. I'm bored. So bored! I'd better be careful as I peel my cheek off Grandma's sweaty arm. Slowly. Slowly. There's a sticky sound. I stop and wait. *Tsss tsss*, goes Grandma. Good! She didn't wake up! I can see the police station as I kneel on the bed. But they aren't playing any games there today. It's empty. I get up and walk through the house. It's all mine and it's exciting.

I'm the only person who knows where some stuff is. There's a bobby pin trapped under the carpet in the living room. A pin in a corner of the bookshelf. A button standing on end on the windowsill. There's a flattened lightbulb box in the back of the coat stand drawer. They're all hiding. "Hush," they say. "Don't tell anyone." I check one by one to make sure everyone's there.

The button came off Dad's shirt while he was watching the news, something about the "left-wing militants of the Revolutionary Path."

His eyes stayed on the TV the whole time as he put the button on the windowsill. It rolled and slowed like a little wheel, then came to a stop, still on end. "Oh!" I said, clapping my hands. But Dad didn't notice. He was talking to the TV: "They've executed those boys. God damn them!" We had a good laugh, me and the button.

But the bobby pin got hurt. Mom opened the newspaper in the morning and she was going to make eggs for breakfast. She bent down over the paper, her face close, like a pigeon eating corn, and that's when the bobby pin fell out of her hair. With a tinny little scream, it hit the floor. It was going to stay there, but Mom was feeling around for her slipper and her foot gave the pin such a push that it went right under the carpet. "Aydın! Aydın! Get up! They've taken in İrfan!" Mom yelled. Yes, the bobby pin had slipped under the carpet. I checked, but it wanted to stay there. *Hush*!

The pin that settled in a corner of the bookshelf is sneaky. It titters like the whiskered fox who stole the crow's cheese. It's making fun of Grandma. I was on my way out the door when I got a tear in the skirt of my school uniform—and at that exact moment the school bell started ringing! Grandma came up with two pins.

"Come over into the light. I can't see."

When one pin was enough to do the job, she put the other pin on the shelf. It rolled into the corner without a sound, and there it stayed.

"Be careful you don't prick your knee, sweetie."

That's when the pin first tittered. *Tee-hee, tee-hee.*

"Grandma! The pin's tittering."

"My goodness, the things you say, Ayşe."

Grandma has these blue and red threads under the skin of her cheeks that show up when she bends over.

"That's what pins do, sweetie. Just ignore it."

It made me laugh so hard. But Grandma wouldn't remember any of that now. She forgets things. Just like the way she forgot all about the flattened lightbulb box in the back of the coat stand drawer.

The phone rang. "Yes, how can I help you?" Grandma answered. "What did you say your name was? Önder? I'm sorry, Sevgi isn't home right now. Just a moment, let me write your number down. You did say the Ankara Hotel, didn't you?"

Grandma squashed a lightbulb box, found a pencil stub in the drawer, and scribbled a "seven" with a long crook, a "two" with a curli-cue, and a "one" with a fat line underneath. Grandma whispered some-thing and handed Mom the box with the number as soon as she got home. But Mom tossed the box into the back of the drawer when Dad stepped in right behind her.

"It's nothing important. Leyla called. Mother took down her num-ber."

Mom seemed scared. But why?

I checked the box later. It didn't say Leyla! It didn't say Önder either. There was a number and nothing else. Maybe Grandma forgot to write down the name. Or maybe she doesn't know how to write "Önder." The lightbulb box went *hush!*

I'm also the only person who knows how things really smell. Grandma doesn't know how nice she smells and that her room smells just like her. The muslin scarf hanging on the back of her door smells like, "Oh, that was such a long time ago. I can barely remember." The guest slippers smell like, "My goodness! Bless your heart!" The dresser drawers smell like talcum powder, and her nightgown smells like butter cookies. It makes you giggle if you close your eyes and sniff. The sewing machine smells like a ticking clock and an afternoon nap. It's a Zetina, and it has a brown smell, too, like sugary oil.

The smell of sleep in Mom and Dad's room is gone now. It happens every morning. I slip under the covers of the unmade bed hoping to catch that smell, but it always gets away.

So I go to the living room next. When I'm home all alone things happen to the furniture. They don't have any eyes or mouths, but if you look carefully, without blinking, things happen. That's when the table starts grumbling inside. It keeps quiet in the evening when every-one's home, but in the daytime, when Grandma's sleeping, you can hear it. The table smells shiny. The backs of the chairs ache sometimes, and so do the sides. They smell like ointment then, like Grandma's make-it-well ointment.

The living room is always sad and silent, and so is our house. It's not like Jale Hanım's house. Oh, Jale Hanım's our neighbor. Because she always paints her nails red and wears high-heeled slippers and plays music night and day, her house smells like scented erasers. Fruity, but fake. The news on TV doesn't make Jale Hanım and her family sad. Her husband doesn't have a mustache, so nothing bothers them. Jale Hanım reads bright magazines about movie stars and singers. About happy things. Mom and Dad don't like our neighbors much. I can tell. We're different. We get sad when we read the newspaper, and Dad's mustache is just like the ones on the dead men on TV.

When I grow up, I'm going to be like the women we see in the news—which is a little scary, but I can't help it—and then Mom will see me in the newspaper. Dad will look at my photo. They'll start yelling. "Sevgi!" Dad will say; "Aydın!" Mom will say. That's the only time they talk to each other. When somebody is suddenly gone.

"My goodness, Ayşe! Haven't you slept at all? Ayşe, what's wrong, sweetie? Why are you crying? Did you have a bad dream? It was just a dream, dear. Now come along and help your old grandma. Let's make some Russian salad before your mom and dad come home, for when you go over to Samim Abi's house tonight. Remember? You can help peel the boiled potatoes, and then we'll drizzle some olive oil, nice and slow, and watch it turn into mayonnaise. You always love that part. Come along, dear."

The sweat in the crack between Grandma's boobs is nice and shiny.

Meet My Mom, Sevgi İzmirli Akalın

"Here we are, meeting like this, years later, completely out of the blue, and we still go through the pleasantries. 'How are you, Önder?' 'Fine, and you?' It's a scene straight out of a movie, but our lives . . .

so much of our lives has ended up on the cutting room floor where it belongs, Önder."

The sun breaks out from behind a cloud, lighting up the white tablecloths of the Captain's Restaurant. Önder is trying out his old smile, the one from back in '71.

"Don't talk like that, Sevgi! You sound so mournful. Anyone watching us would think we were here not to *eat* the sea bass but to attend its funeral."

I was unable to force a laugh. I kept my hands in my lap and tried to get a straight answer.

"Önder, why have you turned up after all these years?"

I covered my mouth, as though that's where the tears flow from. Önder started reaching for my hand but ended up grabbing his glass of rakı instead. He blinked at the sun. He opened and shut his mouth. He picked up the manila envelope resting on the next chair.

"Would you hide this for me, Sevgi?"

Now the envelope is resting next to the sea bass.

Anybody else would have asked, "What's in it?" Anybody but me.

"What do you want me to do with it?"

"Hide it in the national archives."

That's when I looked him directly in the eye for the first time since we'd sat down. It's at times like this, when there is serious and clandestine work to be done, that I know how to look at Önder. We were both arrested before we learned to gaze at each other like lovers.

"For how long?"

"Until better days, Sevgi."

Now it was my turn to reach for a glass of rakı, to blink at the sun and gaze into the distance.

"If by 'better days' you mean until the troubles pass, they won't pass, Önder. We'll pass before the troubles do."

"No, that's not true. Listen. I'll tell you what's going to happen."

Önder laughed knowingly as he turned his attention to the grilled fish. He lifted the top fillet off, exposing the white flesh below. Expertly. So, Önder knows how to fillet a fish. I know how he cursed as they beat the soles of his feet, how he lectured the other students at meetings, how he got everyone to chant slogans, how he shouted himself hoarse selling revolutionary magazines on street corners. I even know how he breaks down and cries. But I had no idea Önder could fillet a fish.

"Sevgi, there's going to be a fascist coup soon."

Önder knows how to sever the head, talking all the while.

"I don't know what will happen to me. Back then, after you disappeared . . ."

Önder knows how to lift out the tender flesh of the cheek and deposit it on my plate with the tip of his knife.

"I mean, after you decided to get married, things got really crazy, really intense. Do you remember Nasuhi Abi? He warned us back before the '71 coup that it would get so bad we wouldn't be able to keep track of our friends' funerals. And he was right."

The spine came out in one clean piece.

"I'm getting old. Sevgi, you and I were the same age, weren't we?"

"That's right, Önder. And we're still the same age."

"I'm not so sure about that, dear."

And with that one word, that "dear," he stripped my spine clean! But he isn't done with me yet.

"If you ask me, those who play it safe age more slowly than those who risk everything. What do you think, Sevgi?"

He's lashing out at me for abandoning him in prison all those years ago and for marrying Aydın. I came here prepared for that. He'll carve out my cheeks next.

"Don't misunderstand. Sevgi, I hope you don't feel any regret or guilt. You did what you had to do. We can't go through life wondering how different choices would have led to different outcomes. It's best to assume that there was no other way, that we had no choice. Gazing back into the past is like peering into a kaleidoscope. Blink, and the images shift and change, become jumbled, take on new forms. . . ."

He gently pulls the bottom fillet off the rib cage, still in one piece.

"Perhaps life won't make any sense until it's over. We'll never be able to understand what we went through. I mean, the magazines and the pamphlets, the declarations, the theories—they'll probably come to nothing. I hope I'm not making Lenin spin in his grave!"

He laughed. I, a reluctant companion to his mirth, laughed too.

"Sevgi, here's what I've been thinking. We need a record not of what we lived through—that's already been documented somewhere—but of what we won't be able to remember. There are things we'll never forget, but there are other things we won't be able to remember. Anyway, look inside the envelope if you want. After all, I know there's no power on earth that could make you talk."

The question in my mind flared and fizzled: Would Aydın talk under torture? I'd never wondered that. Would my husband of nine years break under torture? I know Önder wouldn't. I wouldn't. But Aydın? I need to chase these thoughts out of my head!

"Sevgi, if you agree, I'll give you a few more envelopes later. To keep safe. Something of us should be in that damned Parliament building, Sevgi. By the way, I'll be staying in Ankara for a while.

"What for, Önder? What's this all—"

"Because they say the fish is fresher in Ankara than in Istanbul. That's why."

His chuckle caresses my cheek. In the ten years we've been apart, who taught him to laugh like that, to laugh like a man? I'm much better off not thinking. I take the manila envelope. Önder is smiling as he looks at me. I'm sure of it, even though I'm not looking at him. I stare into my handbag, the eyes of my mind resting on Önder as he looks at me. I fumble as I stuff in the envelope, accidentally folding back the corner of a page in *The Lovestruck Cloud* borrowed from the Library of Parliament for Ayşe, creasing the Population Census of 1971 copied for Aydın, and knocking the jar of honey sideways. That goddamned jar of honey!

"Sevgi Hanım, are you saying you let your daughter read Nazım Hikmet?"

So asked Abdullah Bey, the deputy director of the Library of Parliament in carefully modulated tones, an unctuous bass, just as I was about to leave work early. He then produced the sarcastic laugh I associate with members of the Justice Party, that laugh that makes me feel cornered and defensive.

I've developed ways to cope, though. Sometimes I simply change the subject.

"Abdullah Bey, the stenographers sent over the transcripts of last week's general assembly. There were too few deputies in attendance for the assembly to convene this week, only two pages of names on the roll call list. I thought we might combine this week's roll call with last week's transcript, and send a single binder to the archives."

"It's your party that's preventing Parliament from functioning, Sevgi Hanım. If a presidential nominee were finally approved, the nation would be able to conduct its business. But no! Typical leftists. All they ever do is censure, vandalize, and obstruct."

And sometimes I act like I haven't heard.

"Abdullah Bey, I'm leaving early today—I've already told you—to take my daughter to the doctor. I've informed the director."

"Of course. You and that communist director have sorted it all out. Naturally."

Abdullah Bey's fleshy lips glisten beneath his clipped, almond-shaped mustache. There is obscenity in his gaze, a grossness that makes me shudder and look at the floor even as I am absolutely certain that the oaf attributes my bowed head to feminine timidity. The disturbing gleam in that lecher's eyes, eyes that persistently pry and violate.

And then, so abruptly I am left speechless, Abdullah Bey's gaze has turned into that of the earnest peasant with a heart of gold.

"Sevgi Hanım, I brought you a jar of something special. My home province of Erzurum is famous for its honey. They say it fortifies the body. You can give some to your little girl."

Should I refuse his honey? That would be wrong. And Ayşe hasn't had any honey for such a long time. He means well, so why turn him down? I murmur my thanks as I take the jar. I'm just about to turn and leave when I find he isn't through with me.

"One hundred lira, Sevgi Hanım. That's only enough to buy two packs of Samsun. It's chicken feed."

I'm dumbstruck. I can't really give the honey back. I pull out some money and hand it to him, just to put an end to his nonsense. Will I be ambushed by these sly little deceits for the rest of my life?

Abdullah Bey shuffles away, and I walk off in the opposite direction.

"Sevgi Abla! Wait a second!"

Nazlı, the intern, comes running up with a book, holding it against her body so Abdullah Bey won't see the cover.

"Could we put this in the archive?"

"Let me see what it is first."

"*Mini-manual of the Urban Guerrilla*, by Carlos Marighella."

"Have they released a new edition? We used to call it 'the triple-hole book.'"

"What?"

"Back in '71. The cover design had three bullet holes. For some reason, that book was always available when everything else was banned. It was our guide to guns and armed resistance."

"I know what your generation thinks of mine. They think arms cause all the trouble. Arms aren't the cause, they're the result."

I can't believe that book has popped up on the very day I'm meeting Önder! Now's not the time to think back to those months in prison after the coup. To that pair of trousers so like the ones Nazlı is wearing now. Trousers I left behind in the superstitious belief that if I took any possessions from my cell I was more likely to end up back in prison. I tell myself not to think about how I rushed into marriage with Aydın and how I abandoned Önder while he was still serving his sentence. Not to think about how I vowed never to revisit the past when Ayşe was born a year later. Not to think about how I cried as I nursed my baby and my mother said my 'romantic exploits' were over forever. Now Nazlı the intern—Nazlı the naïve revolutionary of today—raises an eyebrow and gives me, the old revolutionary of yesterday, an appraising look.

"Can we put it in the archive?"

I could explain things to Nazlı, warn her. But she has raised an eyebrow at me, and I know she'll need to travel the path we trod and be given jars of honey.

"Go and ask Abdullah Bey."

Stop clawing at the cigarette burn on your cheek. If this shoe keeps rubbing my heel raw I don't know how I'm going to make it through the day.

Nothing ever escaped Önder's gaze, so before I met him at the restaurant I applied some makeup to conceal the burn mark—the scar—on my cheek. It's not very noticeable any more, but Önder might see it, only Önder might see it. Aydın was too tactful to ever ask about it!

And then Önder did spot it, there, in the restaurant. He sighed as he looked at my cheek. That's how I knew.

"We never had time to talk, Sevgi."

"Who needs to talk? There's no need."

"You're right. Maybe later . . ."

"There is no 'later,' Önder."

Don't say it. Don't say it. Don't. But I do.

"We used up all our 'laters.'"

I ran scared, and he never asked me why I blamed him. I'd have cried if he did. I'm glad he didn't.

What did we do after that little exchange about 'later'? Did we eat the fish, or did the fish swallow us up? Did we talk about the opposition leaders, discuss Parliament, mouth platitudes? We were in a movie about a couple of lovers reuniting after many, many years. Why was the dialogue so wrong?

We're shaking hands. Did we always shake hands? I suppose we did. Didn't he use to kiss me on the cheek? I suppose he didn't. So, you can become lovers without making love, even once. I wonder what it's like to be made love to by Önder? Don't think. Don't think.

I should walk. . . . I should walk for a bit. Leave behind the scene with the white tablecloths and the rakı. Return to reality. These shoes are killing me. Now that Önder isn't around to see, I step on the backs of my shoes, exposing the heels of my feet, as though I'm wearing high-heeled slippers. I stride down Cinnah Avenue, shoes flapping, and end up in front of the supermarket with no recollection of having walked so far, but feeling as if, in a sense, I've been walking nonstop for nine years, 1971 to the present. Rubbed raw all the way.

"Lightbulbs! They've got lightbulbs!"

The crowd in front of Gima passes along the joyous news. I get in line. I don't know why. Because I'm sure to need a lightbulb one day? The other day, my neighbor, Jale Hanım, was talking to my mother Nejla in the stairwell as she returned from a meeting of the Children's Welfare Society. I stared at her red, red lips as she jabbered.

"You won't believe it, Nejla Hanım! I heard patients are expected to provide their own lightbulbs and blankets before they're admitted to the hospital. How our nation has fallen! Imagine that, our hospitals don't have any lightbulbs! I blame it on all this anergy, this pitting of brother against brother."

I didn't tell her she meant "anarchy," not "anergy." Nor did I point out that that they aren't "pitting brother against brother." What they *are* doing is arming Grey Wolf commandos to gun down Leftist youths. I knew better than to try to pierce Jale Hanım's thick hide and thick skull.

At the supermarket, I finally reached the front of the snaking line and bought two bulbs, without bothering to check their wattage. I was trying to make room in my handbag when an old man touched my arm.

"Take it, my girl. I happened to have one in my pocket. Put it on your foot."

The man was holding out a small bandage. I studied his face, wondering if he was going to ask for money.

"Go on, take it. Your foot's bleeding."

I walked off without a word, disgusted with myself. I wonder if Aydın is home yet?

Meet My Grandma, Nejla İzmirli

"Young or old, we're all the same distance from death, Jale Hanım. Young people know there's no getting around it, and that's why they're always so agitated, forever running around in circles."

That's what I said to my neighbor Jale Hanım. I was standing in the stairwell, peering at the front page of the weekend supplement. OUR READERS CHOOSE WHICH SUNGLASSES LOOK BEST ON BÜLENT ERSOY, one headline read. Either Jale Hanım didn't understand what I meant, or she was ignoring me.

Or perhaps she really didn't hear me over the music blasting in her apartment. A loud song with nonsensical words that sounded to me like: "Honky Ponky Torino."

Jale Hanım had yelled out to me as she brought a copy of *Weekend* from a back room to the front door.

"Honestly, Nejla Hanım. That family of yours always looks so glum. I suppose they think it's frivolous to have a little fun. Reading about the rich and famous in these supplements makes life a bit more bearable, and they do come with a proper black-and-white newspaper, after all."

I gave Jale Hanım a hard look, but she kept chattering, her flat and unflappable voice ringing in the stairwell.

"Oh my, get a load of this. . . . It says Zeki Müren had some plastic surgery done in France. And look at this picture of Bülent Ersoy wearing bright red lipstick. He's turning into such a fairy! My word, is that hilarious or what?"

"I'm sorry to have troubled you, Jale Hanım. I thought one of your colorful magazines might cheer Ayşe up. The poor thing's cooped up at home all day. We can't let her run around outside, not like we used to. And *Cumhuriyet* newspaper doesn't have horoscopes, or anything about *Dallas*."

"It's no trouble at all, Nejla Hanım, old girl. Come in and I'll make you a Nescafe."

"Nescafe? What's that?"

"Our friends bring it back from Germany, hidden away in their suitcases among their underwear. It's a powder. You add a spoonful to hot water and it turns into coffee, just like that."

"Don't trouble yourself, Jale Hanım."

"What are you talking about? It's no trouble at all! Come in for a bit. We can watch *Dallas* while you sip your coffee."

I regretted having let her badmouth Sevgi and Aydın and wanted to say something with a sting, something to embarrass. That's why I chose the words:

"Young or old, we're all the same distance from death."

Jale Hanım gave me a quizzical look, raised her eyebrows, nodded, shook her head, and burst out laughing. I decided not to have any of her nest-coffee, or whatever it is they call it. I was upset.

I was climbing the stairs holding the supplement when that old song began echoing in my head again.

"Ever since I vented my sorrows I have not known peace."

How auspicious that we woke up to that song this morning. If a song gets stuck in your head, it means you need to give voice to your troubles. There's nothing wrong with having a chat and a laugh with Jale Hanım, but I'm not in the mood for it right now. Some days are like that.

"The world shows no mercy and I have no friends."

Whenever Nesrin Sipahi started singing on the radio, my late husband would say that her voice rose and fell like a flag rippling in a spring breeze. May he rest in peace. He was a stern, unsmiling man, but İlyas Efendi could become lively and eager, if only a couple of times a year.

"In this new world, I find no trace of the old world."

Sometimes Jale Hanım has a point. I'd suggested the other day that we go to a music hall to see Nesrin Sipahi perform. My daughter and her husband reacted by looking even gloomier. Aydın raised his head from the paper to tell me that Nesrin Sipahi sings for fascists now. Sevgi added that she performs at Grey Wolf gatherings. So, even Nesrin Sipahi is forbidden to me now!

We were serious people, too, back in the day. We struggled to make ends meet, but we knew how to enjoy a torchlit procession during holidays, a concert at a music hall, a play at the community center. Young people today never take a break. When I asked if socialism had its own national holidays, they mocked me, not even bothering to answer my question. And my granddaughter is getting bored. It's perfectly understandable. Don't go out in the street, it's dangerous; Independence

Park is full of fascists and off limits; you never know when trouble might break out, so don't sit in Swan Park. What's the poor girl supposed to do all day? I'm at my wit's end when it comes to inventing new games for Ayşe.

"Ayşe, let's make a ragdoll. . . . Come on, sweetie, I'll bake some puff pastry and you can make your own little pastry on your own little tray. . . . Dear, let's make some puppets and we'll put on a show. Would you like that?"

Sevgi warned me that "anything can happen" and we should keep Ayşe unaware of the danger . . . but how, exactly, do we do that? On one side of our apartment building is the student dormitory housing the nationalists, and on the other is the Political Sciences campus crawling with leftist students. The police station is directly across from the window of Ayşe's bedroom, so how can we possibly keep anything from her? One day, they detained some leftist students and didn't give them anything to eat. Mothers were throwing cookies up to the windows of the detention cells, so I had to make up a story.

"Why, what do you think they're doing, sweetie? Can you guess? They're playing a game with their moms, seeing who has the best aim and who can toss the most cookies right through the window."

Now, every time someone is detained Ayşe starts throwing roasted chickpeas at the station, as though—God forgive me for saying this—she were scattering corn for pigeons. How many chickpeas can we get in the window? That's our new favorite game. Thankfully, the detained kids play along. Only leftists would do that, and they're the ones who always get rounded up.

We've also started playing a game we call "Safety Drill," a game I pray we never have to play for real. Sevgi warned me that they might come to our apartment. Ever since, me and Ayşe have been doing a drill every day. "The bogeyman's coming," I say, and off she goes to her hiding place. I've been getting more and more superstitious. It's gotten so bad now that I can't start the day in peace unless I wave my hands over Ayşe every morning, pretending to create an invisible dome to keep her safe.

"Here, and here. I enclose Ayşe in a dome of light and crystal, of satin and pearls. Presto. She is sealed in her dome. May God protect her!"

Ayşe thinks it's funny. She's in stitches every time I do it. Well, at least someone in this house still knows how to laugh. Sevgi has been even more aloof ever since that phone call. I can't really come right out and ask her why this Önder fellow is calling, now can I? Whenever I bring up the past, she always says the same thing:

"Why didn't you visit me in prison, Mother?"

My husband had told me that the military would never mistreat their young prisoners, that our children were safer in prison that out on the streets, where they could fall under the influence of the communist rabble rousers.

I would have visited Sevgi if my husband hadn't said that. Or did I, too, secretly think she needed to learn her lesson? How were we supposed to know? We'd never even heard about torture back then. The torturing of young women. Who could imagine such a thing? How could we have known? And even if we had known. . . .

This Önder of hers must be an old friend from those days. Something's up, or she wouldn't keep it from Aydın. But if Aydın would only act like a man and be more protective of his wife. He should take her out from time to time. My husband was as stern as they come, but he'd still arrive at home once in a blue moon with a basket of Amasya apples or a couple of meringue cookies. "I know how much you love them," he'd say, not realizing I didn't, not really. To this day, I don't know how he got it into his head that I loved apples and meringue cookies. Anyway, husbands and wives should try to please each other. My daughter and her husband never even smile at each other anymore. Maybe this socialism of theirs forbids flirting and romance, too. Socialism wants its followers to be drab and stern and prepared.

Jale Hanım's blotchy husband is supposedly devout, but she's always all dolled up. If it weren't for her, nobody would be talking about was happening on *Dallas*, who's performing at the music hall, the latest fashions. But whenever Ayşe lets slip something she has heard at Jale Hanım's, we both get scolded. Just the other night, when Ayşe put on the dress Jale Hanım had the tailor make out of some leftover satin from her evening gown, Aydın became furious when he saw his daughter decked out like a little bride.

"Nejla Hanım, we're not raising our daughter to be someone's bride," he said to me, all stiff and huffy. Sevgi said nothing and looked the other way. I guess she wanted Ayşe to learn a lesson. My, how that child sobbed herself to sleep that night. What was the big deal? She's just like any other normal girl.

If only Ayşe had a playmate. There aren't any other children her age in our apartment building. If only she had a friend. Ah! Now I understand why that Nesrin Sipahi song has been running through my mind all day: *The world shows no mercy and I have no true friends.*

Young people today don't know what true friendship is. Jale Hanım is fine enough, but I'd never consider her a true friend. Bless her soul, there's something a little vulgar about her. Whenever Sevgi demands an explanation for why I've been over at Jale Hanım's, I tell her the fuse blew and I needed some copper wire. Jale Hanım's daughter, Feride, popped down to the basement and fixed it in no time, I tell her.

The last time I fibbed, Sevgi asked, "Does the fuse blow every single day, Mother?"

"It blows every day, dear. Every day! The current is too strong in our flat. I have to keep it grounded. If I didn't, we'd all be dead by now!"

I've been feeling sleepy all morning. I wish noon would come so I could read to Ayşe from that book with the peaches and then have a long nap. When everyone goes off to Samim's for a potluck dinner and some vodka, I'll stay home and listen to the radio for a while. Maybe they'll play Nesrin Sipahi, and I'll flick though *Weekend.* I might even pour myself some almond liqueur! I'll wear nothing but my slip, nice and cool. And I really should finish that poem I started the other day. I'm not at all happy with it so far. *The leaf does not fall, the tree casts it forth / The spirit perseveres, the body wastes away.* I wish it were evening and Sevgi and Aydın were home, safe and sound. How much longer is our country going to go without a president!

Meet My Dad, Aydın Bakar

This place is thick with cigarette smoke again. I wonder if the detective has come yet?

"Welcome, Aydın Bey. The detective is waiting for you at the usual table. He's already ordered a drink. Shall I get you a double?"

"Get me a rakı, but don't set a place for me. We're going out to dinner tonight. I won't be staying long."

"Let me give you a hand. You're all weighed down. I can carry something for you. What's that? *Report on Deaths in Turkey and Their Causes.* What's that all about, Aydın Bey? Is the state making you whitewash the murders it commits?"

"I'll keep that binder, Reşit. Just take this box off my hands, would you? Please put it somewhere safe and don't let me forget it when I leave."

I can see Nahit biting his nails over at our table. What kind of detective bites his nails? It must be something important or he wouldn't have wanted to meet up on such short notice.

"Aydın Abi! I'm over here. Good to see you. How's it going?"

"I'm exhausted, Nahit. I've been carrying a box around ever since I left the office."

"A box of what?"

"A chandelier, Nahit. A chandelier."

"What for? You can't even get lightbulbs these days."

"A friend of mine is one of the experts fired by our beloved Nationalist Front government. He's selling chandeliers now. He has a master's from Harvard, but you know what it's like. He's been replaced by a fascist. They stuck him right in my office."

"So you've done it again, huh?"

"Nahit, what else could I do? He and his wife just had a baby."

"Last week you bought a set of duvet covers, and the week before that a set of steel pans. Do you think you can subsidize the whole Turkish Left by buying all that junk?"

"And do you think you can make a difference by catching the odd killer?"

I tried to smile, but couldn't. I could see Nahit was in a foul mood, too.

"Are you reading that disgusting newspaper again, Nahit? Please don't bring that crap in here."

"Look at this column here."

"Please don't, Nahit. I deal with those kinds of guys at work every day, wondering when one of them will stab me in the hallway."

"I was looking at something Necip Fazıl wrote: 'Ode to the Grey Wolf.' And to think they have this crap on TV every day! Listen to this. '*You, the scourge of the communist, the terror of the godless, the horror of the stateless, the dread of the dishonorable—*'"

"Please, Nahit. Spare me."

"Just listen for a couple more lines. You haven't heard anything yet. It calls on the Grey Wolves to—"

"Nahit, do you read this to torture yourself or what?"

"It's my job to monitor right-wing terror organizations, and this is the kind of thing they read for inspiration."

"I know that. But I can't bear it."

"And not only that, the bastards write letters to each other in this paper. Look, they have a column called 'From One Grey Wolf to Another.'"

"It sounds like some kind of lonely hearts column for fascists."

"Things have really heated up since those left-wing militants killed Gün Sazak. The fascists are out for revenge. They say they're going to make the sky crash down on the communists. I've got to monitor what they're up to."

"Put that paper down for a minute. Why did you want to see me today? Has something happened?"

"Yes, it has. But you looked so bummed out. What's the matter?"

"Bummed out! You sound like one of those American wannabes."

I immediately regretted having snapped at him. He shrugged it off, but I could tell I'd hurt his feelings. I decided to change the subject.

"I heard a pack of Samsun costs fifty lira on the black market now. Is that true, detective?"

He fixed me with a stern but sympathetic look, as though he were about to grill a suspect he knew was innocent.

"What's bothering you, Aydın?"

"I don't know what to do, Nahit. I really don't. Our tea man at work, Hasan Efendi . . . he lives in the shanty town in Rambling Gardens. Anyway, his house burned down. To be more precise, his house was burned down. He says the Grey Wolves did it. I know he and his family are left-wingers."

"I'll investigate it if you want. We'll find out who did it."

"Investigate what? His house has been torched. Now his family's homeless. And I was already saddled with this damn chandelier. I didn't haven't anything to spare, couldn't give him a cent. I guess that's what's been bothering me. And he told me a story about a well—"

"Let's not get into—"

"What do you think's at the root of all this, Nahit?"

"The root of all what?"

"All this hatred. It's spinning out of control. I mean, what makes two men in the same socioeconomic class, both of them at the bottom of the heap—"

"Well, you're a lot better at political analysis than I am, but—"

"Political analysis! All I know is that there's a curse on this country. Sometimes I feel like we're being made to pay for something, some original sin. I look back at our history. There was the coup in '71, when they hanged so many of our kids. But that wasn't the first time it happened. So, I go further back, to the '30s, the early days of the republic, when so many people were executed. But that wasn't when it started either. Perhaps, I say to myself, things first went downhill when the Ottomans moved out of tents and into palaces. You know, when the early Ottomans first began seizing young boys in Balkan villages to put them into the service of the sultan. Some of those orphaned boys later rose to high positions of power, ran the state even. Perhaps those boys' mothers cursed us way back then. Or could it be that—"

"Hold that thought for a second. A friend of mine just stepped through the door. A rookie journalist. Timur! Out on the beat, are you?

What's with the raincoat on a sunny summer day? Who do you think you are? Columbo? Aydın, Timur covers criminal cases for *Cumhuriyet*. He's all bundled up so nobody knows he's packing. Don't worry. He's one of us."

Panting, the young man named Timur placed his hands on the table and shouted: "All hell's broken loose! They're trying to avenge Gün Sazak!"

Everyone in the *meyhane* was looking at us.

"Shit! Sorry for not introducing you. Timur, this is Aydın. He's a demographer from State Planning. Aydın, mark my words, this Gün Sazak business is going to be the breaking point."

Timur wasn't going to give Nahit a chance to sit, that much was clear.

"Nahit Abi, I was wondering if you could point me to one of your guys dealing with left-wing terrorism. Are there any leads on who killed Gün Sazak?"

Nahit downed the last of his rakı, grabbed his cigarettes and lighter, and motioned for Timur to follow him.

"Aydın, let's get together again soon. We found a new witness in that case you were wondering about."

I changed the subject to stop Nahit from blabbing about it in front of the journalist.

"Have you heard anything about Liberation, Timur? That's my neighborhood."

"Things are going to heat up in Liberation tonight. The Grey Wolves have already set up an interrogation room in their dorm. I heard they kidnapped some leftist kids in Liberation Park and took them there. And if the leftists from the Political Science Department decide to retaliate . . . well, it's going to be one hell of a night."

"Damn it! We live right between the dorm and the department."

I'd better get home before dark. The strings securing the box are digging into my hand. At the entrance to Liberation Park, two young guys wearing suits have stopped a family with four kids. The family look like they've just arrived from some village. There's no way they could have known that the park was under the control of the Grey Wolves. One of the young guys gets up in the face of the father, who must be in his forties.

"Where are you from? Are you a leftie?"

"No, brother. I swear it!"

"Show me your ID. Are you a commie?"

The pregnant woman pulls her children closer as one of them starts crying. The girl looks like she's about Ayşe's age. I wonder if I should get involved. The principal of Liberation High School tried to help someone the other day and that's when they nabbed him. Then he was tortured for days. The village mother is still trying to gather her children close, and she's hitting one of them. Typical response to oppression in this country. Bullies are never confronted; the weak are bullied.

These strings are really cutting into my hand. I wonder if Sevgi got home safely?

UNIT 2

This Is My Neighborhood

The Akgün Family
RAMBLING GARDENS, ANKARA

"I think it's flying. Is it flying, Ali? Pull in the line a little. Then we'll know for sure."

I pull in the line like Hüseyin Abi says. It cuts at my palms. Does that mean the kite's flying? I think I can hear it: *flap, flap, flap.*

There's so much noise in the garden of our burned-down house. Black ashes rise into the air as the girls sing and dance. They're having another fake engagement party. The fake bride-to-be has green eyes. She's pretty.

I wonder if the kite's flying?

Hüseyin Abi is good at building things. He goes to the Technical University and he's going to be an engineer. Not just anyone gets to go to that university. Only the guys and girls who wear green leftist parkas. I heard Hüseyin Abi say he wanted to cheer me up after my house burned down. That's why he made me a kite out of red paper.

I can't see the kite because the big sisters are dancing in the lantern lights so the big brothers can meet out in the back garden. And anyway, the power has been cut again, so the streetlights are dark. Tomorrow morning I'm going to tell everyone how Hüseyin Abi made me a kite and we flew it at night. I hope I can get all the words out and speak fast, like everyone else.

Hüseyin Abi reaches out and feels the line, real quick. He's in a hurry. When the electricity comes back on the fake engagement party will end. The girls will take off their dresses and be wearing jeans. The secret meeting will be over. Everything will stop when the lights come on. The guys call out from the backyard:

"Hüseyin! We're starting!"

"I'm coming," Hüseyin Abi says. They can't have the meeting without him. He's the chief of the neighborhood cell.

"Ali, I know you can't see anything right now. The kite was flying, but it must have got tangled in something."

I can't answer right away. It's not that I'm retarded. I'm "introverted." That's what the *dede* from the village told my mother. He called me a "serious boy" and said they should let me be. The dede is such a wise old man that everyone listens to him, even my mother and father.

"Ali . . ."

Hüseyin Abi tugged the line. He swallowed, making the lumpy thing on the front of his throat go up and down.

"We're going to have to cut it loose. It got stuck somewhere. We'll never find it in the dark."

Now nobody will believe me when I tell them in the morning that we flew a kite. What if Gökhan says it was just one of my dreams! I can't tell Hüseyin Abi not to cut it. I can't even ask him if it really flew.

They're calling Hüseyin Abi again.

"Hüseyin! They can't keep dragging out the engagement party. The fascists will bust in on us if we don't hurry."

Hüseyin Abi pulled out a switchblade and cut the line. The string in my hand went limp and died.

"We'll make another one, don't worry."

Hüseyin Abi is playing with his mustache, his hand on his hip, his body bent like a question mark. He pats me on the head and grabs me by the shoulder, pulling me against his leg.

"Revolutionaries don't let little things like this upset them. Don't pout. We'll do it again. We can always do it again."

When I wouldn't let go, he sliced through the line so he could take the ball of string. I was left with a piece of string in my hand. It was light as air and all I had left. My favorite book burned up in the fire. *The Paul Street Boys*. Ernő Nemecsek burned up, too.

"Come on, I'll take you over to the meeting with me."

My school uniform burned up. I can't go to school or to the library. I can't look at *The Wonderland of Knowledge* encyclopedia set.

"You're eight years old now. You've grown up. You got circumcised last week, you and all those other boys. You're not a kid anymore."

I put the piece of string in my pocket. The left one. I've got my other strings in the other pocket. I've got a list in that pocket too, a list nobody should see. My head got all heavy again. But I'm going to the meeting with all the revolutionary big brothers. Hüseyin Abi is still playing with his mustache.

"If you're like this because your house burned down, don't be sad. We'll all pitch in and build a new one. Some of my friends from the university will come too. We'll do it together. Don't look so sad! What's a house anyway? It won't take more than a day to build a new one."

We walked past the giant pot in the front yard. They're cooking bulgur. Enough to feed everyone. The water I got must be gone. The container is lying on its side. I got so tired carrying the water down the hill from the fountain and then up the hill to our house. It was only enough to make tea. The girls are carrying the tea over to the guys in the back yard. I can see their jeans under their skirts. They shouldn't let anyone see. They mustn't. They're revolutionaries. The TV sits in the dirt against the fridge. Uncle Laz saved them both. But the cords are all white, like they're dead. As dead as my strings.

Mom's sitting cross-legged on the ground, her head in her hands. A couple of the aunties are rubbing her shoulders. The aunties talk so much, especially when someone is sad. They keep talking and talking. I listen to them.

"Aliye Hanım, you can stay with us until you get a new house. We'll take turns. Stop worrying. Let the kids finish their meeting. . . . It won't take more than a few days to throw up some walls and a roof. Aliye, you should be grateful nothing happened to the children. . . . How did they know you weren't at home? . . . What do you think? The bastards are always watching us from the opposite hill. Aliye Hanım, you didn't have any valuables in the house, did you?"

Mom looked up at the women. "There was the picture of my brother Sait. It's the only one I had."

Hüseyin Abi is tall and he keeps looking over at the hill across from us as we walk.

"Never mind, Ali! Don't let those fascists see you looking sad. They'll be watching us from the hilltop. They burned down your house, but we'll get our revenge. Do you understand that they were getting even with us for capturing their hill last week? Well, what else could we do? It was the only way we could get water. We'll decide what action to take at this meeting. And now that Gün Sazak's been killed, they'll really go wild. We'll stand strong, and we won't be intimidated. All right? Now cheer up. We'll all stick together."

Dad is looking at the black ashes of the house. There are some socks in the ashes. The men clasp their hands behind their backs. That's what grown-ups do. Dad doesn't say anything, but the other uncles keep talking to him.

"I'd never have expected it of Laz the Muslim. Turns out he's not such a bad guy after all. He hauled out the fridge on his back, all by himself, didn't he, Hasan Efendi? Good for him! He's a real hero."

"We've got to teach those fascists a lesson, Hasan Efendi. Those bastards will burn all our houses down if we don't do something. The boys will decide how to deal with them."

Hüseyin Abi looks at one of the girls passing by, watches her dancing and singing.

Hüseyin Abi laughs.

"They must be so fed up at having to sing and dance. It's a good smokescreen for the fascists, but the police are going to realize something is up. I mean, who holds an engagement party at a burned down house? Right, Ali? Anyway, don't worry. The police wouldn't dare come here. They're a bunch of boneheads. Boneheads! Come on, Ali. Laugh!"

I never know when I'm supposed to laugh or not.

"Ali, I'm going to tell you something important. I know the other kids make fun of you for not talking much. Don't let them get you down. You're smarter than them, you know that? You'll be going to Technical University one day. Ali, pay attention when I'm— Shit!"

The power came back on and the streetlights started burning. They could see us now. Mom stood up. The uncles and my dad started clapping their hands to the music. I pulled all my strings out of my pockets.

My Name Is Ali Akgün

"Ali, what will you do if they cut yours all crooked? Or snip it right off?"

"Ali, you'll end up like Bülent Ersoy."

Hamit started yelling at the other boys in the bed of the truck. But why is he trying to sound like a woman?

"Poor little Ali swallowed his tongue again. That's how scared he is."

They're all laughing now. But like they're crying, too. Everyone's wearing the capes and the sashes and the fancy hats with the feathers that the municipality gave us. Hamit yells at Gökhan.

"Gökhan! Your buddy's scared."

"Get off him and leave him alone," Gökhan says. That's what Gökhan always does. Because he's big and I'm skinny. He gives Hamit a shove. The truck bed is rocking, but Gökhan makes his way through the boys, comes up and throws his arm around my shoulder.

"Ali, don't cry! You hear me? Are you getting all weird again? They won't cut off very much. Just the skin at the tip. Don't cry, okay?"

I'm not going to cry. It's just that everyone is shouting so much. They're probably thinking about the times their pee-pees got caught in their zippers. That's why they're talking so much and so loud.

"Ali! If you're scared, just think about going to the fun park after-wards. The mayor closed the park today just for us. There will be hun-dreds of boys, all the ones whose parents can't pay to get their kids circumcised. They even have bumper cars!"

The boys are all laughing and talking about their pee-pees. So is Gökhan, but then Hüseyin Abi sticks an 8-track into the player. He turns it up so loud! He always plays Cem Karaca.

Here in prison everyone is full of advice.

It's so noisy. It's happening again. The weirdness. Gökhan takes off his hat and pulls off some silver braid.

"Here, take it."

I hold the braid between my fingers, hunching over it. I bring it right up to my face. I'll hold it just so, between my two fingers, and stare at it. That's what I'll do. At least until it passes. The weirdness.

"Ali! Don't let them see you doing that. You know what they're like."

I turn my head from side to side. I hold on to the string, tight. It helps me, makes it all stop. When I look at the string, I don't see any of them. Everything is still. The string doesn't move. Not unless I make it move. But when the others look at me, I put the braid into my pocket. Right away. I keep it in my pocket, along with all my other strings.

"Ali, look at me. Look at me! Okay. That's better. Are you listening to me? Was it the fascist boys down the hill who took your red car? If it was, tell me. You said Hüseyin Abi made it out of tin. Did he really? Or were you having one of your dreams again?"

I shake my head. That's all I do. I don't need to speak.

"Why didn't you ever show your car to me? If it was a dream, just tell me."

I shake my head. That's what I'm supposed to do.

"Hüseyin Abi is nice to you, isn't he?"

I open my eyes and look at Gökhan. But I keep my mouth shut.

"He's a revolutionary, just like us. They captured the hill across from us the other day. Did you see Hüseyin Abi that day?"

Of course I saw him. I even helped Gökhan gather up the bullet cas-ings. We can't let the police find any casings, that's what Hüseyin Abi said. They mustn't see. They mustn't see. We went to the stream that smells like shit and threw the casings into it. Gökhan always wants to talk about what we've done. I remember everything. Maybe my head will explode one day because I never forget anything.

"What do you mean you want water? Are you an Alevi? What's your name?"

I don't say a word. I don't talk to fascists.

"Speak up. Are you a rightist or a leftist?"

I don't say a word. I don't talk to fascists or the police.

"Leave him alone. He's a retard. He can't even talk, the Alevi bastard."

How am I supposed to know if they are fascists or not? It's better not to talk. Ever.

"We beat this kid up the other day. He was too stupid to yell. We took his toy car, but we let him keep his string."

They're making fun of me, because they're fascists. When I grabbed the string, it cut my hand. It even bled. That string's in my pocket now.

I never forget anything.

"Children, forget all about your old teacher. I'll be your new teacher from now on. Your former teacher was involved in anarchistic activities and is now gone. He was a terrorist. I understand he distributed some subversive materials in the classroom. Please hand in everything he gave you."

I'm not giving her *The Paul Street Boys*. I haven't even finished reading it yet! And besides, Teacher Ruşen had a mustache just like Hüseyin Abi's.

"Children, at our special year-end show we're going to do ballroom dancing. Now what are we going to do?"

"Ballroom dancing!"

I kept my mouth shut. The only ones shouting were those from the other neighborhood.

"Now, I want all the boys to tell their mothers that they'll need white shirts, black trousers and a bowtie."

A bowtie? Is that something fascists wear?

"What is that? That's a terrorist symbol, isn't it?"

The new teacher with the shiny red lips pulled my eraser so hard that the string dug into the back of my neck. Gökhan was the one who made an eraser with a fist and a star on it. It was his eraser, not mine. But I didn't say anything. The teacher might be a fascist. I don't have any money to get a new eraser. All I have is the string the eraser was hanging from. I put the string in my pocket.

I will never forget.

"Where will we get a bowtie?"

How would I know?

"How much does a bowtie cost?"

How would I know?

"We haven't got any money, son. Your father gave half of his wages to the union. We'll find a way. We'll get one. We still haven't got you shoelaces, but we'll find a way to get a bowtie. Here, take this and use it to tie your shoes."

The string is short. Way too short. I put it in my pocket.

I can't forget. My head's going to blow up. I wonder if the boys in the back of the truck ever feel that way? Maybe they do, but they feel better when they talk. Maybe that's how they forget. That's why everyone talks so fast all the time. Sometimes, when Mom says something is wrong with me and they should take me to a doctor, when she is really, really upset, I try hard to make long sentences and to finish them fast.

"I've got so many things in my head, Mom. I feel better when I read, when I look through the encyclopedia. I don't just look at the pictures. I read the whole page. Don't tell my teacher, though. She doesn't like me. She likes the boys from the other neighborhood and she doesn't like Teacher Ruşen. He would let me run the flag up the pole and hold the string. He would teach me the words to folk songs. The red-lipped teacher wouldn't like Hüseyin Abi either. She makes us sing: *Walk the path of honor, the path of victory. Awaiting you is the dawn.* She doesn't like us because we live in Rambling Gardens. Hüseyin Abi lives in the Gardens, too, but he's going to be a civil engineer. Mom! Do you know what that is? It says in the encyclopedia that it's 'the branch of engineering concerned with the design and construction of such public works as dams and bridges.' Civil engineers know how to make little red cars, too. But the fascist boys stand guard at the fountain and beat up anyone who comes with a water container. And they steal our cars, too. That's because we're proletarians: 'a social class comprising those who do manual labor or work for wages.' Fascists hate proletarians. Fascism is 'a political theory advocating an authoritarian hierarchical government.' Fascists make fun of boys scared of getting circumcised. Mom, don't worry about me. Workers of the world unite! When the revolution comes, my strings won't get mixed up anymore."

When I do that, talk fast and long, sometimes my mother looks scared. She gives me a bunch of string. I stop talking and I stare at the string. When I don't talk, Mom gets sad. But when I do talk, she gets scared.

The truck is rocking back and forth, the music is loud, and Gökhan won't stop talking.

"You know, that day when Hüseyin Abi and the others planted a flag with a star and fist on the top of the hill. Remember how he shouted? What was he shouting?"

I say it to the silver braid in my hand.

"Workers of the world unite!"

"What? Speak up."

"Workers of the world unite!"

I shout it out. The music stopped. Everyone is looking at me. Gökhan yells at the other boys.

"Didn't you guys hear that slogan? Say it again!"

"Workers of the world unite!"

Slogans should be said three times.

"Workers of the world unite!"

I hold tight to the silver braid. Gökhan slaps me on the back.

"Good one, Ali. You made everyone say it!"

Then everyone starts laughing. Their hats get all crooked from laughing so hard. Their capes get wrinkled. They make so much noise I hold my strings tighter, the ones in my pocket too.

Meet My Mom, Aliye Akgün

"Is he breathing? Doctor, is my baby boy breathing?"

If only the doctor cruel as a gendarme hadn't slapped him so hard, maybe he wouldn't have turned out that way. Oh, the way that doctor smacked my little lamb on his bottom, the way he jerked and shook the poor little thing. Nobody's lifted a finger against Ali since that day, the day he was born. And Hasan wouldn't dare hit him, not with me around!

Ah, Hasan. Ah. He told me the shantytown would have a view of the presidential palace in Çankaya. Ah! Way back when we were married, I should have come right out and asked him why he thought that mattered. Did he think we'd get our water from the president's well?

"Let's have another baby," he says now. "One child isn't enough." Does he think our children will grow up playing in the president's garden? I mean, when has the state ever done right by us? It's true we were barely making ends meet in the village, but here they're trying to kill us. We nearly got burnt alive. We lost everything we had . . . everything except for that damn bowtie! The whole house burned down, but not that bowtie. Why couldn't the shopkeeper have let me return it? Would his shop have gone under if I had got my 100 lira back? No! But he knew what I was. If I hadn't been there at the same time as those two women in their showy head scarves, maybe he'd have taken it back. But he'd figured me out. So no way!

"Peace be with you, Hadji. Have you got any red nylon thread?"

"Have a blessed day, Hadji. I wanted to ask you something, too. Have you got any 50-weight ivory thread for lacemaking? Fifty-weight would be about right for that cushion cover, wouldn't it, girl?"

"Peace be upon you, ladies. Let me check and see if I have any."

"Hadji, you wouldn't believe how hot it is out there. And to go without water in this heat!"

"Hadji, it's those shameless anarchists who are to blame. Well, when the mayor is a closet communist you can expect water cuts and power cuts."

"Isn't it the truth, sisters? They keep collecting the neighborhood kids to take them to those anarchistic theaters. Instead of putting on plays for children, why don't they collect the garbage? The stink and the filth is everywhere. And they call this the capital city!"

"Some play about peaches, probably? Like anyone would want to see that!"

"Ma'am, what are you using the red thread for? I've got all different sizes."

"Well, Hadji, we're signing up for a contest for housewives. I'm going to make a heart-shaped cushion, in red. Just give me whatever's cheapest."

"Speaking of red, have you heard the news? They torched the house of one of those communist Alevi families living up in the Gardens. The whole house went up in flames!"

"Those people have got bombs and rifles and even submachine guns. May they burn, may their houses crash down on their heads."

The bearded shopkeeper in the prayer cap turned his attention away from the two head-scarved women and gave me such a dirty look!

"Yes? What do you want?"

I've got a bare head and I wear baggy pants under my skirt. He'd figured me out.

As I pulled the bowtie out of my handbag the two women looked me up and down. They'd figured me out, too. They don't know much, but they know an Alevi when they see one. If only I hadn't needed to return that damn bowtie! It's all that teacher's fault!

"No, something hand-sewn or fashioned out of ribbon won't do. The students must wear matching costumes. That's how it's done. If you're unable to get Ali a real bowtie, I'm afraid I'll have to pull him out of the dance performance."

And then that teacher with the yellow hair got all high and mighty. That cruel woman was threatening my boy's pride! She's the daughter of an army officer, she says, and wanted a position in the shantytown so she could do good, and the children here all have dry, peeling hands, so she'll get them lotion, and they should eat more fruit and get more protein or they'll grow up retarded. Oh, the way she looked at me when she said the word "retarded." I couldn't ask her if she was mocking us, or what good all that protein had done her. And then there was the way she said I needed to take my boy to the doctor. Supposedly in a whisper, but everyone heard her. Everyone! I know she's the type to report young revolutionaries, but I'll still try to be the bigger person. What would she do if she saw her name written on the wall: FASCIST TEACHER NALAN, GET OUT OF OUR NEIGHBORHOOD! She'd run around saying, "They're trying to kill me!" Her officer of a father wouldn't be able to help her then. This is our neighborhood!

The shopkeeper hadn't yet had a chance to open his mouth when one of the women said, "Look, the edge is scorched"—as if it were any of her business. But I held my tongue. Then the other woman whispered: "That's what they wear at their Alevi candle rituals." That's when the shopkeeper snickered and I said:

"You know an awful lot, lady!"

I don't know why, but that's what came out. I said it again, without meaning to:

"You know an awful lot."

Then the words came rushing out:

"All our problems come from bigots like you. Here's something else you don't know. Well, listen and learn. This is called a bowtie. A bowtie! It's what modern people wear!"

The shopkeeper started shouting.

"No talking politics in my shop! Move along, lady. It's burned anyway. I won't take it back. Get going! Godspeed!"

I'd surprised myself and felt a little embarrassed. I stepped outside. Why on earth was I sticking up for bowties, anyway? You'd think I wore one myself. I felt like laughing, or crying, and put it down to nerves from all that had happened since yesterday.

We stared at the ashes of the house. The flames had finally died out. The neighbors kept yelling and screaming. Something inside me was gone. When my beloved little brother, my Sait, was tortured to death in prison, the same thing happened. But the first time it happened was long ago, when I was still little, and the gendarmes took my father away. I don't know if it's the heart trying to protect itself, or what, but when someone goes, when someone dies, when the house burns down, even, it can feel like nothing has happened. My heart doesn't ache. I'm not crushed. I just feel empty. Now it's happened again. It's as though I never had that house. If you asked me where the kitchen used to be, or asked me when my father brought me a bobby pin from the city, or asked me how much I laughed when he flapped his arms and crowed as he gave me a rooster-shaped lollipop, or asked me what my brother's voice was like, what his hands were like: I don't know if I'd be able to answer. My memory's been wiped clean. My heart's full of holes. Empty. And I don't even know if another hole has opened up now. I don't even wonder if all the things that have flown from my mind ever existed in the first place.

I didn't even feel like lamenting as I stared and stared at the ashes. There was a folk song . . . back in the village, Bercuhi would sing it. The only thing I can remember is: "*Its rose inside a glass*." Poor Bercuhi was the only Armenian left, and nobody spoke her mother tongue. Hasan remembers that song, I'm sure, but he'd get cross if I asked him for the words now. "What on earth made you think of that at a time like this?" he'd say.

If only Ali would grow up fast and go to the university. I'll give him his uncle's green parka, still stained with blood. Now he doesn't even have a photograph of his uncle. It burned up in the fire. All that's left of Sait is a few drops of dried blood. I'm glad I hid the parka in the coal cellar. These youngsters can get their guns from the coal cellar, too, and do what they want with them. It's different now. Death doesn't mean anything. The newspapers don't bother to list the names of the dead. Two revolutionary students were killed, three revolutionary teachers were murdered, five lawyers were slaughtered. I can understand *their* newspapers not writing any names, but *our* newspapers don't do it either anymore! We Alevis raise our kids to be fearless; the front lines are full of them. And they're the ones gunned down the most, too. My Ali is a weakly boy. He wouldn't be able to take it. He needs to grow up quick. Him and that damn bowtie of his.

Ahooga!

"Aliye! Aliye!"

"Teslim, is that you? You scared me!"

"How do you like my new horn? If you're on your way home, I can give you a ride. Don't climb up this hill on foot. What's the matter? Didn't they let you return that bowtie?"

"No, that heartless bigot wouldn't take it. Now where will I get the money to feed the young people coming over to build us a new house?"

"My brother's getting married soon. Give me that thing and I'll give you 100 lira."

"I can't do that."

"Hand it over! Here, take this. I don't need it. It's only enough to buy a couple packs of cigarettes."

"Here, take the bowtie. It's a wedding gift from me. And put your money back in your pocket. There, I stuck it in your pocket myself."

"Don't worry about feeding everyone. Most of their families have plenty of money. They'll get themselves something to eat. Besides, they're revolutionaries."

"I can't do that. They'll get weak and hungry. Drop me off here, would you? I'm going to stop by the corner grocer's."

"Sorry about trying to give you money. . . ."

I can see I've hurt Teslim's feeling. Two packs of cigarettes! Doesn't he know we never talk about money?

Grocer Mustafa never manages to air out his store. It always smells sour from the open tins of sheep's cheese.

"Come right in, sister. Welcome. I'm sorry about your house. I heard it burned down, but I haven't had a chance to come and see you. Is there anything I can do to help?"

"Hüseyin and his friends are going to come over and build a new house—"

"Shall I wrap up some bread and olives for you? Wait, I'll send your groceries with my errand boy. Don't wear yourself out. You're going through a tough time as it is. You know what, sister? It'll all work out for the best. Right? Don't let it get you down. Your old toilet was out in the yard anyway. Now they'll put one inside your house. You'll have the fanciest toilet in the whole neighborhood!"

I couldn't help laughing along with him. It did me good.

That song Bercuhi used to sing is still stuck in my head. *Its rose inside a glass.* Now what was the next line? Hasan would remember.

Meet My Dad, Hasan Akgün

"Is he breathing? Tell me, Hüseyin! Is he alive?"

As I shouted down into the bottom of the well to find out if my boy was alive, I felt something collapse in my chest. I've never been the same since.

"He's breathing, Hasan! Ali! Don't be scared. We'll get you out of there. Keep pulling, Hasan. Keep pulling!"

The boy's been all funny ever since that day. He was too scared to cry. If Aliye had found out that our son fell into the well, I swear she would have divorced me. She'd always said not to dig a well near the house, that the water would be dirty.

"Let's not tell your mother about this. Okay, son? I'm begging you, too, Hüseyin. Don't you go and tell her either."

"Okay. Hey, hang on a second. Ali? Did you swallow too much water? Hasan, we need to make him throw up. Open your mouth, Ali. I'm going to stick my finger down your throat. Don't be scared."

The boy coughed up black water, but he still didn't tell his mother anything. That was the day he changed. Ever since that day he doesn't talk.

The other day, as I was serving tea in the office, I was listening to the story Aydın Bey was telling, not really paying attention. It's funny how the mind works. I was thinking about how Ali was trapped in the bottom of the well while Aydın Bey was telling his story:

"The whole family feasted on that big jug of mulberry molasses all winter long. It was the sweetest molasses ever. So sweet that when it was almost gone they turned the jug upside down to get the last drops. And what did they find?"

He widened his eyes and waited for a second.

"A mouse, in the bottom of the jug!"

Everyone was completely grossed out. Aydın Bey was laughing.

"Just imagine. They'd been eating that molasses all winter long. What a story!"

Aydın Bey turned to me.

"Did you like that story, Hasan Efendi?"

So I took off my cap and sat down. That was the day after the house burned down, and I needed to sit down for a minute anyway.

"If your fascist boss isn't around, I have a story to tell, too," I said.

"He's not around, Hasan Efendi. He's gone off to the mosque with the other prayer bead swingers."

"All right then . . . There are these mystics who go from village to village, kind of like wandering minstrels. Back where I'm from we called them *çîrokvan*. When they spend the night in someone's house, they tell stories and recite poems. They say that the world doesn't have a beginning, that the world has been here for all time. One day, one of them turned up in our village and stayed in the house of yours truly. One of his blue eyes was clouded and blind. I was still a little kid at the time. He scared me. My mother asked him to tell her fortune. She wanted to know if our sheep would have lots of lambs in the spring, and if she would give birth to another son. As if she needed another mouth to feed! We were dirt poor as it was. Mother kept asking questions, and the çîrokvan kept fixing his good eye on the ceiling. Last of all, he said, 'Don't drink the water from your well. Fill it in.' We had a well out in our garden. It was such a blessing. Mother was spooked something terrible. The çîrokvan lowered his blue eye and said to Mother:

'There's a body in that well. They threw one of the Armenians driven out of Elaziz into that well. Don't drink the water.'

My late mother lit candles and mourned for forty days next to that well. We'd been drinking its water for years. Ever since that day my mother would keep vomiting. The poor thing vomited herself to death. Her last words were, 'The well, the well . . .'"

Everybody lit up a cigarette. The sun came out, and the cloud of smoke swirling in the room glowed gray. Aydın Bey offered me a cigarette. I wasn't going to, but that's when I told him what happened.

"They burned down our house, Aydın Bey."

He asked me a lot of questions, whether the house was built of sun-dried bricks or concrete blocks, and then he started talking about how he'd just spent all his money on a light or a lamp or something.

"I'm not asking for money, Aydın Bey! I just wanted to tell you, as a friend. We'll find a way out of this, thanks to our friends."

I'd made Aydın Bey feel a little ashamed, and regretted it. Wanting to change the subject, I brought up politics. There's always something to chew over in this country.

"How's the court case against the labor union going, Aydın Bey? Do you think they'll lose?"

Aydın Bey was still thinking about my house.

"You really shouldn't have come to work today."

"How could I not come? If I miss so much as a day of work, those right-wing bastards will fire me on the spot. I'm lucky I had friends who helped me get this job, but you wouldn't believe the problems I've had because of the union. Have you heard about Alaaddin?"

"Alaaddin? Who's that? Which department is he in?"

"He doesn't work here. You know the State Milk Industry building over by Kızılay Square."

"The nationalists have taken it over from what I've heard. Is that right?"

"That's right, Aydın Bey. One of the nationalist leaders over there—I don't know how they decide this—points out people they don't like as they pass by the building. That bastard Alaaddin is in charge. He pointed to me the other day. I wouldn't care if Ali wasn't so young. And if his mother had a job."

The other guys in the room were talking among themselves:

"I heard they've killed Gün Sazak. Things are going to get even messier."

"How could things get any worse? They're killing ten or fifteen revolutionaries every single day. Just yesterday they shot and killed a leftist municipal policeman and put a bullet through his twelve-year-old son's head. Those damn right-wingers are murdering our young people every day of the week. How could things get any worse?"

Aydın Bey leaned closer and said:

"You were talking about how your wife doesn't have a job."

"She wants to work but . . ." I started saying, but I lost my train of thought.

"Aydın Bey, I don't think we can hold back our kids anymore. Our Hüseyin . . ."

I stopped myself. I was about to say we needed more guns. I'd better watch my mouth, even among friends.

"Shall I bring some more tea? Does anyone want another tea?"

As I walked off with a tray of dirty tea glasses, a song started running through my head. It's funny how people's minds work. What made me think of that old Armenian song at a time like this?

I can't remember the first line of that song. I bet Aliye knows it, but if I asked her she'd say, "Why are you thinking about that song now of all times?" I hope the meeting and the engagement party go off without a hitch tonight.

UNIT 3

Early to Bed, Early to Rise

Early to Bed

LIBERATION NEIGHBORHOOD

"Samim, ask your Aydın Abi who he's bringing to the house."

We're sitting on Samim Abi and Ayla Abla's terrace. Everything is so nice. They don't have any armchairs because they just moved and, of course, "When you're in love you don't need chairs." That's what they say. They both work at Turkish Radio & Television, but they call it TRT for short. Ayla Abla is going to introduce me to the kids from the radio show *Children's Garden*. But right now everyone is talking about politics. On the floor below, "We're Cheerful Kids" is playing in Jale Hanım's apartment. Mom doesn't like that song, but I do. Because I get bored sometimes when everyone is talking about politics.

Dad says, "Things are going to get much worse. The Gün Sazak murder was done for a reason."

Samim Abi says, "You're right, brother."

Ayla Abla says, "And Parliament is paralyzed. How many rounds of voting have been held to choose a president?"

Mom says, "Nobody can even remember! Today, someone sent eight hundred cucumbers to Parliament. The CHP deputies distributed them in the general assembly. Not a single person refused to take one. They really are a bunch of cucumber heads."

Samim Abi says, "The streets are terrible."

Samim Abi always smiles, but when they talk about fascists he frowns and says nothing. I think Samim Abi is handsome, really handsome.

They're all too busy to answer my question.

"Dad! Why does Jale Hanım call Russian salad American salad?"

Mom was cross with Dad for bringing a chandelier home from work. That's because before he brought home a quilt "covered with big roses and branches." That's why she's talking like this now.

"Samim, why don't you ask Aydın who he's planning to bring home. As if that bourgeois chandelier wasn't bad enough."

"Look here, Sevgi!"

When there are other people around, my mother and father keep smiling even when they're mad at each other.

"I'll tell them, Aydın. M'lord has decided we need a cleaning lady."

"Mom! Why does Jale Hanım call Russian salad American salad?"

"Sevgi, like I told you, their house burned down. He won't accept any money. Samim, I'm talking about our tea man at work. His house burned down. So I thought—"

Samim Abi laughed as he cut Dad off.

"You know what they say, Aydın Abi. The road to the petits-bourgeois is paved with decorative tiles. Do you remember what our old grocer used to say, Ayla? 'It's the petty part of the bored-was-he that you gotta watch out for.' Still, I'm glad you got that chandelier. Now you can give us your old ceiling light as you abandon your comrades for middle class respectability!"

Ayla Abla loves Samim Abi because he's really handsome and he makes everyone laugh when they talk about politics.

"Samim, the bottles are ready for you in the kitchen. You can heat up the alcohol now."

Samim Abi picked me up. He's so much fun.

"Come on, little miss! Let's go make that vodka. Aydın, why don't you join us?"

Dad likes coming over here, too. Here, Mom only acts like she's angry, but she doesn't get angry for real. And when Mom does get mad at Dad, he can always start talking to Samim Abi.

"Samim, what are you going to do with all this vodka?"

Ayla Abla pushes back her hair when she lights a cigarette. I think she's beautiful. And she smells so different because she and Samim Abi kiss each other a lot. It's a naughty smell, but it makes you smile. Samim Abi picks me up again. He smells like adventures, like wild horses.

"Samim Abi, why does Jale Hanım call Russian Salad—"

"Because, little miss Ayşe, they root for J.R. on *Dallas*!"

"Oh!"

"My, what big eyes you have when you open them wide like that."

"Tell me, then, who do we root for on *Dallas*?"

"There's never anyone on TV we can root for, Ayşe. But never mind all that! Come on, I'll show you all kinds of abracadabra tricks in the kitchen."

When Mom and Ayla Abla are out on the terrace and Dad and Samim Abi are in the kitchen, I always stand in the doorway of the kitchen. That way I can see everyone and never miss a thing. Right now, I'm listening to Dad and Samim Abi.

". . . when the alcohol reaches the boiling point."

"Aydın Abi, the Soviets put on an amazing opening ceremony for the Olympics. You'll see. I did my own montage from all the footage that was cut."

"You're the king of the cutting room floor, Samim."

"Have I told you about the censored footage from the Maraş Massacre? So much is never broadcast. TRT even burns some footage."

"Samim, why haven't you talked to your landlord about that locked room?"

When Mom and Ayla Abla sit across from each other, they cross their legs and lean across the table. They flick their cigarettes toward the ashtray, their hands like pigeons pecking at feed.

"Ayla, why don't you open up that locked room of yours? Just tell your landlord that—"

When Ayla Abla gets asked a question, she plays with her hair and leans back:

"Why? What for?"

"Well, you might have a baby one day and need the spare room for a nursery. And it's not like you have a huge apartment, even for just the two of you."

"Hmmm . . ."

"What's in that room, anyway?"

"Oh, nothing. There's something I wanted to talk to you about. You know the Captain's Restaurant, in Çankaya. . ."

Mom sat up straight and took her elbows off the table. Ayla Abla kept talking.

"I thought I should tell you that a lot of people from TRT go there."

Mom leaned on the table.

"It's not what you think, Ayla. He's an old friend. I—"

"I didn't think anything of it."

Now neither of them speaks. Ayla Abla bites her lip and finds a way to smile.

"This is no time to talk about babies, Sevgi Abla. Not with so much killing going on."

Sometimes Mom doesn't answer. She does it to Dad, too.

"Sevgi Abla, back in your time there was time to think, time to create. Now people are just trying to survive."

Samim Abi came over to the doorway and patted me on the head.

"Sevgi, is my wife lecturing you about politics? Flee to the kitchen. Your husband is hopeless in there!"

Mom and Ayla Abla are smoking in the kitchen doorway now.

Samim Abi has a cigarette hanging from the corner of his mouth. He's standing on a chair, and he looks even more handsome.

"Look, Ayşe. According to what I've learned from the Russian classics, the most important thing in vodka is the water. Oxygenated water is best. Do you know what I mean by that? Remember how when we go to Çubuk Reservoir the water spills down the dam? That's how the water gets oxygen, how it breathes. So if we pour the water from a high place, like up on this chair, the water will breathe."

Sometimes I think Samim Abi says these things just to make me laugh.

"Aydın, could you check and see if the alcohol has heated up yet? And now I'll jump right down from this chair to check on the alcohol because Aydın Abi is hopeless. . . . Yes . . . the alcohol is nice and warmed up. And now, little Ayşe, it's time for the hocus-pocus part. Be sure to stand far enough away, over by the door. That's right. Now you can help me."

Samim Abi took the lid off the pot and lit a match.

"Don't be scared, Ayşe."

With a *puff*, a huge flame shot from the pot. Samim Abi stuck the lid back on, but he wasn't scared, not a bit.

"Count to ten, Ayşe. One, two, three . . . Ten! I'm taking off the lid and throwing in three sugar cubes. Your mom will add two drops of glycerin. That's it. Now, watch what I'm putting inside the funnel, just so. A coffee filter I bought at the American Market, opening myself up to all kinds of criticism. We're supposed to put charcoal in the filter, Ayşe, but when I couldn't find any I got some Eucarbon from the pharmacist. It's a stomach medicine that has charcoal in it. Our country has fallen so far into the clutches of imperialism, is so firmly under the boot of the oligarchy, is so crushed by monopoly capitalism, that we don't even produce our own charcoal. You hear that, Aydın Bey? I'm educating your daughter, if you don't mind. Hey, where did Ayla go?"

I could hear Dad talking to Mom in the other room.

"Sevgi, I'll let Hasan Efendi know then. Let's have his wife come soon."

"All right, Aydın. Have her come."

"Which day should she come?"

"Thursdays."

"So, I'll tell her Thursdays are good?"

"Right. Okay."

Samim Abi turned around and laughed. I love the way he laughs.

"That's great to hear, Aydın. You dodged a bullet yet again. Now let's get back to our real mission for today, which is making vodka. Let's get Ayla in here, too."

Mom and Dad finally laughed for real. I was just starting to laugh too when I got scared.

Bang! Bang!

"Where's Ayla?"

Bang! Bang!

"Fighting's broken out! Where's Ayla!"

Samim Abi dropped everything. The doorbell rang. He ran to the door. Mom tried to grab me, but I ran after Samim Abi. When he opened the door, you wouldn't believe what I saw on the doormat.

"Mischa! Look, Mom, it's Mischa!"

Ayla Abla came up behind me.

"Look! It's Mischa, the Olympic mascot. She's come all the way here just to visit Ayşe."

Samim Abi hugged Ayla Abla.

"Ayla! When I heard the gunshots—"

"Calm down, Samim. I snuck out through the terrace and then around the—"

I picked up Mischa and gave her a hug. She's visiting from Moscow. Grandma shouted out of the window of our apartment.

"Sevgi! Are you all okay?"

"We're fine, Mother. Don't stand in front of the window. Close it right away!"

Then Mom said something in a tiny voice, but I heard it, even if nobody else did.

"We're fine, just fine."

Mom and the other grown-ups always get excited when the big kids are playing out in the streets. The same way I get excited when the swing in the park goes too high or too fast. But when the guns stop going *bang, bang,* Samim Abi sets up the projector and we see a huge place where lots of people walk in a line and carry flags and stuff. They say it's Moscow. When the projector is running, even when you close your eyes the light still comes in. It's kind of like what happens before your afternoon nap, when you squeeze your eyes shut and you can see fish and bugs swimming right in front of your eyes, and when you try to follow them with your eyes you feel like your eyeballs are going to roll out and away. It's like that. If you look right into the projector and then look away, you see all kinds of lights. And if you look here and there, blinking and blinking, the projector becomes the whole sky. Mischa the Bear smells like another country. Just like the map room at school.

Early to Rise
RAMBLING GARDENS NEIGHBORHOOD

"Hüseyin, ask my husband who fell into the well. Go on, ask Hasan!"

There's going to be a fight. And there'll be lots of noise. What if Dad hits Mom? I hope he doesn't. But he won't, not in front of Hüseyin Abi.

Everything was done. The engagement party was done. The meeting was done. Nobody shot at us from Almond Stream on the other hill. We could all go to sleep. Come on, let's go to sleep. Come on! I want quiet. I'm so tired. I feel like my head's going to explode!

A little after the power came back on, the big sisters at the party gave the signal. They shouted out the words of the song:

"*Oh petrol, dear petrol!*"

One of the big brothers near me heard the signal.

"The police must be on their way. The girls are singing 'Petrol.' We need to get all our stuff, quick. What do you say, Hüseyin? Those fascists over at Almond Stream have heavy weapons. Our pistols are no match for them. Can we ask your connections for something else, Hüseyin?"

The light of the lantern is dim now. It's a lantern with its own gas canister and a little white bag that burns, but you mustn't touch it

when it's on fire. If you do, it'll turn into dust, that's what they say.
Hüseyin Abi is playing with his lighter.

"There's no need. What are we going to get, an anti-aircraft gun?
What more do you want?"

Nobody has a lighter like Hüseyin's. It's an Ibelo. Silver. He's thinking hard, flicking his lighter. It clicks, but it doesn't burn.

"Well, for one thing, we need more ammo."

"Okay, I can understand that. What else do we need?"

"We need a couple of assault rifles, Hüseyin."

"Okay, okay. I'll ask. Now let's get out of here. The cops are on their
way. Figure out how much money we can raise. We don't want to bleed
the neighborhood dry. We'll end up looking like extortionists."

"Hüseyin, they're burning houses down now. Unless someone stands
up to them, they'll be gunning down women and kids next."

The big brothers pushed down on their knees with their palms as
they stood up. They were all twisting their mustaches between their
fingers. Then they scattered into the darkness. It's always the big sisters
who talk with the policemen.

"We're having an engagement party, officer."

"This house just burned down. Why are you having it here?

"We still need husbands, officer."

The pretty big sister said that. The other ones aren't as pretty as her.
She's prettier because she goes to Middle East Technical University, just
like Hüseyin. She made a notebook out of all the paper left in her old
notebook and gave it to me for New Year's. She really likes Hüseyin,
and that's why she gave me a present.

The other girls pull the prettiest one to the side.

"The party's over, officer."

The policeman pushed back his cap with the tip of his baton.

"There's a rumor going around that a group from Almond Stream
torched this house. It's not true. You better tell your people to lay off.
We saw you raising a flag on their hill the other day. We see everything,
but we don't want trouble. Where are the guys?"

The pretty big sister shouted at the policemen.

"They went to the tennis club!"

"Look, I'm trying to be patient. But only because you said you were having an engagement party."

If the policeman gets mad, he'll beat her. I hope he doesn't. I hope he doesn't.

White-haired Uncle Dürüst comes up. He's not really old; he just has white hair because they tortured him a lot in the '71 coup. They zapped his pee-pee. That's why he went crazy. And because he thinks too much. He always carries a bunch of books. And he's carrying a flower, too. He picks them. He goes to the cemetery every day, picks a flower, and then gives it to one of the big sisters. Now he's holding out a flower to the policeman. I hope he doesn't get beaten.

"Get out of here! This guy gives me a flower every time he sees me. He's nuts!"

The pretty big sister runs up and takes the flower.

"Give it to me, Dürüst. Come on, come over to us."

She puts the flower in her hair and takes Uncle Dürüst over to the fire. Uncle Dürüst always has a smile on his face.

"Have kids. Have lots of kids."

Uncle Dürüst always says that. But he doesn't say much else. When the policeman leaves, the big brothers come out of the darkness and go up to the big sisters. They walk differently in front of the girls, real serious, like they're not scared of anything. The pretty sister puts her hand on her hip.

"So, what are we doing now?"

Hüseyin Abi pulls her closer.

"Settle down. I'll talk about that in a minute."

Mom sits next to the fire again. She doesn't speak. She's letting all the other women do the talking tonight:

"How dare that cop come up here! If he's so brave, let him go and patrol the fascists' neighborhood."

"The cops aren't afraid of anything when the power's on. Is it any wonder those Almond Stream fascists dare to come up onto our hill?"

"Let's put out the fire. Aliye, you're welcome to stay with us tonight."

Mom shakes her head. She cries when everyone else leaves. Hüseyin Abi sends the pretty girl off with the other ones. Uncle Dürüst is sitting in front of the fire. Someone always takes him away when it gets late. I don't know where they take him. He always wears a black suit. An old one. He went crazy from thinking too much. I wonder if I'm going to go crazy too. Maybe my hair will turn white.

Everyone's gone but Hüseyin. He's talking to my father.

"Hasan, could I have a word with you for a minute?"

"Sure. What it is, Hüseyin?"

"The other guys are saying . . ."

Mom is wandering through the ashes of the old house. Dad and Hüseyin Abi watch her as they talk.

"Well, they're saying the neighborhood needs more protection after what happened to you."

"Right. But how?"

"Me and the others decided tonight that . . ."

Now Mom is crying in what used to be the house, but she doesn't make a sound. I think she's saying, "Sait, Sait." He's my uncle, but I never met him.

". . . we need to get a couple of assault rifles."

When Mom starts wailing and sighing in the ashes, Dad calls out to her.

"Aliye. Come over here. Don't walk over there! Sorry, Hüseyin. I'm listening."

"Everyone agrees we need heavier weapons, so I'm—"

Mom wails louder now. "Oh! Ah!"

She sits down in the ashes. Dad goes up to her.

"Aliye! What is it? Stop moaning. We're going to build a new house. It'll be better the old one."

Hüseyin Abi joins Mom and Dad.

"We'll all help. My friends from will come too. Tomorrow."

It scares me when Mom starts crying on her knees in the ashes.

"Aliye! Get up. Come on. I told you I'd build a new house. With an indoor toilet. And we'll cover the well this time so Ali doesn't fall in again."

Mom froze. She looked at Dad.

"What? Did Ali fall in the well?"

She looked at me. I felt scared.

"Ali, did you fall in the well? Did you? Tell me, Hasan. Did you let Ali fall in the well and not tell me?"

Nobody said a word. Dad always lights a cigarette right away when he gets scared. Mom stood up. She was so angry. And that's when she said it.

"Did you hear that, Hüseyin? Hasan let Ali fall in the well and nobody even told me!"

"Okay, okay. He didn't get hurt."

"Hasan! Is that why my boy turned out like this?"

Turned out like what? How have I turned out? Nothing happened to me. I just get all funny from too much noise. Does Mom not love me because I don't like noise?

"It's okay, sister. Nothing serious happened!"

Mom stamps out what's left of the fire.

"You listen here, Hasan. This changes everything. I'm getting a job. I don't need your wages. You give most of it to the union, anyway. I'm going to make my own money and my boy's going to go to university. I'm not asking you for permission. Come on, Ali. We're spending the night at Nuran's house."

Mom shook her finger at Dad.

"Don't try to follow me, Hasan. Go stay somewhere else. Hüseyin, take him away. I don't want to see his face tonight."

I turned around while we were walking away. "Don't look at him!" Mom said, her hands shaking. But I looked anyway.

"Damn it," Dad said. He kicked a pile of ashes.

They forgot about Uncle Dürüst tonight. He's still by the fire ring. He was talking in a low voice, just like me. I heard him:

"Have kids before you die. Have lots of kids."

I hope they don't forget him. I'll give him some string. He can look at it.

I shared a bed with Hamit that night. He kicked me in his sleep. I pushed him. Our neighborhood is so crowded. It's so noisy. Nobody else has an encyclopedia. I think morning came before I fell asleep.

UNIT 4

This Is Our City

We Love Our City

"They're here, Grandma! Grandma! Come quick or they'll leave!"

I run straight to the door. The "helper"—we're not supposed to call her a "cleaning lady"—is bringing her kid. Someone about my age, Dad said. A new friend!

Grandma has been cleaning the house ever since she got up. Dad is mad at her.

"Nejla Hanım, why are you cleaning? The helper is on her way here now."

"Aydın, we don't want her to think we live in a dirty house."

Grandma's tired and her face is red, so she can't walk to the front door very fast.

"Don't be silly, Ayşe. They can wait for a moment. They won't leave."

The door opens and . . . Oh no! It's a boy!

—

"Listen, Ali. Don't make any noise while we're there. Okay, son? Make your mother proud."

When Mom said that, I knew she was scared. She was holding my hand so tight it hurt. I didn't say anything, though. She kept fussing with my clothes and my hair. She washed my dress shirt twice, with lots of soft soap. There's a friend for me in that house, she said. Maybe we can play together. Or even read books.

The door opens and . . . Oh no! It's a girl!

—

When they came inside, Grandma picked up the envelope. Then she set it back down. There's money in the envelope. Grandma told Mom and Dad that's what she'd do.

"I can't hand her money! That would be so awkward. I'll put it in an envelope."

—

"Welcome. I hear your name is Aliye."

"And you . . . you're Nejla Hanım, right?"

"Please come in, my dear. You can take your shoes off inside. And what's your name, little man?"

Everyone was looking at me. I looked at my mother. Why did she let my hand go? The girl screamed.

"I'm Ayşe."

Everyone laughed.

—

I run straight off to my room, looking back over my shoulder to see if he follows. He's not coming. That's because he's a boy. They're laughing in the living room.

"Ayşe was so happy you were coming, little man. The two of you can play together."

Oh, why did Grandma say that!

—

The old lady put her hand on my shoulder. She's taking me to where that girl went. I look at Mom. "Run along now," she says in a whisper. There are so many books in that girl's room. Ten! The girl screams again. She's jumping up and down on the bed. She must be crazy.

"I've got lots of books. I have *One Peach*. I have *A Thousand Peaches*."

I sit down in the chair.

"They're the same book. That's only one book."

She stopped jumping.

She screams again. I think she's going to cry.

"Grandma!"

Now the girl's running back into the room with the old lady, her grandma. The girl is holding a plate, and the plate is full of börek.

—

"Go on, Ayşe. Look, your friend's name is Ali. Get to know each other. I'll be in the other room helping Auntie Aliye. Would you like some börek, Ali? Help yourself. I'll leave the two of you here, like brother and sister."

Grandma leaves, and I look at the boy. He's not bad-looking, but he's really skinny. That's because they're poor. His collar looks nice against his skin. He's the color of coffee. I put my arm next to his while he was eating his börek. It made me giggle. My arm is so white. He didn't laugh, though.

"I can't read the tiny letters yet. Can you read them? I mean, I can't read the letters in *Cumhuriyet*, but there are some biggish letters that I can read really easy. Do you get *Weekend*? We don't, but Jale Hanım does. Do you get it?"

—

The girl keeps talking and talking. Even more than Hamit the Laz. She puts her mouth close to my ear.

"Jale Hanım is rooting for J.R. in *Dallas*."

What is *Weekend*?

She gets back up on the bed.

"Do you want to play 'music hall' with me? I'll be the singer. Then it'll be your turn. Stay right there! I have to get my feather."

She ran out of the room. She never stays put.

"When I stick this feather in my hair, I turn into Seyyal Taner. Ladies and gentlemen, let me introduce Seyyal Taner! '*I told my heart it was fired. How could he have left me?*'"

She jumped off the bed and held out the feather.

"Okay, now it's your turn. Be Bülent Ersoy."

I can't scream for my mother. I don't want to scare her.

"Oh, all right then. Don't be Bülent Ersoy. You can be . . . Cem Karaca!"

—

That boy doesn't even want to play with me. I wish he'd go home. I knew I wouldn't like him.

"Want to look out at the police station? Sometimes they play games there."

—

The girl scoots over to the window by the bed and puts her face up against the glass. They don't play games at police stations. What's she talking about?

"Come here. You can't see anything from way over there! You have to look from this spot. See! There they are. They put the big brothers

and sisters inside. Then they try to get out. I throw them dried chickpeas. But we can't do it right now. Nobody's there today."

———

Ali always looks like he's about to cry. It makes you want to be nice to
him. To make him laugh somehow.

———

"They're not playing a game," I told the girl. I think I scared her. She
shuts up when she's scared.

———

"Ayşe! Come into the living room for a while. Auntie Aliye is going to
start her cleaning in your room."
    What does he mean? They're not playing games? What are they
doing then? He's just saying that because we can't throw any chickpeas
at the windows over there right now. Of course they play games. It's a
game!
    "Ayşe, I'm putting these pastries on the coffee table. You and Ali can
help yourselves. Okay?"

———

She stopped talking. It's so quiet. Oh! A shelf full of books. An encyclopedia set!

———

"Like I told you, they're playing. You just don't know it."
    How could he know? He's a boy. And I think he's not very smart.

—

"Have you got *The Wonderland of Knowledge*?"

"So what if we do? You can't read tiny letters, can you?"

"Yes, I can."

"Not the tiniest ones!"

She put her hands on her hips. She looks like she wants to hit me.

"Yes, I can."

"I'm talking about the really tiny ones. This big."

She's holding the tip of her thumb and her finger together. Yes, she must be a little crazy.

"Well then, let's see you read! Here it is! *The Wonderland of Knowledge*. But give it back when you're done. What shall we look at? What about—"

"Ankara!"

"Hey!"

I took the encyclopedia out of her hand. She's still talking. She never shuts up.

"You know what? I was going to say 'Ankara' too. I swear it. Because . . . Because . . ."

Now she's talking like me. She keeps saying the same word. I wonder why she wants to look at Ankara. I know why I do. Because of Hüseyin Abi . . .

—

Mom and I stayed at Nuran Abla's for two nights. Until Dad said, "Okay then, work. Aydın Bey needs a cleaner. You can go there." Hüseyin Abi really laughed.

"If at first you don't succeed . . . Right, Aliye Abla?"

It turned out that Hüseyin Abi was going to Liberation, too. That's what he told Mom.

"Let's go together. I've got some business over there today. The local shared taxi takes that route. And you can learn how to get there in the future."

The people in the shared taxi were so tired. I kept looking at the prayer beads hanging from the driver's wrist. They shook every time he changed gears. At first it was noisy. Music was playing and people were talking the whole way.

". . . can't go the normal route. There's a demonstration. . . . Are they still out on Sakarya Avenue? Those nine guys have been on strike for two years now. . . . No, Dikimevi Hospital isn't in Hacettepe. But where is it, exactly? . . . That's not why. They're going to start building a metro. They'll be digging for years. . . . Driver, I didn't get my change!"

I can't look at my strings right now. Hüseyin Abi would ask me about them. I like being in a moving cab. I can look out the window. When I see the apartments for rich people, I feel like we're in a different city. I'm looking at them now. I'm also looking at the graffiti saying, DOWN WITH FASCISM! and the posters of big brothers stuck on all the walls. Hüseyin Abi is holding a magazine called *Gong*. There's a different magazine inside it, though. I saw it. It's his real magazine. They better not see it. They better not see it. Hüseyin Abi starts clicking his Ibelo lighter again.

"Ali, try to do a lot of reading this summer. You'll forget how to read unless you practice. Okay, little lion? Ali, can you read the fine print, too?"

I can't read when the cab is shaking back and forth, but I don't tell Hüseyin Abi. He'll think I can't read. I can't tell him my stomach feels all funny.

"Can you? Here, try to read this. But do it in a whisper. Just loud enough for me to hear. Read this part, the bit that's underlined."

Hüseyin Abi stops clicking his lighter.

"In this battle for surv—"

"Survival. Right?"

". . . for survival, do whatever it takes to stay alive and always remember that there is no other path. Everyone must comp—"

"Comprehend. Continue."

"Comprehend this reality, and act accordingly."

"That was great! You really do know how to read. Like I said, though, you need to keep reading a lot so you don't forget how."

Hüseyin Abi puts his lighter in his pocket. The silver Ibelo. I try to understand what I just read.

"But are we . . . are we . . ."

"Yes, Ali?"

"Are we fighting for our survival?"

He pats me on the head and gives my shoulder a squeeze. He points, touching his fingertip to the window.

"Look at that, Ali. They're going to build a metro in Ankara. They've already started digging and they'll dig deep down into the ground. What do you think is underneath Ankara, Ali? What do you think they'll find when they clear away the earth and the stones?"

I don't know! Hüseyin Abi is getting a funny look in his eyes. He looks like how I feel when I'm having one of my dreams.

"Ali, I think they'll find a lot of things under Ankara. Like a clay pot belonging to the man and woman who reached this steppe thousands of years ago in search of food and shelter, interpreted the winds ushering in the spring rain as a fortuitous sign, and erected their tent poles. Or the jug of a Roman aristocrat who, having fallen into imperial disfavor, arrived on this steppe, threw up a couple of columns for appearance's sake, and indulged in some wine as his throne was being toppled. Ali, did you know that Ankara is the first and only place where an Ottoman sultan was held captive? They'll find the ashes of the opium Timur smoked to celebrate the capture of Sultan Yıldırım Beyazit."

Hüseyin Abi stares out the window. He's talking to himself, not me.

"And there are the shoes worn to tatters by youths stuck somewhere between the stars and the fly-covered cheeks of the kids back in their villages, the youths who trudge to university with dreams of becoming nuclear physicists. There are World War II bread ration coupons belonging to the scores of doctors and teachers and accountants who poured their hearts into poetry to save their country. The thousands of typewriters, mimeos, and lead types churning out essays on 'How to Save the Homeland' have mingled with the shells of pumpkin seeds cracked open during blue movies shown in the Yeni Maltepe Cinema. Ink pots and sealing wax, prayers written with reed pens and nibbing implements, and hidden away, amulets are jumbled in with plastic pen cases scrawled with 'Revolution Is the Only Way.' The T-squares snapped in street protests, the remains of barricades built of constitutional and administrative law books, the unsent letters written by provincials to cheer up the intellectuals gloomily contemplating the Bosphorus in Istanbul, the drumsticks of the band girls who marched in thousands of official parades, the mandolin picks that dropped to the ground as children from the Village Institute played Turkish tangos. Ankara comes from the word *ánkura*, the ancient Greek for 'anchor.' The anchor cast from a ship on an imaginary journey. And Ankara is also the city of King Midas, who knew that all kings had donkey ears and who feared wells because he believed they would shout out his secret. We shout out our own version of 'the king has donkey ears,' and as we run away from the police, falling from our pockets are telephone numbers, photos, fake ID cards. . . . It's dangerous to dig too deep, Ali."

Hüseyin is back from his dream. He pats me on the head again. That's when I ask him:

"Are we fighting a war, Hüseyin Abi?"

He gives me a weird look. Mom hasn't been listening to us, but now she asks Hüseyin what business is taking him to Independence.

"I'm meeting with someone."

"Oh?"

"It's nothing important. It's about the pieces."

"Hüseyin, the stuff in our coal cellar—"

"Don't worry. I'll take care of it."

Mom gives Hüseyin Abi a hard look. A long, hard look. He looks right back at her. They don't say anything after that.

—

"I think Ankara is beautiful!"

I get up on the end table and yell it really loud. Jale Hanım and the lady who comes to sell all kinds of cloth make me so cross! Why are they laughing at me?

"Stop laughing!"

When Grandma asked how much to pay the cleaning lady, Mom said she didn't know. Dad didn't know either, so we went to Jale Hanım's house to ask her.

"Jale Hanım, what's the daily rate for a cleaning lady?"

"Come on in, Nejla Hanım. The cloth peddler is here. I'm looking at things for Feride's trousseau. You too, you crazy little munchkin!"

Jale Hanım's house smells like fruity chewing gum and giggles. Jale Hanım laughs all the time because she has really big, jiggly boobs. And when she walks in her high-heeled house slippers her bottom goes up and down and all around. That's because she's always laughing. Feride Abla has hair down to her waist. She always chews gum. Mom won't let me chew gum because she doesn't like the sound. She says the "popping and smacking" gets on her nerves. The hope chest is open. It smells like soap, like it's saying, "Don't touch me or I'll get dirty." I remember the cloth lady from before. She walks through the street with a big bag yelling, "Cloth! Linen! Lady's clothes. The cloth peddler is here!" There's always a lot of lace and cloth in her bag. Cloth peddlers always sit cross-legged on the floor. They can tell your fortune using beans and beads. Sometimes it scares me. There's a shiny bead, or maybe a button, right in the middle of the beans, and the cloth peddler makes her eyes get really, really big while she's looking at it and talking. She does it when she brings out her lace, too.

"Jale Hanım, let me show you some petit point. Sister, you'll love it. It's just the thing for any bride. There's a set of five, and the biggest one is the perfect size for the middle end table or the coffee table. I've got it in pink, too. Here, have a look. Touch it."

When the cloth peddler pulls out her lace the living room smells like roses.

"Why don't you have a look too, Auntie? I've got a beautiful memorial service coverlet right here. Look at that fine stitching. Silver embroidery. I'm letting it go for a song. This is the last one. The young ladies don't appreciate workmanship. But then again, memorial services aren't what they used to be. Do you know, there's a group of young women who go from service to service, not taking any money, but saying all kinds of things in between prayers. They tell the other women that they'll burn in hell if they don't cover their heads. That retired teacher in the building opposite yours gave them such a tongue-lashing the other day! Anyway, why don't you get something for the little miss? There won't be any lacework this fine when she's grown up. I always say it's never too early to start putting together a trousseau. I've got a nice set of bed linen here, and I'll throw in four pillow cases. Auntie, I'll tell you what: I'll let you have the bed skirt for free if you buy the set."

Jale Hanım keeps lace on her bookshelf. A whole set. Everything has to match. We don't have any matching sets in my house. I like them, though. It's like playing house. Jale Hanım's got books on her bookshelves, too. There's one called *Prayer Hodja*. The cover shows a girl doing her prayers on a carpet. Next to the *Golden Plate* recipe book is *Our Reproductive Life*, and next to that a *Romance Series*. Those books are about love, and Feride Abla reads them all the time. Jale Hanım and Feride save coupons, too, enough maybe to get a free holiday in Cyprus. "Moderno detergent is sending you to Cyprus!" On a shelf below the coupons is a set of coffee cups from Germany. They're orange, but the edges are gold. Some of the cups lie sideways, and they smell like dust even though I can't see any.

"Nejla Hanım, the groom-to-be is from Istanbul, and I thought I'd bring his family something when we go to visit. What about this quilt? It looks tasteful to me."

Now Grandma's asking something about Istanbul. Grandma is different when we go to Jale Hanım's. She laughs different. I don't like it.

"Even the air and the water is something else in Istanbul, Jale Hanım. And it's not all gray, like here in Ankara."

"But . . . but . . ."

Nobody's listening to me. When Grandma gets like this I feel lonely.

"And you can see famous people walking down the street. There aren't any stars in Ankara."

"But . . . but . . ."

I look at *Weekend* when I get bored:

Is Bülent Ersoy getting a boob job? In an exclusive interview conducted by phone, Ersoy said she will consider a sex change "when the time comes." The famous singer plans to return from overseas with costumes that will "astonish" concert goers at the İzmir Fair.

"Nejla Hanım, some of the plane trees in Istanbul are so tall you can't see the top branches. They were planted back in Ottoman times. And the mulberry trees aren't all stunted like in Ankara. They're full of fruit."

"But . . . but . . ."

Grandma has forgotten all about me. I think she's forgotten about our house, too. She's starting to look like Jale Hanım. That's when I shout:

"Ankara is beautiful!"

I wish they wouldn't laugh, though! Why do they keep laughing at me?

I don't like the way they laugh. When Dad laughs, it's like he's drinking water. Mom laughs like a flock of birds. Grandma normally laughs like a tray of pastry. Samim Abi laughs like racing horses. Ayla Abla laughs like little Heidi running down the mountain. But Jale Hanım laughs like a schoolmistress just slapped everyone's hands with a ruler, except hers.

Stop laughing!

—

The girl talks and talks. She won't let me look at *The Wonderland of Knowledge*.

"I think Ankara is beautiful. What about you?"

If I don't answer her, will she shut up? She doesn't.

"It's like in *1001 Peaches*, isn't it? You know, when the tree grows up it belongs to the children, because even though the field isn't theirs, they're the ones who watered the tree and made it grow, so it belongs to them. Right?"

"Right."

"Ankara belongs to us because we love it. It's better than Istanbul. Only rich people live there. Ankara is just like the peach tree, isn't it? Ankara is ours."

"Right."

"Do you want to go out on the balcony and look at the street?"

Now we're leaning against the balcony railing.

She puts her mouth next to my ear.

"Do you want to be friends?"

Hüseyin Abi! That's Hüseyin Abi down there in the street. He's running, looking right and left. He ran away. I can't see him anymore. I couldn't yell down to Hüseyin Abi. Come back, Hüseyin Abi! The girl's still looking at me. Still talking.

"Your hands smell like iron after you hold an iron railing. See?"

I give her one of my strings. Maybe she'll be quiet. The list almost came out of my pocket. But it didn't. I gave her the silver cord. It made her happy. She wrapped it around her finger to make a ring. Girls are weird.

—

Grandma made macaroni with meat sauce for lunch. I gave Ali the plate with the most macaroni. I need to explain again about the game at the police station. He didn't understand.

—

She gave me the plate with the biggest portion. But I put some meat from the sauce on her plate when nobody was looking. It's only fair.

—

When Jale Hanım opened her windows, music came out.

"*We are a pair of roses blooming on the same branch . . .*"

Ali knows some songs, but he won't sing. He says he only knows "anthems."

—

The girl looked a little sad when I took my silver cord back. Me and mom got out at Gima on our way home. They have meat there like in the TV shows. We got a little of it. And we got some chicken necks, too. Mom cried. She said it was because she's happy. She made some money. I didn't tell her I'd seen Hüseyin Abi from the balcony. He was running, maybe because he was scared. He tries hard to protect us. He loves us and he doesn't want any of us to die. If I told that girl about Hüseyin Abi and our neighborhood, she wouldn't understand. Her name is Ayşe.

UNIT 5

Our Friends the Animals

Ayşe Visits Parliament

"Sevgi Hanım . . . How should I put this? I'm not very good with words. Unlike you. But . . . *I toss rose petals even to my enemies.* I mean . . ."

That's what Muzaffer Abi said. His eyes tiny as fleas behind brownish glasses, and he's a little scary. When Mom brings me to Parliament, I don't like Abdullah Amca and Muzaffer Abi most of all. Not one bit. Their trousers are too short because they're always washing their feet in the mosque courtyard before prayers. We don't like them, and it makes me mad when Mom smiles at them. When we were down in the archives, I got so mad I kicked Muzaffer Abi in the shin. He was scaring Mom. I could tell.

First, we were upstairs in the library. Then Mom yelled, "I'll go down to the archive myself." She did that because a "pompous" deputy from the Republican People's Party came in and bossed her around.

"Sevgi Hanım, I need newspaper clippings on the '78 Alevi Massacre in Maraş. Have them brought up from the archives. I also need to know how many times martial law has been extended since then. Have it added up and written out."

At first Mom just said she'd go down herself and do it. Then she got mad.

"You'd think his majesty was ordering the butler to arrange a cup of tea! What's the grammatical term for that, Nazlı? The causative verb?"

Nazlı Abla is new so they call her an "intern." Mom's veins stand out on her neck when she gets mad.

"Have it brought, have it sent, have it done! That's how they order you to boss someone else around. It's an Ottoman throwback, but it's as widespread as ever in our republic today."

Mom is holding a big envelope. It's yellow. She secretly took it out of her handbag, but I saw her. Then she put it back in and took it out again.

Uncle Abdullah Bey has a bunch of bottles of honey under his desk. He keeps looking at them. I don't talk to him because we don't like him.

Then one of the lady clerks comes in.

"Sevgi Hanım, we're all going to Youth Park on our lunch break. They say there's a new fortune teller there. We'll have our fortunes told. I don't know if you've got any old nylons with you, but afterwards we're going to that darner in Ulus who can fix runs and ladders."

After that, the director, Uncle Ali Rıza Bey, came in. We like him because he's one of us.

"Ladies, if you're going to the marketplace in Ulus, could you stop by Rasim Kaygusuz's office on the way and pick up *Jinn Ali*. I'd like to have the complete set in the archives."

Jinn Ali! I clapped my hands as Mom smiled.

"Why'd you get that look on your face, Sevgi Hanım? Surely you agree that *Jinn Ali* should be in the national archives? Rasim Kaygusuz has created the most popular stick figure in the land. Do you know how many generations of children have learned to read by following Jinn Ali's exploits at the circus and in the zoo? Right, Ayşe? Shall we get the whole set of *Jinn Ali* for our library?"

"Let's get it!" I said. Everyone laughed. Even Mom looked a little happy.

"It's perfect, and so Turkish. A stick figure hero for the kids of a country with no luxuries of any kind, even fully fleshed out storybook characters."

Uncle Abdullah Bey always looks at the floor when everyone else is laughing. He has a belly, but Uncle Ali Rıza Bey doesn't, because he's one of us. I think he's funny.

"Well, Rasim Kaygusuz did model his stick figure on the thousands of poor, skinny children he taught over the years. Can you imagine Jinn Ali with a belly?"

He's being funny again. I was trying to imagine a fat Jinn Ali when Muzaffer Abi came in. He always wears green trousers. And his mustache isn't like Dad's. It's a thin line just above his lip. I think that's why we don't like him. I can tell Uncle Ali Rıza Bey doesn't like him either. He always scolds Muzaffer Abi.

"Ah, Muzaffer Bey. Come in. I wanted to have a word with you. How do you manage to get your finger on the microfilm of the newspapers you archive?! Why can't you be more careful?"

"It won't happen again, sir. I'm sorry."

When Muzaffer Abi said that he kind of looked like Salim, the boy in our class who learned to read last. I saw the look on Mom's face. She pitied him. That's why she tried to sound nice.

"It's not a big deal, Ali Rıza Bey. What could be more natural than for an archivist to leave his mark on microfilm?"

Uncle Ali Rıza Bey doesn't show any pity. He reminds me a bit of the teacher in 1-B, the one who sometimes hits his students.

"Muzaffer is the only one who can't keep his finger out of the way."

When Muzaffer Abi left, Ali Rıza Bey said something to Mom in a quiet voice.

"Your Muzaffer must be spending a lot of time on his prayer rug. The other day he asked why we didn't have a copy of *How to Perform Your Prayers* in the archives. Are you okay, Sevgi Hanım? You haven't been looking well for the past few days. How did it go when you took Ayşe to the doctor?"

I never went to the doctor! Am I sick?

When we were alone with Abdullah Bey and his jars of honey, Mom pulled out the envelope. She took my hand as we left the room.

"Mom, am I sick?"

"Ayşe, I'm going to take you down to the archives. We've got a little job to do. But don't make any noise, daughter. Okay?"

She called me "daughter." That means we're about to do something secret. Maybe we'll have an adventure! I love the archives. Mom always says the same thing when we go into it: "It's all here, Ayşe!"

It's huge with high shelves so they can fit everything in. Even Mom looks tiny standing next to them. Mom always talks in a quiet voice here, like there's a sleeping monster and we mustn't wake it up.

"Ayşe, we're storing everything that's been published here so that when you and all the other children grow up you'll find out what we did. So you remember. So you don't forget."

I'll tell Ali about the archives. He can't come here!

"Mom, isn't not forgetting and remembering the same thing?"

She looks surprised. It's the look she gets when I ask a hard question.

"Well . . . actually . . . they're not the same. I'll tell you later what I mean."

She reached down and grabbed my chin.

"Let's see what you'll remember and what you won't forget."

She let go of my chin. I start touching the books on the shelves. Books for grown-ups don't smell like books for kids. They smell black. They smell serious. I can only read the names on their covers. Maybe Ali can read what's inside them too.

Ali is super smart when he's reading. He's a regular Jinn Ali! He gave me that ring made of cord. Well, I made the ring. But he still gave it to me.

Now Mom's over by *Weekend* . . . Hey, that's the newspaper Jale Hanım reads. Mom's sticking the yellow envelope back behind *Weekend*. But we don't like *Weekend*, so why's she putting it there? I can see another newspaper. *Hürriyet*. We don't like that one, either. There it is! *Cumhuriyet*. That's our newspaper. Or is Mom secretly reading *Weekend* too?

Mom was going to open the envelope, but she changed her mind. There's another envelope back there. I know that envelope! It was in our house, in Mom's underwear drawer. I saw it there. So that means my mom brought it here. It was full of letters, but I couldn't read the writing. They were in green ink. And there was a black stamp on each envelope: SCREENED. And Grandma looked at those letters too. She doesn't know I saw her. I also heard what she said to Mom in the kitchen when they were frying vegetables:

"They're from that guy, Önder, aren't they? The one who telephoned the other day. I saw them. Sevgi, don't keep them here at home. Aydın mustn't see them."

The metal door of the archive room slammed into the wall. Mom got scared.

"Who's there?"

"Sevgi Hanım, it's me, Muzaffer."

"Oh, so it was you, Muzaffer."

"Sevgi Hanım, I wanted to tell you something."

"I was just looking for some files from 1978. For the deputy."

"I wanted to thank you. For what you said to the director. For sticking up for me."

"It was nothing."

"Sevgi Hanım . . . I can't express myself the way you do. But . . . I do write poetry, Sevgi Hanım."

"Of course, you do, Muzaffer Abi. Of course."

"Please hear me out. I liked it when I saw the outline of my finger on the microfilm that first time. It was . . ."

Muzaffer Abi took off his glasses. It turns out he has huge eyes.

"It was funny. I'd left an image of the person doing the archiving. Proof of my existence. I even thought to myself, perhaps, years from now, someone will look at my finger and laugh. Making people laugh is a virtue in God's sight."

"Well, as far as what's in God's sight, I can't really claim—"

"You performed a good deed for me just now, upstairs. We might be saying the same thing using different words. Mightn't we?"

"I'd rather we talk outside, Muzaffer. It's not appropriate—"

"Sevgi Hanım, we can't talk outside. We all play a part outside, but here—"

"I know what you mean."

"You do? Sevgi Hanım . . . How should I put this? I'm not very good with words. Unlike you. But . . . *I toss rose petals even to my enemies.* I mean—"

"I see. I see."

"Don't be alarmed, Sevgi Hanım. I've hidden things here too."

"Hidden things?"

"You know, things that would be lost in the middle of all this fighting. Who knows, there may be others who have hidden things here. You can trust me, Sevgi Hanım. Believe me. You aren't cut out for this war. Neither am I. Nobody is, actually."

That's when I kicked Muzaffer Abi in the shin. How dare he scare my mom! She acted like she was angry with me, but I could tell she wasn't.

Mom took my hand and led me outside really fast. When we got to the parliamentary gardens, she lit a cigarette, her hands shaking. Then the orange butterflies came. Millions of them! People came out of the building for a closer look. There was a cloud of butterflies. A storm of butterflies, beating their wings against the walls of the Parliament.

"Mom, the butterflies want to go inside!"

"They can't." Mom sounded sad. When Uncle Abdullah Bey came out carrying a jar of honey, he jerked backwards. The jar fell out of his hand and broke.

The aunties didn't make it to the darner in Ulus. The one with glasses told Mom why.

"We were unable to go, Sevgi Hanım. There was trouble in front of the State Milk Enterprises building, so we headed back. Just look at all these butterflies!"

Another Auntie joined in.

"Sevgi Hanım, you wouldn't believe what we saw. Go on, someone tell her."

The aunties made their eyes big and talked over each other.

"The municipal workers were trying to take a swan out of the park. They failed, of course. You should have seen how that swan resisted!"

Then the one with glasses butted in.

"Why would they want a swan, anyway? You'd think they had better things to do."

"Mom, they're not going to hurt the swan, are they? Don't let them hurt it."

The aunties had moved on to *Dallas*. Nobody answered me.

"Mom, what did they do to the swan? Mom!"

Muzaffer Abi came out into the garden. Mom looked at him and then looked away. He was trying to talk to Uncle Abdullah Bey, but Uncle Abdullah Bey was watching the pool of honey growing on the ground, and he didn't listen. I'm sure I didn't hurt Muzaffer Abi's shin. My foot isn't very big.

On our way home, we got *Ulduz and the Crows*. Mom said it's a story about a boy and a girl who rescue a baby crow. A tiny crow. I asked Mom something in the shared taxi.

"Mom, are you ever scared, too?"

"Who else is scared, Ayşe? You?"

I didn't tell her Dad was scared. He might not want her to know. I wish butterflies could get into Parliament. But they can't.

Ali Visits the Office

"Jump in, Hasan!"

"Şeref Abi? Is that you?"

"Jump in!"

Me and Dad are waiting for the bus. We left the office. I went there with Dad today because Mom was taking one of the neighbors to the doctor. But I was forbidden to leave the little kitchen where my dad makes tea. Ayşe's dad works on a floor upstairs. I couldn't let anyone see me, though. I sat in the kitchen without making a sound. After we left the office, Dad started reading *Cumhuriyet* while we waited for the bus. He read it aloud to me because nobody reads the newspaper alone. And because he gets mad when he reads the newspaper.

"Civil servants are expected to sign a form pledging to work diligently, and without favoritism or discrimination. People are killing each other over politics and they think they can stop favoritism at the workplace by making civil servants sign a pledge? And they're also passing new regulations to provide firearms to anyone who feels threatened at work. As if everyone didn't have a gun already! It says here that the academic year was bloody. Just this year, three hundred ninety-five teachers and students have been killed. Turgut Özal, the undersecretary to the prime minister, is in Paris working out some kind of deal with the IMF. That beady-eyed Özal is up to something, just you wait and see. Ecevit, the leader of the Social Democrats, considers the socialist left to be too radical. He wants to exclude them. Well, what else is new? The trade union DİSK claims that the bourgeoisie is trying to foist a fascist dictatorship on the country. Foist? As if we haven't been ruled under martial law most all our lives! Parliament keeps meeting to try and give the army more power. The garbage collectors' strike is over and there are fourteen tons of garbage to be collected. Cats are being let loose in the train compartments to solve the rat infestation. They're all crazy, the whole lot of them."

Dad didn't see it, but I did. A group of men started marching down the street. They were chanting all together:

"*Ya Allah bismillah Allahu ekber!*"

Dad folded up the newspaper and stuck it inside his jacket. They'd better not see him reading *Cumhuriyet*!

"Shit! It's that fascist Alaaddin and his pack of dogs!"

He took my hand, but there was nowhere to go. They were getting closer. The man leading them all pointed to my father. At that moment, a van stopped right in front of us.

"Jump in, Hasan!"

Dad knew the driver. It was Uncle Şeref.

"Şeref Abi! Is that you? Talk about arriving in the nick of time!"

Dad was surprised but happy. It's good when something happens "in the nick of time."

Uncle Şeref didn't look at us when we got in. Dad leaned forward and looked right at his face, but he didn't look at us. That's when Dad talked to me.

"Look, Ali. It's your Uncle Sait's old comrade, Şeref. Let me get a good look at you, Şeref Abi!"

Uncle Şeref was acting like he didn't know us. There were two men in the back of the van. A van belonging to the municipality. Şeref Amca said a few words. But he still didn't look at us.

"We're going to the park. We're supposed to get one of the swans."

Dad looked a little hurt. One of the guys in the back tried to explain.

"Şeref never talks. Don't take is personally, brother. Just be glad we saved you from those fascists."

Uncle Şeref wasn't listening. He's older than the guys in the back, but they don't call him "abi." Dad gave them a dirty look. Uncle Şeref is tilting to one side, like he's weak. Or maybe he's tired. Dad grabbed his arm, like he was trying to wake him up. But Uncle Şeref kept driving without looking at Dad. Even so, Dad didn't give up. He kept talking.

"Şeref Abi, they said you'd gone to Istanbul and stayed there. So you came back?"

"Yeah. I'm working for the municipality."

"Are you doing all right?"

"I'm okay."

One of the guys in the back laughed.

"Like I told you, he doesn't talk much. Don't waste your breath."

Dad looked at the guys in the back and bit the end of his mustache. Then he kept talking to Uncle Şeref.

"How's Istanbul? They say it's even worse than here. Is that true?"

"There's a lot of bad blood . . . infighting."

Dad looked at Uncle Şeref's shoes.

"So, you're still wearing those rubber galoshes. The strikes today aren't like the old days, Şeref Abi. I remember the strike at the galosh factory. Then you and Sait went off to Istanbul."

Şeref Amca's head sank so low it looked like it was going to touch the steering wheel.

"We had some good laughs back then. There was that time you and Sait were talking about Raziye Abla. It was the fourth or fifth month of the strike and you were thinking of agreeing to the boss's terms. Raziye Abla—if I remember right, she was a widow with two kids—reached under her skirt and pulled off her long underwear. She told you to wear her underwear if you were going to settle with the boss. Sait cracked us up by saying, 'Raziye Abla's underwear with the pink roses had a more powerful effect on the working class than Lenin ever did!'"

The less Şeref said the more Dad talked. Like he was a kid.

"Do you remember that ironworker? Now what was his name? Remember how Sabri Ülker, the big industrialist, came and asked that ironworker to have a look at his industrial oven because the cookies were getting nice and crispy on top but the bottoms were still uncooked? And the ironworker—don't you remember his name?—found a way to bake the biscuits standing on end, with the heating element on the side. Sabri Ülker gave him money even though he didn't want any, and he donated the whole amount to the party. I remember how that guy said it was important that everyone found out that communists are the best workers. Was that guy an ironworker or a carpenter? Do you remember?"

"Osman the Ironworker," Uncle Şeref said. And that's all he said. After that, Dad kept his eyes on the road and his mouth shut. It was Uncle Şeref who broke the silence.

"How's Aliye doing?"

"Our house burned down. We're building a new one."

Uncle Şeref looked at Dad for the first time.

"Sait's parka?"

"It didn't burn up in the fire. Aliye wants to give it to Ali when he grows up. You remember that photo, though? The one of Sait wearing that parka? Burned to ashes. Aliye kept it on the wall right near her climbing rose. She kept moving that photo so it was always near a rosebud. Anyway, she was really upset when we lost it in the fire. Şeref Abi, have you got any other photos of Sait?"

Şeref Amca rubbed his face, smiled, and pointed to his forehead.

"They're all in here."

Şeref Amca sat up straight. The guys in the back were talking about Bülent Ersoy.

"Zeki Müren is still a man, but that Bülent Ersoy is a real queen."

"Well, it was Zeki Müren who started wearing those weird costumes."

"But Zeki didn't go and get himself a big pair of tits like Bülent."

They laughed. Dad got mad at them. That's why he said we wanted to get out at the next corner.

Dad told Şeref Abi where we lived and where he worked, but Şeref Abi won't ever come. He wasn't even listening.

"Don't go it alone," Dad said.

"I'm okay," was all Uncle Şeref said.

When we got to our neighborhood, the lanterns were burning. They're going to build our house tonight. Mom's smiling, and her cheeks are red. She's been working all day moving bricks. The aunties always mix the plaster, and the big brothers from the university lay the bricks. Mom told Dad that they sang all day while they worked. When she smiled, sweat ran down her face. The neighbors brought bread and tomatoes. We had them for supper. Mom put a whole tomato in her mouth because she was working all day. She made lots of noise chewing it. She had another tomato in her hand when she told Dad where she wanted to put the toilet. Mom and Dad looked at the spot together in the light of the gas lanterns, tomato juice running down their hands. Mom's hands are all red, but I think it's the dust from the bricks, not the tomato juice. I've seen it many times before: when people build houses, their hands get red and their faces look like tomatoes.

The revolutionary big brothers and sisters come in the morning. They stand with their hands on their hips except for when they point at the ground. They hold their tea glasses with two fingers and use their middle fingers to hold their cigarettes. They stand in a circle stirring their tea. Finally, they say, "Okay we'll build this here and that there," and their tea spoons stop moving. The spoons click against the glasses twice. Nobody makes a sound as they all stare for a while at the place the house will be built. That's when they hold their glasses and think. Next, they drive sticks into the ground and stretch string between the sticks, showing the outline of the house. The big brothers and sisters put their empty glasses on a white tray with pictures of flowers. The glasses will be waiting there for them when they start digging. Everyone smiles as they carry bricks from the truck. They sweat and they smile. Kids like me eat bread and wait on the sidelines. They shout out to us when their hands are full:

"Hey, come take off my hat for me. . . . Pick up that trowel and bring it here. . . . Get a rag and wipe the sweat off my face."

When you close your eyes and listen, there are all kinds of sounds: Ugh! Hey! Hold on, hold on. Come on, one more time. Wait! Give! Hold! Move! When the sounds turn into a song, you know the house is being built. At noontime, everyone squats on the ground and has their lunch, talking the whole time. Then they drink water. Lots of water.

As soon as a wall is finished they put a picnic stove by it to make tea. The next morning, more walls go up and a roof gets put on top. When the house is finished, everyone comes to look at it, and they're always surprised, as though they hadn't built it themselves. "Look at that!" they say. "It turned out really well! We'll add another room right over there when we have some more money." The big brothers and sisters start joking around in the garden by the front door. Everyone watches them, like they're watching a movie. Nobody understands their jokes, but they laugh anyway. Even the bricks seem to join in the laughter. After a short while, the big brothers and sisters stop laughing. They go back to stirring their tea. They start thinking again. There are other houses to build, other things to do. They get serious, and they make plans. And that's how our house was built. With everybody laughing like a ripe tomato.

Ayşe's Outing with Dad

"Pain doesn't necessarily bring wisdom, Aydın. Do you know what I mean?"

Those were Uncle Selahattin's words. Then the birds sang like crazy.

I went to the office with Dad because Grandma had to go to the doctor to get her blood sugar levels checked. Mom said, "The other day, she went to work with me. Today, she can go in with you." I don't like Dad's office at all. There's nothing there but a stapler. They don't even have a paper puncher. Then Detective Nahit called my dad. "Let's meet in Sakarya," he said on the phone. "Then we'll go to Selahattin's bird shop." Dad got upset.

"Please, Detective. Let's not get Selahattin mixed up in this if we can help it. You know how shaken up he gets."

Then we went to Sakarya. It has a stand named "Picnic." "Picnic" means eating a sandwich standing in the street. Everyone seems happy because the air smells like grilled sandwiches, and it's nice. What's more, when you squint all kinds of colors swim in front of your eyes. That's what I was doing while we stood there waiting for Uncle Detective. Dad starting talking to me about the people passing. He always does that.

"Look, Ayşe. Look at the people's hands. They're telling each other how they ran away. You know, those games they play in the streets. They're letting each other know which streets they took. See that guy over there! He's making a chopping motion. That means he ran in a straight line. And that one over there making a kind of sideways scoop with his right hand? He's showing how he rounded a corner. It's kind of funny, isn't it?"

I say yes right away just so Dad will keep talking.

"Your mom gets mad at me, Ayşe, because those guys are out playing in the streets but we're not doing anything."

"Dad, is that because we're scared?"

"Do you think we're scared?"

"But Mom gets scared too, doesn't she?"

Dad laughed.

"You'll have to ask her. When she's all on her own, she might get a little scared."

I already asked Mom, but I'm not going to tell Dad.

Uncle Detective came. He's got a denim jacket. When he walks, his head wobbles from side to side. He and Dad stood and talked for a bit.

"I didn't feel like going inside without you, Detective. Selahattin's always so quiet, you don't know what to do."

"Cihan was a good friend of yours, but he's Selahattin's brother. Don't you think he has a right to know how the investigation is going?"

"Well yes, but . . . Oh, I don't know, Detective. It's like Selahattin died too. Or lost the will to live. Like so many others in this country. Now they stay out of sight in their stationery shops, in their photo ID shops, or, like Selahattin, in their bird shops. Do you realize how many leftists have lost their jobs, are scraping by selling pots and pans and chandeliers?"

"Aydın, I don't know anything about all that. It's my job to catch people and arrest them. That's all."

"You should spare a thought for the walking dead, too, Detective."

"Speaking of which, shall we take a little walk first?"

They took big steps, so I ran. I had to run extra fast when they forgot all about me. Mom never forgets me, but Dad does.

"Detective, every time I visit Selahattin Abi, I feel terrible, but then I remember some of the things that happened and I can't help laughing.

After Cihan was killed, the photo of him they picked for their posters showed him at his most serious and scowling. He'd have been so mad if he'd seen it! 'Where on earth did those dopes dig up that photo?' he'd have said."

"Everyone who knew Cihan said he was a lot of fun."

"Boy, was he ever! Another thing that would have made Cihan mad was their chanting 'Cihans never die!' at his funeral. 'What do you mean, never die?' he'd have said. 'As you can see, those bastards killed me. I'll be six feet under in a couple minutes.'"

Dad laughed, but down into his shirt. When grown-ups do a sad-laugh, that's what they do. Uncle Detective clapped him on the back a couple of times. Dad's fun friends all died a long time ago.

"Uncle Detective, do you know Detective Columbo?"

They stopped and laughed. But then Uncle Detective tugged at his mustache and forgot all about me again.

"Before we step inside the shop, let me give you a quick update. Aydın Abi, we found a new eyewitness, an old lady in Bahçelievler who lives next door to where Cihan and his friends were living—Oh, hello Selahattin Abi. I hope you don't mind us showing up unannounced like this."

Uncle Selahattin always gives me a piece of chewing gum. His shop smells like bird's wing dust. That dust is all over the place, you see. And it smells like roasted chickpeas, but chickpeas forgotten in the bottom of the cupboard. Uncle Selahattin looked at me one way, and at Dad a different way. He didn't look at Uncle Detective at all. Even so, Uncle Detective kept talking really fast.

"Aydın Abi, let me finish and go. Selahattin Abi, we've had a new lead in the case, in Cihan's homicide."

All at once, Uncle Selahattin seemed to grow smaller. Dad squeezed his legs together on the chair, like he had to pee.

"Detective," Uncle Selahattin said. He turned to Dad and said, "Aydın."

The birds started singing.

"Listen—"

The birds want to get away. They sound like they're hurt really bad. They're singing like crazy, so loud I can only hear some of what Uncle Selahattin is saying.

"I don't want to know. I don't want to know anything about the case. Say what you want about me. Call me a disgrace who doesn't give a damn about his brother. . . . I can't believe you're making me say this!"

Uncle Detective looked ashamed. Uncle Selahattin lit a cigarette. Grown-ups smoke when they're sad. They were standing there not saying anything when a lady came in. She reminded me of Auntie Jale.

"I wonder if you've got any nightingales?"

Uncle Selahattin didn't look at her. "No!"

"But there's one right over there. I can see it!"

The birds were singing like crazy. Uncle Selahattin was scaring me.

"What the hell do you need a bird for?"

"Are you nuts or what?"

Uncle Detective smiled to himself. Then Uncle Selahattin waved his cigarette and made a sound like a laugh.

"Just leave me alone, lady!"

Dad was smiling too, but he pretended he was wiping his mustache so nobody would see. The birds finally stopped singing, and Uncle Selahattin forgave everyone.

"Guys, I beg your pardon."

"No, we beg yours," Uncle Detective said. But Uncle Selahattin spoke to my dad, not him.

"Pain doesn't necessarily bring wisdom, Aydın. Do you know what I mean?"

Uncle Selahattin puffed on his cigarette so hard that it burned down halfway.

"Cihan's friends come here from time to time, asking if there is anything they can do. They say they'll never forget him, that they named their sons after him, that they'll do this and they'll do that. Why don't they go and have another child and bring it up right? What do we do when a forest burns down? We go out and plant new trees, don't we, Detective? What the hell else can we do!"

"Brother," Dad said, but I don't think Uncle Selahattin heard. He started talking.

"Listen. In Swan Park, there are three trees onto which they carved the names Deniz, Yusuf, and Hüseyin. The three sacrificial lambs of our generation. What they forgot was that those trees were going to grow tall and those three names were going to be so high up nobody would be able to see them anymore. People find comfort in vowing they'll never forget. But Cihan's friends will remember other things, not the things we're trying not to forget. Aydın, it's life we remember, not death. Harping on someone's death means you might as well be dead, too. Do you know what I mean, Detective?"

Uncle Selahattin looked at me. Sometimes, everyone looks like they pity me. I wonder if I'm pitiful?

Uncle Detective started talking really fast again.

"Selahattin Abi, we found another eyewitness. A woman who says she heard four people talking about Cihan's building and his apartment number. She's afraid, but we'll get her to talk."

"Detective, are you even listening to me? I don't give a damn! I'm angry with myself for being alive. Don't take it personally. Please. It's just that I can't take it anymore. Here I am in this shop, with all these birds . . ."

Uncle Selahattin looked like he was going to cry. I was embarrassed for him. I turned around and went straight to the back of the shop to give the birds some seeds. Dad tried to change the subject. I knew what he was doing.

"Hey, Selahattin Abi. What's this? What are you doing with this diagram and these papers? You haven't started operating on your birds, have you?"

"Oh, that. A friend from the Department of Veterinary Medicine left that here. I guess he forgot it. They've got some plans for the swans in the park."

The swans! What are they going to do to the swans? Uncle Detective has a radio that pops and crackles sometimes. He stepped outside when it started doing that.

"What are they going to do to the swans?"

"The martial law commander of Ankara—I can't remember the bastard's name—took one of the swans from the park and put it in his garden."

"You're kidding."

"With all the commotion these days, I guess nobody cared. Anyway, the swan decided it didn't like its new home and tried to fly back to the park."

Dad laughed.

"Well, what do you expect? It's an Ankara swan, a revolutionary swan."

They kept talking, but I followed Uncle Detective outside. I was so curious about that radio. Terrible men talk in it. It's not like a normal radio. It never plays music. And Uncle Detective smells funny, a smell I can't put a name to. But it's a scary smell. Like . . . like . . . It was only when Dad took my hand that I realized he'd come outside. Dad looked at Uncle Detective but didn't say anything. Uncle Detective started talking really fast again.

"Don't get angry with me, brother. What can I do? It's my job. Do you think I want to upset Selahattin Abi? I've got to catch whoever did it. I'll go out of my mind if I don't catch somebody, anybody."

Uncle Detective put his hands on his hips and bowed his head. When Dad is talking with other men, I sometimes look up at their chins and their whiskers and at that thing like a ball that moves up and down in their throats. It makes me forget to listen to what they're saying.

The auntie who came into the bird shop is going into the aquarium shop. Fish don't shiver in the winter, so you don't need to put them on the radiator. If you do put a fish tank on the radiator, the fish die. But

God doesn't punish children who put their fish tanks on the radiator, because they were just trying to make it warmer for the fish and they didn't know any better.

Ali's Outing in Swan Park

"What are you saying, Bahri Abi! Not our Turgay? The Turgay from Middle Eastern Technical University?"

We're in Swan Park. Hüseyin Abi lets go of my hand and puts his in his pocket. Maybe he keeps string in his pockets like me. His chief just came to meet him. Hüseyin Abi brought some pots. I know what's inside of them. But I mustn't tell. I mustn't tell. When his chief, Bahri Abi, says, "We've lost Turgay," the pots Hüseyin Abi is holding in one of his hands start going *clank, clank.*

"Chill out, Hüseyin! Put those pots down."

Hüseyin Abi puts the pots on the ground and they go quiet. Now Hüseyin Abi has both hands in his pockets.

"Are the pieces in the pots, Hüseyin?"

"Brother, you promised Turgay wouldn't get mixed up with guns. So how'd he get shot?"

"Chill, Hüseyin. Chill."

Hüseyin Abi is shrinking. This is my first time in Swan Park. We were going to look at the swans. I love those birds. They don't make any noise.

Bahri Abi picks up the pots and says, "Let's go get some tea. It's not like you think."

They ordered me a soda. I don't like soda, but that's what they always get kids. Hüseyin Abi kept stirring his tea. On and on, without stopping. He can't hear the spoon going *clink clink* against the glass. If he could, he'd stop stirring. Bahri Abi takes the spoon from Hüseyin Abi's hand and puts it on the saucer. He leans closer to the table.

"Hüseyin, Turgay didn't get mixed up with any guns. That's not what happened."

Hüseyin Abi looked over at me. Like I was dead. It was the same look he gave me when he pulled me out of the well. That time I vomited black. People do that sometimes. They look at me like I'm dead.

"Hüseyin, have you calmed down? I'm going to tell you once. Then I'm out of here. I've got to meet the guys who are taking those pieces to Dikmen."

"Okay, brother. I'm listening."

"Nobody killed Turgay. It was suicide."

Suicide is when you kill yourself. It was like Hüseyin's face curled up and hid in his mustache.

"Hüseyin, are you listening to me? A few days ago, they arrested Turgay out on the street. A special team has begun operations in Ankara. I've been hearing about them for a while. They're something else. Professional. I don't know what they did to him. He was detained for three days. Then they let him go. He went home and killed himself. That's all we know."

"Bahri Abi—"

"Hüseyin, I need you to decide if we should have posters at his funeral. This is complicated. You know, as a suicide . . . Talk to the guys at the university and decide. Do we write that he was a 'martyr to the revolution,' or not? Now, moving along . . ."

Bahri Abi rested his hand on top of the pots. That meant he wanted to know what was inside.

"There's a Port-Said. It jams sometimes. And there's a 14-caliber and a STEN."

"Okay. We've also got a couple of automatics arriving from another neighborhood. I need you to go and pick them up from a friend in Liberation. You're expected there."

"Okay, brother."

"Have you told everyone in the neighborhood? These are on loan. Get a couple of shots off at the opposite neighborhood. I'll get them in a couple of weeks. Just let the fascists know you've got automatics so they don't mess with you. If you need the automatics later, you can take them back and use them on night watch."

"Okay, brother."

"How many magazines have we sold, Hüseyin?"

"Um . . ."

"Never mind. We'll talk about the magazine and the poster later. Hüseyin?"

"What?"

"This will all be over in a couple of months. There are three or four neighborhoods left in Ankara that we don't control. It'll be over soon. We'll do our mourning then, not now."

"Okay, brother."

"There's one more thing, Hüseyin. I need you to listen good. I know the news about Turgay—"

"I'm listening."

"After the Çorum Massacre, we're expecting more assassinations. We've decided to provide protection for some writers and intellectuals. If you've got any level-headed guys in your neighborhood who could help us out—"

"Who are we going to protect?"

"We're asking around. Those who agree will get close protection. Those who don't will be protected from a distance, and won't even realize what we're doing."

"Okay, brother."

"Hüseyin. Don't go it alone. This is no time to go it alone."

Revolutionaries don't go it alone. That's something bad, like being "opportunist." It means thinking only about yourself. If you stay all alone you get sad, like Uncle Şeref. Now, because Hüseyin Abi is sad, I can't go and look at the swans. That would make me an opportunist. But I can look at them from far away. I can look a little. From far away. Bahri Abi left us. There were two other big brothers with him. He doesn't it go it alone.

Right when they left, two men came up. They chased one of the swans. I know those men. They were in the van with Uncle Şeref.

I didn't tell Hüseyin Abi that I knew them. Maybe that's a secret too.

"Catch it! Catch it!"

"It's huge!"

"Grab its wing. Don't screw up again."

"I couldn't help it! If that brat hadn't started yelling, we'd have caught it! Hey, the commander only wanted one more. Why are you chasing after that one? I've got hold of this one. Come on, let's take it away. People are going to kick up a fuss if we go after a second one. You heard what the commander said. One at a time!"

Hüseyin Abi was like me, talking in a dream. He looked at the swans. He looked at the men. When he talked, it was to the air in front of him, not to me.

"Ali, there was a composer named Tchaikovsky. You'll learn about him when you grow up. He wrote a ballet called "Swan Lake." Turgay Abi loved it. You know, Turgay Abi could play the guitar too. He was so smart. Smarter than the rest of us. But in thousands of years of human history he had the bad luck to end up in a civil war. Now the magazine people are going to argue about whether he should be called a martyr. If you slip through the cracks, are you a martyr? Turgay Abi was a physicist, and totally opposed to guns and violence. But when I first introduced him to Bahri Abi, he said he could pull off the perfect heist. Bahri Abi was furious. 'We're organizing for our survival,' he said. 'We're not crooks! Oh, by the way, Turgay, what do you know about grilled sheep's intestines and egg and onion sandwiches?' We all burst out laughing, but within five days Turgay Abi had become an expert on both of those foods. After three days in Beşevler Square studying our *kokoreç* and *gobit* vendors, he went up to Bahri Abi, report in hand, and said: 'You know, I was thinking, if we redesigned the vending carts like I sketched here, and if we added a few more items to the menu, the ones I've listed here, we could increase daily profits from five thousand lira to eight thousand lira.' That's when Bahri Abi nicknamed him 'Turgay the Intestine Researcher.' Turgay wore glasses with a missing lens, and when he poked his finger in through the empty frame and scratched at his eyelid you knew he was about to blurt out some bright idea: 'You know, I was thinking, the highest cost in the citrus business down south is labor. If we got our people to do the picking and we pre-purchased the harvest in the summer months, we could sell it at a nice profit in Ankara come winter, especially considering we have our guys in the wholesale market hall.' He'd put down a book by Spinoza or some such and start scribbling calculations on a slip of paper about our souvenir sellers in Kuşadası. He laughed a lot, Ali. He always carried a sandwich wafer in his jacket pocket. He'd give one to a girl and walk away saying, 'If a wafer won't make a girl happy, nothing will.' Damn you, Turgay! Don't forget any of this Ali. Remember it all. Never forget any of it!"

I asked Hüseyin something, but I guess he didn't hear me.

"Hüseyin Abi, are remembering and not forgetting the same thing?"

Hüseyin Abi went to the restroom. I looked at the swans. The men chased a swan. The swan didn't make a sound. None.

Alone with Grandma

"When troubles arise . . ."

"Ah! Do you hear that, Ayşe? I turned it on just in time!"

In our house, we have a bottle of almond liqueur and Grandma pours out a little bit. Later, she pours a little more. I eat a little dab of hazelnut cocoa spread, and then a little more. Until it becomes a whole lot. Mom and Dad went over to Samim's apartment, leaving me alone with Grandma. She turned on the radio and sat down in her slip, "all nice and cool." Grandma has long, thin boobs. She pulled out one of Mom's cigarettes and lit it, but she doesn't smoke like my mom. She kissed the cigarette with a *puff puff*. That's when the song started playing on the radio.

Grandma did another *puff puff* on her cigarette. She poured some more almond liqueur, looked at me, and laughed. "Let me give me you a little bit," she said. She filled a teeny glass. Then she said, "Hold it like this, with your pinkie cocked." I sat down at the table next to her.

"Take tiny sips, Ayşe."

Grandma has a scrapbook. She opened it up.

"What do you think of this, Ayşe? I'd got as far as, *The leaf does not fall, the tree casts it forth / The spirit perseveres, the body wastes away.* Then I added, *If you do not come to me, the world shall turn and bring you.* I suppose these verses are in memory of bygone days and of your grand-father, İlyas Bey. I wonder if you'll bother to read any of this when you grow up."

She laughed to herself. It kind of scared me. There was something strange in her laugh. Grandma's a little tipsy now, and I can see bloody threads in her eyes.

"I've collected so much for you in this scrapbook, Ayşe. Comical clippings, poems, holiday congratulations, all kinds of things to help you remember that these days weren't always filled with gloom and doom."

Grandma really has filled up that scrapbook with all sorts of things from newspapers and magazines. They don't smell like paper, though. They smell like her hands. Like talcum powder and börek. I sniffed them.

"You enjoyed having Ali over the other day, didn't you, sweetie? He's a clever little thing, sitting there so serious with an encyclopedia or a book. And so well-behaved, too. It's obvious his mother has given him a modern upbringing. Bravo to her! I'll ask Sevgi to tell her to bring her boy around from time to time. You two can become friends. And the Sugar Feast is coming up. Jale Hanım calls it 'Eid.' I should sew him some clothes so the poor boy has something nice for the holidays."

Grandma should sew Ali a shirt. I think he only has one.

"Ayşe, why don't we take Ali to the Citadel one day soon? Per-haps we can visit the museum as well. Would you like that, sweetie? And I need to stop by Cavit Bey's to get some more vanishing cream. Ah, Cavit Bey! He's still a fine-looking man in his beautifully pressed trousers and his spotless white lab coat. And he's so jolly he makes you forget all your worries. The last time I saw him was in the winter. I was wearing my best wool skirt, and when I stepped through the door he called out, 'Oh, I think my heart just skipped a beat. For a moment, I thought Sophia Loren was stepping into my shop. Welcome, Nejla Hanım!' Can you believe it? The silly goose!"

Grandma laughed so hard her head went back and her boobs went forward. Then she sat like she always does, with that hump on her back.

"Your mother thinks Cavit Bey's creams don't work, but every time I see Jale Hanım she says, 'My word, Nejla Hanım, your cheeks are as smooth as a baby's bottom.' Well, it's all thanks to Cavit Bey's vanishing cream."

I'm getting a little scared because one of Grandma's straps slipped down. *Pull it back up, quick!* Her boob mustn't show. And if Grandma falls, I won't be able to pick her up. I'm taking tiny sips but my mouth feels sticky. Grandma isn't talking to me like I'm little, but like I'm a grown-up. It's scary.

"Back in '63, a passenger plane collided midair with a military aircraft over Ulus, killing dozens of people out shopping, and many more got badly burned. Some of the survivors used Cavit Bey's special creams and—would you believe it?—none of them ended up with scars on their faces! Sevgi doesn't know anything about that. A whole generation recognized the burn scars on one another's faces. They'd whisper to each other, 'The plane collision, right?' It always came up when marriages were being arranged: 'She doesn't have any burn marks on her face, does she? No? Well that's a relief.' Ah, those were the days!"

The other strap just slipped down. *I don't want to see Grandma's boobs!*

"And in 1960, when a woman watching the public hanging of the Adana Monster in Samanpazarı Square nearly had a miscarriage, it was Cavit Bey who saved her baby. They hanged that monster for murder, but these days the streets are full of killers and nobody calls them monsters. . . . Back then, some women claimed that his mentholated hemorrhoid cream worked wonders for dark circles under the eye. I've never had that problem, though, so I wouldn't know."

Grandma stroked her cheek and ran her fingers through her hair. Like that singer, Ajda Pekkan.

"I haven't stopped by to see Cavit Bey for ever so long. He must be wondering why. He'd never come out and admit it, though. Nobody tells anyone anything anymore. Sevgi certainly doesn't. She thought those letters of hers were a secret. I know she took them away so Aydın wouldn't see them. The other night she came home a little drunk. Something's going on with her, but I can't come out and ask her, now can I? She doesn't pay enough attention to her little girl, but she'll bite my head off if I say anything. At this rate, the poor girl's not going to have any memories of her mother."

I'm right here, Grandma! Stop talking like I'm not here!

"Aydın always keeps his feelings bottled up, and Sevgi is so aloof, so high and mighty with him. If she treated him with a little tenderness, he'd be over the moon, but she always holds back. Who knows? Maybe it's better that way. They say one loves and one is loved. She's got her husband wrapped around her little finger. Not that it does her any good. All she wants is for him to be miserable. Nothing he does is ever quite good enough for her. It's been that way for years. As though she wasn't the one who wanted to get married, the one who ran into Aydın's arms the minute she got of prison. Well, she's the daughter of an officer and he's the son of a worker, and he's always going to fall short, no matter how many handsprings he does to impress her. As a relationship begins, so it continues. He's so attentive to her fears and phobias, though. I know my daughter through and through. She holds her head high and puts on a brave face, but she's a bit of a coward at heart. Yet she bosses Aydın around, asking why he didn't do this or that. Why doesn't she do it herself? If she didn't have a husband, she wouldn't be able to be so demanding. Try doing that when you're single. Try getting mad and telling someone to leave you alone when you're already all alone. She treats Aydın badly, but she'll stick with him through thick and thin. Not that he realizes that. I think he's terrified she'll leave him one day. Like I said, maybe it's better that way. What do I know? I think I'll pour myself another glass."

Grandma has completely forgotten me. *This isn't funny anymore.* I feel like Mom and Dad will never come home.

"Look at this one! After Parliament voted to give a medal to Özcan Tekgül, the belly dancer, one of the opposition MPs introduced a motion asking where they planned to pin it. Well, he did have a point! Anyway, in an interview she said, 'Pin it to my heart.' I'll cut that out and paste it in the scrapbook. It'll make you laugh one day. In this article, it says that an MP from the Justice Party has a lion chained in his garden. He claims a female admirer from Africa gave it to him! We'll keep that too."

Grandma doesn't look at me at all. *I think I'm going to cry.* She's trying to stand up.

"Nobody tells anyone anything anymore. Oh, my word! I feel a bit dizzy."

The tears come.

"Ayşe! What's the matter? I can't bear to see you so upset! Here, let me give you a kiss. Ayşe! What's come over you?"

Grandma pulled up the straps of her slip. The doorbell rang. Mom and Dad have finally come home.

What Happens at a Funeral?

I wasn't going to go to the funeral with my mom today, but she took me with her because she couldn't find anyone to look after me. The aunties filled the bus. The women made Auntie Seher their "chief" for the day—but the real chief is Hüseyin Abi. Also on the bus was our Laz neighbor, Nuran Abla. Auntie Seher sounded mad when she talked to Nuran Abla.

"Now listen here, Nuran. You insisted on coming with us, but this funeral will be different. I hope it's not too much for you."

"What do you mean, different? Communists bury their dead too, don't they?"

"I'm not saying you shouldn't come, but if fighting breaks out, stick close to me. I need to keep an eye on you and on Şükriye, with her bad leg."

My mom didn't become the chief. Hüseyin Abi is staying with us, the guns are in our coal cellar, and they put the television in our house because that's where everyone meets, but Mom still didn't want to be the chief. She said it's someone else's turn. Because my uncle is dead.

It's so noisy on the bus. The aunties talk and talk. Auntie Seher sat next to Nuran Abla and looked her in the eye.

"Nuran, you should be coming to the resistance meetings, like your husband. I know you like to stay in the background, but the neighborhood is yours as much as anyone else's. And those girls from the university will teach you to read and write. You don't know how to read, do you?"

"No, sister."

Nuran Abla's face is snow-white. Laz Hamit's face is beet-red. He's her son. I think she has a daughter, too, but I've never seen her. Nuran Abla's son and her husband are fat, but she's thin. She makes lots of bread and they eat it all. She does all the work, and that's why her face is so white. She wears a headscarf, and that's why she never talks. Nuran Abla is always scared. Auntie Seher fills up her seat and half of Nuran Abla's seat while she's talking. I think she's "organizing" Nuran Abla. I once saw Hüseyin Abi doing organizing. He kept saying we had to "unite."

"Nuran, we'll win if we unite. If we're divided, they'll break us. Do you remember what we did when the demolition team came? We put all our children in front of the bulldozer. And then what happened? They left without tearing down a single house. That's how we win! United! If we all pitch in, there's not a problem we can't solve. Your problems are everyone's problems, and ours are yours. And anyway, the fascists control only three of the neighborhoods in Ankara. We'll finish this within the year."

"Sister, I've got a problem."

The bus stopped. The pretty girl stood up. I found out her name is Birgül. When she talks, her cheeks are even more beautiful. I've seen Hüseyin Abi petting her cheeks.

"Ladies, don't go off on your own at the funeral. Stay together and look out for each other. When the service is over, we'll all take the bus back to the neighborhood. Don't scatter if the police attack us."

Auntie Seher frowned.

"What is it, Nuran? Tell me about your problem."

Just then, beautiful Birgül Abla started shouting out slogans so the other women would learn them.

"We are many! We are united!"

I hear everything. I can hear what Nuran Abla is saying to Auntie Seher.

". . . hard to tell you, sister."

"Go on, tell me. There's a solution for every problem."

Beautiful Birgül Abla shouted again. Her hair falls in front of her cheek sometimes.

"You'll pay for the Çorum Massacre!"

". . . the thing is, down there, between her legs . . . it's kind of stuck. We can't say anything to her father. He'd only make her feel worse. She pees sideways. She's just started school, and she holds it in until she gets home, crying all the way."

Auntie Nuran held the corner of her scarf over her mouth, but I could tell she was crying. Birgül Abla yelled again.

"Revolution is the only path!"

Nuran Abla wiped her eyes.

"We can't wait until the revolution happens."

"Don't let it upset you, Nuran. We'll find a solution. That's what revolutionaries are for!"

"I don't know, sister. They guard at night, but I can't tell the revolutionaries about my girl."

"Trust me. Don't be scared. Don't be ashamed. There's no place for fear in a revolution."

I looked at my mom. She didn't hear what Auntie Seher was saying because she was too busy chanting slogans. That girl is "stuck" down there. *What does that mean?*

Hüseyin Abi got on the bus. A rifle! We were sitting by the back door, so he saw us first. He looked right at my mom.

"Where's that rifle from, Hüseyin? What happened to the other pieces? Did you take them out of the coal cellar?"

"It's been taken care of, sister. This one's new. You and Seher Abla are responsible for these women. Birgül will help, too. Be careful."

"Hüseyin, wait a second. What's the matter? You're acting strange."

"We lost one of our comrades. I'll tell you about it later."

Beautiful Birgül Abla's got a sandwich wafer in her pocket. The end is sticking out. She didn't give it to me. Hüseyin Abi would have.

Auntie Seher grabbed Nuran Abla by the arm.

"It'll be taken care of. I just talked with the one of the revolutionary girls. They'll arrange a doctor and we'll take your daughter there together."

Nuran Abla started crying.

"God bless you."

"Nuran, God doesn't bless revolutionaries."

"Never mind, sister. Never mind."

Later, the funeral began. Everyone lined up. The dede leading the service was there. His bushy mustache was white, but with yellow tips. The lines in his face were many and deep, as though carved with a knife. His eyes were always watery. I felt like crying when he talked. *Be quiet! Be quiet!*

"Bismishah, Bismishah! Our friend alighted in this world. He ate, he drank, he laughed, he cried, he departed. Our friend, who sided with the oppressed and opposed the cruel, has returned to God. He has taken on a new form. When he is reborn, it may be in the form of a pigeon, of a lion, of a swan . . ."

Birgül Abla whispered in my mother's ear, loud enough for me to hear.

"Your dede must have visited Swan Park today."

Mom didn't laugh. She was a bit put out. The dede kept talking in a voice that sounded like he was crying.

"Only the Shah of Shahs knows the form in which our departed friend shall return to the world. What kind of person did you know the departed to be? Do you freely renounce any claims you might have on him?"

Nuran Abla shouted it the loudest.

"I do!"

"May God-Muhammed-Ali be content with those tongues that gave their blessings. May the cycle continue for all time!"

I can hear Nuran Abla saying, "Allah, Allah," with the others, but then she hides her mouth behind her scarf and says, "Amen."

"Pain is lesser if shared; love is greater if shared. May suffering decrease and love increase. May God grant a long life to the living. May God grant favor to Haji Bektash Veli, Pir Sultan. Attention to the truth; *Hû*! Ya Ali!"

Now they are chanting "hû," I wish they'd stop. *Please stop!*

Dad came. Mom held her handbag close to her belly and frowned.

"What are you doing here? Did they let you leave work?"

"Never mind about that. He came and helped us when we were fighting for water. I wanted to pay my last respects. Hüseyin got a new rifle. Have they taken the pieces in our coal cellar?"

"I'll tell you about that later. Tomorrow's a Thursday. I've got work. I'll take the boy with me."

"What are we having for dinner tonight?"

"If we get out of here alive, flour soup. Don't look at me like that. The money ran out yesterday. We'll eat either stones or flour soup."

"Is that Nuran over there? Well, good for her! I asked her husband to come, but he didn't."

"You must not have asked him the right way. Why are you looking at me like that?"

Then the police attacked us. The police always attack us. They want to kill us. Nuran Abla fought back the hardest. My mom and Auntie Seher and all the other aunties kept patting her on the back when we were back on the bus. "Good for you," they said. Everyone seemed extra happy. Even the ones who'd got hurt were laughing and joking. It was exciting, and they couldn't stop talking about it.

"Nuran, you're the lion of Rambling Gardens!" Auntie Seher said.

Nuran Abla got embarrassed. She covered her mouth with her scarf, but her eyes were smiling.

There was a meeting in our house that night, so I went out into the garden and looked at the silkworms. Gökhan got them from the market, lots of them. He gave me some. My dad and Gökhan's dad came out into the garden. Dad laughed.

"I'm surprised they're still alive. Silkworms usually die about May."

I'm going to take Ayşe some silkworms. She'll love it. She loves everything. Then I heard Gökhan's father—he works for the municipality—say that they were going to catch all the swans in the park, and that they were going to do something to their wings so they couldn't fly anymore. Ayşe might get scared when I tell her. But I don't want to scare her.

UNIT 6

The Attractions of Our Fair City

Visiting Museums Is Fun

Ayşe took my hand. In the garden of the museum. She put a daisy in her hair and spun around in the sunlight. Arms open wide, she sang a song I didn't know: *You're slender and white as a daisy.*

She twirled her skirt. "Now you look just like beautiful Birgül Abla," I said. Because . . . because . . . Her hair stuck to her cheek while she was singing. She laughed. Then she came up and took my hand. My mom would love it here. There's a climbing rose, just like the one in our house before it burned down. The one that used to be next to the photo of my Uncle Sait.

—

When Ali looked at me I wanted to twirl my skirt. He doesn't say a word. He wanted to give me a daisy, but he didn't. I took the daisy from his hand, but I'm sure he was going to give it to me. Ali gave me a daisy! That's why I sang a song, because it makes you want to sing when Ali looks at you. He'd never been in a museum before, but he's still smarter than all the kids in my class. He can read the tiny letters,

not just the big ones, and he brought me silkworms. Baby worms.
Eensy-weensy worms.

—

Mom asked me why I wanted to take Ayşe silkworms. She said a box
of bugs was no kind of present.

My mom can be a real opportunist. I didn't say anything, but she
let me in the end. When I don't say anything, I get what I want. I put
the silkworms in a box with some mulberry leaves. Hüseyin Abi picked
them straight from the tree. He asked me where I was taking them. I
didn't answer. I'll tell him later. People think silkworms don't make a
sound, but if you listen carefully you can hear the *crunch, crunch* of
their munching on the leaves. They don't have any teeth, but they eat
a lot. They'll make a cocoon and sleep inside it. Then they'll be quiet.
Our neighborhood is so noisy they'd never fall asleep. It's quiet where
Ayşe lives.

—

When Ali came to my house and gave me the box of silkworms, I
gave him *Ulduz and the Crows*. Mom already read it out loud to me.
It's about a boy and a girl who rescue a baby crow. The grown-ups
don't like the boy and the girl, and they never talk to them. So the
boy and the girl fly away with all the crows. The box of silkworms is
on the bookshelf now. Ali put it right in front of the *Wonderland of
Knowledge* because he loves that encyclopedia and he says everything
we don't understand is inside it. Everything! I told him everything
is in the archive in Parliament, but then he said everything is deep
in the ground under Ankara. Then I told him about the butterflies.
They were orange and they couldn't get into Parliament. When we got
home, Mom told me more about the butterflies. She said they weren't
allowed in Parliament because nothing nice is allowed in this country,

especially in Parliament. I wish the butterflies could get into Parliament. They wanted to. Wouldn't it be great?

Then I told Ali about the swan. How they were going to take it away. I heard Dad telling Mom that a swan trying to get back to the park from the commander's yard flew into a building and died. Now they're going to get another swan from the park, and they're going to do something to its wings so it can't fly anymore.

It was when I told him about the swan that Ali spoke for the first time that day.

—

Ayşe knows about the swan. How did she find out? I told her about the dede and how he said people can come back to this world as a swan. She said you go to heaven after you die and never come back. She's so stupid sometimes. I told her the fascists were going to do something to the swans. Ayşe doesn't even know what a fascist is. She's never had to get water from the well and fight fascists. She wears white stockings and has a scented eraser. When I told her that butterflies were going to come out of the silkworm cocoons she screamed, "Orange!" I wish she wouldn't yell. And I don't think she understands about the swan.

—

Grandma was so happy this morning.

First, she told my mom that we were "cooped up all the time" and she wanted "to take the children on an outing" since she needed to stop by the pharmacy anyway.

Grandma has only one stick of lipstick. It was almost gone, so she had to reach inside with her fingertip. She spread some red on her lips. I sat next to her in front of the mirror and sniffed the drawer of her "vanity table." It smells like the theater in there. Mom never wears lipstick, but Grandma wears it to go to the pharmacy. She let me try it.

"Ayşe, just a little bit. Like this. That's right. Now pucker up. That's it. Okay, press your lips together. No, not like that! Now you've got some on your chin. Silly goose!"

Grandma says I'm pretty as a princess, but Mom and Dad better not see me. I bet Ali would like me with red lips, smelling like the theater.

Grandma was surprised to see the silkworms.

"Ayşe, you know that mulberry tree in the garden of the police station? We can go and ask the police for some fresh leaves. Then the silkworms will make themselves cocoons until they're ready to become moths."

"But Ali said they'd become butterflies!"

"Well, Ayşe, moths and butterflies are nearly the same thing."

When Grandma said "police," Ali pulled out his string. He didn't say another word until we got into the shared taxi.

—

Ayşe wants us to get mulberry leaves from the police station. *This isn't a game!* When Hüseyin Abi was picking mulberry leaves this morning, he made his eyes into slits because of the sun. He looked like he was going to cry.

I remember that day he came home crying when I was real little. He'd been at the police station. Dad had to help him stand. He had a broken arm and no shoes because they'd beaten the undersides of his feet. Hüseyin Abi didn't want to talk about it in front of me, but Mom said, "We all live here together. We've got nothing to hide from each other. This isn't a game!" Hüseyin Abi's lip got fat and his eyes were slits, like he was looking at the sun.

He didn't smile even once when he was talking with me this morning.

"Hüseyin Abi, what does it mean to come back in the form of a swan?"

He took out a cigarette and whistled, long and low. Then he looked for his lighter. He couldn't find it. He cursed and pulled out a box of matches.

Hüseyin Abi lost his Ibelo lighter. It was a nice lighter. I sat down under the mulberry tree with him. He hugged me, squeezing my arms against my sides. I felt like the letter "I." Hüseyin Abi sounded so sad.

"To be reborn in the form of a swan . . . means dialectical materialism. One day, we die . . . No, let me put it another way. We stop living one day, but we don't stop existing. Ali, everything in existence lasts forever. But sometimes things continue in a new form. So a dead person—a person who is no longer living—might come back to the world one day as a swan. Now, say it with me: di-a-lec-ti-cal ma-ter-i-al-ism. It's the continuous cycle of life."

Hüseyin Abi started looking at his cigarette, not me. He put the burning end of it near his finger. Like he wanted to burn himself.

"What did they do to the swans, Hüseyin Abi? The ones in the park."

"Let me give you an example. Let's say I have a friend who's no longer living. He might have become a swan. He's alive, he's just not Turgay anymore."

"What did they do the swans, Hüseyin Abi?"

"Huh? Oh, the swans. They're doing to the swans what they do to us. Those fascists have even found the time to oppress the swans. Never forget, Ali. Fascists always have plenty of time. They lie in wait, ready to strike again and again."

I won't forget, Hüseyin Abi. I remember everything. I picked up the mulberry leaves, put them in a box, and set the silkworms on top of the leaves, one by one. I put my ear close to the silkworms and listened.

"Ali, are you really going to give your silkworms to that rich girl? What makes you think she'd want them? We'll buy a sandwich wafer and you can take it to her."

I walked away. I was mad at Hüseyin Abi. He doesn't know Ayşe. She's not that kind of girl. I gave her one of my strings last time. She's silly sometimes, but she's not that kind of girl. Hüseyin Abi gave a sandwich wafer to beautiful Birgül, not me. I remember.

—

Ali doesn't know anything about downtown Ankara, so I keep telling him: "This is Red Crescent Square, Ali. . . . Look! That's Soysal Marketplace. . . . Right now, we're passing Yeni Karamürsel department store."

Ali pulls a piece of string out of his pocket. He pulled out a folded-up piece of paper, too, but he put it back. *I wonder what it is?* He just sat there staring at his string. I tugged at it. At first, he wouldn't let go, but then he let me have it. I made a ring out of the string and showed it to him. I laughed. He didn't. "You can't get mulberry leaves from the police," he said. "The fascists might do something to the silkworms, too." He looked so scared. "They're doing something to the swans. You don't know." Ali is trying to scare me. I hugged him, but he pulled back. I decided never to talk to him again. After a while he said, "I can't get you a sandwich wafer." I couldn't help but smile. He smiled too. "The silkworms are so cute," I said. "Eensy-weensy worms." I wiggled like a worm and he smiled again. The taxi went over a bump and Grandma cried, "Oh my, oh my." Then we both laughed and laughed. Everyone stared at us. It was the first time I heard Ali laugh.

—

When I laughed, it came out really loud, like the kids I see on TV. Then I called that girl by her name.

"Look, Ayşe. That's Youth Park."

Ay-şe. It doesn't scare her when I talk, and it doesn't scare her when I don't talk. I'm going to tell her. She should know that they're not playing games at the police station. If she goes there, and she doesn't know, they might break her arm. And we need to find out what they're doing to the swans. Hüseyin's friend might be one of those swans. It's possible. That's what he said. He's been so cross lately, like he's looking into the sun. I know Hüseyin Abi won't help me with the swans. He's busy.

—

Ali's never been to the Citadel, but he knows everything because he looks it up in the encyclopedia. Just before we left home he ran over to our bookshelf and, under *D*, found "dialectical materialism." He said it was too hard to explain to me. Then he went to *S* and found "silkworm." He said the silkworms will come back to life as moths. I asked him if they'd try to fly into Parliament, but he told me not to go to the police station. He looked all scared again, so I said, "Look, Ali! That's my grandma's favorite pharmacy. That's where we're going."

—

"Good morning, Cavit Bey."

"Good morning, Nejla Hanım. Welcome. Come in, come in. Let me order you a lemonade. Soda for the little ones? Welcome, young lady. Welcome, young man."

Pharmacist Cavit Bey always wears a white coat and stands up very straight. The only time Grandma wears lipstick is when she goes to his shop. That's because she puckers her lips when she talks to him and she laughs a funny laugh.

"I've run out of vanishing cream again. I thought I'd stop by and pick up another jar. It's so nice for the children to get some air."

"Who is the young man?"

"He's the cleaning la— I mean, the helper's son. He and Ayşe have become great friends. Ali's always got his nose in a book. He's sharp as a tack."

"Wonderful!"

Pharmacist Cavit Bey ordered two orange sodas for us and a lemonade for Grandma. She holds the glass like she holds her almond liqueur, with her fingertips. Ali is looking at Uncle Cavit Bey's bottles of medicine. Grandma calls out like she's singing a song.

"Children! You can look, but don't touch!"

"Do you have medicine for girls?"

Grandma and Uncle Cavit Bey can't understand why Ali would ask that.

"Why would you want medicine for girls, young man?"

"I know someone who's stuck down there."

Nobody said a word, but when Uncle Cavit Bey started laughing, Grandma did too. I think Ali said something shameful, because after they laughed they didn't say anything. Like they hadn't heard him. Ali got mad again. He pulled the strings out of his pocket.

"It's terribly hot this summer, isn't it, Cavit Bey?"

"They say another heat wave is heading in from Africa, Nejla Hanım. Still, Ankara summers are always hot. I've never understood why everyone acts so surprised, year after year."

"How true, Cavit Bey. Ah, but wouldn't it be lovely if we could go somewhere cool together. The Beer Garden in Atatürk Forest, perhaps, or a picnic on Mt. Elma."

Cavit Bey stopped what he was doing. Then he laughed. *I wonder if Grandma said something shameful?*

———

I need some medicine for Nuran's daughter. She'd never be able come here. They don't have enough money. I need to get it for them! I have to! Ayşe puts her hand on her hip. Her soda bottle is on the floor. She's pushing it with the tip of her shoe. She's going to spill it. She's looking at her grandma, but her grandma isn't looking back. She's doing it to make her grandma angry. I don't want her grandma to get angry. I don't want her to yell. "Don't do that!" I say to Ayşe. She shrugs her shoulders at me. I know what to say to make her look at me:

"I think I know a way to get the butterflies into Parliament."

It works. Ayşe looks at me. When she looks at me like that, I get taller or something. Nejla Hanım is looking at the pharmacist the same way Ayşe is looking at me.

"I suppose every lady in Ankara visits your shop, Cavit Bey. There's nothing like your vanishing cream anywhere else."

"You're the fairest lady of them all, Nejla Hanım! Your lemonade must be getting warm. Shall I order you another one?"

"No, thank you. I was wondering, Cavit Bey, if you ever went to the CSO concert hall? Perhaps you and your wife—"

"If you're free, let's go together next Sunday."

"Oh! I've spilled my lemonade. What a mess I've made!"

"Don't worry about it, Nejla Hanım. My apprentice will clean it up. Let me splash some of my cologne on your hand. I made it just today. It's tobacco-scented."

The pharmacist wiped Nejla Hanım's hand with a cloth.

Ayşe's still looking at me.

"How?"

"I'll tell you. Later."

"Cavit Bey, your cologne is so wonderfully fragrant," Ayşe's grandma says.

—

We left the pharmacy to go to the museum. It's being renovated, so we sit in the garden. Grandma keeps looking at her hand. She's even happier than she was this morning. She keeps humming to herself. Ali and I chase each other around the rosebushes. Then he picked a daisy. I took it from him. But he gave it to me.

—

In the shared taxi, Ayşe put the daisy in her buttonhole. That's what her grandmother told her to do. The taxi stopped near Liberation Park. It couldn't go any farther because there was fighting. Nejla Hanım was shaking, and Ayşe got scared too. "They're playing games," Nejla said to Ayşe. "Like I always tell you, they're playing games." Ayşe looked at me instead of listening to her grandmother. How could I tell her it wasn't a game?

—

Grandma got all sweaty.

"Children! Don't be scared. We'll cross the park. Come along. Stay together!"

She took Ali's hand and my hand. It was so exciting. It was like we were rescuing Grandma, because she couldn't run as fast as us. We pulled her along. Ali pulled harder than me.

Men were shouting: "You'll pay for the İnciraltı Massacre!"

The other men didn't shout. They had big guns. *Rat-a-tat!* "This way!" Ali said. Grandma listened to him. We ran along the edge of the park until we reached the street to our apartment.

—

I need to protect them. They don't understand. Even when we were safe, Nejla Hanım's hands kept shaking. She got a cigarette out of her handbag, but she couldn't light the match. We sat on the stairs in front of the apartment, with Ayşe's grandma in the middle. I lit a match for her. Grandma puffed and puffed behind a big cloud of smoke. Her hair was messed up. Ayşe fixed her hair, then sat down next to me. "You're really smart," she said to me. Later, I'll tell Hüseyin Abi what I did today. *It isn't a game!*

—

When we got home, me and Ali looked up the swans in the Wonderland of Knowledge. There were pictures of the swans in Swan Park. They're called "mute" swans, and they can't make any sounds. Poor things. I can't wait for Ali to tell me how to get the butterflies into Parliament. He's so smart. Grandma asked Ali's mother if he could stay overnight at our place on Saturday and go to the concert Sunday morning. Auntie Aliye looked at the cloth she was holding in her hand and said, "Okay."

UNIT 7

Moral Values

Industriousness

When night came, Hüseyin Abi went onto the rooftop of Gökhan's house with beautiful Birgül Abla. I was going to ask him about the swans. And I wanted to know if it would be opportunist to get mulberry leaves from the police station. But I couldn't ask him anything. He's on duty tonight. He sounded sad when he was talking to my mom.

"Aliye Abla, something's happened to our neighborhood. People aren't as willing to volunteer for guard duty. Have you noticed that, Hasan Abi?"

When my dad and my mom said nothing, he turned to Birgül and said, "Come on, you and I will stand guard tonight."

"Hüseyin, that's not right," Mom said. She raised her eyebrows at Birgül. "You've got to sort something out. It's time you two got married. There's talk in the neighborhood."

I followed Hüseyin and Birgül. They couldn't see me in the dark. They hung their rifles over their shoulders and went up onto the rooftop. I followed them a little way up the stairs, but stopped and sat on a step. I can hear them talking, and when

I poke my head up, I can see their hands cupped around their cigarettes.

"You've lost weight, Birgül. Are you on a diet?"

"I've been fighting and running around every bit as much as you, Hüseyin. Could that be why?"

"You get mad so easily! Anyway, we need to discuss something. It's important."

"Go on, Hüseyin."

"Birgül, these are—"

"Troubled times. That's what you were going to say. Weren't you, Hüseyin?"

"Birgül, soon we're going to be living under a fascist dictatorship. That much is obvious. And it'll happen sooner rather than later. Our central committee is talking about registering as a political party and running an independent candidate in Ankara or Adana. As if they'd ever let any of us into Parliament! They're as naïve as little Ali and his talk of getting butterflies into Parliament. I'm worried our leadership isn't up to the task anymore. The rank and file wants more. The people are expecting a revolution, and our leaders are busy calculating how many deputies to run. We're letting the people down. We're not recruiting enough members. There's so much to do, Birgül. Funds are needed for the striking miners in Yeni Çeltek, so we have to start raising money from the tea kitchen at the Chamber of Architects. Then rush off to Çorum after the attacks on the Alevi there so it won't turn into another Maraş Massacre. When I get back, we'll organize a strike among bread sector workers. We need to protect leading writers and intellectuals, and that means arranging pairs of bodyguards for dozens of people. Revolutionary high schoolers are getting beaten up in Gazi, so we have to go there. Fighting has broken out in Cebeci, and we've got to pitch in there, too. Sleepless night after sleepless night. Writing up manifesto after manifesto. Ammo's arriving from the Aegean hidden in crates of mandarin oranges, so somebody has to go and organize wholesalers at the market hall. We're collecting cartons of cigarettes from the state monopoly workers and recruiting vendors to sell them on the black market. We're sending a shipment of weapons to revolutionary teachers in central Anatolia, and we've persuaded Yeni Karamürsel to donate boots to our cadre in Kars. It's impossible to keep up, Birgül. It's like a pool of water is collecting, and it's growing much bigger than we ever expected, and we have no idea where it's going to flow or how to stop it. We're trying to create a new country out of nothing, but the only thing our leadership can focus on right now is the elections. Will the people be satisfied with seating a couple of deputies? After all we've gone through? We were promised a revolution! We were promised paradise on earth! Birgül . . . I'm going to Çorum tomorrow. Perhaps never to return."

Birgül Abla stood up.

"Hüseyin, weren't you going to ask me something?"

Hüseyin Abi stood up, too.

"I wanted to ask . . . if you'll marry me."

They heard me hiccup. I was caught.

"Come here!" Hüseyin said. "You can be our witness. I just proposed to Birgül."

Hüseyin Abi was smiling. He hugged me, pulling me tight against his leg. But his fingernails dug into my cheek. He was too excited to notice.

"So, what's your answer, Birgül?"

The next morning, Mom said, "Why put it off? Let's hold the ceremony right away." When Hüseyin Abi came home with a ring in the afternoon, they got married in our garden. They put two rifles on the wedding table. Hüseyin Abi thought it was funny. He laughed when he was talking to my mom.

"Well why not, Aliye Abla? We need to swear on something, and our rifles are as good as anything. This is a revolutionary wedding, after all."

Hüseyin Abi laughed a lot. Birgül Abla turned pink that day.

Then Hüseyin Abi went to Çorum. *Perhaps never to return.*

When the aunties came to their lesson that night, one of them said Birgül should have a henna party. Birgül Abla got even pinker. The women began singing folk songs to her.

"Bring the henna, Mother. Dip in your finger, Mother.
From afar he comes, his kisses hot and sweaty."

Birgül was smiling, but she turned to my mom and said, "It doesn't feel right. We don't know what will happen to Hüseyin in Çorum, yet here we are—"

"My girl," Mom said, "you're one of us now. Listen to me. You're married now. You've got a man. Live it up. Every moment, every touch."

The aunties danced in a circle around beautiful Birgül Abla. None of them studied their ABCs that night.

Hüseyin Abi is too busy now to help me with the butterflies. I'll do it myself. That's what revolutionaries do. They take action. I know that because I'm a revolutionary too.

Philanthropy

I knew I shouldn't kick him. Girls, especially, shouldn't kick. His name was Önder. I knew that name. I never forget. Mom's voice tinkled like a cymbal when she was talking to him. It made me mad that Mom sounded so happy. But he was handsome. When Uncle Önder put his hands on his hips, the collar of his shirt opened wide. The hair on his chest was shining in the sunlight. That's why Mom was so happy. I could tell. And I didn't like it one bit.

Mom had taken me to Parliament again that day. She was giving me "a tour."

"Ayşe, this is the general assembly hall. The deputies debate weighty matters here in this hall. Or so they claim!"

There's a strong smell. Like the seats of a bus or a teacher's big wooden desk.

"Listen, Ayşe, Ecevit is about to address the assembly."

We used to love Ecevit for being a social democrat. Now we don't really like him. He didn't keep his promises, or something bad like that. When Ecevit begins speaking in the hall, the men with fat bellies laugh at him and the skinny men keep clapping.

"Çorum is not the first massacre to occur, nor will it be the last unless your government embraces a new approach. The number of so-called 'liberated' provinces has increased from twenty to forty. These provinces are under the control of the paramilitary organization calling itself the Grey Wolves. The mass murders committed by this organization, which enjoys the protection of the government, are spreading across the country. The governing coalition is being held hostage by its junior partner, a fringe party."

Men in dark suits started shouting at Ecevit.

"The Nationalist Action Party is not a fringe party! The real fringe party is the party that gets its marching orders from Moscow."

I can see Demirel. He's laughing. Ecevit gets mad at him.

"The prime minister is laughing when he should be hanging his head in shame!"

Mom points to a different man not far from us.

"Do you see that tall uncle right there, Ayşe? He's a writer. Your father and I like him a lot."

The writer is talking to the woman next to him. We move a little closer.

"It's all a diabolical game. The massacres, the murders . . . They'll do anything to foist economic liberalization and the Decisions of January 24 on us. So much death and destruction just so we abandon Keynesian policy for Friedman's monetarism."

I didn't understand a word the tall uncle said, but Mom kept nodding her head, so it must have been true.

Next, we visited Muzaffer Abi in what they call the "microfilm department." Mom gave Muzaffer Abi a book by Nazım Hikmet. He's our greatest poet. That's what Mom says.

"I think you'll enjoy this, Muzaffer. It's an old edition published in Bulgaria. My favorite line is—"

"Sevgi Hanım, I've read Nazım. Of course, I did it in secret. . . . As you know, my circle doesn't think much of him."

"This, right here, is my favorite line."

Muzaffer Abi read it aloud.

"*In the people we trust.*"

Mom's been acting strange all day. She's even smiling at Muzaffer Abi as she talks to him.

"It's a simple sentiment and it doesn't rhyme."

"In real life, there's no rhyme or reason when it comes to believing in people, is there, Sevgi Hanım?"

"Beautifully put, Muzaffer. And like you said before, any number of people might be hiding a lot of things somewhere in this Parliament building."

They both laughed.

"You know what, Sevgi Hanım? I think you're right. I think we should believe in people."

"But believing in people can lead to even greater disappointment than believing in God. Wouldn't you agree, Muzaffer?"

Mom laughed, but Muzaffer didn't. We left.

Mom's spreading some glue on a run in her stocking, secretly, with her leg under her desk where nobody can see.

"Mom, what's an opportunist?"

"Where did you learn that word?"

"What does it mean?"

"Well . . . It's someone who thinks only about herself and what's best for her. Someone who believes the end always justifies the means. It means you'll do anything to get what you want."

"It's a bad thing to say about someone, isn't it?"

"It certainly is. Was it Ali who taught you that word?"

I start kicking at my mom's desk, little kicks with the tip of my shoe. I don't want to answer her. Maybe she'll get mad at Ali.

"What other words has Ali taught you?"

"Mom, are we rich?"

"Oh dear! No, we're not at all rich. What made you ask that?"

"Ali gave me a daisy. And he can read small letters."

"Hmmm! You don't say. What else can he do?"

I better not tell her about the butterflies. Ali's my friend, and I don't want to be a snitch.

"You're very fond of Ali, aren't you?"

I ran away, escaping into the other room where aunties sit at their desks. Mom followed me. The aunties were laughing and gossiping, like always.

"And that song, 'Petrol.' It's Arab music, and we made such fools of ourselves singing it at Eurovision. Even so, they still play it everywhere."

"Never mind that. Have you heard the latest about Bülent Ersoy? The crowd started chanting, 'Bülent's a spinster!' while he—or she, or whatever it is—was singing up on stage. He started crying and drank two glasses of rakı, right on the stage."

"The whole thing was staged! It's not funny anymore. If our country's going down the drain, it's because of this kind of indecency!"

I was playing with the auntie's paper puncher when Mom came in. They acted like my class does when the teacher comes in. Everybody stopped talking.

Then my mom took me to Sakarya Avenue. She said she needed to meet with an old friend. And she promised to get me a hot dog. A hot dog!

That's when Uncle Önder came. I think my dad's mustache is bigger than his. I'm sure of it!

They drank beer. It was a hot day, so the outside of mom's glass kept getting wet and she kept wiping it with a napkin, until there was a pile of soggy napkins on the table. They didn't talk much. Uncle Önder gave Mom a big yellow envelope.

"Aren't you going to tell me what's in these envelopes, Önder?"

"Look inside if you want to know."

"If it's anything about me—"

"What? Of course not, Sevgi. You didn't think it was full of our correspondence, did you?"

Mom is giving the leg of the table little kicks, just like me. She can't run away, though. She goes quiet. He starts talking about politics. That's what grown-ups do when they don't know what to say.

"Have you heard what Demirel just said? That bastard of a prime minister said we should be worried about the leftists in Fatsa, not the fascists in Çorum. They're cutting down leftists in Çorum, but he couldn't care less. The columnists at *Tercüman* and *Hürriyet* seem hell, bent on provoking people. They claim the revolutionaries are trying to set up a state within a state in Fatsa, that they've set up checkpoints and won't let anybody into the city. The state will be targeting Fatsa next, that much is clear."

Mom kept wiping her glass, so Uncle Önder kept talking.

"I don't know if you've been following the news. The chairman of the joint chiefs of staff has extended his tour again. He's been traveling around the country for weeks now. He was just in Çorum, and he'll be visiting Fatsa. It's obvious what he's up to. The army is inspecting conditions on the ground before they stage a coup. They got the green light from America. There's going to be a coup."

Mom turns to me and says, "Ayşe, shall we order some fried lamb's brains?" She's not really looking at me, though. So I don't answer.

"Önder, shall we order some fried lamb's brains?"

Uncle Önder waves to a waiter, and that's when the blue veins come out on his arm. Mom's looking at his arm too.

Önder keeps talking about "the working class" and "labor unions" and "the Decisions of January 24," but Mom isn't really listening to him. Finally, she puts down her glass of beer and speaks.

"Önder, say whatever it is you have to say— Just a moment."

Why is she looking at me like that? I didn't do anything!

"Ayşe, look over there. There's a little girl about your age. Why don't you go and play with her?"

I shake my head. *No!* Mom doesn't want me to sit with her and Uncle Önder. The only reason I get up and go is that I'm mad. I don't even talk to that girl. She's just a baby.

I can see Mom moving her hands in the air and talking, talking. Uncle Önder rubs his face. Mom leans back and crosses her arms. He leans back and chews on his mustache. Mom waves to me. I go back to the table. We're about to leave, but Uncle Önder grabs my mom by the arm. She stares at him, like she stares at my dad when she's mad. He lets go. I was going to kick him, but I knew I shouldn't.

"Sevgi, you and I happened back before all of this madness. Back when life had meaning. Maybe that's what I miss. Maybe—"

"Önder. This isn't a good time."

Mom didn't talk to me at all the whole time we were walking. I asked her if we could go to Uncle Selahattin's shop and she said no. So I said, "But I went with you to meet your friend." I kicked the ground. She looked at me and said, "That's what it means to be an opportunist, little miss Ayşe." I think my mom was scared of me at that moment. I shrugged my shoulders. Then we went to Uncle Selahattin's shop. I had to get something there for Ali. It's about swans, and it's some pieces of paper. I remembered my dad talking about it. Uncle Selahattin ordered Mom a tea. He showed her a green parrot in a cage by the door. That's when I went to the back of the shop and pretended to look at the birds.

The papers were still there on the table. I stuck them under my shirt, against my belly. They touched my skin, and it was like swan's wings were touching me. I was excited to show them to Ali. We're going to be heroes. We're going to have an adventure. All the way home those papers made a soft sound, like mulberry leaves in the wind, but Mom didn't even look at me. If she'd asked, I might have told her I'd taken papers about swans because Ali is really smart and he'd understand. But she didn't ask. Today, Mom wore the nice shoes that make her feet hurt. She was limping a little. I walked slow, too, and the papers didn't make very much noise. Not that Mom was listening to me. Ali's going to be so surprised!

Charity and Friendship

It's Saturday night. Mom and Dad are drinking rakı out on Samim's terrace. Because Ali is spending the night, he's visiting Samim Abi and Ayla Able with us. Tomorrow, we're going to a concert with Grandma. Ali and I are watching TV in the living room. I can hear the other guest talking out on the terrace. Her name is Süheyla.

"It happened at Tuncer's burial service. Everyone was shouting slogans and crying. The guy who dug the grave—one of 'the people' we always glorify—was scrambling up out of the grave when a National Lottery ticket fell out of his pocket. Everyone was looking at him. Anyone, he went back down into the grave, picked up the ticket, checked it was legible, and put it in his pocket. This is the guy who a minute ago was singing revolutionary anthems with his fist in the air. It got me to thinking. . . . 'The people' inhabit a world we'll never understand. A precarious dream world, a world of survival."

Because Süheyla Abla is from Istanbul, she has long hair and a long dress with flowers on it. She writes books. She wears lots of rings, really different rings. She has Bodrum sandals made of leather. Her toes are pretty: long, thin, white, and clean. When she talks, she crosses her legs and jiggles her foot. And she makes her hair move back and forth, like it's windy, except there isn't any wind. She's got yellow hair, and when she stands under the light it looks like Lucy's hair in *Dallas*. She's not famous, but she looks famous. That's because she's from Istanbul. I've seen pictures of "Istanbul Nights" in Auntie Jale's *Weekend* supplements. When Süheyla Abla is talking, Mom looks at the table and secretly smiles. Some of the girls in my class smile like that when another student is at the blackboard and doesn't know the answer.

Süheyla Abla laughs a lot while she's talking. Mom and Dad and Samim Abi and Ayla Abla keep looking at each other, but they don't laugh.

"But our revolutionary men get on like a house on fire with 'the people.' That's because there's one thing they have in common: fear of women!"

Ali's not talking right now because he's playing with his string, but he'll talk later. Mom's sitting sideways, tearing off little pieces of her rolling papers and making them into tiny balls. She's lifting her eyebrows and making her mouth small. That's what Mom does when she doesn't want to talk. Or maybe it's because she doesn't like Süheyla Abla's flowery dress and loud voice. I think she's talking extra loud so the others will look at her. I can hear music coming up from Jale Hanım's house. Ali is thinking. He says he needs to "take action." I gave him the swan papers. He couldn't believe it. I might become a revolutionary too! But first we have to get the butterflies into Parliament.

They started playing in the street again. *Bang bang*! Ali says it was a handgun, not a rifle. Dad and Samim Abi pulled the table close to the living room door. For a while, everybody was quiet. Then Süheyla Abla started talking again. She holds out her fingers and rubs her rings together while she's talking.

"This country wakes you up in the middle of the night to a sense of dread, and, in the morning, to a sense of shame. Overnight, while you were in your bed, terrible things were happening somewhere, and with the morning light you blame yourself for the deaths of people you've never met. You're constantly under siege. It's paralyzing!"

—

I can't tell Ayşe about those "terrible" things. She'd be scared. But they told me about them at the cinema. "They gouged out the eyes of the bodies in Çorum. . . . They're murdering more leftists in Çorum. . . . They're massacring Alevis." Hüseyin Abi is going to rescue the people in Çorum. It was at the outdoor summer cinema in Öveçler that they told me. We went there on the bus to see *Revenge of the Snakes*. But first the big brothers and big sisters got up and gave a talk. Then they all shouted together: "Down with fascism!" They said lots of things, but I couldn't understand it all. Hüseyin Abi would have explained it better. He opens his arms when he talks, and everyone understands. When he explains, I don't get scared. When he explains things, we always win. I should tell Ayşe the way Hüseyin Abi tells me.

"Ayşe, we can get the butterflies into Parliament if we are united. If we're united, they can't break us."

—

Ali got up. I can't see the TV because he's standing in front of it. He's talking like I do on "show and tell" days at school.

"The revolutionary path is . . . it might be covered with broken glass, but together . . ."

Ali is holding up his arms. Now he puts his hands on his hips.

"We must resist, Ayşe. If we don't resist, there will be a dictatorship, and they'll gouge out our eyes. Listen to me: our eyes! But you should get mulberry leaves from the police station. You won't be an opportunist, because you have no other choice. Get some leaves tomorrow morning. I can't go. They'll know I'm a revolutionary."

—

Ali makes me laugh! He's so funny. He got mad at me, though. When he started playing with his strings again, I went over and gave him a hug. "You're really clever," I told him. He likes that. He put his strings back in his pocket. Süheyla Abla is still talking out on the terrace. How can she have so much to talk about and why isn't anyone else talking? I want to get some Coca-Cola for me and Ali. But I don't want Mom to add water to it this time. We're old enough to drink it without water. We're old enough to "resist," too.

Süheyla Abla laughed to herself again. They're still not looking at her.

"If you ask me, we're wasting our time."

Mom is still making her mouth small, but she opens it and talks.

"Is that what they're saying in your artistic circles in Istanbul?"

"As if everyone in Ankara has joined a guerrilla movement, Sevgi Hanım."

Mom picked up a plate off the table and went to the kitchen. I followed her. A second later Ayla Abla came into the kitchen too.

"Sevgi, I'm sorry about that. Sühelya hasn't been the same since her fiancé was tortured to death."

"We can't make everything about us, Ayla!"

"She's had a little too much to drink."

"We're in the middle of a civil war, Ayla. If everyone gave up as soon as they lost someone . . . I wish she wouldn't talk like that today of all days. They've just launched an operation in Fatsa. People are being tortured. The 'common people' are who she's ridiculing. How dare she!"

They went back to the table. I got a bottle of Coca-Cola, holding it in both hands. I'm going to pour me and Ali a glass, the exact same amount. Exactly equal!

The bottle of Coca-Cola is teetering on the tray, but nobody's looking at me. They're looking at my mom and Süheyla Abla, who's laughing like Sue Ellen now. You know, when Sue Ellen gets sad and laughs with a drink in her hand. Süheyla Abla leans close to the table and lifts her hand at my mom.

"There's something I've never understood. That quiet arrogance you've all adopted out here in the sticks, in Ankara. What have any of you done? You get together with your friends and try to stay alive, just like everyone else."

I made it all the way to the coffee table without spilling a drop. And I didn't spill any when I poured it into the glasses either. If I had, I'd have given the bigger glass to Ali. When he sits in the armchair his feet poke into the air. His feet aren't dirty, he's just got brown skin.

—

I need to be brave, like Hüseyin Abi and the other big brothers. But I can't talk like he does. I'll sit here, and I won't try to hold out my arms.

"Ayşe, you know that lunchbox you have? Let's put the silkworms inside it. Then we'll put in lots of leaves. A whole lot. If the silkworms get hungry, they won't be able to sleep. And if they don't sleep, they won't grow up. We don't want their tummies to grumble. After that, you need to go with your mom to Parliament."

I'm going to protect her. Hüseyin Abi would. When the teacher with the yellow hair asked me to bring her a stick, Hüseyin Abi got mad. He went to school with me the next day and said, "Shame on you! It's bad enough you beat these kids, but you can at least get your own stick."

She never beat us after that. Hüseyin Abi will say, "Shame on you!" in Çorum, too, and they'll stop hurting people. It worked when he told Uncle Laz not to hit Nuran Abla. Uncle Laz never hit her again.

—

It sounds like Mom is shouting at Süheyla Abla. I mean, not really shouting, but her voice is sure loud.

"What matters is principles and the establishment of a new social order. That's what they've tried to do in Fatsa, even if on a very small scale. They're establishing a new way of life. In the middle of fascism, surrounded on all sides, they're trying out a new way of life."

Süheyla Abla laughed like a wicked-hearted woman again.

"Friends of mine went to that festival in Fatsa. There you are, an intellectual visiting from Istanbul, and they tell you not to drink alcohol, not to do this and that, not to upset the locals by—"

Dad jumped in to help Mom. Together, they'll make Süheyla Abla be quiet.

"I'm sure your friends have every opportunity to drink rakı to their heart's content in Istanbul. The fascists are afraid of what's happening in Fatsa not because there's been a bloody uprising—there hasn't—but because the people there are peacefully showing that a better life is possible. It's not revolutionary violence the fascists fear, it's the success of a revolutionary order. Fundamentally, they fear life itself. And our moral shortcoming is that we've become too entrenched in our middle-class lifestyle to join them in Fatsa."

"Well you can say that again," Süheyla Abla said, with a wicked laugh.

Now they're all standing up and talking at once. That's what grown-ups do when they get excited about politics. Ali ignores them and tugs at my arm.

"Are you listening to me? We need to get lots of mulberry leaves. I checked the *Wonderland of Knowledge*, and it says they're going to spin cocoons soon."

"But I want you to come with me to the police station."

"No. Go with your grandma."

"No. What if they hurt me?"

"They won't hurt you. You're different."

"You're just saying that because I'm not poor. You're the one who said it wasn't a game. You said it, not me!"

"Okay. We'll go together. If they beat us and we're together, it won't hurt very much."

I sat down next to Ali so he wouldn't get scared. He gave me a piece of string from his pocket. Ali made himself a ring out of another piece of string.

—

I'll go to the police station with Ayşe. We'll stay together, shoulder to shoulder. United. I don't drink much of my cola. It burns my lips. Soda does that too. Ayşe loves it, though. She takes a big swallow and goes, "Ohhh!" Maybe her lips don't burn. There's so much food on the table out on the terrace. They don't eat it all. It just sits there. They eat slowly, just a few bites at a time. I wish I could take some of that food home.

But how can I? If I can't take any food home, I shouldn't eat any. They think I don't like their food. That's not it, though. It's just . . . if Mom can't eat it, I shouldn't either.

I don't understand those papers about swans. Maybe I'll understand better tomorrow morning. Or maybe, when everyone's in bed, I'll turn on the light—because they have electricity here—and try to read it again. All you have to do is press the switch, like in school.

—

I can't read small letters like Ali, but I looked at those papers. I can tell from the drawings that they're going to do something to the swan's wings. I think it'll hurt. Ali says he'll read it later. He's smart. He'll understand. But what if he doesn't? Sometimes even grown-ups can't agree on words.

That's what they said when I went to Kızılay Square with my dad a couple of days. Dad's friends were living in a big tent in the square because they were on strike. They work at the Turkish Language Institute, and they fight over words all the time. Some words are bad—not because they're dirty words or curse words, but because they're "loanwords." The Turkish Language Institute wants to give those bad words back to their owners. Anyway, me and Dad went to the tent because the strike was ending that day. Everyone was playing drums and dancing, because that's what happens when a strike ends. One of the uncles started yelling.

"We have been striking not just for our social benefits but to protect our language. This is a victory both for our union and for our mother tongue."

Samim Abi came up to us.

"Hey, look who's here. Aydın Abi. And you brought little Ayşeyevich, I see."

Everyone was happy, and nobody wanted to go home. Dursun Dede came over. He smokes all the time, and he plays games with me. He always talks to me first. He can make a whistle out of a piece of rolling paper. One time he made a rabbit. It wiggled its ears when you pulled its tail. He's a teacher. When I grow up, I'm going to read his books.

Dursun Dede can't get to the end of a sentence without coughing. He stood in a cloud of smoke and talked to my dad and Samim Abi.

"Things aren't looking good. *Khoff khoff!* We're in for some terrible times."

Everybody was happy. Dursun Dede tried to be happy, too.

"We're still waiting for your revolution, guys!"

Then he looked at me.

"Don't get me wrong, little miss. It'll happen one day. *Khaff khak khak!* But the grown-ups aren't working hard enough. When it's your turn, you'll do a better job."

Dad shook his head and looked serious.

"I worry about the kind of world we're passing on to our kids."

Samim Abi put his hand on his hip. His face got all wrinkly, like Dursun Dede's, because the sun was getting in his eyes.

"What worries me is that we're not going to be able to pass anything on. They've started censoring everything. We had to cut half of the footage from Çorum. All this history, straight into the rubbish bin."

"Store everything you can," Dursun Dede said. "Hide it for our kids. Have you heard the latest about the language committee? They've recommended the official dictionary drop the word 'resistance.' And it's not even a loanword!" Then he went over and started talking to some other uncles with white hair and beards.

Samim Abi shook his head.

"Nothing makes sense anymore, Aydın."

That's when I asked my dad.

"Dad, what are they going to do to the swans?"

"What swans?"

"The ones in the park."

"Nothing, I guess."

"That's not what Uncle Selahattin said!"

"What did he say?"

Dad forgot! He doesn't remember. I got a lump in my throat. It hurt to swallow. I'm not going to tell Dad I took the swan papers from Uncle Selahattin's office. I hope Ali can read them tomorrow.

—

I wish I could take home some bread at least. The other morning, Mom and the other women were doing a bread boycott. Soldiers brought us bread. We don't have money to buy store bread. The soldiers don't understand. They came in a jeep with GMC on the front. The back of it was full of sacks of bread. They wanted to give the women the bread, but the women wouldn't take it. That's because the women were cooking their own bread on iron plates over a fire. Up on the wall was a piece of cardboard with big letters saying: "Bread, equality, freedom!"

Flat bread is revolutionary. That's why the soldiers brought us the opportunist store bread. Mom shouted at them.

"Look here, soldier! Take your bread back. Don't make me throw it away!"

The bread fell onto the ground, because they were fighting. Uncle Dürüst came up, quiet as a swan. And his hair is white not because he's old but because they gave electric shocks to his pee-pee in the coup. He slowly picked up the loaves of bread. Everyone was fighting. A soldier kicked over the metal plates. Cinders flew up. Hüseyin Abi was in Çorum, so he couldn't "organize" us. Some of the aunties' muslin scarves fell to the ground. Birgül Abla swung at a soldier and said, "Shame on you! How can you hit an old woman?"

One of the soldiers went back to the jeep. He was quiet as a swan too. Uncle Dürüst said something to him, but I couldn't understand any of the words he used. The soldier took the bread from Uncle Dürüst one by one, put them in the back of the jeep, and left with the other soldier. The women celebrated by waving poles in the air, the long, thin poles they turn the bread with while it's cooking. The dark-skinned aunties made a loud, high sound, like a screaming bird. That's what they do when they're happy. They're from Diyarbakır, and I can't understand a word they say.

Mom took Birgül Abla's arm, and they sat down next to the open fire.

"Listen, Birgül. This isn't working. We're getting scattered."

"What do you mean, Aliye Abla?"

Mom laughed.

"Birgül, you always call me 'abla' even though we're the same age."

Birgül Abla laughed.

"That's because you're . . . well, you've got Ali and all."

"I don't mind. Call me whatever you want. Anyway, with all the fighting I haven't had a chance to talk to you. You know about Çorum. Now they're clamping down in Fatsa. What are your chiefs telling you? What are we facing?"

"They're discussing a response."

"Discussing isn't enough. We had the bread boycott today, there's a funeral coming up tomorrow, we've got a water protest to do. It never ends and everyone's getting worn out."

"When Hüseyin comes back—"

"Don't get me wrong, Birgül. I worship the ground you young revolutionaries walk on. You know, don't you, that my brother fell on your path. I've still got his bloody parka. You know best, but I wish we'd do more than just protest and boycott. It's time the people rise up. And I don't give a damn what happens if we do!"

"I understand. Okay."

"You're a wonderful girl and a wonderful new bride! You've got the weight of the people on your shoulders. I know you must be tired out too."

"Never. As long as we're united, as long as we're standing shoulder to shoulder, nothing's a burden and I'll never get tired!"

Mom was stroking Birgül Abla's hair when Aunt Seher shouted, "If we are united . . ."

Uncle Dürüst went and squatted a little further along. With his rounded back and his hands on his knees, he looked like a bird. I squatted next to him. He patted me on the head.

"When it's your turn, you'll do better."

He said it in a whisper. That's how he talks. Then someone led him away. I just sat there.

The Coca-Cola is tickling my nose. Maybe it's my turn now. I'll have to figure out those papers about the swans tomorrow.

—

Mom and Ayla Abla put their arms around Süheyla Abla's shoulders. Is she crying? Her hair's fallen over her face. Samim Abi and Dad went to the kitchen. Men always leave when women cry. They get embarrassed. Now Mom, Ayla Abla, and Süheyla Abla are all laughing. But they're crying, too, I think. Grown-ups sometimes do that. They can laugh and cry at the same time. Süheyla Abla lifts her head. Her nose is red. She brushes back her hair. She doesn't look like Sue Ellen anymore. Now she's more like Pamela. She laugh-cries.

"I feel like a pane of glass. On one side of the glass, it's yesterday. And on the other, tomorrow. But today is see-through, completely transparent. We're in this transparent moment in time, and reflected onto us are mixed-up images of both the past and the future. . . . I'm not making any sense, am I?"

Sometimes Süheyla Abla doesn't make any sense because she's from Istanbul. She picked up a bottle of rakı and looked at Ayla Abla.

"Have you got a pen?

Ayla Abla gave her a pen.

"I doubt any of you Ankarans have heard of the '(Not) Dying Day.' Turgut Uyar and Edip Cansever started it in Istanbul a few years ago. They were gathered at a *meyhane* in Rumeli Hisarı with a bunch of their fellow poets when the conversation turned to fear of death. Turgut Uyar asked the waiter to bring a bottle of rakı. Then he asked everyone present to sign their names on the bottle and pledge to meet exactly one year later, on the 26th of March, to drink that bottle of rakı. And they did meet the next year, and the year after that. They still meet every year. It's become a tradition. Now, I'm going to write today's date on this bottle, and I want everyone to sign it and to promise that nobody will die before we meet again in a year. I'm writing it right here: July 30, 1980!"

Mom laughed a laugh without tears this time and lit a cigarette. Smoke came out of her mouth when she said, "And under that, write: 'In the people we trust.'"

I remember that!

When Samim Abi came out of the kitchen, he looked at me and Ali. Then he yelled out to the women on the terrace.

"You know what? When I look at these two kids it makes me realize something. The real truth is the shortest distance between two kids."

—

Ayşe's dad smiled at Samim Abi as he came up to us.

"Aren't you two sleepy yet?"

He's got an unlit cigarette in his mouth. He needs a match or a lighter. He looked inside a bowl on the coffee table.

"Samim, that's some lighter you got yourself. No wonder you're hiding it in here."

It's an Ibelo. It's Hüseyin Abi's! I put it in my pocket when nobody was looking. I'll give it back to Hüseyin Abi.

UNIT 8

Music Is Food for the Soul

Classical Western Music

Everyone was whispering.

"The chief of staff is here. . . . Evren is coming."

Ali and I were walking into CSO Concert Hall with Grandma when two giant men cleared the way for a smaller, older man, the one everyone calls "chief of staff." As he passed, people pressed their lips together into a smile. He nodded to the left and to the right. Grandma let go of our hands and tried to find something in her handbag. She didn't even look at the chief of staff. I think that's because we're waiting for Pharmacist Cavit Bey.

—

This place is nothing like the Gardens. Nobody shouts. Everyone whispers.

"Kenan Pasha is coming. . . . You know, it's so refreshing to have a military chief who appreciates the arts, unlike those peasants in the government. . . . They say our pasha never misses a concert or a ballet performance. . . . I'd read in the newspaper that he was touring the country. After the Çorum Incident, he visited Fatsa."

The Çorum Incident? Is that the same as the Çorum Massacre? I wonder if Hüseyin Abi's come back from Çorum yet. Ayşe's grandma keeps looking inside her handbag and at the door. She's probably afraid that man from the pharmacy won't come.

—

At the CSO and the State Theater, everyone dresses like they're going to a Republican Ball. The men have shiny shoes, and the women wear lots of perfume. Men in white bowties and black jackets show us to our seat. We're supposed to say, "Thank you, sir."

—

Were we against the chief of staff? I think we were. He's making a dictatorship, or he's letting the fascists in Almond Stream make one. Something like that. I'll have to ask Hüseyin Abi. Ayşe's grandmother wouldn't know. When she heard me say "dictatorship" to Ayşe, she said, "That's an inappropriate word for children." In Liberation, kids get to eat hazelnut cocoa spread on their bread, but they're not allowed to use certain words.

—

Ali's in a bad mood because he didn't eat any bread this morning. Mom spread hazelnut cocoa on our bread because it was a Sunday morning. She never leaves empty spaces on the edges and the top is always smooth. But when Grandma spreads it, it's so thin you can see the holes in the bread and it never reaches the edges. Ali picked up his bread and licked the top. I told him you're not supposed to do that. Then he didn't eat any of it. I was embarrassed. When my mom wiped the dirt off Ali's shoes this morning, I was embarrassed too.

—

Ayşe's grandma said, "Where could he be?" But she was talking to herself, not me. Her lips are painted red. When she talks, she tries not to move her lips and keeps her mouth in an "o" shape.

"Cavit Bey will never find us if we take our seats in the third row. Ah! There he is over there. Cavit Bey! For a moment, I thought you weren't coming."

"Nejla Hanım, I wouldn't miss the concert or the chance to see you for anything in the world. Here's a program. I picked up an extra one."

"Ever the gentleman! You needn't have troubled yourself—"

"Oh, there's my wife. Zeliha! We're over here. Let me introduce you to Nejla Hanım. I was just telling you about her."

—

Grandma's mouth was open, but she didn't say anything. Then she bowed her head. She didn't say, "Pleased to meet you." She didn't shake the lady's hand. We walked off to our seats without a word. When we sat down, Grandma pulled her handkerchief out of her handbag. She wiped the lipstick off her lips, sitting low, like she didn't want anyone to see her, especially Bala Hanım, who always gets a seat next to Grandma at concerts. There was a still a speck of red in the corner of her mouth, but I didn't tell her. Grandma tossed the program onto my lap. If we hadn't been at the CSO I would have kicked Cavit Bey.

—

I grabbed the program from Ayşe's lap. She can't read as good as me. Under "Program," in big black letters, it says "Selection of Waltzes" in smaller letters. Not another waltz! I hope they don't make me wear a bowtie . . . or make me dance with Ayşe. I want to leave. I want to go home.

"Ali, put that string back in your pocket! And give me back that program. Grandma gave it to me, not you."

—

Ali's no fun when he's in a bad mood. I asked him to help me read the program, but I get to hold it, because Grandma handed it to me.

"It says, 'Selection of Classical Waltzes.' The first one is 'Swan Lake Waltz.'"

"Swan Lake? Does that mean everyone knows about the swans?"

"No, of course not."

"Well, what if they do?"

"If they knew, they'd call it Swan Park. And our swans swim in a pond, not a lake."

The chief of staff sat down in the very front row, and the giant men sat down in the row behind him, right in front of us. Ali put the string back in his pocket.

"Ayşe," Ali whispered. I think those men in front of us want to hurt the swans."

"But why?"

"Because they're fascists!"

The two men turned around and looked right at Ali. Grandma said, "Shhh!" Then she smiled at the two men and said, "Enjoy the concert, gentlemen." When they turned back around, she looked at us. But mostly she looked at Ali, and her eyes got small and scary. Then she started going through her handbag again.

Ali held his head in his hands, like he had a terrible headache.

"Ayşe, first we have to get the butterflies into Parliament. Then we can save the swans. Okay?"

—

Men and women in black clothing came onto the stage. Everybody clapped. Then it was quieter than quiet. Like everyone was holding their breath and waiting for something wonderful to happen. I wanted it to last forever. It's never like this in the Gardens. It's always noisy, and when there's a lot of people together, it's even noisier, and we wait for terrible things to happen. Maybe you need to be rich to be this quiet. Maybe after the revolution it will be quiet everywhere, even in Rambling Gardens. Then the music started. When I closed my eyes, pictures started moving in my head.

First, I saw Uncle Dürüst, his white hair getting longer and longer. He took my hand and we jumped. Up into the air, higher and higher. Down below, the houses got smaller and smaller. Then something like giant horns started playing and fighting broke out. I could see Hüseyin Abi running from the fascists. He fired his gun, but he'd run out of bullets. Birgül fired her gun, but she'd run out of bullets. They held hands and jumped, up into the air. Mom grabbed two loaves of bread and jumped. Then Dad jumped. Everyone was floating through the air. Nobody was talking. They were laughing. And then we saw a whole bunch of swans flying toward us. When we saw the swans, we knew we'd won. One of the swans waved and smiled at me. It's Turgay Abi. The revolution happened. I was so happy I wanted to cry.

—

When I saw Ali close his eyes, I closed mine too. I could feel the music, not just inside me, but on the outside too. I could feel it on my face and on my neck. I could feel the drums in my belly. Like a giant butterfly was in my belly, and it opened its wings. Everything smelled nice too, sweet as flowers. When the flute played, a butterfly came and flapped its wings right in front of my face. It's peeking at me, at my cheek, my nose, my ear. Then I saw myself running and running, and behind me there were rabbits and cats and baby horses, and they were running too. There's a swan, flying high over my head. A lot of swans, dozens. And I'm growing bigger and bigger, until I can put my arms around my mom and my dad and Ali, all at the same time.

The music stops and I rub my eyes. Grandma says it's the intermission, and she wants to "stretch her legs." Me and Ali follow her and Bala Hanım up the aisle.

"How have you been, Nejla Hanım?"

Grandma and Bala Hanım always talk during the intermission. She's fat, so she has big legs, and they help her stand up extra straight when she walks. She has elastic bands that help keep her stockings up. You can see them when she's sitting. Grandma said she's one of the founders of the teachers' union, but even if Grandma hadn't told me, I'd know she was a teacher. Her shoes are clunky and old. She doesn't wear makeup, just like my mom. We usually sit next to Bala Hanım when we go to a concert. This one time, I saw inside her purse. She had a handkerchief that was white, but brown with dust on the fold, a hand mirror with a crack, a little book with "Constitution" on the front, and a cellophane packet full of tiny white mints.

"Fine, thank you, Bala Hanım. I hope you're well?"

"How could I be well? With the state of our country . . ."

Grandma likes Bala Hanım, but not a lot. Bala Hanım always asks questions, but she never listens to the answer. She starts looking around when Grandma is speaking, and it's "irritating." I think Bala Hanım does that because she's so big. When people look at her, she wants to look somewhere else. She's always looking at something. Once, in the middle of a concert, I saw her pull out her cracked mirror and look at her face. She eats her mints in secret, one by one, without making a sound. And she never gives me one.

". . . and the military of today is nothing like it was back in 1960. Back in the day, they knew how to stage a proper coup. The elite of Ankara applaud Evren Pasha whenever they see him at the opera house and the ballet, foolishly hoping he'll save us from this descent into anarchy and lawlessness, but, mark my words, Nejla Hanım, this isn't going to turn out well. I mean, just look at them toadying up to him over there in the corner!"

Grandma isn't listening to Bala Hanım, and she isn't looking at Evren Pasha and his toads. Grandma can't take her eyes off Uncle Cavit Bey's wife. Bala Hanım looks over where Grandma is looking. They watch as Uncle Cavit Bey puts his arm around his wife's waist and leads her back into the hall. Then Bala Hanım leans close to Grandma.

"That pharmacist has been foisting his worthless creams and potions on the women of Ankara for as long as I can remember."

"You took the words right out of my mouth, Bala Hanım!"

At the end of the concert, we left while Bala Hanım was still clapping. We were going to get a shared taxi, but Grandma said, "Let's walk. Some fresh air would do me good." Grandma starts walking extra fast, and she doesn't slow down until she is huffing and puffing. Grandma says we should wait until she catches her breath, and she tells us not to let go of her hand.

That's when I ask Ali: "Did the music make you feel like you were getting bigger and bigger?" He says, "No. I was flying."

A group of people came around the corner. They're holding signs and shouting on the other side of the street.

"You'll pay for Fatsa!"

Ali tugs Grandma by the hand and tries to cross the street.

"Stop it!" Grandma says. She yanks him so hard. I hope she didn't hurt Ali.

I think Grandma feels bad. She says she's going to get me and Ali sesame bread rings from the vendor on the corner. She pays the man, and then I say it.

"Grandma, why can't we go over there? Aren't we revolutionaries? Or are we like Uncle Cavit Bey? Or J.R.?"

Grandma laughs.

"Ayşe, sometimes you say the most extraordinary things! All right. We'll go over there. But only for a few minutes and only if you promise not to let go of my hand."

We go up to the people with the signs. Me and Ali give them our sesame bread rings. They're so excited and happy. We shout along with them. "You'll drown in your blood! . . ." "Shoulder to shoulder against fascism!" They pick us up and put us their shoulders. Even Grandma shouts along.

I feel like I'm getting bigger and bigger. Or even flying, like Ali.

—

Ayşe danced and skipped all the way home from the protest. When Ayşe dances, it's much better than at the school recitals. She was happy, like she's forgotten what we talked about last night. Then we ran into that neighbor, Jale Hanım, in the hall. She started talking to Ayşe's grandma.

"Things are going from bad to worse, Nejla Hanım. I blame it all on Bülent Ersoy and his new breasts. One thing leads to another, and the next thing you know everything's spun out of control. Everybody thinks they can do whatever they want. Everywhere you go, the streets are full of queers. Why, I even saw a demonstration in Kavaklıdere, of all places. They stood up on top of a red convertible. And it was brand new! It's gotten so bad families are afraid to go outside."

—

Auntie Jale Hanım is wearing lipstick because she's coming back from her Children's Welfare Meeting. The more she talks, the darker red the tiny cracks in her lips get. She says they had chicken salad with walnuts, palace halvah, and rice pilaf at their meeting luncheon. *Hürriyet* newspaper came and took pictures, because they're going to build a "children's village" to help poor people. I don't think it's for children like Ali, though. He's poor, but he never looks like he's about to cry. Auntie Jale Hanım patted Ali on the head and talked to him like he was one of the sad poor kids.

"What do you have for dinner? Do you ever get any meat? Do you drink a glass of milk in the morning? Growing boys should eat a piece of cheese about the size of a matchbox at breakfast. Do you do that?"

Ali jerked his head away. Later, he told me why he got mad.

"She's just like the teacher with the yellow hair. They always ask what we eat. What difference does it make!"

Ali doesn't like to talk about food. When he talks, he always talks about exciting things. He has a list, and he showed it to me last night. We were in bed, and I asked him if he could hear his heart beating in his ear when he lies on the side of his head.

"You can hear your heart here because it's quiet. I never hear it in Rambling Gardens."

"It's echoing, like there's a big cave inside me."

"You're too little to have a big cave inside you."

"But you can have a little cave inside, can't you, Ali?"

"I guess."

"Ali?"

"What?"

"Do you think they'd love us more if we were dead?"

"Yes. But I'm not going to die. There are lots of things I want to do."

"Does thinking about them crying when you're dead make you sad?"

"No. I'm not going to die. I have too many things to do."

That's when Ali showed me his list. He got up and turned on the light, and he helped me read it.

TO DO LIST

1. Read the *Wonderland of Knowledge* from cover to cover.
2. Wear my uncle's parka and do something important.
3. Get the biggest gun ever for Hüseyin Abi.
4. Get Mom a whole roomful of bread (like in *Heidi*) and meat (like in *Hagar the Horrible*).
5. Get the butterflies into Parliament (then Hüseyin Abi can get into Parliament, too).
6. Save the swans. (Or as many as possible. Maybe they're too big for me to save all of them. *The wingspan of a mature mute swan is typically between 79 and 94 inches.*)

I got up and turned off the light real quick. In the darkness, Ali told me not to tell anyone. I promised I wouldn't. But I told him he'd never be able to do his list, not all alone.

I'm glad Ali's not going home tomorrow. When we got home from the concert, Dad said Ali's father called. Ali's allowed to stay for another night, if he wants. I screamed, "Yay!" but Ali didn't say anything.

"I'm going to help you, Ali."

I closed my eyes, and didn't hear my heart after that.

UNIT 9

The Republic of Turkey Is a Parliamentary Democracy

A Nation Is Composed of Individuals Who Desire to Live Together

As I was walking up the hill to our house with Dad, I kicked at the dirt road. Dad told me twice not to "kick up a dust cloud." He doesn't understand. Ayşe's mom wiped all the dirt off my shoes. I don't want my friends Gökhan and Hamit to see my shiny shoes. They'll know I went to a concert or something. Ayşe's mom gave me a slice of Şokella-covered bread wrapped in a napkin with little blue flowers on it. She said I should eat it at home, since I didn't eat it at her house. Mom hugged me when I got home, real tight. With wet eyes, she said, "What did you eat? Did you sleep?" When I gave her the bread, she pulled off the napkin. It was a little greasy, but she folded it up and put it on the shelf. "Where's Hüseyin Abi?" I asked. Mom turned around with her back to me.

I could hear Hamit and Gökhan.

"Ali! Come outside, Ali!"

I thought we were going to play ball with the other guys. But that wasn't why they wanted me. I asked them too: "Where's Hüseyin Abi?" I wanted to give him his Ibelo lighter. "He's bummed out," Gökhan said, taking a drag on his cigarette. He smokes because he's grown up now, and that's what revolutionary big brothers do. Gökhan's brother gave him a pocket knife a while back, and he always carries it. "Did your silkworms make cocoons?" I asked him. "Who cares about those dumb silkworms!" he said. "We've got more important things to do. Now listen good." When we got to the vacant lot, Gökhan threw his arm around my shoulder.

"Where have you been?"

"Nowhere."

"You stayed with those rich people, didn't you?"

"They aren't rich. They're just richer than us."

Something happened while I was gone. Everyone seems different. Older. They walk with their elbows out and their hands jammed in their pockets. They look hard and tough, like revolutionaries. Gökhan breaks the news.

"We decided something while you were away. We're going to do a protest."

He leans close and speaks in a low voice.

"All of us. All the guys in the neighborhood have been collecting yoghurt containers for the last couple days. You know, the plastic white ones. It's against the law now to sell old tires in Ankara. We can't find any tires anywhere. So we went through the garbage for yoghurt containers and we asked restaurants for them. We have plenty now."

So much has happened while I was at Ayşe's. Does time pass more quickly in my neighborhood than in Liberation?

"Ali, are you listening?"

I can't pull my strings out of my pocket, not in front of all the other guys. Gökhan looks at them. Then he looks at me. I have to ask him. I have to.

"Does Hüseyin Abi know about this?"

"No. We're strong enough to do it alone. Like Mahir Çayan!"

When I looked at Gökhan for a long time without saying anything, he got mad. Everyone gets mad when I do that.

"Stop dragging it out, Ali! Are you in, or are you out?"

The other boys are all looking at me. I put my hand in my pocket and squeeze my strings. I want to close my eyes. If I close my eyes, maybe I'll be back at the concert. And even though a part of me wishes I was there, another part is ashamed for wishing it. Hamit is trying to smoke a cigarette, but he's so useless. I look at Gökhan and nod "yes." He smiles and slaps me on the back.

"I knew it! I said to everyone, Ali never talks but he's got guts. He's brave."

Nobody laughed. They all grew up while I was gone, I guess. I was going to tell Gökhan about the swans. I read about them last night, and I think I understand now. But he's changed, or I haven't changed. I know he wouldn't even listen to me now.

Gökhan pointed at the ground. When the big brothers have a meeting, they all squat on the ground. That's what he wants us to do. He's trying to cup his cigarette in his hand. He's learned how to flick the ash with his middle finger. We're doing the protest early tomorrow morning. When the bus stops between our neighborhood and the one down the hill. It'll be empty then.

Evening came, and still nobody told me where Hüseyin Abi was. Mom and Dad aren't talking, and I don't know why. After dinner, Mom divided the slice of Şokella bread into three pieces. We ate it together. Dad asked what the "stuff" on top was. He smiled while he ate. He asked three times.

"What's this stuff called?"

Mom said it was "Çukella," and then, "Like I told you, Çukella!" I didn't say, "It's called Şokella." We'll never have it again anyway.

I went up on the rooftop. That's when I saw him. Hüseyin Abi! He's in Gökhan's house, sitting there with Birgül Abla, still as can be in the light of a candle. Gökhan's uncle died in the fighting, so I guess they have an extra room for Hüseyin Abi. He has to live with Birgül Abla, so he can't sleep at our house anymore. Hüseyin Abi has his head in his hands. Birgül Abla is petting his hair. I got down from the rooftop and sneaked straight over to Gökhan's house. If I sit real quiet under the window, they won't hear me. But I can hear them. And I can see them if I peep real careful. When Hüseyin Abi talks, it sounds like something is stuck in his throat, or like he needs a glass of water.

"My stomach's turning, Birgül. I can still smell the blood. I feel like I'm going to throw up."

"Darling . . . My love."

"They say that if it weren't for us revolutionaries, Çorum would have turned into another Maraş. After seeing Çorum, I can't imagine what the Maraş Massacre was like. Those fascists gouged out the eyes of children! I saw it."

"Victory will be ours, Hüseyin. Never forget that. A reckoning will come one day, and they'll pay. Think about that, and don't think about anything else."

"Birgül, I can't think straight anymore. You're the only person I can confide in. My brain's not working anymore. Not like it used to."

"Don't say that! It's not true. Forget everything. Tomorrow's a new day, and we have to mobilize. The fascists are escalating the violence, but the people are ready for all-out war. Pull yourself together. I mean it. My love . . ."

Hüseyin's snot is running. I can't see it, but I know it's running. Down his throat, kind of warm, kind of sweet. That's why he was talking like that. He makes a fist and punches his knee. He needs to talk and talk so he can get the snot out of his throat.

"Do you remember, Birgül? I've already told you about what happened to me and Guerrilla Zeki in Giresun. But I don't think I said anything about a man we met in Gökçeali village. That guy was so proud of us. Zeki Abi had just talked for an hour and a half about the exploitation of the hazelnut workers. Then that man insisted we go home with him and be his guest. When we got there, he showed us a calendar and said, 'Go on, read it! Read it good!' He shouted it out, like everything he said. It was an old calendar from '68. One of the dates was circled, and written there, in pencil, was: 'Hüseyin Cevahir, Nahit Töre, and Ziya Yılmaz came today.' The man looked at us and said, 'You're sitting in the exact same spot as the revolutionaries who came before you.' It knocked the wind right out of me. We drank *ayran* with that guy and we all cried. It seems so silly now!"

Hüseyin Cevahir. I know who he was. He was friends with Ulaş, and Mahir. All of them got killed. But I get it mixed up. I don't remember who died where. I shouldn't forget. I mustn't.

"I remember something else from that night. When Zeki Abi was talking about exploitation, he got the crowd to chant: 'Down with the Oligarchy!' A man in the front row kept saying that slogan, over and over. But instead of saying 'oligarchy,' he was saying, 'Down with Aligarısı.' I guess there was some bad blood between him and another villager named Ali, and he got a kick of out of changing the words to 'Down with Ali's wife!' Anyway, the guy named Ali came up to him, mad as hell. The fists were flying! Me and Zeki Abi managed to pull them apart. Our lecture on ruling-class theories was completely upstaged, but we just about died laughing. I remember looking at the crowd and saying, 'This is what it is to be alive!' That feeling, like splashing your face in a mountain stream. Mad Hasan made me feel that way, too. Have I told you that one? No? The army was in Keçiören, searching for Mahir and the others. Mad Hasan the Woodchopper marched right up to an officer, waved the ax he always carries, and said, 'Look here, major. I'll bring this down on the middle of your skull and make two majors out of you. Leave those kids alone!' Oh, how we laughed."

Hüseyin Abi isn't laughing. He's talking about laughing, but he's not laughing at all. He wasn't like this before. Is it because of Birgül Abla? Girls can mess with your head.

"And there were those women in Büyükkayalı village, in Uşak. 'Comin' is how they pronounced 'commune.' They couldn't get enough of it.

'Tell us more about comin. We don't care about Marx and Lenin. We want to listen to comin.' We planted lots of pine trees along the village road there. The women tittered when we named it 'Love Road.' One morning, as we all headed to the fields together, there was this girl on that road, early one morning, the sun not yet up, the sky all purple, and she started singing: '*And there was Ulaş / Ulaş like the sun / Comrade Ulaş giving up his life / My heart burnt to ashes . . .*' Wow! What a voice! The song ended. Complete silence. My heart was bursting in my chest. For a moment, the world was one. Then that girl said to me, 'Hüseyin Abi, people need to feel the revolution deep in their souls, or it means nothing. You know what I mean?' Such pure goodness. I could feel it. Do you understand, Birgül? Because I sure as hell don't. How can such goodness and such evil exist under the same sky? I don't understand!"

I didn't cry. But I felt like I did that night when Hüseyin Abi made me a kite, and the kite was swallowed up in the darkness. I think Birgül Abla is hugging Hüseyin Abi. It sounds like he's talking into a blanket.

"Birgül, I'm going to Fatsa next. Everyone in the city's been rounded up. They're being tortured. Our comrades are hiding out in the mountain villages. They have no other choice. We haven't been allowed to build a new life. Now we have no choice but to fight to the death."

I could hear them breathing, the two of them. I peeked through the window. Hüseyin Abi kissed Birgül Abla. Right on the lips. Then on the neck. Like in the movies. After that, I didn't look anymore. It's shameful. But it's nice to do what they're doing. If it wasn't, Hüseyin Abi and Birgül Abla wouldn't do it. It's revolutionary, so it can't be shameful.

"Ali. Ali."

Gökhan whisper-yelled my name outside the door. Dad was having bread and olives for breakfast, but not "a piece of cheese the size of a matchbox." Bread and olives are plenty nice, that's what I think. I went straight outside. All the guys were there. They were carrying yoghurt containers in big black bags. Hamit said to Gökhan, "Birinci's no good. I wish we had Bafra." He's been smoking only since about yesterday but Birinci's not good enough for him! Gökhan flicked his ash and spoke.

"Hüseyin Abi gave a talk when he came back from Çorum. You missed it because you were staying with those rich people. Anyway, he said we need to attack "with all our might" and 'overthrow this whole fucking order.' He even said 'fuck.' We all laughed, but Hüseyin Abi didn't. Something's happened to him. I don't know what. But we decided to cheer him up. We've collected 702 yoghurt containers, sonny boy!"

It was still real early. The sky was purple. Hamit threw his arm around my shoulder. Gökhan smiled. We were all carrying giant black bags, and we were so happy walking down the hill. Our feet went *clop clop* on the road and the jiggling bags went *plop plop* on our backs. It was all mixed up at first, but then our feet clopped together and the bags plopped together and we were making one sound. Nobody else was out on the road. Gökhan went out ahead of us and started walking backwards. We were laughing as we repeated it after him, quietly, so we didn't wake everyone up.

"*Hey, Revolutionary Youth / Battle time has neared / Take up your weapon / Against imperialism . . . Deniz Gezmiş, Mahir Çayan / They died for the revolution / Revolutionaries might die but / The revolution lives on.*"

At that moment, I understood what Hüseyin Abi was saying to Birgül Abla, about the mountain stream. We were walking together, and my heart was getting bigger and bigger. I could feel it in my chest, a huge heart. And I didn't have goosebumps, but I sure felt like I did.

Further along, we hid behind some garbage cans. Then we did just what Gökhan said. Two by two, we went out onto the road and emptied the bags. The bus appeared in the distance. Gökhan yelled.

"Ali! Light it on fire!"

I ran out and lit a yoghurt container. The white plastic hissed and blackened. Then the whole pile burst into flames.

"Ali! Come back! The bus is coming. Get back here!"

The fire was huge, as big as the ones with burning tires. And the smoke was dirty and black, like from tires. And then came the slogan. Well, I didn't yell it, but they all did.

"Hüseyin, Mahir, Ulaş! The revolution lives on!"

We started running back up the hill. "Scatter!" Gökhan yelled. Everyone ran in a different direction. Then we met at the top. We turned and looked.

"The bus rolled over on its side! We made the bus roll over!"

We laughed so hard. Gökhan turned and faced us.

"Let's take the oath of the revolution! Everyone, stand at attention. Do you know the words by heart?"

We shouted the oath together.

"We, as revolutionaries, swear to tirelessly battle imperialism to the last drop of our blood and to the last bullet in our rifles. We swear it! We swear it! We swear it!"

We were about to burst out laughing again, but Gökhan stopped us.

"Stop laughing. There's more. Listen: If our battle slogans shall spread from ear to ear, and if our weapons shall pass from hand to hand, and if the lamentations of our comrades at our funerals shall be the sound of machine guns and victory cries and war cries . . . then do we say, in the name of our cause . . . Death! How welcome; how sweet!"

None of us knew that part of the oath. But Gökhan had become something like our chief, and we tried to say it. We couldn't get it right, though. We were all looking at each other and messing up. "Death! How welcome; how sweet!" Gökhan was yelling again when Hüseyin Abi came out of nowhere and gave him a big smack. Right on the side of the head. Knocking him off his feet. It was no joke.

"What the hell are you doing? Are you out of your mind? Who taught you that?"

Gökhan was saying, "Abi! Abi!" But Hüseyin was a stranger.

"What's all this about death and machine guns and battle cries? You're still kids!"

The rest of us went quiet as death. Hüseyin stopped and turned. He looked right at me. He had black circles under his eyes. Gökhan was still on the ground, crying.

"Abi, we did a protest for you. Hüseyin Abi, please!"

But Hüseyin Abi was looking at me. "Ali!" he said. And I ran away. I ran as fast as I could. I ran until my chest was tight and I couldn't breathe. I ran until I was no more than a speck. Now I can't give the Ibelo lighter to Hüseyin Abi. Maybe later? I wish Ayşe was here.

The People Are Represented in Parliament

I'm standing in the garden of the police station. Mom is standing outside the gate. She doesn't want to come in. Before we left home, Mom and Dad talked to each other, but through their teeth, because they were fighting.

"Aydın, you're acting like that's the only mulberry tree in all of Ankara! Why insist we get it from the police station?"

"Sevgi, just step into the garden and get what you want without going inside the actual building."

"I can't do it."

"Why? Will you lose your revolutionary credentials?"

Mom stopped talking.

Mom and I reach the gate. She lights a cigarette.

"Go on, Ayşe. Go in and ask them."

In a little bit, after I get the leaves, I'm going to go to Parliament with Mom. I cried a lot so I could go. Anyway, Grandma didn't wake up this morning. When Mom and I listened at her door, we could hear *tsss tsss*. She does that when she's sleeping. Grandma hasn't left her room since the concert. She hid a bottle of banana liqueur in her room, and all she does is listen to the radio all the time. Mom lifted her eyebrows and looked at Dad.

"Mother's a little out of sorts. Will you take Ayşe to work, or shall I?

"You take her. I'm already taking Ali to his dad."

My dad's "a little out of sorts" too. He called Ordu last night and talked to my granddpa. There's "trouble" in Ordu, Grandpa said. Dad told Grandpa not to go outside. He talked about it to Mom after he hung up.

"What shall we do, Sevgi? He says he's having spasms again. I wonder if we should bring him here?"

Mom didn't answer. Grandpa has "a bad heart."

I brought my lunchbox with me. Me and Ali put the silkworms in it last night. I didn't tell my mom, though. I had to cry a lot before she let me bring my lunchbox. Mom's wearing her new shoes again. She put Band-Aids on her heels. We all left home together, but Ali and Dad walked off real fast. Ali turned and looked at me. I waved to him. We were going to go together, but he mustn't go to the police station. I know that now. Last night, when Ali was reading the swan papers, we looked out the window together. I heard what they could do to Ali. That's why I told him I'd get the leaves without him. Mom took another puff on her cigarette.

"Go on, Ayşe. Go inside and ask them. Get your leaves and let's go!"

Mom wouldn't go into the garden with me. A policeman came outside. "May I pick some leaves from your mulberry tree?" I asked him. He held me up in the air. I grabbed a branch. *Why isn't Mom looking at us?*

Just then, that shout came from inside the police station.

"You be a star and I'll be a fist / We'll meet in Fatsa."

Then there was an "Ow!" and an "Ouch!" Other men started shouting. The policeman holding me in his arms laughed.

"Sounds like they're having fun in there," he said.

"Come on, Ayşe! Hurry up!"

Mom started walking away. I picked and picked. The police won't get any leaves, not from this branch. Our silkworms are going to eat them all up. I didn't say "Thank you very much" to the policeman. I just ran away.

When I caught up to Mom, we walked real fast for a while. Then she stopped, threw her cigarette on the sidewalk, and waved her finger at me.

"Listen, Ayşe. Don't you ever, ever . . ."

Mom's too mad to talk. But she's mad at everything, not just me. I know that.

She didn't talk to me again until we got to Parliament.

But she sang that song, under her breath, the one about prison and the bridge, and she sounded mad. When we got to the gates of Parliament, she stopped, because the song is about rifles, too.

It'll be terrible if Mom doesn't go down to the archives today. I won't be able to hide the silkworms and Ali will be sad. We'll both be sad, I mean. Please God, let Mom go down to the archives today. Lunchtime came, and still she didn't go. Please!

We went to lunch together. To the big restaurant with the old men like the ones at the concert hall. We sat down at a table next to theirs. They have shiny faces, and they walk with their heads high. That's because they're senators. When I hear that word—"senator"—I think of the merry-go-round at the amusement park. To get there, you have to go through a turnstile. And it goes "*tor tor tor*" as it turns. Ali would understand what I mean, but nobody else would.

In front of each of the senators is a plate with a big artichoke bottom. It's like an artichoke cup, and it holds little squares of carrot and some peas. One of them cuts off a little slice and eats it. Then he turns the artichoke on his plate, like a wheel, and cuts off another slice.

"How many rounds of voting has that been?"

"That was the 112th. And we're still no closer to electing the next president."

"Frankly, I sometimes wonder why we trouble ourselves to vote at all. Even if our party leaders were to agree on a compromise candidate, it wouldn't matter in the slightest. Brace yourself. A coup is coming."

"If it weren't for the prime minister's little act of defiance, the Americans would never support a military takeover."

"The prime minister? What do you mean?"

"You can't have forgotten what Demirel said last January. He put the Americans on notice, told them they would no longer be able use their military bases in Turkey for irregular activities without our permission. And that, I suspect, is when the Americans decided that perhaps they could do without Mr. Demirel. And so the delicate balance of power tilts once again, this time toward the Armed Forces. Now all we can do is hope for the best."

"Amen."

The senator turning his artichoke around like a wheel looks mad.

"This artichoke is terribly stringy. How's yours?"

None of them talk about swans or butterflies, like I hoped. But this restaurant has such big windows. If only they opened them. Millions of butterflies could get in. Millions!

Me and Mom went back to her desk after lunch. Something's bothering her. She goes "Ohhh!" and "Ahhh!" loud enough for me to hear, just like Grandma. They don't know it, but they make the same noises, Mom and Grandma. Mom stands up.

"Come on, Ayşe. We're going to the microfilm department."

I grab my lunchbox and follow her.

"Why are you carrying your lunchbox everywhere?"

I don't say anything.

"How was the concert yesterday?"

"Mom, did you know that music makes your arms feel longer?"

She doesn't say anything.

We go up to Muzaffer Abi at his desk. I think we kind of like him now. He's writing something. Mom leans over and reads a bit out loud.

"*Faithful Muslims and true believers have been posing questions peculiar to this era in which we live, the 20th century, delving into certain matters in their quest for answers, while were I to do such a thing, I would tumble headfirst into ruin.*"

Mom laughed.

"So, asking questions makes you tumble headfirst into ruin. Is that so? What on earth is this, Muzaffer. And why's it so badly written?"

"I'm transcribing a sermon by a popular preacher. Fetullah Gülen. One of his followers asked for my help. I was happy to be of service."

"Well, I'm relieved you didn't write it yourself. I hadn't pegged you for a reactionary."

"Reactionary? What do you mean by that, Sevgi Hanım?"

"I mean our whole country's going up in flames, and while some of us are racking our brains trying to figure out what to do, or at least taking a stand, there are others who refuse to ask any questions and who even discourage others from doing so. They're the ones who scurry off and play it safe. They're smart. Real smart. Pure provincial cunning."

"Sevgi Hanım, aren't you being a little unfair? The hodja's simply citing the hadith to—"

"Don't get me started! I remember what a friend said a long time ago. The Prophet's teachings, especially in the early days, were truly revolutionary. We know whose side he would be on today. But you wouldn't know that from listening to these provincial preachers! I'm sorry, Muzaffer. I didn't come here to argue. In fact, I came to ask you for a favor."

"Sure. What is it?"

"Something urgent just came up. Would you mind if Ayşe stayed here with you for an hour or so? I didn't have a chance to tell the director I'd be leaving work for a bit, and I don't want him to see Ayşe getting underfoot or playing in the library."

Mom didn't tell me! She didn't tell me she was going out. But she did wear her new shoes today. That means she's meeting with Uncle Önder. I knew it.

Being alone with Muzaffer Abi got boring right away, so I started kicking at his desk, but not too hard.

"What would you like to do, little lady?"

"Let's go to the archives!"

"What for?"

"I love it down there. I want to play hide-and-seek."

"Okay. Come on then . . . but you can leave your lunchbox here."

"No!"

I tricked him. He was counting "one-two-three" when I ran over, took the leaves and silkworms out of my lunchbox, and stuck them behind the stacks of *Weekend*. I peeked—but really quick—into one of Mom's yellow envelopes. I couldn't help it. *Oh! So that's what's inside.* Right when Muzaffer Abi got to "eight-nine-ten" I put the envelope back and whispered to the silkworms, "Now be good and don't make a peep!" They were all sitting on the mulberry leaves with their heads up, listening. Then I ran out into the open so Muzaffer wouldn't find my secret spot, and the game was over. Silly Muzaffer Abi was so excited to catch me.

We went back to the microfilm department after that. Mom came a little bit later. Her face was all pink and sweaty. She must have been running.

When she asked what me and Muzaffer Ai did, and I said, "We played hide-and-seek in the archives," Mom made her eyes big and grabbed both my arms.

"Did he do anything to you? Did he touch you?"

"We played hide-and-seek," I said. *I already told her!* Mom didn't see Muzaffer Abi standing near the doorway, didn't see him shake his head and walk away. "Goddamn it, Muzaffer!" Mom said. But Muzaffer wasn't even there. Mom took me by the hand, and we went to the library. "Did he do anything to you?" she asked again. I screamed, "What are you talking about?" Mom said, "Okay, it's okay."

I was going to tell Mom about the silkworms, but I didn't. Not after that. She's acting weird. Like she's somebody else's mom, not my mom. On the way home, after we got out to the street, she walked on the backs of her shoes and she didn't talk to me, not once. It made me kind of sad. I wonder what Ali's doing? He's going to be so happy about the butterflies. I bet he's going to love me even more than before.

A Nation Shares a Common Language

"You and I are going on a little walk. Okay, Ali?"

Hüseyin Abi was standing in the doorway, his hands on his hips, when he said that. He sounded a little mean. I pulled out my strings and looked at them. I didn't answer. Mom said, "Ali, Hüseyin Abi's talking to you. He's going to take you out."

"Ali!" Hüseyin Abi said again. I put the strings in my pocket without looking. I went over to him without looking at him. He squeezed me against his leg, like before, and I shook him off and went out into the garden. "Me and Ali are going on a little trip," Hüseyin Abi said to my mom. "Don't worry. We'll be back soon." Mom said it in a quiet voice, but I heard her:

"Hüseyin, please. Don't be too rough on the boy."

Hüseyin Abi was standing in the doorway again, the sunlight hitting his face this time. And I got a funny feeling. Like I was taking his picture with my eyes. I don't have the words for it, but it was like I suddenly grew up a lot and it was much later, and I was remembering the way Hüseyin Abi stood in that doorway. Then the funny feeling passed.

Me and Hüseyin Abi went down to the bottom of the hill, *clop clop clop*. We both stuck our hands in our pockets. Hüseyin Abi didn't talk all the way there. I'd already made up my mind not to say a word. *Why did he smack Gökhan like that?*

When the road got flat, we stopped.

"Where do you want to go, little lion?"

I didn't look, and I didn't speak.

"Ali, shall we go to Swan Park? All right then, we'll go to Swan Park."

Hüseyin Abi walked slowly. Even when he doesn't talk, even when he doesn't make a sound, it's like his chest is talking, like something is always moving deep inside him. But right now, nothing's moving inside Hüseyin Abi, nothing I can hear. He's not even talking to himself without saying anything. Maybe something happened to him in Çorum. Maybe he wants to hide it, and he's ashamed for wanting that.

Maybe it got too noisy there and his head hurts. I took hold of Hüseyin Abi's hand. *I'm here, Hüseyin Abi! Don't go it alone!* He patted me on the head and squeezed me against his leg a little. Then he let me go. We kept walking. *Clop clop clop.*

"Whatever happened to that kite, Ali? Did you find it later, see where it got tangled?"

I went "I don't know" with my shoulders.

"I guess that kite must have flown up and away until it was free. That was one clever kite."

Hüseyin Abi thinks he can make me talk.

"What about that little red car I got you? Did it fly away too?"

I waved my hand; "Who cares?" He laughed. I played with the strings in my pocket, but Hüseyin Abi didn't see me.

We stopped in front of a patisserie. Hüseyin Abi pulled his money out of his pocket and looked at it.

"Come on! Let me get you an Ankara Sarması."

It smells awfully nice inside. Forks and knives are clicking, and ladies are talking. Nobody there is like us, but when you're with Hüseyin Abi you don't care, because it always feels like we're the strongest and we have the nicest clothes.

"I'll have a tea, brother. And an Ankara Sarması for the little guy. Do you want a lemonade, too, Ali?" *Lemonade is for kids!*

"I want tea, too!"

"Okay then. Make that two teas."

My arms are sticking to the tabletop. It's "formica," and formica is brown. I know that because of the tables at Dad's workplace and because of the teachers' tables. *Oh good!* Ankara Sarması means cake!

Hüseyin Abi presses his cigarette between his lips and narrows his eyes against the smoke as he cuts the cake in half.

"Dig in, little lion!"

They brought us both a napkin. I put mine in my pocket for Mom. The cake's really different. There's a soft part, and it's like yoghurt, and then there's a bready part, and it's yellow. And the whole thing is rolled up. It's better to get both parts on your fork, the exact same amount. I'm lifting the fork to my mouth, and it smells so good. I bet Ayşe knows this smell. It smells as good as when you're about to fall asleep with your head in your mom's lap, but she's talking to someone so she forgets she has her hand on your back, and she leaves it there, her hand on your back, nice and warm. I wonder if Ayşe ever tasted Ankara Sarması? It's so, so good. I keep the soft, sweet, yoghurty stuff in my mouth, between my teeth, on the insides of my cheeks.

"Ali, we're going to have a man-to-man talk today. Because you've grown up now. That's right! Today, I announce to the world that little Ali has become a young man."

I swallow with a loud gulp. Why did I grow up today? Hüseyin Abi is trying to smile, but he can't, not really. He's making a serious face, and he's making a funny face. So his face gets all mixed up, and he doesn't know what to do with it.

"Ali, first things first. I want to talk about what happened the other day. I shouldn't have done that."

I put down my fork and look straight ahead. *I need my strings!*

"Listen to me, little lion. Being a revolutionary . . ."

He lowers his voice, because we're in a patisserie.

"Being a revolutionary isn't the same as causing trouble. And it's never about making a bus roll over. What if there had been kids like you inside that bus? That was wrong! Revolutionaries try to make the world a better place, a more beautiful place. Do you understand, Ali? You see us walking around with pieces in our hands and you imagine . . . It's not like that. Don't believe anyone who says, 'The revolution is written in blood.' That's not true. The revolution is written in patience, in love, in hope. In conviction. And if the day comes when you have no choice but to . . . Never mind!"

Hüseyin Abi got mad at himself. He's smoking really fast now.

"You stopped eating. Don't you like it? Go on, have some more."

I start eating again. Now I'm taking big forkfuls and swallowing fast, because I want it to be over.

"Ali, remember when I first came to the neighborhood? You were what, four years old? Do you remember those days? Never forget them. It was a wonderful time. We marched for water, all together, and you learned when to stop and run, when to keep marching, when and how to chant a slogan. We got back to the neighborhood from a demonstration that one time and you were running back and forth with a rolling pin in your hand, so excited."

I don't remember, but I nod "yes" because Hüseyin Abi's head is hurting something awful. I smile a little. To make him happy. The sweet yoghurty stuff gets all over the inside of my mouth. If I finish it, maybe then we can go. Because Hüseyin Abi's going to tell me sad, sad things. I know it.

"Ali, we were born into troubled times, you and me. That's just the way it is. But to make it through these times, we have to swallow our fair share of the grit kicked up by these times. And if we don't make it, who gives a shit! I'd rather die fighting than live like rabbit shit . . . too timid to make a stink, too timid to make a mess. Good for absolutely nothing. You know, nothing is as glorified in this land of ours as the ability to make it through life. Deception, cunning, hypocrisy . . . Do whatever it takes. Survive at any cost. Some, a very few, are prepared to make the ultimate sacrifice. The others watch, waiting for the danger to pass, waiting for the others to fall by the wayside, waiting for the chance to take over, to make our country theirs alone. Time after time, all through history."

Hüseyin Abi looked at me and stopped. Because I couldn't swallow, my mouth was so full my cheeks got puffed out.

"Ali! What are you doing? You're going to choke. Quick, drink some tea. I can't believe you!"

I got it all down. No more cake. Hüseyin made his hands into fists, one on top of the other, and rested his chin on them. He looked into my eyes and smiled, like we were best friends.

"Ali, never mind what I was just saying. I'm about to tell you something I've never told anyone. Do you understand?"

Hüseyin Abi dipped his finger in the yoghurty stuff on his plate and licked it off.

"This is really good! Isn't it, Ali?

"I bet you didn't know my mom and dad are engineers. Do you know where my home is, the one I grew up in? In Istanbul. On the Bosphorus. In a neighborhood called Bebek. There was this man who looked after our apartment building. I guess I was about your age. One day, while he was out working in the garden, I decided to pitch in. It didn't feel right for me to be playing while he was working. Me and my family were going to visit friends that day, and I was wearing a white shirt and a white pair of trousers. Well, I completely threw myself into it. A part of me wanted to work so hard he wouldn't have to lift a finger. It wasn't until I stopped to catch my breath that I realized I was covered in mud. And that's when I noticed that the man was smoking a cigarette and chuckling to himself. He'd figured he might as well take it easy since I was doing all the work. Just then my mom came out and saw me. Boy, did she ever yell. She was tugging and tugging at my ear! I looked over at the man. He didn't say a word. He just turned around and started working, as though he'd been working the whole time. Can you believe it, Ali? Sometimes, especially lately, I wonder if it'll be like that when this is all over. I mean, like that day my ear was being tugged and I realized I was all alone."

It popped into my head, and I said it without thinking.

"You've got me, Hüseyin Abi!"

Hüseyin Abi laughed. And he shouted, so loud everyone looked at us.

"Yes, I do, Ali! I've got you. And that's what this is all about. That's what makes us go on. Ali, there's something I wanted to tell you today. I'm leaving, and you might not see me again. I didn't want you to have any hard feelings when I left."

I didn't like that Ankara Sarması one bit. It's like yoghurt, like choking.

"I need to be somewhere else, Ali. Some new big brothers will come to the neighborhood, and you'll like them a lot. They're brave as can be. But as for me . . . well, I've got to go, Ali. Do you understand, little lion?"

That's when I heard the men yelling outside. The waiter knew Hüseyin Abi was a revolutionary, I guess. Because the waiter was dark, too.

"You might want to get out of here, brother. Nihat Erim was killed today. The Grey Wolf commandos are marching this way, from Liberation. Don't worry about paying."

Hüseyin Abi grabbed my hand and we ran outside. We began walking really fast toward Swan Park. I'd never seen Hüseyin Abi like that. His hand got sweaty and they were shaking.

"Don't be scared, Ali. We'll walk toward Cinnah and decide what to do when we get there. Okay, little lion?"

But he's not looking at me. He's talking to himself. The fascists are behind us. As they get closer, everyone runs into the shops. We walk faster and faster. As we pass the park, I can't say anything, not a word about the swans, because we're running now. Hüseyin Abi picks me up, and I hold on tight to his neck. The blue veins in his neck are going pit-a-pat. We go through a door, up some stairs, through another door. It's dark everywhere. But there are purple lights, spinning round, people dancing. But they dance like Americans, and the song isn't Turkish.

"*One way ticket. One way ticket. One way ticket to the moon!*"

Hüseyin Abi puts me down. He's looking for something, but he can't see. It's too dark. Purple lights blink and blink on Hüseyin Abi's face. Purple and black, purple and black. Someone comes up and talks to Hüseyin Abi.

"Sinan! What are you doing here?"

Sinan? Hüseyin Abi looks at me. He knows I heard, but he doesn't say anything.

"Hide the boy!"

Hüseyin Abi goes over to the shiny place where everyone is dancing. My eyes are on him the whole time the other big brother is carrying me away. Hüseyin Abi is dancing just like the Americans. How does he know how to make like an American? Like an opportunist!

I got taken to the kitchen. I waited there, but not for long. Why did that big brother call Hüseyin Abi Sinan? Doesn't he know Hüseyin Abi's name? Maybe he doesn't. Hüseyin Abi came and took me away. We got in a shared taxi and went home. As we were walking up the hill to the house, he said it.

"Ali, not a word of this to anyone."

"Why did he call you Sinan?"

Hüseyin Abi stopped and looked at me. He was going to say something, but he didn't. He thought I'd tell someone if he did. I understood. And that's when I let go of his hand. I didn't give him his Ibelo lighter, either.

Where are you, Ayşe?

A Sense of Trust Binds the Citizenry

"Samim, has a tree ever come crashing down, right in front of your eyes? You know, split right down the middle and toppled over? If you did see something like that, happening right in front of you, you'd probably think, for a moment, that your eyes were playing tricks on you. Trees don't just topple over, in the blink of an eye, for no reason. That's not what trees do. It wouldn't register. Well, these days, it feels like we're watching as a mighty tree comes crashing to the ground in slow motion. It's happening in front of our eyes, but we can't process it. The whole thing's crashing down, Samim."

Mom told me to stay home with my dad. Grandma's still "out of sorts," so she and Mom went out together. That's why Dad invited Samim Abi over. He said he wants to have a couple of drinks and some *meze*, just the two of them. Ayla Abla's out at a union meeting, you see.

They sat in the kitchen, on stools. Since Mom wasn't home, the table was a mess. The food to go with the rakı wasn't in serving dishes and the glasses didn't match either. That's what happens when mothers aren't home. Things get ugly. There weren't any paper napkins. There were small forks, but in the evening we use big forks. Dad and Samim Abi dripped melon juice all over the table and sliced the cheese still in the package. I watched *Train Theater* on TV for a while, but then, because of Ramadan, TV got boring. So I went over by the kitchen door and listened. That's when I heard Dad say, "The whole thing's crashing down, Samim." He had his elbows on the table. Samim Abi was sitting like a hunchback, looking at him, holding *Gırgır* magazine, all rolled up in his hand.

"Have you seen that interview in *Hürriyet*? The provincial chairman of the Nationalist Action Party claims they've got five thousand people monitoring everyone. I used to think it was paranoia, but we really are being followed. There's no way of knowing who's an informant. What a joke!"

Dad laughed.

"Well, I'm not an informant, Samim. That much I know."

They laughed, but not really. They had to drink some more rakı before they could talk again.

"Samim, have you heard that wiretap story?"

"No."

"I think it was a journalist or something. He was on the phone with a friend and he heard a cough. 'Brother,' he said to whoever was listening, 'You've been working too hard. Let me suggest a nice hot cup of lime tea with honey. It'll do wonders for that bad throat.'"

"Now that's funny!"

"And the guy listening in thanked him!"

"Aydın Abi, that's the one thing they can't take away from us."

"What?"

"Our sense of humor. We're still able to laugh."

"You call that laughing, Samim? It's more like a nervous reaction. We love to claim we Turks have this unique sense of humor and our satirical magazines are the best in the world. People will laugh at anything when their nerves are shot to hell!"

"They wrote in *Gırgır* this week that the Japanese are deeply troubled by the Çorum Massacre."

"If the Japanese really did have to accept responsibility for every disgrace in our country, hara-kiri would lead to the extinction of their entire race."

They both laughed again. Then Dad got serious.

"How's Ayla doing? I mean, how are the two of you?"

"Good. We're thrilled every time one of us makes it back home in one piece. We hug each other and all that. Everything's fine."

Dad had half a glass of rakı left. He finished it in one swallow.

"And how's Sevgi Abla?"

"Angry, Samim. Always angry."

"Is anything the matter?"

"Let me give you some brotherly advice: Never let a woman lose her respect for you. And if she does, don't make a fool of yourself trying to regain it."

Samim Abi looked at the table, and Dad looked at him. Then Samim Abi lifted his head, and Dad looked at the table. Nobody laughed. Nobody talked.

When Dad did talk again, it was in a loud voice.

"That detective friend of mine asked me to attend a deposition yesterday. I was real close friends with one of the guys killed in the Bahçe-lievler Bloodbath."

"Brother, you're kidding!"

"They'd identified a possible witness. I was allowed to sit in as the detective questioned her."

"How'd it go?"

"She was petrified. Who can you trust these days? Certainly, not the state. If you decide to talk to a cop sympathetic to the revolutionaries, you could find a cop sympathetic to the Grey Wolves waiting on your doorstep. And she was elderly, too. It was awful."

"Did she say anything useful?"

"I don't know. I left early."

"What? How could you leave, Aydın Abi?"

Dad looked at Samim Abi with a sad smile.

"You sounded like Sevgi just then: 'How could you, Aydın? Why didn't you do anything? Why didn't you fight back? Why didn't you go to prison?'"

"Hey, that's not what I meant, Aydın Abi. It's just that you . . . I wondered if . . . anyway, I've got a brother who—"

"Samim, I've got another piece of brotherly advice for you: Live bold. Don't be afraid to take risks. Yes, you'll probably end up paying for it. You might get tortured. You might get imprisoned. You might lose your job. You might even go out of your mind. But it's better than living like rabbit shit. If you've played it safe, but those you love haven't, you'll find it's too late and—"

"Rabbit shit? Aydın Abi, my brother says—"

"They'll make you pay the heaviest price of all, and that is—"

"I've got a brother who—"

"Please hear me out, Samim. I need to get some things off my chest."

Dad poured another glass of rakı. Samim stuck his hands between his legs and listened.

"I don't know if you know this, but Sevgi was imprisoned in the military intervention of '71. I was studying the history of language. While my sympathies lay with the Left, even chanting slogans made me feel a little silly. I was completely engrossed in my studies and literature, off in my own little world. We didn't have much in common, she and I. If Sevgi hadn't ended up in prison, and if she hadn't been so terrified when she got out, she'd never have given me another look. She was beautiful, tough and fearless, always spoke her mind. But that was before prison. She came out of there too scared to cross the street on her own. One day, me and Sevgi ran into each other again in Yenişehir. She was holding her books against her body like a shield, her shoulders drooped, her face pale. She'd tried to cover it with her hair, but I could see the burn mark on her cheek. Right about here. They'd stubbed out a cigarette on her face! I didn't ask about it, of course. She'd hadn't met up with anyone or seen any of her old friends. Some were missing, some scattered, others were broken in body and spirit. And yet . . . I should have realized. There was a strange light in her eyes. 'Let's have some tea,' I told her. It was the tea that did it. She'd made up her mind long before that, though. She might even have decided to play a game with fate. You know, she might have told herself, 'I'm going to marry the first man who talks to me in Yenişehir.' At first, she was happy to nestle under my arm. And there she stayed. We never went out together, always stayed in. But I was so puffed up with pride. *Sevgi loves me*. I'd become a man. And then one day, much later, while she was nursing Ayşe, she turned to me with tears in her eyes and said, "How did you manage to stay out of prison, Aydın?" I could tell from her voice that I'd let her down and that there was nothing I could do about it. Samim, you can never know the dreams you've inspired in a woman and how badly you've let her down, but I could tell from the fury in her voice that she'd had such high hopes for me. That day, I sensed that Sevgi's dreams were big. And she made me feel small. I've felt that way ever since. . . . Why the hell are you letting me jabber like this! I wish you'd stopped me, told me to stop being such a bore. But you just sat there and listened! I wonder what Ayşe's up to? I'd better go and check on her."

"Aydın Abi, you can tell me anything. You know that. We've got nothing to hide from each other."

"I don't know about that, Samim. Now that you mention it, I've been wondering about that extra bedroom of yours. Are you hiding something in there? Why do you always keep the door locked?"

"Aydın Abi, look! If it isn't little miss Ayşeyevich, sitting there in the hallway, all bug-eyed, listening to every word we're saying."

"Ayşe! What are you doing out there? Get in here."

Dad pulled me onto his lap. His eyes are all red. And he smells like rakı. It feels like we lost. It feels like there's nothing we can do about it, either. Mom's always weird, and now Dad's being weird too. I'm sitting in his lap, but my dad forgot all about me. I wish Ali was here.

Faith Binds the Citizenry

"*Religious movies have become all the rage. Currently, the top actresses in the land are vying for the plum role of Rabia Hatun, the Muslim saint and Sufi mystic whose life and times are to be portrayed in a Yeşilçam production*—Sorry about that. I keep yawning my head off—*Our sources tell us that the top contender for the title role is none other than a curvaceous beauty best known for her steamy scenes and bared skin.*—I wonder who they're talking about?—*Throughout the month of Ramadan, our readers can look forward to multiple airings of two faith-based epics*—Oh, there I go again!—*We particularly recommend the critically acclaimed* His Holiness, Ömer."

Jale Hanım's daughter, Feride, was reading out loud from a magazine, yawning and yawning. Then she tossed the magazine onto the middle coffee table. If I did that, Mom would get mad. You're not supposed to toss things. It's wrong. But here at Jale Hanım's house it's fine. It's okay to yell here, too, and to call each other "idiot." They think it's funny. Here, they play Okey out on the balcony, and they don't care if the tiles go *click* on the table and *clack* on the racks. Sometimes they even dance out on the balcony, *snap-snapping* their fingers and *smack-smacking* their feet. Jale Hanım has a housecoat made out of lace, and she chews gum, just like her daughter Feride. I'm not allowed to chew gum because it goes *smack smack*. Jale Hanım's house slippers go *clippety-clappety*, and she doesn't care how much noise she makes when she stirs her tea. We don't do that in my house. We rest our teaspoons on the bottom of the glass and stir extra slow and careful. And we don't laugh *hah hah hah* with our heads back and our teeth showing. But they're "not that bad, actually," are Jale Hanım and Feride Abla. When Jale Hanım kisses me on the cheek and I rub the mark she leaves, it looks like I'm wearing rouge. It's not that bad, actually.

Me and Grandma are at Jale Hanım's house for iftar because they invited us over. "We don't fast," Grandma whispered to me, "but don't eat anything until they do." Grandma feels like she's "going downhill" these days, so we have to be extra nice to her. That's what Mom said. I can't be naughty, not when I'm with Grandma. Mom and Dad laughed when Jale Hanım invited us all over to iftar, but me and Grandma came, and they didn't. İftar means starting dinner with an olive. I just learned that. "Well, what do you expect? She hasn't had any religious instruction," Jale Hanım said, screwing up her mouth and raising her eyebrows. She's "bad-tempered" right now because she's "fasting." While we're waiting for iftar, Jale Hanım showed us Janin Cosmetic Products.

"It's a new system, Nejla Hanım. You invite a group of housewives over to pitch the product. Then, not only do you get a commission if you make a sale, you get a cut of their commissions, too, if they become Janin Ladies. You just sit there and make money! What could be better?"

Grandma was confused.

"One doesn't sell skin cream to one's guests, Jale Hanım!"

"What's the big deal? It's called free enterprise. Besides, it's my life, and I'll do what I want."

Grandma put down the jar of skin cream, wrinkled her forehead and tilted her head to one side. That's the "it didn't turn out right" look she gets when somebody cooks a dish wrong. Jale Hanım handed me something that looked like a camera. One of her "chums" brought it back from "the hajj." When you look inside, you see a whole bunch of people dressed all in white walking around a big black box. "Have a look at the Kaaba. Not that anybody ever taught you what it is," Jale Hanım said. And the "chum" also brought Feride Abla green lipstick that turns pink on her lips, which doesn't make any sense. Grandma shook her head at the plastic bottle of Zamzam water and said, "It's full of germs." She didn't drink any.

Then it was time for iftar. They fired the cannon! When it goes *boom*, you can eat. They've made so much food. And there's this thing called cornflakes. It's American, and you're supposed to eat it with milk. The "foreigners" have it for breakfast, but, because it's "easily digestible," you can eat it at *sahur*, too, before the sun comes up. I tried some. It's like paper. But the box, now that's nice. All red, and there are smiling people on it. They're Americans. They all have yellow hair. I guess if you eat enough cornflakes your hair turns yellow. Just like Lucy, in *Dallas*! I pop a handful into my mouth. The *crunch crunch* is fun, but the smell, well, there isn't one. Well, maybe a little bit, I guess, but like paper.

There's so much food at Jale Hanım's. *Slurp slurp*, stuffed vegetables and stuffed vine leaves, *chomp chomp*, meatballs and fried potatoes. They haven't eaten anything since *sahur*. They're so hungry I can't watch them. Especially when lettuce hangs from their mouths. And then there's a horrible cough, like choking, that Jale Hanım's husband makes before he has a big drink of water. "Ah!" he says, "that was delicious." He laughs and says, "Fasting makes everything taste better, Nejla Hanım." Jale Hanım says, "Fasting purifies the body." Feride Abla says, "But it's tough to do in the summertime." Grandma doesn't say anything. She's not looking at them. She's listening to the TV, because that man with the deep voice is telling her the news. Grandma drops her fork and says, "They've killed Nihat Erim!"

Jale Hanım can't really talk with so much meatball in her mouth, but she says, "Oh, you mean . . . now who was that guy?" I listen to the news with Grandma.

Former Prime Minister Nihat Erim has been assassinated by unidentified gunmen near his summer home in the Istanbul suburb of Dragos. The terrorist organization Revolutionary Left has claimed responsibility for the attack. Nihat Erim served as prime minister from March 26, 1971, to May 22, 1972.

Grandma dropped her fork. "He tortured your mother," she said. Just like that. Her mouth opened and closed before I understood. I don't think she understood. It was that quick. For the first time, nobody was eating. Grandma started putting salad on her plate, a huge pile of salad. She looked at me to see if I was looking at her. And I was. Nobody said anything until the news was over. They just ate. A sign saying ENTERTAINMENT came up on the TV, and still they kept eating.

They were about to burst like balloons. Then Füsun Önal sang "One Way Ticket" on TV, easy and free, just like the Americans. Jale Hanım and the others got all sleepy and sank into their armchairs with their arms folded over their bellies. Feride Abla was chewing gum again. "Sugar-free gum doesn't count," she told her mom. "Gum spoils your fast only if it has sugar in it." She was reading *Weekend* when her dad asked what was on TV. That's when she got the red magazine and told us about *His Holiness, Ömer*.

"For crying out loud," Jale Hanım said. "Those are the only kinds of movies they show during Ramadan."

Her husband said, "Good, good. We'll learn something." Jale Hanım and Feride Abla kept talking even though their eyes were closing.

"Mom, I heard the ladies in the apartment building next door are having this '*mukabele*' thing all through the night. Have you heard about it?"

"It's some kind of meal, right?"

"No, Mom! It's chanting passages from the Koran together, because of Ramadan."

"Well, let them pray the night away for all I care. If you ask me, they're a little backward, the whole lot of them. I think everyone in that building is from Yozgat or some godforsaken place like that. Oh, except for that lady Sevgi visits, Ayla. But she and her husband are communists, from what I hear. Why can't more people be like us? Fast during Ramadan, say your prayers at Bairam. Everything in moderation. But if I do say so myself, we did go a little overboard again tonight. We really must try to eat less. I say it every night, but . . ."

Then they got quiet. Jale Hanım's eyes closed, and so did her husband's. Feride Abla took the phone into her bedroom. She's calling her fiancé. I know that because Jale Hanım told Grandma once that Feride Abla always calls her fiancé "in secret" and it's "hilarious."

When the Ömer movie started and everyone else was snoozing, Grandma talked to me real quiet.

"Listen, Ayşe. God told people to fast so they would know what it's like to go hungry. That's why."

"But they ate so much!"

"That's because they'd gone hungry since dawn."

"Why did that man torture Mom? And when? Was I born yet?"

"Forget I said anything. It never happened. I'm not thinking straight these days, Ayşe honey. It looks like everyone's fallen asleep. Would it be terribly rude if we let ourselves out?"

"Let's turn up the TV. That'll wake them up!"

Grandma laughed. "Go ahead, turn it up." Then Ömer yelled really loud on TV, and Jale Hanım and her husband almost jumped out of their seats. She went to the kitchen to make tea, and he went to the bathroom.

When Grandma went to the kitchen to help Jale Hanım, I went out on the balcony. I looked over at Samim Abi's house. I wanted to see Ayla. To wave to her. But all I could see was their terrace, empty, and the back room, the one that's locked. It was dark. I looked over at the police station and at the mulberry tree. The silkworms are growing bigger in Parliament. Mom's going to be so surprised when they turn into butterflies. And they'll be flying around! She doesn't know I don't have them at home. She didn't ask about them, even once. And Grandma forgot all about them, too. Then the light went on in the locked-up room. I could see a shadow on the curtain. Samim Abi? The room went dark again. Ayla Abla went out on the terrace. She looked over at our apartment building. She looked the other way. She looked down at the street.

I was going to yell, "Ayla Abla!" But I didn't. I ducked, but I didn't know why.

When Grandma yelled, "Ayşe! Ayşe!" I went back inside. Feride Abla turned on her tape player.

"Shrugging it off we arrived in this place
By mistaking a smile for a friendly face"

The People of a Nation Share a Common Land

"I think most of you already know Vedat from the coffeehouse or the public fountain. But I'll introduce him anyway while we're gathered for our committee meeting. I want you to see comrade Vedat as the new Hüseyin. They say there's no need to praise a brave man to his face, but let me say that we have full confidence in Vedat, that he's proven himself time and again, and that he's as brave as they come. He'll be handling all the problems and questions in your neighborhood. Now, here he is, comrade Vedat."

Hüseyin Abi introduced the new big brother. I heard Birgül Abla say that he's handing "vigilance and mobilization" over to Vedat Abi. Hüseyin Abi has been "reassigned" to another place. Later, maybe Birgül will be reassigned too. Vedat Abi doesn't talk much, and he never smiles. I don't really like him. But Gökhan says, "He's our revolutionary big brother, so we have to trust him." Gökhan still carries that knife everywhere and tries to act like a grown-up.

Then one of the uncles in the audience—I couldn't see which one—said, "Hang on a second, Hüseyin!" The uncle didn't stand up to talk, and that's wrong. He coughed, was quiet for a minute, and talked again for a long time, stopping now and then to cough.

"Hüseyin, these are blood-filled times and, I mean, everyone is expecting a coup, so it kind of feels like this is being done outside our initiative. *Cough cough.* Is it, or isn't it? I think it is. And there's another thing—don't take this personally, comrade Vedat—but it's never a good idea to change horses in the middle of a stream. *Cough cough.* I mean, don't get me wrong, but this is all so . . . Do you see what I mean?"

Hüseyin Abi said, "It's like this," and stopped. Everyone was looking at him. He wasn't smiling anymore, and he was hanging his head.

"It's like this . . ."

He stopped again. That's when Birgül Abla stood up and said things I didn't understand. I don't think anybody understood. Because nobody said anything. The uncle said nothing, but he was shaking his head from side to side. There was a lot of whispering. When the room got quiet again, it was time to move on to "the other items on the agenda." That day, the main "item" was "neighborhood defense." If a coup's coming, you must make "preparations." Vedat Abi spoke, his voice so low nobody could hear him. Well, I did, but his words didn't mean much to me. Anyway, the meeting was soon over. As we all walked out of the "Fruit and Vegetable Cooperative," people talked to each other in low voices. Even the women were saying, "This is no good." Mom yelled at Nuran Abla.

"You've been revolutionaries for all of two seconds, and you think you know what's best?"

"But Aliye Abla, we don't know this young fellow."

"Did you know Hüseyin when he first came? You'll get to know this one too."

Mom took my hand, and we walked home with Dad. Again, she made flour soup for dinner. We'll have money tomorrow after we go to Ayşe's house. Mom will make soup out of a chicken neck, but right now, the flour's floating on the soup and we're watching it. Dad ate fast. Mom ate nothing. They didn't talk. When I sat down on a cushion and started reading *Ulduz and the Crows*, they blew out the candle on the table and went out in front of the door to talk.

"Aliye, this will never work if they keep sending members of the organization all over the place. That guy was right to ask about it. That's just what I was thinking. The only reason I didn't say anything was that I didn't want to make trouble for Hüseyin. They say we're headed for a dictatorship. If it doesn't happen today, it'll happen tomorrow. But they're still sending our people away."

"Hüseyin's off to Fatsa, he says. He's probably joining the guerrillas. I don't know what they're doing, Hasan. And what about the guns they stuck in our coal cellar again?"

"I didn't see anything. What did they put in there?"

"I don't know if it's new rifles or what, but they stuck a big sack in there. Nobody's thinking straight these days. Before Hüseyin goes, ask him to clear out the cellar."

"Listen, Aliye. There's something else I want to ask you. Are you putting money aside without telling me?"

"I'm setting aside a little something for Ali. So he can go to a special doctor."

"What happened? Are the revolutionary doctors not good enough for you?"

"They're up to their necks in work already."

"You've been acting different ever since you started cleaning for rich people."

"Not again, Hasan! Anyway, there was something else I was going to tell you. You know Zarife the Kurd? Followers of Apo keep coming to their house. They've been telling Zarife's sons to go down there to Kurdistan."

"Kurdistan," Mom said. It's "down there," she said. Maybe it's far off in a different Turkey. Zarife and her friends speak a Turkish I can't understand. And they scream like birds, making their tongues and their throats show when they're really happy or really sad. So they must be from a different Turkey. I didn't tell Mom about the other big brother and how he called Hüseyin Abi "Sinan" at that dance place. Because that's a different Turkey, too.

"Aliye, do you think Hüseyin and the others are going to go underground?"

"Why would they do that? We're not in enemy land!"

"I don't know. They seem so strange these days, so troubled. They keep it inside. They don't tell us anything, but if they did . . . If they said, 'Come on, let's do it!' Maybe, all together, we'd—"

"Let's say we decided to do that. Where we would go? How can we go underground with our families, our kids?"

"That's true, but will the slaughtering ever stop?"

"Slaughter or not, it's still our country. Isn't it, Hasan? If it's not, we should just pack up and leave for good."

So, Turkey has an underground. A different country, down there under the ground. But how will they get there? By digging and digging, like an ant? Maybe the ground under Turkey is already full of tunnels. There are a lot of things under the ground in Ankara. Hüseyin Abi told me. There must be people living down there, too, only we don't know about them.

"Aliye!"

"Yeah?"

"They say a lot of people are going to foreign parts."

"And?"

"They say they made themselves a country over there."

"And?"

"Maybe we should apply for Germany too? It's like Turkey now. That's what they say."

"I don't want to go anywhere."

"I don't either, but we could think about it."

Is there a Turkey in Germany? That means there's a different map than the pink and yellow and blue one at school. There's an underground map, there's a map of the Turkey "down there," and there's a map of our country. There are other places, other maps I don't know about.

Dad burped really loud.

"That flour soup gives me gas. I'm puffed up like an inner tube. Feel that!"

Outside, Mom and Dad laughed. Dad's belly went *goop goop* because Mom spanked it. I didn't have much flour soup, so I'm hungry. My belly's going *grrr grrr*. It'll stop by morning. It'll stop when I have tea. When you smoke, you don't get hungry. That's what Gökhan said: "Have a cig and you won't get hungry." I wish we had bread with Şokella. Maybe they'll give me some again at Ayşe's house tomorrow.

What kind of name is "Sinan"?! That's a rich person's name.

Our Oath

"They're here, Grandma! They're here! Come quick!"

Grandma doesn't put her hair in a bun anymore; it just hangs down on the sides. She's sleepy all day, every day. She walks so slow. She's always asking, "Huh? Huh?" It took so long for her to get from the hallway to the front door.

—

My mom rang the bell. We're waiting at the front door. I could hear Ayşe inside, yelling, "They're here!" But nobody's opening the door. Ayşe probably forgot to take the silkworms to Parliament. Hüseyin Abi forgot his Ibelo lighter. Maybe Ayşe forgot everything too.

—

Maybe Ali told everyone about the swan papers. I'll be mad at him if he did. Only the two of us should know. It's ours and it's for us only!

—

If Ayşe forgot about the swan papers . . . She doesn't know any marching songs, so she can forget important things. She probably went to the concert again and ate Şokella bread without me. She made new friends. They told her the swan papers were stupid. They all laughed and teased. Maybe her real name isn't even Ayşe. Maybe she has a rich person's name too.

—

Ali has boys for friends and they're more fun for him, of course. They kick balls. They hang out in the street. They play cowboys and Indians. "Ayşe's just a stupid girl!" That's what he tells them. "She can't even read the little letters." I know it. He said that. Maybe he won't even come here anymore. I feel like crying. First Dad got weird, now Ali.

—

When we were reading the swan papers, Ayşe said it was for us, only for us. But she went and told her mom, I'm sure she did. She doesn't have a chief in her neighborhood so she blabs. That, and because she's a girl. I don't care! Let her tell everyone!

—

Grandma opened the door. Ali! I knew he'd come.

—

Ayşe was happy to see me!

—

"The butterflies are in Parliament! Hooray!" That's what I yelled when I saw Ali. I shouldn't have done it right away, shouldn't have yelled, but I was so excited. Grandma won't know what I meant. And Ali's mom doesn't know about it. It's okay.

—

Ayşe got the silkworms into Parliament. I knew she'd do it. Because, because . . .

—

Me and Ali decided together.

—

Because we decided together.

—

That night, Ali said to get out the swan papers. Everybody thought we were asleep. It was when we got back from the concert and we went to bed early. The papers were hidden in my lunchbox. There were six pages. All full of writing in little letters. We turned on the little light on my desk. Ali bent over the papers, and I bent over too:

"Ayşe, we have to read it all. Every word. We have to understand. Everything depends on us."

"Ali, why does it depend on us?"

"Try to understand. They're making a dictatorship. Nobody knows that but us. They act like they know, but they don't. Not really. Not all of it."

"Who? What?"

"The fascists! They're coming, Ayşe."

"What does—"

"When the fascists come, they're going to hurt the swans. We have to save them. Because we're revolutionaries. Don't you understand?"

"I understand, Ali! I know all about revolutionaries. Dursun Dede's waiting for our revolution. And his hair is white and he can't do it. We have to do it. We have to work hard. Right?"

"I guess. Revolutionaries save everyone, or something like that. Ayşe?"

"Yes?"

"If I can't read these papers . . . can't understand, I mean . . . Hey, don't put your hands on your hips like that."

"You can read it. You're smart. I put the silkworms in Parliament, now you can read these papers. Come on!"

Ali started reading. We didn't understand anything at first. But then Ali said, "Here it is, right here!" Ali read and read, because everything depends on us. That's why.

To date, an Avian Deflighting Technique has been applied once at the Animal Clinic of the Faculty of Veterinary Medicine of Ankara University.

A mute swan (*Cygnus olor*) was attempting to return to Swan Park after its transfer to the residence of the general chief of staff when it struck several buildings and trees while in flight. When it was brought to our clinic, it was in a semi-conscious state. Despite our efforts, the bird expired. The martial law commander of Ankara then instructed the municipality to inhibit the flight ability of the remaining swans in the park, upon which the municipality applied to us for assistance.

We responded by performing for the first time a tenotomy of the *extensor policis brevis*. This simple surgical procedure on a healthy specimen from the park was a success—i.e., the wing extension property was reduced, rendering the bird incapable of flight. Furthermore, the literature on this technique reports that the ability to groom and breed is not impeded in any way.

The procedure consists of a few simple steps, of which the most critical is the excision of a portion of the tendon while the wing is fully flexed. With young birds, operated on before flight has developed, the ability to extend the wing is lost and it remains permanently flexed.

There is no reason the procedure outlined above cannot be performed on the remaining swans in the park, thus preventing their escape without compromising their utility as an ornamental display for the public's enjoyment.

We looked at the drawings of a swan. I wanted to cry. They were doing terrible, terrible things to it.

They opened its wing all the way and then they cut a hole, right in the wing. And out of the hole, they pulled something—a bone, or a muscle—and they cut that too. With scissors. It hurt. It hurt so bad! And Ali said they're going to do it to all the swans. Because of the dictatorship.

Fascists are so awful. When I looked at the drawings, my arm hurt.
Like I had wings and like they were cutting into *me*.

"Don't cry, Ayşe."

"My wings hurt."

"Stop crying!"

"Ali, what are we going to do? Ali? . . . So you don't know either!"

"We're going to save the swans."

"But how?"

"We have to be smart. We have to take action."

"Maybe we should tell Mom?"

"No. We're strong enough to do it on our own. That's how to do it."

"The two of us, together?"

"Yes. Let's take an oath."

"Like at school?"

"No, not that one. The other one."

"I don't know any other ones."

"Just repeat after me. Okay?"

"Okay."

"Have you got the *Wonderland of Knowledge* with the swans?"

"Here it is."

"Put it between us. Okay, now put your hand on top. Like that.
And I'll put my hand there too. Now we'll say it. But I'm going to
change it. We're taking action so we need different words. We . . . as
Ali and Ayşe . . . swear to fight fascism to the last drop . . . until the
swans are saved."

"Don't forget the silkworms!"

"Okay. Until the swans are saved . . . and the butterflies get into
Parliament . . . Even if we get really tired, even if we get sleepy . . . we
will resist. . . . I swear it! Okay, we're done."

We kept our hands on the book for a little bit. The lamp was our only
light. And that's when I said it.

"Ali, is it okay if we look at the police station?"

We opened the window and looked outside. We saw lots of shadows in the police station. All the lights were on. People were yelling. Because of torture, Ali said. Then we looked out of the window, at faraway places.

—

Something happened to me. Like I was talking for the first time. Like there was something in my throat. And out it came:

"Ayşe, after the revolution everyone will have bread. And even Şokella. We'll have electricity in my house, too, and Mom will grow roses in the garden. We won't eat flour soup anymore. And the things that used to be at one end of my strings—the kite, the red car—they'll all come back. Because the fascists in Almond Stream will finally understand. They won't want to be fascists anymore. It'll be quiet everywhere. And everybody will have *The Wonderland of Knowledge*, too. And, and . . . And then Turgay Abi, and everybody's who dead, all the revolutionaries, all the big brothers and the big sisters, I mean, will come back. But as swans. They'll be flying. That's why we need to save the swans, Ayşe. They're swans, but they're dead revolutionaries. We can't let them do anything to the swans. They need to fly when the revolution happens. Do you see, Ayşe?"

"You can't save dead people."

"If we save the swans, we can."

"Ali?"

"What?"

"My arms hurt when I looked at that drawing. That's why we have to save the swans, Ali. Because our arms will hurt if they do that to all the swans. Right?"

—

The night we looked at the police station, we fell asleep, together. And that's how I knew, when Ali came today, that he didn't really forget. So I held his hand.

—

Ayşe talked so much. Her mom did something to Muzaffer Abi. What though, I didn't understand. And something happened to her grandma, like she's a little sick, but all the time. Her father got red eyes and acted like he lost at something. And she told me how she got the silkworms into Parliament. "Wow!" I said. It was the first time ever I said that.

—

I asked Ali if he had started "taking action." He said he had.

—

I told Ayşe that I'd got started too, but then her grandma came.

—

Grandma made us Şokella bread. She spread it all the way to the edges this time.

—

Ayşe was laughing and eating her Şokella bread. We were jiggling our feet under the table. That's how they touched. I think Ayşe is beautiful. I mean, because she's a revolutionary.

UNIT 10

How We Liberated Our Country from the Enemy

We Must Never Abandon Our Country

We're waiting for Auntie Günseli, the friend my mom loves best. The one she gets to see "only once a year." Auntie Günseli's a history teacher in that place where men kill bulls and women twirl in pouffy red skirts. She's an "academician." That means she's a teacher, but at a university. She and Mom used to be students and they always smiled. "Before prison" they smiled, I mean. Now Mom never looks happy. If I want to see her smiling, I get out the old photo album. The one with the empty pages in the back. Black and empty. The other pages are full of photos with four little black ears, so they don't fall out. They mustn't fall out. And I mustn't touch them. In the "Happiest Days of Our Lives" album, Mom closes her eyes a lot. She can't even keep her eyes open. That's how big she smiles. In the days before me and Dad.

I'm here alone with Mom. We sent Grandma to Jale Hanım's and we sent Dad out, but I don't know where. I didn't go with Grandma; Mom couldn't make me. "Oh, all right, you can stay here then," she said. "But no snooping." She got so excited she made breakfast and then she made lunch and then she got out the vodka glasses. Everything's on the kitchen table, ready for Auntie Günseli. Everything's "just right," clean and nice. Like Mom's playing house. She won't let me play, though, not with her and Auntie Günseli. I asked if I could help, and she said no. The mixed fried vegetables with yoghurt sauce are on the table, too, shiny and yummy. They're Auntie Günseli's favorite. Mom's happy today. Just like before me and Dad. I wish Auntie Günseli could come every day.

Mom did her hair in a ponytail. Then she smoked three cigarettes. She set the table with matching plates and glasses, with a cigarette in her hand the whole time. She put it out in the sink and threw it in the trash. Three times, the same thing. So the ashtray doesn't get dirty. She turned on the TV for me, a cowboy movie on *Cinema Sunday*. She was humming in the kitchen. Then the doorbell rang. Mom fixed her hair in the mirror. When she opened the door, they screamed:

"Ohhh! My, oh my. Look at you!"

They hugged and they laughed and they cried. "It's so good to see you!" they said. They got tears in their eyes. They coughed and laughed, wiping their eyes with the palms of their hands. I was standing there. Auntie Günseli has big eyes, and I think she always smiles. She looked at me, made her voice high, and said, "Ayşe!" She hugged me, and she smelled like the seashore. But in the morning time. With a breeze blowing. She hugged Mom again. Then they held each other by the arms and looked into each other's eyes for a long time. "Welcome," Mom said. Auntie Günseli said, "It's so good to see you again," She had a present for me and took it out of her handbag. A box, red. With a button. "Go on, push the button," she said. And when I did . . . Oh! Laughter. All kinds of laughter. *Hah hah, hee hee, ho ho*. It came from inside the box. Mom started laughing, too. They laughed, the two of them, so hard their bellies wobbled and their legs squeezed together like they had to pee.

Auntie Günseli's shoes are bright and orange. She didn't take them off. Mom had slippers ready for her, but she let Auntie Günseli wear her orange shoes in the house. While they were walking to the kitchen, I pushed the button, again and again. I wanted to count how many people were laughing inside the box. There were a whole lot. Just think if we could be in the box, too. Me and Ali. Laughing our heads off.

Mom and Auntie Günseli said funny things in loud voices. Then they got serious, and I couldn't hear them. So I hid just outside the door and listened, because they forgot about me. I want to play, too, but I know Mom won't let me into the kitchen.

"Önder? I don't believe it! Why on earth would he show up after all these years?"

"How do I know? He said something about my belonging to a time when things meant something, and he's in search of meaning, I suppose. But there's something else, too: Every week he gives me an envelope and I hide it in the archives."

"What? You hide envelopes in the archives? What's in them?"

"I don't look."

"Bravo, Sevgi!"

I know what's in the envelope, but I'm not telling. Mom won't let me play, so I'm not telling. I'll tell Ali, though.

"Günseli, you got here in the nick of time. I'm about to burst. I really need to talk."

"What's going on, Sevgi?"

"Aydın's turned into a . . . I don't know how to put it. An air bubble? I'm barely aware of him these days. He doesn't ask any questions, doesn't wonder about me, doesn't even make his presence known, not really. When Önder reappeared . . . I don't know if we have a future together, me and Aydın. Mother's not doing well, either. I know she's getting on in years, but she's become so forgetful lately. She seems a little disoriented. It's gotten so bad I'm afraid to leave Ayşe with her. And as for Ayşe . . ."

Mom's whispering so I don't hear, but I do. Every word.

"Ayşe's growing up in an unhappy home, and I don't need to tell you how bad things are getting in Turkey. Günseli, sometimes I just want to get away. And Önder . . ."

"And Önder, what?"

"It's stupid."

"What is?"

"He's leaving. Going abroad. He asked me to go with him."

They've stopped talking. A curl of smoke noses out of the kitchen and into the hallway. Somebody gets up. Heels *click click* on the kitchen floor. It must be Auntie Günseli. She's getting something out of the fridge. Ice cubes land in glasses, *tink tink*. Then the cupboard door opens and closes. Vodka? But it's still morning. Glasses *clink clink*. Mom goes, "Ahhh." Is Mom leaving us?

This time, Auntie Günseli doesn't laugh when she talks.

"I want you to know that I'm behind you all the way, no matter what you decide. But this 'getting away' business is more complicated than you think, Sevgi. Take it from me. And you're not even fleeing for your life."

"I'm not going anywhere. I've got Ayşe. And my mother."

"Listen to me. You wouldn't have brought it up unless you were considering it. But there's something you need to know. When you do 'get away' and try to settle in a strange country, at first you feel like . . . well, like a child. Like an orphan, in the beginning, and then like a child. You expect your country to call you back, you wait for its call like a devoted dog. Or like a child who's rebelled, but come to regret it. You wouldn't be able to cope, Sevgi. You have no—"

"Look, I get it. I see what you're saying."

"Do you know where I live, Sevgi? Where I really live?"

"What do you mean?"

"I reside in Spain, but that's not really where I live. I live in the air-waves. In the waves of sound bringing news from Turkey. I spend the whole day listening to the radio. It's the only thing I truly listen to, the only thing I truly hear. It's awful, Sevgi!"

They went quiet for a while. Then Mom said, "Look, I've made your favorite, fried vegetables with garlicky tomato sauce." Auntie Günseli snuffled and sniffed and laughed.

"You're the best friend ever!"

They got serious again.

"Sevgi, sometimes you act as though everything just happens to you. Don't forget that you chose Aydın precisely because he was insubstantial. He's always been a bit of an air bubble. You chose him because he doesn't ask any questions, because he isn't curious. And now, you say that's the reason you're—"

"Günseli, I'm not doing anything. I'm not going anywhere. I was trying to explain how I felt, that's all."

"All I'm saying is that the act of remembering is a tricky business. We all play games and rewrite the past. You can play those little tricks on yourself, but don't mess with history. It's dangerous!"

They fell quiet again. Mom sounded bright and loud when she talked again.

"Look here, Günseli. Are you going to have some of those fried vegetables, or not?"

"I can't wait to have some. I miss those spicy green peppers most of all. You're such a dear, Sevgi. There was something else I was going to tell you . . ."

After that, they talked about funny things. The things that make them laugh. They didn't call me for lunch. I went to the living room and pushed the laugh button over and over. Mom didn't even look at me again until her "best friend" left. Auntie Günseli wanted to kiss me good-bye, of course, but I ran away to the kitchen. Then I went back and sat in front of the TV.

When Auntie Günseli was gone, Mom came over to me. She sat next to me, on the floor. Mom never sits on the floor. "What are you up to?" she said. I didn't answer. I'm mad at her. She hugged me real tight.

"I love you so much."

I love Mom, too, but I'm mad at her. Mom might leave me. I need to tell on her, to Dad.

The phone rang.

"Önder? . . .Okay, this week . . . actually, no, let's make that next week. . . . All right. I need to talk to you, too. . . . All right."

Mom looked at me. She wanted to know if I heard what she said. I looked at the TV. It's Sunday, so there's TV all day long. I'll know which day Mom is meeting Önder. She'll wear the nice shoes, the ones that hurt. I'll know.

When the Nation Mobilizes, Soldiers Report for Duty

The water flooded Almond Stream. Not yesterday, the day before yesterday. "They killed Kemal Türkler, that's why," Mom said. He was the leader of the Confederation of Progressive Trade Unions. They shot him, right in front of his house. It was the fascists, of course. Mom said it can flood even in the middle of summer if someone good dies. The houses of the fascists in Almond Stream were all underwater. Our house was dry, but the streets got muddy. All the kids in the neighborhood got the runs and had burning fevers. I looked at Kemal Türkler in the newspaper. He was a worker. Birgül Abla told the other women about him.

"He called on the workers to rise up, so he was murdered by the dark forces who want to establish a fascist dictatorship."

Birgül Abla doesn't smile now. Not after yesterday.

I got up early in the morning. I looked out the window. Nuran Abla and Auntie Seher had already got water from the fountain. The clean sheets were hanging on the line. They do the wash early because later, after everyone gets up, only a string of water comes out of the tap. The sheets in the garden were flapping in the wind. Some were flowery, others white. There were a lot of them. They looked so nice, I watched them for a while. *Flap, flap, flap.* I could hear them, too. It was then that I saw Hüseyin Abi. Wearing his jacket, slowly walking through the mud. Now and then, one of his feet getting stuck in the mud. He'd take a step back with his unstuck foot, and push his foot and toes way down into the stuck shoe, so he could lift it out of the mud. Then he'd take another step forward. Then his foot would get stuck again, so he'd take a step back and a step forward, again and again. . . . Hüseyin Abi didn't want to keep walking, that's how it looked.

He stood in the mud in the middle of the flapping sheets. I'd see him for a moment, then he'd disappear. And it happened again, that feeling. Like I was grown-up and I was remembering, but it was happening now. The feeling passed. Hüseyin Abi was still standing there. He pulled out a cigarette. He stood in the middle of the sheets, turned around, all the way, slowly, looking at the neighborhood. He lit a match and held it to his cigarette. Nobody else was around. I was the only one looking at him. He looked at our house, but he didn't see me. And I felt like I was having a dream, the kind where you shout but no sound comes out. I wanted to yell, "Hüseyin Abi, I've got your Ibelo lighter," but no sound came out. Hüseyin Abi smoked half a cigarette. He threw it in the mud. Since he's wearing a jacket, and smoking like that, and looking at the neighborhood, Hüseyin Abi must be leaving. He stopped, just as he was about to go. He scraped the bottom of his muddy shoe on a rock. The mud came off. He's cleaning the mud off his shoes. *We never clean mud off our shoes!* Hüseyin Abi's doing it, though. Because he's not one of us. We take off our shoes at the front door. They're muddy, all of them. Hüseyin Abi wants to get away from us. And the mud. The sheets flapped again, and Hüseyin Abi was gone. My head hurt just then, real bad.

I'd fallen asleep. It was noon and everyone was up. But I'd had a fever and stayed in bed. Mom was next to my bed. "My little lamb," she said. Then she yelled, "Hasan, he's come back to life. He opened his eyes. Thank God!"

Did I die?

"Mom, I had a dream about Hüseyin Abi and sheets."

Mom started crying. She hugged me.

"Darling. My little lamb."

I woke up again, later. I thought the whole thing was a dream. I felt fine, got out of bed. The sun was setting. The other kids were out in the field. I walked over to them, but slowly. I couldn't walk fast. I was too tired from that dream. When I went back to the house, I walked over to the garden and saw the footprints. Hüseyin Abi's footprints. He was gone. He was really gone.

I sat down. Just stayed there. The sunlight hit my face, the red light of the sinking sun. I touched a footprint. Then I leaned over and kissed it. Because Mom always says, "I could kiss the ground you walk on." Because I had to kiss something. Then I lay down on the ground, in the mud. It was cool on my back. And I wanted to stay there. I felt like I couldn't do anything. Like I was dead. What would life be like without Hüseyin Abi? It still felt like a dream. But I knew it wasn't, none of it.

It was getting dark. I got up and I looked at his footprint. I put my foot inside it. Mine was still so small. I could get both my feet into Hüseyin Abi's footprint. I stood there until the stars came out. Nobody saw me. Maybe there was no more "me" anymore, and that's why. Not a sound came out of me, not even from the inside. Not even my breath. Then Mom came, picked me up and carried me home. We didn't talk. I slept a lot. In my dreams, I kept seeing the kite Hüseyin Abi made me. It's in Almond Stream, way up the hill. Hüseyin Abi says, "Wait, I'll go and get it," but he's stuck in the mud. His feet are walking backwards. The only thing I hear is the kite: *flap, flap, flap.*

We Must All Defend the Motherland

"We can't, Aydın. I don't trust Mother with Ayşe. You take her today and I'll do it tomorrow. We'll have to manage for the time being. Perhaps Mother will come right once she's rested."

Mom and Dad were whispering in the kitchen. They were standing in front of a big pot of strawberry jam. And in the jam, there was a lot of pepper, because of Grandma.

"She hasn't been herself for a while now. Haven't you noticed? I mean, little things like getting up late, absentmindedness, just generally letting herself go. . . . And now this."

Grandma made the strawberry jam the night before. And then, when we tasted it in the morning . . .

"Mother? What did you put in the jam?"

"Strawberries."

"I know that. But I can taste . . . Did you put black pepper in it?"

"Strawberry jam doesn't have any pepper, Sevgi. Why would I do that?"

"Mother, I was thinking you might . . . It might be a good idea for . . . Oh, never mind. We're taking Ayşe in to work. Get some rest today, all right?"

"We make it with cinnamon, don't we? Why would I add black pepper?"

"That's right, Mother. Be sure and get some rest today, okay?"

That's why I left home with Dad today. Mom's not wearing the nice shoes that hurt, so I don't need to go with her.

All morning, until noon, nothing happened in the office. That's because there's a "nationalist" in Dad's room. The government sent him. Dad said the government's a "coalition" and it has three parties. They're "right-wing" and "religious" and "nationalist." And they don't really like each other, but they made a coalition so Ecevit doesn't get to be prime minister, even though he got the most votes. The government man in Dad's office has a bald head. He walks on the backs of his shoes. He wears yellowish socks. He's skinny, but his jacket is big. He seems mad all the time. There isn't any paper on his desk. Mostly he stands in front of the window, looking out. He keeps his hands behind him, right above his bum, and plays with his prayer beads. He's good at it. The black beads slide so fast on the string, one at a time, between his thumb and finger, *click click click*. He doesn't even have to look at the beads. When he goes back to his desk, he puts down his prayer beads and picks up his pens. He likes his pens to be lined up on the desk, just so. He tilts his head to one side until they're perfectly straight. His key chain is a skeleton man and he keeps his keys in the lock of his top desk drawer. It looks scary when the skeleton swings back and forth. When he leans back in his chair, it goes *creak creak*, and he leans back a lot. He doesn't go anywhere or do anything, just sits at his desk and stands at the window and looks at his watch. The yellow watch that's too big and slides up and down when he moves his arm.

Nobody talked to the government man, so he came up to me. I was drawing a picture. He stuck his arms behind his back again and clickety-clicked his beads. "Is that a lamb?" he asked. "It's a cloud," I said. "Is that a lamb down there?" he asked. "There aren't any sheep in my picture," I told him. Then he left. He didn't come back. The uncles in the office all laughed. "Way to go, Ayşe. I guess you showed him," they said. I don't understand. What did I do?

At lunch time we left the office. Dad and I are going to meet with Detective Nahit, down the hill in Ayrancı. On the way, I'm going to tell Dad what Mom said. I'm going to tell him she might leave us. Dad and I walk along for a while.

"Dad?"

"Yes, dear? It's so hot! Isn't it, Ayşe?"

"Mom said something."

"Oh? What?"

"But don't get mad."

"Ayşe, when do I get mad at you?"

"Not at me, at Mom."

"Why would I get mad at her? What's going on, Ayşe?"

"Mom said something."

"Just tell me what she said!"

Dad stopped. I got scared. He's sweating. His face is red. His eyes are scrunchy, and they have lots of wrinkles, in the corners. He's scared, and it's making me really scared.

"Tell me!" He's yelling at me. Doesn't he already know? Dad grabs my arms and shakes me.

"Ayşe, tell me this minute. What did your mother say?"

I was going to cry. Then a whole bunch of big brothers came out of nowhere. Lots of them. They shouted, all of them, in the middle of the street.

"Down with fascism! Turkey will be a graveyard for fascism!"

Their eyes got big and the veins popped out on their necks when they yelled. They're sweaty, their faces shiny in the sun. Some ladies ran away. Some others, men and women, young and old, went into the street and yelled too. They put their fists in the air and yelled. There were people everywhere. I could smell them. Two of the big brothers had rifles. They were looking around. Men like my father went up to the big brothers with the rifles. We didn't go, though. I wanted to, but Dad pulled my arm, pulled me into a pickle shop. A sour place with lots of jars and a roly-poly man. "Come on in, quick," the man said. "The anarchists are at it again." Dad took a step toward the door but the pickle man was quicker. Down rolled the shutters, so loud, so metal, I couldn't hear anything else, not Dad and not the people shouting out in the street. We were trapped with the pickles, behind the metal shutters, and the air felt heavy and sour. Dad kept wiping the sweat off his forehead. He got out a cigarette. "Mind if I have one?" the pickle man said.

Dad handed him a cigarette. We could hear the shouting outside. The pickle man laughed.

"They say they want a revolution, but all they do is smash things. Nobody asks what us normal citizens want. Well, these anarchists' days are numbered. Things will be back to normal soon. What do you think?"

"Normal? I don't think so."

"What do you mean? It's all because of a handful of troublemakers. The soldiers will beat some sense into them. Then those kids will go back to school where they belong."

"Could you open the shutters? We're in a hurry to get somewhere."

"You can't go yet. They've got guns. What about your little girl?"

"Of all the things!"

They started clapping outside, for a long time.

"Do you want some pickle juice?"

"No, thank you. Not in this heat."

"And what about you? Do you want some pickle juice, little girl?"

I don't like him. He called me "little girl." Why did Dad bring me here? Why didn't we join the big brothers? They have mustaches just like Dad's. The pickle man's mustache is little and sad. And now we're stuck in pickle man prison.

"You look like an intelligent guy. So tell me, how long do you think it'll take the army to get rid of all these anarchists? I say a week, tops."

"It won't be that easy."

"I've got the best pickle juice in Ankara. Come on, have some."

"No, thanks."

Dad's sweating even more now. It's hot in pickle man prison, and dark. Dad forgot he was holding a cigarette. He got out another one, then put it back.

"Hasan Efendi!"

That's what Dad said when the pickle man pulled up a shutter to look outside. There was a man with a nice mustache right outside the window, and he looked at my dad for a long time. He didn't say anything, though. Dad opened his mouth, but he didn't say anything either. Only when the man walked away did Dad say, "Oh no!" Dad threw this cigarette on the floor.

"Hasan Efendi won't understand."

"Who was that man, Dad?"

"He's Ali's father. I don't believe it!"

"What won't he understand?"

Dad didn't answer, so I yelled.

"Let's go outside, Dad!"

I kicked the ground.

"Let's go outside. Dad! Dad!"

Nobody was shouting anymore. The big brothers and sisters were gone. The pickle man pulled up all the shutters and we left. I looked at Dad like Mom looks at him. He looked at me like he looks at Mom. He tried to smile.

"Why don't I get you a toy, Ayşe. Would you like that?"

I didn't say anything. We went to pickle prison because of Dad. He was scared. I could tell. It was all because of him!

"Ayşe, what did Mommy say? Remember, you were going to tell me."

Dad scooched down and pulled me close. He's being extra nice now.

"Ayşe, what did your mother say?"

I had to say something. I was scared not to.

"Mom says . . . those nice shoes, they hurt her, but she wears them anyway. She doesn't want to wear them, but she still does."

Dad's mixed up now. "And?" he says. I go "I don't know" with my shoulders. He stands up straight, and we start walking again. That's all. He doesn't ask me again. I might have told him. I was mad at him, but I might have told him. But he never even asked me!

I still want my toy. Dad promised me a toy, and I won't let him forget. I told him to get me string for jump rope. He found the kind you hang clothes on. Dad picks it out, blue, and I wrap it around my arm. "It hurts," I say. I ask for a different one, something softer. He gets me a soft one. It's nice and thick, too.

Never Flee the Enemy!

"Nuran! Give these to Hamit and Gökhan. They're for the houses down the way. And tell Hamit he'd better not eat any on the way. I swear I'll skin him alive if he does!"

Auntie Seher has been making halvah since morning. She built a fire in the garden under a huge tin pot. All day, she's been stirring the halvah and putting it in bowls for the neighbors. She's made so much halvah that Mom said, "Next thing you know, she'll start sending it over to Almond Stream, too." Auntie Seher's making halvah because her son escaped. He was in prison, but he escaped. Through a tunnel! A tunnel under the ground to another Turkey, where nobody can find him. Auntie Seher took her radio outside. Every time the news comes on, she shushes everyone and turns up the volume full blast.

"Shhh! Quiet. They'll say it again. Listen, everybody."

She grins and opens her eyes wide. She holds up a finger, like she wants to ask the teacher a question in class. Then the lady on the radio says it.

"*Fifteen terrorists escaped from maximum security prisons in Niğde and Konya early this morning. The terrorists, who are members of an illegal left-wing organization, reportedly fled through a tunnel they had dug. The names of the escaped prisoners are: Halil Taşbaş, Fahrettin Elveren, Cem Tokmakçı . . .*"

Auntie Seher waved her giant wooden spoon in the air and did a little dance.

"They said it! They said it again! That's my boy, my Cem!"

Auntie Seher's face is red and dripping, from the fire. It's the same reddish-brown color as the halvah. The other women are laughing and clapping as she wiggles her hips and shakes her shoulders. One of them says, "I wish my boy would escape." Another one says, "Well they got out of Metris. There's not a prison our boys can't escape from. They dig a tunnel, and out they go! Nobody ever finds them again." "Seher Abla," the first woman says, "is Cem going to leave Turkey? Can he come and see us first?" Auntie Seher doesn't listen to anyone. She keeps saying the same thing.

"Sisters, we're having a feast tonight! I took a vow back in the day. I only have one gold bracelet, but I promised to sell it if my boy escaped. It was a promise, so now I'm selling it. I said I'd have a sheep sacrificed and pass out the meat to everyone in the neighborhood. When this halvah's gone, I'm going to make a whole cauldron of ground wheat stew with chicken, too. Thanks be to God!"

Mom's smiling at Auntie Seher. The whole neighborhood's happy today. Just like when other sons and husbands escaped from Metris. And we had fun that day, too. Back before Hüseyin Abi left. He danced the *harmandalı* with a cigarette stuck in his mouth. He was the best. Who'll do that dance now? Vedat Abi can't. He's too short.

Birgül Abla is helping Auntie Seher. Mom said that ever since Hüseyin Abi left, Birgül Abla "has a broken wing." Like that swan, and she never makes a sound either. I stand next to her, so she won't be sad. I don't say anything. She doesn't say anything. We just stand there, side by side. I gave her some string yesterday. "What's this?" she said, with a small smile. "String," I said, and she smiled again, but small. That was all. She didn't understand, not like Ayşe did. Later, when I was getting water, I found a yellow flower up there on the hill. I gave that to Birgül Abla, too. Because of her broken wing. She put it in the buttonhole of her shirt, just like Ayşe.

I go up to Birgül again. She strokes my hair.

"Have you had some halvah, Ali? Shall I get you a bowl, too?" I didn't say anything, but she got us each a bowl of halvah. We stood side by side, eating.

"Birgül Abla, does it hurt when a wing breaks?"

"What wing?"

"Your wing. Mom said it's broken."

Birgül Abla put her fork in her bowl and put her hand on my cheek.

"It hurts a little, Ali. Are you telling me your wing hurts, too?"

I pushed my fork into my arm and looked at Birgül Abla. She looked right back at me. Then I pushed harder, and a bit harder. Birgül Abla kept looking at me. I pushed harder, a bit harder.

"It hurts this much."

She hugged me.

"Don't worry, Ali. He'll come back."

I didn't say anything.

I stayed next to Birgül Abla until nighttime. When it got dark, they lit a big fire. It was time for fun. There's a song they sing, but they sing it one way when they're happy and a different way when they're sad. *"Drama bridge is narrow, O Hasan; it can't be crossed,"* they start singing, all together, happy as can be. When they get to the last line, they shout it out, loud as they can: *"Shoot your Martini rifle, Hasan from Debre; let it echo through the mountains. Let the friends in Drama prison listen to it."*

Auntie Seher cried. Then she danced when they sang, *"The roads to Evreşe are narrow."* I stayed with Birgül Abla the whole time, so she pulled my head against her leg, like Hüseyin Abi. But not so hard, because of her wing. Everyone else was dancing, so we sat down in front of the house. Mom came, too. I can see the flames on their faces, glowing orange, then back to black, orange, then black.

Mom got a stick, and she's scratching in the dirt. She's going to tell Birgül Abla something.

"Birgül."

"Yes?"

"I'm going to say something. It's a little important."

"Go on, Abla."

"I'm going to say it right here in front of Ali. But don't tell anyone. Not even Hasan. You hear that, Ali? Let's not tell your dad. It's just that he doesn't need to know, Birgül, not that I'm keeping secrets. Ali? Okay?"

"Is something wrong, Aliye Abla?"

Mom looked at them dancing. She scratched in the dirt again.

"Has everyone gone crazy? A little funny in the head? One minute they're whooping it up, the next minute they're mourning. Sweet and sour, hot and cold. They dance through it all. Look at them now, letting loose, letting go. You can't tell if they're laughing or crying. Look at them!"

Mom points to the women with her stick, then to the men. They're all dancing. And their faces are breaking up, going to pieces. Their eyes aren't looking at anything. I can see something in their faces, and it's a terrible thing. I look down at the ground. Mom keeps talking.

"Birgül, have you ever heard that story about the sultan and the villagers? You know, the one where the sultan comes down hard on the villagers, breaking their backs with heavy taxes, hanging everyone who can't pay up. The villagers weep and weep. Then, a year later, the sultan's soldiers come back for more taxes. But the whole village is dancing in the square. When they report it to the sultan, he says, 'Leave them alone. They're too far gone.' Sometimes I feel like that's what's happened to us. We're too far gone."

"Don't say that. It'll all be over in a few months."

"No, Birgül. No, it won't. Are you telling me it makes sense to you? This new fellow, Vedat or whatever his name is, says to build barricades, to dig trenches. Okay, he's one of us. I know that. But does it make any sense?"

Mom scratched in the dirt a little more. Then she looked at Birgül.

"What are we supposed to do? Dig our way under Ankara? Hide out with our children? It'll never work, Birgül."

"Vedat threw that out. It was just an idea. What we're doing—"

"I've had enough! There's something else I wanted to say. Listen to me, Birgül."

Mom pointed at me with her stick.

"You see Ali, here. He doesn't talk much, but he's one clever kid. My boy's going to go to university, Birgül."

Mom wiped her face with her hands, real hard. Like she wanted it to hurt.

"Oh, Birgül, oh my! Now listen. Birgül, if anything happens, you know, to Hasan or me, there's something I want you to do. It's about Ali. I'd have asked Hüseyin, but you two are one flesh now, so I'm asking you. If anything happens to us, Birgül, will you—"

"Don't say that, Abla. Nothing will happen! And if something did happen to you, don't you think it would happen to us, too? Let's not talk about this in front of the boy."

"You think he doesn't know, Birgül? My little lamb knows everything. I'm not scaring you, am I, Ali? Don't be scared."

"Just tell me what you want me to do."

"You know that house I clean, in Liberation. They're good people. If anything happens here in our neighborhood, take Ali to them. He knows how to get there. Will you do that?"

"Yes, but—"

"No, not like that. Swear to it. Promise me."

"All right. You can entrust Ali to me. I swear it."

Mom scratched the ground a little more. Then she smiled.

"I didn't think much of Seher's wheat and chicken stew. It should melt in your mouth. Right, Ali?"

Mom's trying to make us laugh. Some women came up and asked Mom to go and dance with them. She did, just a bit. Then she laughed a little, got embarrassed, and ran home.

"Ali, what should we do now?" Birgül Abla asked. I told her I needed a sack. I knew she'd ask me why, so I was ready.

"Me and the other kids are having a sack race tomorrow."

"I'll find you one. Whatever Ernő wants, Ernő gets."

Birgül knows Ernő Nemecsek from the Paul Street Boys! I liked her even better after that.

"And I'll get you a wafer sandwich, Birgül Abla."

She laughed a lot, the first real laugh since Hüseyin Abi left.

Me and Birgül Abla sat there together watching the dance. Everybody got happy, a little. Nobody knew what we'll do when the fascists come. I banged my heel against the ground Mom was scratching earlier. The dirt is hard as rock. We'll never get to underground Turkey. We can get there only with lots of Revolutionary Youth. Only if Hüseyin Abi and the others come back. If we get things started, that's when they'll come back. But first we need to do revolutionary things. Like saving the swans. But nobody else understands. They just keep dancing. They keep lifting their arms like their wings were never broken. Only Birgül Abla knows about broken wings.

I kissed Birgül Abla, right on her wing. She laughed again. She doesn't understand, either.

Beware the Enemy Within

Grandma's whole face is crying. When she sits on the edge of the hot marble stone, her boobs fall to her knees. We have cloths wrapped around our waists; Grandma, me, Jale Hanım, and Feride Abla. Sometimes a drop of water lands on Grandma's head, but she doesn't know. The ceiling is so high and round, and it drips water on Grandma.

There's a lady, real skinny, with black hair and brown skin. She has a special cloth for scrubbing. She gets the women all foamy, gets them to scream: "Ohhh! Ohhh!" When they're washed and scrubbed clean, she wraps them in cloth and has them sit on the edge of a white bench made of stone, so they're all lined up in a row, like dolls. When the dark lady walks, her wooden clogs go *takka da takka da*. She has a cloth wrapped around her head, and it's tied in a butterfly on the tippy top. Her skin hangs off her legs, that's how skinny she is. Her face is hiding behind her wrinkles. That's because she works in a hamam and "sweats buckets."

When you go "ooh" and "ahhh" in the hamam, the wet walls and the high dome and the slippy slidey floor all talk to each other. Maybe that's why Grandma is so quiet. She doesn't want noise. Her eyes are dry, but water comes running out of all the tiny lines on her face. Everyone's talking and laughing, but Grandma sits there, her head to one side, like a quiet bird. I'm playing with the water. I scoop it out of a basin with a copper bowl and pour it over my toes, a little at a time. Now my feet are as white as the stone Grandma's sitting on. And wrinkly, too. I think my big toenail looks like a TV.

Jale Hanım brought stuffed vine leaves and baskets of fruit and other "goodies." They're eating and laughing. The dark lady turns Jale Hanım over and over, scrubbing her head to toe with a cloth.

"They kidnapped Bobby last week. I wonder who did it?"

"Jale Hanım, our whole country has turned into *Dallas*. Never mind what's happening in Texas!"

"You're right. Our country's become a regular Çıfıt market."

"Do you know what 'Çıfıt' means, Jale Hanım?"

"How am I supposed to know? It's just an expression."

"'Çıfıt' means 'Jewish.'"

"You're kidding!"

"No, really. It's an old word for Jewish. And did you know that this place, Şengül Hamam, used to be in a Jewish neighborhood?"

"There were Jews in Ankara? I thought that sort of thing only happens in Istanbul: Armenians and Greeks and what have you."

"There are still Jews here, too. But the Christians are gone. I wonder where they went? Maybe their ghosts still wander around."

"You're creeping me out! Don't talk like that. We've got enough dead on our hands as it is. Don't go and conjure up ghosts."

"They say the spirits of the dead pile up, layer after layer, right below us, like a big ball of wool."

"We're in a hamam, for goodness sake. This isn't the place for ghost stories. You're supposed to talk about juicy things. Have you heard about Princess Caroline? Her husband cheated on her. And with a low-class Italian, no less. That tramp's not even pretty. The only thing she's got going for her is her big breasts. Poor Caroline is such a beauty and so refined."

"Speaking of breasts. You know that sports thing, with the gymnastics and all. There's that girl from a Communist country. I've got her name on the tip of my tongue . . ."

"Nadia Comăneci!"

"That's it! Anyway, I don't know if you watched her on TV the other night, but she's filled out like you wouldn't believe. I don't know how she manages to balance on that beam, what with her breasts going one way and her body the other. We laughed our heads off watching it."

Ferida Abla joined in, squeezing the water out of her hair.

"She was just a kid in the last Olympics, but she's a grown woman now."

"Feride, what was the name of that other beautiful princess? You know, the one who became the wife of the shah of Iran."

"Farah Diba?"

"No, not her. The other one. The shah's first wife. The one who couldn't give him any children, so he divorced her . . . She had a Turkish name."

"Oh, hang on a sec. You mean Süreyya, but they call her Soraya."

"Right! Well, they had a photo-roman in *Hürriyet* about her life. It ran for ever so many days. How she met and married the shah of Iran. And that gorgeous wedding gown she wore. Feride, I was going to tell you about that. You wouldn't believe how elegant it was. Do you think we could have one just like it made for your wedding?"

Jale Hanım's skin turned bright red and then the dark lady started foaming her up. She's lying in the middle of the white stone, like a big balloon. It looks funny. Grandma doesn't laugh. Fifteen drops of water have fallen on Grandma's head, but she hasn't wiped her face. She doesn't even know.

Feride Abla sat next to Grandma. "Nejla Hanım, is anything wrong? You've gone all funny today."

Grandma just sat there with her hands in her lap, huffing and puffing. She looked at her hands.

"My dear girl, I've been feeling rather . . . faded these days. Insubstantial as the flickering flame in one of those old lanterns. I've never enjoyed a particularly vigorous constitution, but this, this sense of being so insubstantial, and yet so heavy. There are mornings I wake up with an ox on my chest. I don't know what's happening to me. Yes, I'm getting on in years. Perhaps, I say to myself, this is what is meant by 'having one's foot in the grave.' And yet, my body is strong enough. It's my mind that flickers. It appears that God will call me only when He is ready and perhaps not while I'm in full command of my senses. There is nothing to be done. It's kismet. But there is the fear—"

When Feride Abla laughed, the ceiling and the walls and the floor laughed, too.

"I don't believe it, Nejla Hanım! You're depressed. It's your nerves, I mean. That's so interesting. I didn't know old people got like that."

Grandma lifted her hand. Almost like she was going to hit Feride Abla. Jale Hanım came over and grabbed Feride Abla by the arm.

"Get up. Go get another scrub or something. I'm sorry, Nejla Hanım. Young people are so clueless these days. They blurt out whatever comes to mind. She's about to get married and set up her own home, but she's as ill-mannered as a child. Sometimes I blame myself for not raising her right. Perhaps her mother-in-law in Istanbul will have better luck with her. You can talk to me, Nejla Hanım. Tell me what's on your mind. Go on, I'm listening."

Jale Hanım is treating Grandma like a child. And Grandma is acting like a child. She's holding Jale Hanım's hand.

"I'm gripped by fear, Jale Hanım. I don't dare touch anything. My ears ring, and I worry someone is saying something bad about me. I get a twitch in my eyelid and wait for the news to arrive, but will it be good news or bad news? They say that if you drop your teaspoon on the ground a guest will come. But who will it be? I find an eyelash on my cheek, and try to make a wish, but I can't think of anything. If I forget, and get out of bed on the left side, my heart starts pounding. I find a slipper backwards on the floor, and we all know what that means. Sevgi leaves her blouse inside out, a sure sign she'll never come home. . . . I don't know what's come over me. These superstitions have paralyzed me with fear. I see the devil's work in everything."

Jale Hanım is holding both of Grandma's hands now, and rubbing her wrists. "Nothing bad's going to happen! For God's sake, Nejla Hanım. Stop bottling everything up, that's the problem. And that home of yours, if you'll forgive me for saying so, is always so gloomy. That's why you're feeling out of sorts. I'll tell you what, after the Sugar Bairam is over, but before the wedding, I was going to have some lead poured for Feride. Why don't you and that saucy little granddaughter of yours join us? We'll chase away the jinn together."

Grandma likes what she's hearing. I can tell. And she likes having her wrists rubbed. Mom never does that. Because Mom takes her to the doctor. Grandma closed her eyes. She looks like a crybaby.

"Let's do that, Jale Hanım. I can't go on feeling as though war is about to break out, we'll all starve, we'll all die . . . feeling as though a black string is coiled in my throat."

"Why don't you go to that pharmacist, Cavit Bey, and get something to soothe your nerves?"

"Never!"

Grandma yanked back her hands.

"Not on your life!"

Grandma pushed back her hair and lifted her chin.

"He's clueless. What would he give me? He'd have no idea."

"Well, your troubles haven't mysteriously fallen from the skies in a *zembil*. Once we figure out the root of the problem, we can solve it."

"Jale Hanım, do you even know what a zembil is?"

"I have no idea. It's just a turn of phrase, isn't it?"

"We used to have baskets called zembil, during the war. They'd hide bread and mulberry molasses and other food in it, and hang it from the ceiling so children couldn't reach it. When it was time to eat, you'd lower the basket on a string. That's where that expression comes from."

"Oh, who cares about all that! Olden times and wars and stuff. Listen, you won't believe what I read in the paper yesterday. As always, Bülent Ersoy is having costume after costume made for the İzmir Fair. You know, he always headlines there. But this time . . . he's having women's dresses made!"

"Forgive me for asking this, Jale Hanım, but has this man-woman . . ."

Grandma leaned close and continued in a whisper.

"Has he had it cut off?"

Jale Hanım howled and howled.

"No, Nejla Hanım. Not yet. He's still fully equipped."

All the women in the hamam started laughing. Copper bowls fell to the floor, waist cloths came undone, boobs and bellies jiggled. The hamam turned into a giant laugh box.

When Grandma looked up at the ceiling, a drop of water fell. Not on her head, in her eye. I laughed. Grandma didn't, though. I felt ashamed.

Who Saved Our Country from the Enemy?

"If anything happens to my mom and dad, I'm coming to your house."

That's what Ali said. We were stretched out on the living room floor together looking at the Memorial Tomb in *The Wonderland of Knowledge*. We were lying on our bellies and waving our feet in the air. Grandma was sitting by the window in her nightdress, smoking. She stayed there all morning. *Puff puff.* Ali's mom was cleaning the bedrooms. I thought it was a good time to tell Ali.

"My mom's leaving, maybe. Without me. But I didn't tell Dad."

"Did your mom tell you not to?"

"No. Me and Dad left his office and then some big brothers started yelling and they did a little anarchy, so Dad stuck me in a pickle shop. But it felt like a pickle prison."

"That's called an 'illegal demonstration.' They were breaking the law."

"They didn't break anything. But they yelled a lot."

"Did the police come? What happened?"

"No. First they yelled and then they left. Then me and Dad walked away. We were in the pickle shop. I think Dad was scared. So I didn't tell him about Mom. I didn't want to make him more scared. I was mad at him, though. Oh, and I forgot to tell you, we saw your dad."

"What was my dad doing?"

"He was breaking the law. But we didn't."

"Of course you didn't!"

"Why do you say that?"

——

Ayşe's grandma is taking us to the Memorial Tomb tomorrow, in "the morning coolness." That's why I'm spending the night. It's what Ayşe wants. And it's her grandmother who wants to take us out. But my mom wants me to stay here, too. Maybe nobody will come and get me ever again. I asked Mom, and she said, "Of course you're coming home." Then she hugged me.

The photo in *The Wonderland of Knowledge* is a little scary. Me and Ayşe are reading about it together.

The Mausoleum of the Memorial Tomb complex, the final resting place of the Great Leader Atatürk, is reached via an 860-foot-long walkway called the Road of Lions. It is flanked by 24 lions representing the 24 Oghuz Turkic tribes. The lions are in pairs to symbolize "togetherness and unity," and are seated to symbolize "peaceableness." The gap of just under two inches separating the paving stones on the Road of Lions ensures that visitors maintain an appropriately deliberate pace and keep their heads solemnly bowed as they approach the Mausoleum of the Father of the Turks.

I'm trying to read all about the Memorial Tomb before we go there tomorrow. Ayşe might ask me lots of questions. She's twirling her feet and she keeps poking her nose into the encyclopedia so I can't see. Then she whispers to me.

"Ali."

"What?"

"I got some string. Did you do what we agreed? There's only one more thing for me to do."

"I couldn't. Some things happened in the neighborhood. A kind of transfer."

"Well, what are we going to do now?"

"I need to do a little organizing. Birgül Abla, and maybe some others. But she's got a broken wing, too. I need a little more time."

—

I looked in Ali's eyes, but really close, to see if he was scared.

"Ali, you aren't scared, are you?"

"Nope."

"Ali, if your mom leaves you here, we can open up the laugh box and see what's inside. Don't be scared."

"I don't like it."

"Why not?"

"Why is it laughing all the time? All it does is laugh."

"Because funny things always happen in Spain. And in other countries, too. Ali? Can you look up 'silkworm' again? Maybe they turned into butterflies."

"Not yet. I know how long it takes. Not for another two or three days."

"But what if you're wrong and they don't have any food and they die?"

"I know how to count."

"Okay."

"Look, this is 'O! Turkish Youth!'"

"That's too hard. That's for fourth grade, isn't it, Ali?"

"But what if they ask us to say it at the Memorial Tomb?"

"They won't do that, smarty. I went there before. They don't make you take a test."

———

Ayşe's grandma made some lemonade and börek. We sat in the kitchen and ate, but Mom stood in the doorway and gobbled hers down. Ayşe's grandmother told Mom to have a seat at the table, but she wouldn't. She looked at me and smiled. She looked at me like I lived in this house. Like it's okay for me to sit, but not her. She took big swallows of her lemonade, too. I was embarrassed, so I didn't drink mine. A little after she left, I got up and followed her. She was in the bathroom, scrubbing the toilet. I stood in the doorway, so she'd see me. So she'd know I wasn't sitting at the table. She smiled at me and whispered.

"Go on, little lamb. Go and play in the living room."

I kept standing there. She stopped smiling. That's when I understood. In Ayşe's house, my mom isn't supposed to talk or sit or eat slow or drink lemonade slow. I ran back to the kitchen. Ayşe and her grandma were still sitting at the table. I stood in the doorway and waited for Ayşe to finish her lemonade. When she didn't, I said, "Come on! Let's go out on the balcony!"

—

Ali doesn't like lemonade, but he loves tea. We're looking out at the police station. They brought in a whole bunch of big brothers and sisters today. But we can't hear anything. They yell more at night. Ali counted as they went into the police station.

"That's seventeen. Twelve guys and—"

"Wait, I'll tell you how many girls. Seventeen take away twelve is . . ."

"Is?"

"Wait, I'll tell you. I'm doing it in my head."

"Okay."

"Four?"

"No."

"I can do it on paper. We don't learn to take away the big numbers until second grade, I think. Right, Ali?"

That night we went to Samim Abi's house. Ali wanted to go out on the terrace this time. He sat next to Samim Abi and kept looking at him. "I need to understand something," he'd told me. He's going to tell me later what it is. He's got something hidden in his pocket, and he's going to tell me about that, too. But later. Samim Abi is talking to Dad.

"Comăneci's really letting us down this year. It looks like she'll have to share some gold medals with the Russians. Here in Turkey, they'll blame her performance on Socialism, of course."

"Nothing gets them as excited as the end of Socialism. Have you seen the headlines about Poland? They're thrilled there's a labor strike going on in a socialist country."

"Yet not a word about all the strikes right here in Turkey."

"Exactly. *Hürriyet* put it right on the front page: 'Labor Unrest Grips Poland.'"

"You should see the cartoon in this week's *Gırgır*. A union leader says, 'We're holding our next strike in Poland so we can make the news.'"

Dad and Samim Abi are laughing a lot tonight.

—

Hüseyin Abi left his Ibelo here, so maybe he's friends with Samim Abi. They both tug on their mustaches when they listen. And when Samim Abi stops talking, his eyes look like Hüseyin's. I'm watching him, but I'm trying to listen to Ayşe's mom and Ayla Abla, too. They're looking at the newspaper and being serious.

"It's the most amazing photo. It almost looks she's posing."

"That's no pose, Sevgi Abla. All I can say is, good for her! Pulling out a gun and stopping traffic right in the middle of Istanbul. That takes guts. We've reached a fork in the road. From now on—"

"For goodness sake, Ayla! How many times have we said that? A fork in the road, indeed!"

"This time is different. It's going to get rocky. Everyone knows a coup's on the way. Some are going to bend, others are going to fight back. There are two camps. It's reached the point where you have to choose one or the other."

"Oh, I don't know, Ayla. Mind if I use the bathroom?"

"Give me a second, would you? Let me check first."

—

That's what happens when you're a guest. They want to check the bathroom, so they make you wait in the hallway the first time you need to pee. And that's why, when I followed Mom, I heard her yell to Ayla Abla.

"It looks like you still haven't opened up that spare room."

"Mom, it is too. It is open. Right, Ayla Abla?"

Mom looked at me. And then Ayla Abla came out of the bathroom and looked at me. It was such a weird look that I ran back to the terrace.

Ayla Abla talked all night. Mom didn't say anything. Dad kept looking at Mom; Ali kept looking at Samim Abi. Maybe Ali got scared. I saw him stick his hand in his pocket and play with his strings.

—

Samim Abi pats me on the head and pulls me against his leg just like Hüseyin Abi. I can tell he's one of us. The others don't know it, but I do. Maybe Samim Abi knows I'm one of us, too. I stuck my hand in my pocket and flicked the lighter, *click click*, so he'd know. He didn't hear it. He was talking to Ayşe's dad.

"Aydın Abi, did you read that column in *Tercüman* by . . . now what was his name?"

"First the detective, now you! I don't understand how you can stomach those papers."

"All the papers are delivered to us at TRT. And I think we should know what the other side is saying. Anyway, this columnist wrote that Kemal Türker was a Marxist, so it would be a sin to perform prayers at his funeral. Go figure!"

"Ugh! Some things never change. I remember what a friend of mine, a law student, did. Erol was his name. Erol Abi."

"What happened?"

"The body of an activist was delivered to Erol's home village for burial. It was summer, and Erol was there. Well, can you guess what happened? The local imam starts muttering about how he won't lead the funeral prayers for a 'godless anarchist.' Erol looked at the imam and said, 'Get out of the way. I'll do it.' Nobody thought he'd be able to, but he did."

"Why can't we come up with our own funeral rites, something for revolutionaries?"

Samim Abi patted me on the head. "I hear you and Ayşe are going to the Memorial Tomb tomorrow." I didn't say anything, but I clicked the lighter a couple of times. Why can't he hear it? I don't want to do it too loud. Because it's only for him. "If Atatürk had worked something out with Lenin back during the War of Liberation, nudged us a bit closer to Russia, we wouldn't be in such deep shit today. Ali, I want you to say something for me when you're standing in front of Atatürk's tomb, a message from your Samim Abi. Tell Mustafa Kemal: 'Samam Abi sends his respects, but you left the job unfinished!'"

I stopped clicking the lighter. Everybody was laughing too loud for Samim Abi to hear it.

—

Ali ran inside to the couch, so I followed him. Mom looked over at us and said, "We embarrassed them." Dad said, "Sometimes I wonder how they see the world, with a child's perspective." Ayla Abla said, "They see it a lot more clearly than we do, I guarantee it." Then Samim Abi said something about "the children of a country alone and apart," but I didn't hear it all. Later, they took us home and put us in bed. Me and Ali fell asleep on the sofa, but when we got in bed we didn't sleep right away. We could hear the police station, and we got up and looked. A man was yelling but like he was crying. He cried and yelled for the longest time. Me and Ali listened:

"O! Turkish Youth! Your first duty is to preserve and to defend Turkish Independence and the Turkish Republic forever. This is the very foundation of your existence and your future . . . Youth of Turkey's future! . . . You will find the strength you need in your noble blood."

Ali got a little mad at me. He said, "I told you! Tomorrow they might ask us to say 'Turkish Youth.' Because Atatürk said it first, and we're visiting him." When I fell asleep again, the man was still yelling. Or maybe the words were stuck in my head.

—

When me and Ayşe were walking to the Memorial Tomb, our shoes kept getting in between the stones. Just like the encyclopedia said. It was worse for Ayşe's grandma. She was wearing high heels. We kept our eyes on the ground so we didn't fall. Everybody else was looking down, too. Ayşe brought her laugh box with her, but she dropped it. Twice. Maybe she broke it. Her grandma acted like a teacher giving us a lesson.

"Children, it was Atatürk who saved our country from the enemy. Oops! There goes my shoe again. I nearly broke the heel off that time. He and his comrades in arms liberated our nation—oh, dear. Not again. I'm surprised nobody's twisted their ankle. I should have remembered to wear my shoes with the crepe soles. I'd forgotten how bad this road is. Why couldn't they have a nice paved road?"

"Are Atatürk's dead soldier friends buried here too?"

"My boy, Atatürk isn't buried. He's been 'entombed.' And no, his comrades are not here."

"You mean Atatürk's all alone? He shouldn't be alone!"

"Ali, look at the lions. Would you like to climb on top of one?"

—

Me and Ali don't want to get on top of the lions. Some other kids do, but we think the lions are spooky. They've got big eyes and open mouths. What if they came to life? And anyway, we want to get there, to Atatürk. It's a long, long road, and we can't run, not on these stones. Grandma didn't tell us if we should be happy or sad. On November 10, we're always sad, because Atatürk died. But on April 23, we're always happy, because Atatürk gave us "Children's Day." We get to dance in stadiums and wear folk costumes and everyone says, "Atatürk will live forever in our hearts." But today's not November 10 or April 23, so how should we be?

—

This is such a big place. I closed my eyes, and I was trying to figure out how many houses could fit here, when the music started. It's not our national anthem, "Independence March." I know almost all of that by heart. It starts: "Fear not; For the crimson banner that proudly ripples in this glorious dawn shall not fade." This music is different, sad. Everybody stops. So do we. But nobody sings. Everybody is dressed in nice clothes, like on Bairam or Children's Day. Here, maybe it's National Bairam every single day. We stand there, but not like revolutionaries, like soldiers. I remember this one time at a meeting in the neighborhood. We were all standing and Hüseyin Abi was saying, "The War of Liberation was a popular uprising against imperialism. Mustafa Kemal was one of its leaders. . . ." But there aren't any revolutionaries here, only rich people in nice clothes. The kids aren't from the slums. They all have clean shoes. Maybe that's why Hüseyin Abi cleaned the mud off his shoes before he left?

—

"If only we'd got an earlier start," Grandma says. "Now the sun's right overhead." We're "standing at attention." It goes on and on. Grandma's sweating. She can't get a handkerchief out of her handbag. A drop of sweat is running down her chin. Even the kids littler than me are standing still. A soldier yells, "At ease!" That means we can move and talk. We can't move if nobody else is. They'll think we don't love Atatürk, and everybody loves Atatürk.

—

In front of the museum, the sun is bright and yellow. Inside, the floor is shiny, like glass. Important places always have shiny floors. The people going in look like shadows. Thin, black, quiet. It seems dark inside, in the beginning. Then you can see all the faces. There's a big hall, and a man is talking to lots of people, all close together. The man's excited, and he's saying something real important. Nobody talks. They listen.

"... and Atatürk declared, 'You can strip me of all my awards, but this silver medal I shall never return. For along with this silver medal I carry on my chest the blood of the 250,000 martyred in the Battle of Gallipoli.'"

—

I wonder where they keep the medals of the dead soldiers? The man doesn't say anything about them. He's talking so loud, and he's rocking back and forth on his feet. Sometimes, when I'm reciting a poem at school, I do that too. Rock back and forth. Maybe he can't remember all the words. And he's sweating a lot. There was a girl who came to our class from a special home. She had white hair and white eyelashes, and when she recited "SaBuHa" this one time, she yelled like this, and her face got red and the veins came out on her neck.

—

The man's still talking, but so is everyone else now. It's too noisy! I took Ayşe's hand. She'll go anywhere if you take her hand. We ran down the big hall. Her grandma was looking at medals. We went to another place, with photos.

—

Ali held my hand. There are pictures of serious men on the wall in the hall. I can't tell if they have good hearts or bad hearts. All of them are old. Most of them are pashas. Ali's making me run now. There are lights on the floor in the hall, and we're trying to catch them with our feet. *Thump thump* we go, on and on, the only ones running. Ali takes me to a corner with no people. I know why. It's quiet there. "Here they are!" he whispers. He's looking at pictures. He can read the things written under them. They're old photos, and they're hard to see. Small

and fuzzy. And they're of women, not men. Ali still reads them out
loud to me, though.

—

"*Sergeant Halime, from Kastamonu.* Look Ayşe, this one is just like
Gökhan's granny. She waved a shovel at the police. Then the police
hit her on the head and she fell and hit her head again, on the ground.
Now, she gets all mixed up. For 'bread' she says 'bird,' and for 'water'
she says 'car.' *Havva and her mother, Zehra Hanım.* They're wearing
black sheets on their heads, just like Nuran Abla used to do. Now
she wears headscarves, and they're never black. They're red and yellow
and green. Her husband hit her because she wore so many colors. But
then, after Hüseyin Abi and Birgül Abla talked to him, he never hit her
again. Now they're revolutionaries, too. When Nuran Abla went to her
first funeral the police hit her, but she didn't cry, not once. On the bus,
she even laughed. *Corporal Nezahat.* This one looks just like Birgül
Abla. She has dark eyes and her hair sticks to her cheek, especially
when she laughs. Your hair does that, too, Ayşe. *Hatice Hatun, from
Adana.* When's there a protest, all the women in the neighborhood do
that, you know, stick out their chins and close their mouths hard. And
she's holding her rifle just like Auntie Seher did that one night. She
went up on the roof for guard duty because there wasn't a man to do it.
Senem Ayşe. She's named Ayşe too! *From Maraş.* Look at them! I swear
it, that's just how the big sisters from the university sit. I wonder if the
women in the pictures killed anyone? The men did, because they're
pashas. But these women were helping Atatürk, too. Maybe they killed
lots of enemies. Ayşe! That one looks like my mom. Doesn't she?"

—

Ali yelled. His eyes got big. He never does that. Something happened
to him. He's talking, and I think he's not going to stop. He can't stop.

He wants me to read this one myself. I think I can, if I go slow, but he wants me to go fast.

"*Er-zu-rum-lu Ka-ra Fat-ma.*"

"Well, doesn't she? The same face, the same eyes."

Ali's so excited he's jumping up and down. Or maybe he has to pee.

"They put all the revolutionaries in the corner. All together."

He stuck his hand in his pocket and went *click click.*

Strings don't click.

"What have you got in your pocket, Ali?"

"A lighter. An Ibelo lighter. It's Hüseyin Abi's. I wanted to give it to him, Ayşe. But he left. He's fighting imperialism. I wish he was here. I wish he could see these pictures."

Ali grabbed my hand. We ran toward the light. And when we were running, he yelled again.

"I didn't think any of us were here. But we are. There are lots of us!"

—

"You children gave me such a fright. I thought I'd lost you. There will be no more running off like that. Once we've visited the tomb, we're going straight home."

—

Grandma's heel broke off. She walks funny now. Me and Ali took her hands so we can go and see Atatürk. There are lots of lights there.

—

It's so quiet here. Ayşe's grandma is standing on one foot. "I can't be expected to perch here like a magpie for much longer," she says. "Let's finish up and go."

—

I asked Grandma what we were going to finish. And she said, "Perhaps we should recite al-Fatiha. But would that be appropriate?" So, when nobody said anything, I pushed the button. Ali said the laugh box was broken. But it wasn't.

—

Ayşe's grandma opened her mouth when the laughing started. It made me laugh. Ayşe laughed a lot. We both did. Her grandma tried to run out with us, but she can't go fast, because of her heel.

—

We got outside. Grandma didn't even get mad. She was scared. She thought the soldiers would get mad at her for letting us laugh. There was a soldier outside, and he didn't move, even a teeny bit. He stood there like one of those stone lions. Then I looked up and saw it in giant letters behind him:

"Look Ali! It's 'O! Turkish Youth!'"

"I told you!"

"But we don't have to say it. They wrote it in the stone. Nobody's saying it."

"The big brothers at the police station were saying it. You heard them. And then they got beat up because they didn't know all the words by heart."

The soldier's eye moved. He was looking at Ali. We ran down the steps.

I begged Grandma to take us to Swan Park. I even cried. But she said no. "How can I go anywhere with a broken heel? We'll go next week." Me and Ali will wait.

When we got in the shared taxi, Ali went *click click* with his lighter again. "Did Hüseyin Abi give you that?" I asked him. "I found it at Samim Abi's, but it's Hüseyin's," he told me.

The other passengers were quiet mostly. Maybe because they were thinking about Atatürk. I did hear a man say to a woman that he wished the army would come and "save us." He thought everyone needed to "fall into line" and only the army could "whip them into shape."

Grandma sat with one shoe in her lap, trying to fix the heel. She was talking to herself, so everyone looked and smiled at her.

"It's a bad omen! A bad omen!"

UNIT 11

The Great Turkish Nation

We Are a Compassionate People

". . . and then some particles lose energy and slow before they drift outward and away from the swirling core. Detective, they form that which we call 'order.' They make up our buildings, our bridges, our banks, our systems, our lives, our marriages, and anything else in this world you could name!"

While Dad was talking, Detective Nahit chewed and chewed on his fingernails, and blinked and blinked. He bit his lip and said nothing. Then he spit out a piece of nail.

"Aydın Abi, I'm trying to tell you something important, but you're blathering on about particles!"

I'm in the *meyhane* Dad always goes to. That's because Mom's taking Grandma to the doctor after work. She said she could get an appointment only in the evening, so me and Dad would have to eat out. She and Grandma handed me over to Dad in Kızılay Square. I love the *meyhane*. They make me meatballs and fried potatoes. And there's this funny sign on the front door:

COME TO YOUR SENSES, AND ONLY THEN COME TO THE MEY-HANE

BECOME PHILOSOPHICAL BEFORE COMING TO THIS HOUSE OF
    PHILOSOPHY
FOR THIS PATH IS FOR THOSE WHO HAVE PREVAILED AGAINST
    THEMSELVES
IF YOU ARE GREEN AND RAW, SEEK AMUSEMENT ELSEWHERE

Whenever I come here, Uncle Reşit, the *meyhane* man in the bow-tie, always reads that sign out loud. Then everybody laughs. And that's what they did this time, too, before they brought me meatballs and fried potatoes. Dad's eating, but only foods you can spear with a fork and eat a little at a time, between drinks. If you're drinking rakı, you're not supposed to eat fast. It's shameful. And you're not supposed to talk loud, either. That's why I can hardly hear Uncle Detective when he talks to Dad.

"Don't get me wrong, Aydın Abi, but you've been so absent-minded. The last few times we've met you've been off in space. If anything's wrong, and there's something I can—"

"Don't worry about me, Detective. Just tell me if there's any news."

"You remember that witness I interviewed concerning Cihan's homicide? The elderly lady. We're corroborating her sworn testimony. Something kind of shitty has happened, though."

"They haven't shot her?"

"No, no. It's nothing to do with her. We nabbed this poor sap. One of the two guys sentenced to death in the Balgat Bloodbath case. To be honest, I feel kind of bad for him."

"Why? Who is he?"

"Mustafa Pehlivanoğlu. The other perpetrator had apparently threatened him. 'The local coffee houses are full of communists. Open fire or I'll put a bullet through your head,' he was told. So, this Mustafa character opened fire, killing five and wounding dozens. Aydın Abi, sometimes I . . . Look, you know how determined I am to catch these guys. We all are. And everyone in law enforcement is a prime target. You know that, too."

"Hey, hang on a second! Didn't those two escape from prison? I remember seeing it in the paper."

"Yeah, somebody helped them escape from Mamak Military Prison. They got as far as Kütahya. I didn't tell you about it at the time. We were tipped off. There were four guys holed up in a village house in Kütahya. We burst in on them—"

"Dad! I need to go to the toilet. I mean, the restroom. Can I go alone?"

When we're not at home, we call the "toilet" the "restroom." I'm old enough now to go by myself, even at the *meyhane*. I walk through the thick smoke, waving my arms to clear a path. Each table has its own cloud of smoke, and the people talk and talk in their own little cloud. I hear them as I pass, but the things they say get all mixed up in my head.

"Twenty! On average, twenty people a day are getting killed in this country. Not to mention all the armed robberies."

"It says here that our heroic army is determined to stamp out the so-called 'insurrection' in Fatsa. Apparently, the Soviet Union hopes to invade Turkey from the Black Sea with the help of local collaborators. Who dreams up this stuff? Fatsa's just a small town on the coast."

"I'm hearing reports from back home in Adıyaman that Apo's organizers are busy recruiting followers from among the city's Kurds."

"Our male authors are such phonies. None of them deigned to take Sevgi Soysal seriously when she was alive, but now . . ."

"Am I the only one? I don't know how to describe it. I feel as though this is all happening in another country. I should be horrified, outraged, terrified. . . . I should feel *something*. Is it apathy? Stoicism? Am I protecting my heart, or my sanity? Is there a clinical term to . . ."

I wave my arms faster and faster, until I'm a butterfly floating though a smoky cloud.

I get to the old auntie sitting at a small table outside the toilet. She's got huge earrings and a white kerchief. And she's got a son. He's big, but he's like a child. He never talks. His face is kind of scary, and so is the way he moves his head. I asked Dad why he does that. It's because he can't see anything. I'm afraid to go into the toilet with him sitting there, so I wait for someone else to come. The old woman's reading the newspaper out loud to her son. He's smiling, but at the air. His eyes are white.

"Listen to this, my boy. Zeki Müren's begun posing for the press with a woman or two on his arm. The fuss being made over Bülent Ersoy must have scared him. Some people are pointing out that Zeki Müren was the one who started it. He's been mincing around in a cape and a skirt and platform shoes for years now. Bülent's just taken it a step further. You should see this photo! Zeki Müren's more womanish than the woman he's kissing. He's wearing mascara. And lipstick. And yet it's Bülent who's taking all the heat. Well, it always pays to be two-faced in this country. It says here that Bülent's posters got torn up at the fair. Somebody even drew a mustache on one of them. I'm telling you, these maniacs are no better than a pack of wild dogs. Bülent thinks his fame and fortune will protect him. Well, he's in for a terrible surprise. Nobody can get away with being that different. They'll gouge out his eyes sooner or later."

The lady stroked her son's head, then his cheek. Tears came out of his eyes, and she wiped them away with her fingers. Then she saw me.

"Hi, little miss. Got to pee?"

You're not supposed to say 'pee'!

I ran back to Dad's table. He didn't even notice me at first. Maybe because it's so smoky. Dad's eyes were all red again. Uncle Detective was leaning back in his chair with his arms crossed.

"Aydın Abi, do you realize what you're saying?"

"Detective, this isn't simply about my being jealous. This guy Sevgi's seeing is from her old organization. I'm worried."

"Well, have you considered talking to her? Can't you?"

"No, I can't do that. She doesn't talk to me anymore. Could you do me a favor and tail her for a few days?"

"Tail your wife? Have you gone out of your mind?"

Then Uncle Detective saw me. He said, "Ayşe!" like I'd caught him doing something wrong. Dad didn't look at me. I didn't even get to tell him I still had to go the restroom. Uncle Detective smiled at my dad.

"Don't get angry, but let me give you some advice. In matters like this, you're better off ignoring your suspicions."

"In matters like what, Detective?"

Dad yelled it. Uncle Detective chewed on his nails. He looked over at me like he was scared. He leaned close to Dad.

"I can't promise anything. But I'll see what I can do."

"There's something else."

"Yes?"

"Our neighbor. Samim. He works at TRT, but there's something funny about him. I can't quite put my finger on it."

"I'll make a few inquiries. Aydın Abi . . . Why don't you take it easy for a while? You're not looking well. I hope you don't mind me coming right out and saying so."

"I'm fine, Detective. In fact, I'm starting to feel like myself again, like I've regained my footing."

"That's good to hear."

I couldn't hold it in anymore.

"I have to pee!"

The smoke stopped swirling. The clouds giggled. I started crying. Dad didn't care. He didn't stroke my hair or wipe my eyes.

A People Steeped in Common Sense

"Let's put a bullet in his head!"

Snot flew out of Auntie Seher's nose when she yelled that. She pulled her salwar all the way up to her boobs. Pointing, she yelled again.

"What else can we do? Let's shoot that dog in the head!"

Nobody said a word. Pulling Auntie Seher by the arm, Birgül Abla tried to get her to sit in a chair.

"Easy, Seher Abla. Calm down."

"Let go, Birgül! Let me go. You'd understand if you were a mother. Let's kill him, Vedat! I won't know peace until we do."

Everybody in the hall of the cooperative went quiet. Even Mustafa Abi the grocer. But before that, he was kind of crying as he talked.

"Let me go. I'm begging you, Vedat. I swear on the life of my family, of my baby, that I'll never come back to the neighborhood again."

When nobody else said anything, he stopped talking, too.

The day before, in the morning, Birgül Abla gathered with all the aunties. They were telling each other about the Maraş Massacre. Birgül Abla was wearing trousers under her skirt and a scarf on her head. She's trying to dress like us. But her shoes are different. She put her hand on her hip when she talked.

"And that's why we need to take our own self-defense seriously. As you can see, the law doesn't protect the oppressed. As if it weren't bad enough that the state's arming and training Grey Wolf commandos, they're not rounding up any of those responsible for the massacre. That's why we must be completely self-reliant, not dependent on help from anyone, and why we must always remember that the law is designed to protect the bourgeoisie and can never be trusted."

Vedat Abi and the men were gathered at the cooperative. There were tables set up in front. Vedat Abi was "talking inside his mouth" again. That's how my mom put it. He was playing with his mustache, his hand blocking his mouth. Everyone was trying to hear him, so they poked their heads up to the right and up to the left, like they were watching a movie they couldn't see.

"Now . . . The government decision on Maraş leaves no doubt that all the might of the state . . ."

I couldn't understand the rest, so I ran back to Birgül Abla and the aunties. They weren't done yet. Auntie Seher was talking to Birgül Abla, and my mom and I went over to them.

"Birgül, a call came to the corner grocer. That's how I know."

"Did Cem say anything important?"

"No, just that he would call me on the grocer's phone come night. I waited outside the grocery until morning, but the phone never rang."

"He didn't have a chance to call. Look, your son's on the run. We'll have to wait for his call. Except for the grocer, who knows about this?"

"Nobody."

"I'll still get my friends to ask around in Istanbul."

"Sure, do that. Ask around. Sure."

Auntie Seher's rubbing and squeezing her hands together, first one, then the other. It makes a *shush shush* sound. Her hands are dry and red, from all the laundry she does for rich people. Mom gives Auntie Seher a little poke with her elbow.

"Come on, stop gnawing at yourself. Your boy managed to dig his way out of prison. He's not going to get caught now, out in the open."

Auntie Seher made a small smile. She went home without another word. Mom and Birgül Abla looked at each other. I knew something bad was going to happen. I felt it right away. There are three old aunties, and one of them is Gökhan's granny. All three of them have this veil over their eyes, a bluish white covering. They can't see, but they knit nonstop. They stick their balls of wool in their salwars, and their knitting never ends. That day, they sat in the shade and knitted. And while they knitted, they wailed for Maraş.

Dad and the other men cursed a lot. They tugged at their mustaches. They listened to Vedat Abi. I sat in the garden and listened to all the sounds. I closed my eyes so I could hear better.

> *The cranes fly high over Maraş*
> *Broken-winged, circling and crying*
> *Mothers whose brave boys have been shot*
> *Are bleating like ewes to their lambs*

"Death songs won't get us anywhere, brothers. We need to take action."

"That's easy enough to say, Vedat, but what difference would it make if we did some kind of protest here in the neighborhood? If we're going to demonstrate, we need to do it right in the middle of Kızılay Square."

"Hasan Abi, those who look, see."

"That's true, Vedat. But they need to see us out there, too."

> *O friend, O wounded friend*
> *Blood flows in times of tyranny*
> *Today, the true-hearted are giving up their lives*
> *And the false-hearted are holding wedding parties*

"Aliye Abla, this grocer—"

"I was just getting to him, Birgül. I like Mustafa. He's a good fellow. He's been kind to us when we were in need, but lately—"

"His behavior has been a little odd, hasn't it?"

"One of the women told me. Strangers are going in and out of his grocery. They've got walkie-talkies. I knew you trusted him, so I shrugged it off."

"Aliye Abla, I trust him until you say otherwise. I mean, I'm something of an outsider in this neighborhood. What matters is that you trust him."

"Birgül, we're kind of ignorant, the whole lot of us. Until we set up the cooperative, his was the only place to shop. And when we had no money, he let us buy on account. He was the most popular guy in the neighborhood."

"Well, what do you think about this phone call business?"

"I don't want to talk behind anyone's back or blame an honest man, but Mustafa's been acting strange lately. He's always got one eye on the ground and one on the sky. What do you think happened with Seher's son? He got caught, didn't he? You and the others will figure out what to do."

> *The dead were burned, the living were not*
> *Children suffer, mothers weep*

Seas are vast, droplets splash
Mahirs never end, new Sinans are born*
Why do you sorrow so, mountain of Maraş?

The three old aunties were still knitting when evening came. They don't know it's dark, and keep knitting. Later, at night, the other women come and take them home. They think it's dark in the morning, too. That's why they sing folk songs. So they're not scared of the dark.

I looked at over at Auntie Seher's house. Their candles were still burning when I fell asleep. The last thing I remember is Mom and Dad talking in the dark.

"It's hot, Hasan. Leave me be!"

"I haven't so much as touched you. I'm hot too."

"Well, stop moving around. Every time I'm about to fall asleep, you start kicking."

"Listen here!"

"What?"

"This Mustafa business is serious. Do you realize that?"

"I was going to say that. He's been acting all guilty for the longest time. And today Birgül told me that one of the—"

"I heard her. Dürüst was trying to tell me something the other day. I didn't pay him any mind."

"Hasan, what did that madman say now?"

"He looked at me, all serious, and said, 'Still waters get mossy. Beware storekeepers.'"

"We all say he's crazy, but maybe Dürüst's on to something."

"Could be."

"These mosquitos keep biting me. But they leave you alone."

"Why would they be interested in me when there's a tasty bite right next to me?"

They laughed for a while. Then we all fell asleep.

---

* Mahir Çayan and Sinan are heroes of the left.

Auntie Seher woke us up in the morning. The sun wasn't up yet. The sky was blue-black. Auntie Seher screamed like a torn sheet.

"No! My heart's breaking. No!"

Birgül Abla was trying to hold on to Auntie Seher. She was outside, tearing at her salwar, beating on her legs.

"Cem! My boy, Cem! What have they done to you?"

Birgül Abla and some other revolutionary sisters are trying to put their arms around Auntie Seher, but because she's fat one swing of her arm knocks them all to the ground. They get up and try again. They all fall again. When they try to pull Auntie Seher to her feet, she gets up so fast the others fall. Mom runs over, still in her nightgown. Auntie Seher hugs her, then collapses on the ground, crying and yelling.

"Aliye! The Wolves caught my Cem, they tortured him, then they hog-tied him . . . Aliye, they tossed his body in a ditch, like a dead dog. Aliye!"

Other women come running up, still in their night clothes, and gather around Auntie Seher. The three old aunties come too, and sit in the garden. They make sounds like birds. It's like the night never happened, like morning never came again, as they sing the death songs of the day before. The balls of wool rest in their laps, but they don't knit. Time has stood still this morning.

> *God, mightiest of mighty*
> *God of day and night*
> *God in name only*
> *God of nothingness, you seem*

Vedat Abi talked to the women. He went down to the bottom of the hill with two uncles. Then I saw them walking with Mustafa the Grocer. He kept shouting. They held Mustafa Abi by the arms and climbed up the hill. "What do you mean, a trial?" Mustafa Abi yelled. "Are you saying I'm a traitor?"

I couldn't hear what the others were saying. They kept pulling him, and he kept jerking his arm away. They all got sweaty. Especially Mustafa Abi.

Some of the women walked behind Mustafa Abi. Until night-fall, Auntie Seher kept quiet and kept quiet, and then screamed and screamed.

Vedat Abi stuck Mustafa Abi in the cooperative. He stayed in there with him all day long. Then the news came. The women said there would be a trial at night. Me and Dad went to it. Chairs were brought from houses. They made Mustafa Abi sit in the middle.

Vedat Abi tugged at his mustache the whole time. The uncles sat in the front row with their arms crossed. They looked at Mustafa Abi like they didn't know him. Everybody was shouting at him.

"The cooperative turned you into our enemy. Is that right, Mustafa?"

"You're the only one who talked to Cem. Did he tell you where he was?"

"Who are those men who visit your store? Huh? And why do they have radio phones?"

"The whole time you were handing out paper money—"

"Let's not go into that, brother."

"Did Cem tell you where he was, or not?"

Mustafa Abi didn't answer any of their questions. Finally, he lifted his hands and spoke, looking at each of the uncles, one by one.

"Hasan Efendi, when your house burned down, didn't I help? Sister Nuran, every time your baby needed milk, didn't I give it to you on credit? You should all be ashamed of yourselves. When I think of all I did for you!"

"Hold on, Mustafa! Don't go mixing things up. If we knew anything for sure, we wouldn't be having a trial."

"What are you going to do? Kill me? Who do you think you are? The state?"

Everyone went, "Ohhh." Mustafa Abi didn't get up from his chair, but he waved his hands in everyone's faces.

"You're living in a dream world. You think you're going to have a revolution and take over the state. How? How many are you? All that work you did to start a cooperative, and what do you have to show for it? A couple of sacks of rice. That's it! You're going to overthrow the government with your women and your children? What a joke! They'd laugh in your face!"

That's when Auntie Seher came in with her collar ripped. Birgül Abla tried to hold her back, but she was too big.

"Let's put a bullet in his head!"

Nobody said anything. Auntie Seher yelled again.

"Birgül! What would you do if they threw your boy's body into a ditch? Vedat, son, what else can we do? Let's shoot that dog in the head! So many have died, our most precious. Why should he live? You call that justice?"

Vedat Abi pulled Mustafa Abi to his feet by the arms. He took him somewhere. Everybody went outside. The uncles smoked and talked with my dad in front of the door.

"Let's chase him out of the neighborhood. Let him suffer some-where else."

"Why should we do that, Hasan Efendi? Let's handle this ourselves. Let's keep him from ratting on someone else, the dirty informer."

"You heard what he said about the revolution."

They talked for a long time.

Mom didn't come back from Auntie Seher's house that night.

When it got dark, they came and took away the three old aun-ties again. One of them dropped a ball of wool and it unrolled and unrolled all the way down the hill. Nobody heard it. It unrolled all the way to Mustafa Abi's grocery store. I wish he'd run away and never come back.

One from Many

Number one, Mom put on her nice shoes. And number two, the but-terflies might come out of their cocoons today. That's what Ali said. It could happen tomorrow, too. But, please God, let them come out today. That's why I cried so much, so Mom would have to take me to Parliament. It wasn't easy, though.

"You're acting like a spoiled brat, Ayşe. I've got too much to do today."

I had to say it. What else could I do?

"But I didn't tell Dad about that man."

Mom understood. But she didn't talk to me again. Not a word, all the way to Parliament, even when her shoe rubbed on her heel and hurt her. As soon as we got inside, she made a phone call.

"I can't make it today. . . No, I really can't. . . . Yes . . . Let's keep in touch. . . . All right."

Mom looked at me. A terrible look.

"We're taking your Auntie Günseli out for lunch today. Then you and I need to have a talk, little miss Ayşe."

Oh no! This is bad. It's because of what I said in the morning. Mom didn't yell at me, and that's scary. She looked at me like she looks at Dad. Like she didn't know me.

Not once until the afternoon did Mom look up from her desk. She didn't look at me at all. I kept walking around her desk, and she still didn't look, not even once.

Two old men came to the library. They can't hear very good because they're old, and they shout. They have those old marks on their faces, round and brown. You're supposed to keep quiet in the library, but they're loud. Nobody stops them, though, because they're "party elders." That's what one of the aunties said. The old men were "crunching numbers" for Parliament, whatever that means.

They finally left, still shouting, to have coffee with the Republican People's Party. There, they talk about politics "in the wings." Mom never takes me there, though. I guess it's like at the theater, where Grandma took me this one time. Everyone hides in "the wings" and whispers. Then, when they're ready, they go out on the stage and talk loud, but not with their own words, and everyone claps.

The phone rang. It was Auntie Günseli, saying she was waiting at the gate. Mom remembered to smile again. I followed her, skipping. Maybe she'll forget to be mad at me. You're not supposed to get too mad at your children in front of your friends. Dad doesn't get mad at me when we have guests, either.

Auntie Günseli was wearing green shoes this time. It was the first time I saw shoes in green. I kept looking at them. So did Mom. Everyone looked at them. We had fish in a restaurant. Mom and Auntie Günseli drank white wine.

When Mom was sitting at the table with her arm on my chair, her hand touched my neck. I didn't move when I felt her hand. Maybe she'll leave it there. Maybe she's not mad anymore. But no, she doesn't know her hand is touching me. She might pull it away at any moment. But if I tell her to leave it there, she won't, because I'm making noise. I sit very still. My neck starts hurting, that's how still I sit. Her hand is still there. But not because she wants to touch me. She's going to pull it away. She's going to, now. Or now . . .

"Sevgi, have you got everything arranged? Were you able to unseal those confidential dossiers for my research?"

"It's all set. We'll go down to the archives together. But not before we have some coffee in Parliament."

The intern girls are having coffee in the garden. They talk about happy things, not politics.

"I don't blame Zeki Müren. He knows what he's doing."

"Nobody's going to fall for that nonsense. Who's going to believe he's made love to all those women or that he's got a girlfriend now?"

"It's not about believing. Do you think anyone believed those romantic movies starring Bülent Ersoy? I mean, Bülent kissing a woman . . . come on!"

"Well then, why do people watch those movies?"

"This is Turkey. As long as you play the part in public, you can do whatever you want in private. It's only a sin if you flaunt it."

"Well, that's what he's doing now, flaunting it. Sooner or later, he's going to get lynched. Mark my words."

"You're right. They've got to attack someone, and he's an easy target."

Mom and Auntie Günseli look so nice drinking coffee. The wind's blowing on the trees, making the leaves move, making the sunlight play on their faces. I like watching them from over here. It wouldn't look as nice if I was up close. And Mom will get mad if she sees me. She doesn't love me that much. I'm a "headache," that's what she said that one time. And she wants to leave, but she can't because of me. That's why she doesn't love me. I can't tell her I know everything, because I love her even if she doesn't love me.

Uncle İbrahim the Supervisor came out into the garden with Uncle Abdullah and Muzaffer Abi. Uncle Abdullah is smiling, but Muzaffer Abi is hanging his head. The supervisor is angry, and he shouts.

"Sevgi Hanım, could you come here?"

I run up to Mom.

"See off your guest, Sevgi Hanım. We need to talk."

"But she's only just arrived. If you'll give me a few minutes—"

"Please do it now."

Mom snapped back her head, she was so surprised.

Auntie Günseli left. I followed Mom to Supervisor İbrahim's room. Uncle Abdullah was there, playing with his prayer beads, and so was Muzaffer Abi. When Mom noticed me, she asked for a moment to take me away. Uncle Abdullah Bey laughed and said, "She should hear about this, too." The supervisor told Abdullah Bey to be quiet. I stayed in the room with Mom. The supervisor was mad at Mom. I could tell from his voice.

"Sevgi Hanım, as you no doubt know and appreciate, we try to put aside our differences here and focus on our work. You are a valued employee. I've always treated you with the courtesy and respect you deserve. But after what happened today, my confidence in you has been badly shaken. We found cocoons in the archives, and winged creatures, and some other things. . . ."

The butterflies!

"I'm giving you a chance to tell me you are in no way responsible for any of this. If you can do that . . . I mean, I would rather not have to launch an official investigation."

"Winged creatures?"

"And some other things, too, Sevgi Hanım."

Uncle Abdullah twirls his beads over his belly, his eyes on them the whole time he talks to Mom.

"Sevgi Hanım, we all knew about your ideological leanings. Apparently, you were quite the revolutionary in your youth. But this . . . even for you, this is astonishingly childish. And that's not to mention the other, far more serious, items we've discovered."

Mom looked only at İbrahim Bey the Supervisor.

"The insects aren't what concern me. But the other things . . ."

"What are you talking about, İbrahim Bey? Just say it. Do you mean the letters?"

Mom knows too! But there's more than just letters inside those envelopes. There are photos, too. But the butterflies! Ali's going to be so happy. We did it! We got the butterflies into Parliament.

"Please come with me, Sevgi. Would you mind staying here, Abdullah Bey? There's no reason to make this more unpleasant than it already is."

"But I found them, İbrahim Bey. I can show you exactly where they are."

"That's enough. You can go back to your desk."

"But we need to launch an official investigation."

"I'll decide what's necessary, Abdullah Bey. Right after you, Sevgi Hanım."

We're going to see the butterflies! I was skipping and dancing when Mom grabbed my arm.

"What are you doing, Ayşe?"

"Nothing. We got the butterflies into Parliament. You said we couldn't. You were sad. Now the butterflies are—"

"Ayşe! What are you saying?"

We got to the archives. The butterflies were crawling on the shelves. Some fell off and flapped their wings, but they hit the ground. A couple of men were trying to catch them. But it wasn't easy, because they crawled between files and books and magazines. The windows were opened wide and sunlight came in. I laughed and clapped my hands. The sun is shining on the butterflies. I clapped and clapped. "Fly away, fly away," I screamed. But they only just woke up from their cocoons, so maybe they're too sleepy to fly just yet.

İbrahim Bey the Supervisor laughed.

"Sevgi Hanım, look . . . Muzaffer, you're here, too. Let's keep this to ourselves. All right? Obviously, this was Ayşe's doing, and she's only a child. We've all watched her grow up. I can't help laughing at what she's done. But as for the other things, the letters and the childhood photographs—"

"What childhood photographs? İbrahim Bey, I can honestly say I know nothing about them."

"I'm returning these envelopes to you, Sevgi Hanım. They contain . . . How do I put this? There are letters and then there are those photographs. I have no choice but to conduct an internal investigation. If Abdullah Bey hadn't seen them, I would have turned a blind eye to the whole business. Naturally, your husband will not be informed. Have no fear of that."

"Thank you, İbrahim Bey. I appreciate it."

Mom's hands are shaking, and her face is all red and sweaty. She tries to pull me away, but I'm watching the butterflies. "Look, Mom," I say, "I think they have orange stripes."

It's like a dream. For the first time, I see the sun shining on the dark books in the archives. Men are running after the butterflies, laughing. But Mom isn't. Even Muzaffer laughs, but Mom doesn't. I wish Ali could be here. I'm glad he's my friend. Nobody understands but us.

Mom walked on the backs of her shoes all the way home. She didn't look at me. She cried a little. But Ali will be glad when I tell him. He said we couldn't help the swans unless we did the butterflies first. Now we can help them! Ali got everything ready, and we can do it now. Me and Ali can do everything.

A Cohesive Society without Class Distinctions

They came real early. The noise woke me up. Mom had just got out of bed, too. She was drinking tea in the kitchen with Auntie Aliye. They'd put Ali on the sofa, with a pillow and a blanket. Mom shouldn't see me, because she's still not talking to me. I listened to them from the door. They were almost whispering. Auntie Aliye said to Mom, "If anything happens to us . . . You've got trouble here, too, but it's worse in our neighborhood. I want to put Ali in your care should something happen to me."

Mom didn't say anything at first. She stirred her tea for the longest time. Then she said, "You've caught me by surprise . . . I'll have to . . ." Auntie Aliye whispered again.

"I don't want to be a burden. Never mind, Sevgi Hanım. And anyway—"

"No, not at all. I mean, he's become almost like a son to us. We'll do what we can, of course."

"If you have any doubts . . ."

"Why would we have any doubts?"

"You're sure, then."

"Of course. I agree."

It went quiet. When Auntie Aliye spoke again it was in a normal voice.

"Never mind, Sevgi Hanım. Forget I said anything. I didn't say a word, you didn't hear a word. It never happened."

Mom talked loud, too.

"Don't say that, Aliye Hanım! I'm sorry. It's just that you caught me by surprise."

"You've got your own life to think about. It's different."

"What do you mean, different?"

"Ayşe! Sweetie, what are you doing up at this hour? Ali, weren't you able to fall asleep, my boy?"

When Grandma came out into the hallway and shouted, Mom and Auntie Aliye stopped talking. Ali had been behind me the whole time! He ran off to the living room. I ran after him. Mom was trying to talk to Auntie Aliye, but she went to the back room to change her clothes.

"Aliye Hanım, I've offended you. Please don't."

"It's fine, Sevgi Hanım. But this is my last day. I'll clean everything before I go."

"You misunderstood me."

"Enough."

"Aliye, I understand. I know what it is to live in the slums. At one time, I used to help organize—"

"At one time!"

"Argh!"

They didn't talk again. I followed Ali into the room with Auntie Aliye. She was mad. She pulled down her skirt. Under it, she was wearing something clear down to her knees. Mom was getting dressed in the room opposite. She got cross because she couldn't hook her bra. She turned her back to the door, but Auntie Aliye didn't. I could see her boobs under her white sleeveless shirt. Auntie Aliye tied a white kerchief over her hair while my mother pinned her hair up in the back, quick as can be. They were both talking to themselves. Mom got fed up while she was buttoning up her blouse, and she left half the buttons undone. Auntie Aliye pulled her salwar all the way up to her boobs and pulled her cuffs up to her knees. Mom turned her gray skirt to the front so she could button it, but then she couldn't turn it back around. Auntie Aliye tried to straighten her slipper with her other foot. She couldn't, and bent over to do it. They came out of their rooms at the same time and stood there, face to face. But they didn't talk. I went and stood between them. Mom had started with the wrong button, so all the rest were wrong, too. Auntie Aliye's shirt was inside out. When Auntie Aliye went to the bathroom to fill up a bucket, Mom got her briefcase and went to the front door.

"Aliye Hanım! You've misunderstood. I couldn't answer right way. Because—"

Her voice got all funny and she slammed the door on her way out. Grandma looked at me. When I didn't say anything, she went off to the bathroom to talk to Aliye Hanım.

"What's going on, Aliye Hanım? And so early in the morning."

"Nothing. Pay us no mind. Today's my last day, so tell me if there's anything extra you want done."

"Your last day? Whatever do you mean?"

That's all Auntie Aliye said. She walked off with her bucket, spilling water on the way, with Grandma following her. "Aliye Hanım, shall I take the children to Swan Park today?" Grandma asked. When Auntie Aliye said "Okay," I screamed out loud.

"Ali! We're going to the park. Ali! The butterflies got into Parliament. And they flew, sort of. The butterflies."

He was playing with his strings.

"Be quiet! Didn't you hear them? We're never coming again."

"I heard, but . . ."

"We're not coming again. We can't do anything."

"But the butterflies got into Parliament. I did all my jobs."

Ali didn't say anything. He was mad at me. I went to my room. He's probably ashamed because he didn't do his jobs. That's why he's like this.

—

Ayşe's grandma got dressed. She told me Jale Hanım was going to come, too. I don't like that lady. Neither does Ayşe. Me and Ayşe aren't talking today. She doesn't understand anything. She doesn't know what's going on. She doesn't know about the trial, about Hüseyin Abi, about Birgül Abla, about Maraş. All she knows is Şokella. She thinks getting the butterflies into Parliament is such a big deal. But that's the easy part. If she's so smart, let her find some chloroform and a wheelbarrow. She gave me all the hard jobs because she's rich. I'd tell her if her Mom hadn't made my mom so mad. This time, I'm standing with my mom. Not with Ayşe. Mom said, "We pay the price while they play at being revolutionaries! I spit on them!" She's awfully mad. Her forehead is sweating. Maybe she's mad because we won't be able to get meat at Gima anymore. She keeps talking to herself.

"It's not as if I asked them to adopt him. Well, who needs them!"

—

I tried to talk to Ali, but he won't leave his mother's side. She's talking to herself, though, not him. She's mad at my mom. But Mom didn't say anything about the letters. She didn't have a chance. I understand, but I won't tell. I promised Mom. It was more than a promise. I swore it on my heart. She won't tell Dad about the butterflies, and I won't tell about Uncle Önder. Mom cried when we talked about it last night.

"Those letters and files were entrusted to me, Ayşe. You'll understand what that means when you grow up. They were given to me for safekeeping and I failed. It's shameful to let anyone down like that. That's how you lose people's trust. Now, I want you to promise you won't say anything to your father about this, and I won't say anything about the silkworms."

I can't tell Auntie Aliye. I won't tell her that Mom hid the letters in the closet. What happens if she hides Ali and then they find him? That's what's worrying her. But I can't tell Auntie Aliye!

Ali stayed with his mom until Grandma told us it was time to go and get Jale Hanım.

We got into a normal taxi, because Jale Hanım said she "can't be bothered with a shared taxi or a bus, not in this heat." She even said she'd pay for it, which is shameful, but that's what Jale Hanım does.

"And then I read that Princess Caroline is no angel, either. You remember her husband's escapades in Turkey with that Italian tramp? Well, she wasn't about to take it lying down. Apparently, she was caught wining and dining with the son of a famous film director."

"Please don't, Jale Hanım. Not in front of the driver."

"What's wrong with that? Everybody talks about everything these days. At least it's normal, what goes on between a man and a woman. It's when a man and another man—"

"Jale Hanım! The children!"

"Little kids know everything. Stop acting like a spinster schoolmistress, Nejla Hanım. The times are changing. Loosen up. And listen to this . . . Why are you covering your ears? It's about Cavit Bey."

"What happened to Cavit Bey?"

"Oh, you're all ears when it comes to Mr. Vanishing Cream. Well, someone at the hairdresser's told me he's leaving his wife. My source has been using his creams for decades and knows what she's talking about."

"At his age?"

"What's his age got to do with it? He's a fine figure of a man. A little bird told me you might want to know he'll soon be single."

"I implore you, Jale Hanım. We can talk about this later, just the two of us."

"My dear Nejla Hanım, I do believe you've gone all pink. Okay, we'll talk later. Chauffour, we're getting out just before Swan Park. A brisk walk will do wonders for our legs."

"It's pronounced 'chauffeur,' Jale Hanım."

"You old-timers really crack me up. Forever correcting everyone's Turkish. And anyway, in case you didn't realize, 'chauffeur' isn't even Turkish. It's French. You're a funny old gal, Nejla Hanım. I'll give you that."

I tried to hold Ali's hand when we got out. But only because Grandma told me to! He pushed my hand away and stuck his hands in his pockets. As if I wanted to hold his dumb hand! I don't care. Then I put my arm around his shoulder. He tried to shake it off, but I kept it there.

"I got the silkworms into Parliament. You can't get cross with me! What's the matter? Is it because you didn't do your jobs?"

"You don't know."

"What don't I know?"

Grandma and Jale Hanım are walking so slow. Me and Ali are in out front of them. Grandma holds back her shoulders and looks straight ahead when she's walking. Jale Hanım keeps taking her arm because she wants to look at the shop windows. When Grandma stops, she smoothes her clothes in the window. Grandma doesn't want Jale Hanım to take her arm, but there's nothing she can do.

"Oh, look over there, Nejla Hanım. It's the famous Goya shoe shop. It's pricey, but they have a layaway plan."

"Who would pay that kind of money for a pair of shoes? It's an extravagance and a waste, Jale Hanım."

"But look at the lamé ones. They'd go great with the dress I want for Feride's engagement party."

On the walls between the shop windows there are posters of men and women. Some say WANTED and others say THEY WERE BUR-IED IN THE SUN, all in big letters. Me and Ali look at the posters while Jale Hanım and Grandma look at the windows.

—

I wish Ayşe would leave me alone. I want to see if Hüseyin Abi's on any of the posters. She keeps getting between me and the posters. Then, when I go to posters farther along, she follows me.

"Ali, what don't I know?"

"Shhh."

"What don't I know?"

"Do you know what this is?"

"M-L-S-P. It's easy. I course I know."

"But what does it mean?"

"You don't know, either!"

"I do so!"

"Ayşe, I hope you children aren't quarreling."

Jale Hanım takes Grandma by the elbow and leads her to another shop window.

"Would you mind helping me pick out some fabric? You've got such a good eye for quality, Nejla Hanım. I want something super classy but eye-catching, for Feride's engagement party."

Ali went up ahead to look at more posters. I followed him.

—

Ayşe's got her hand on her hip again.

"Why do you keep pestering me? And why don't you ask about the butterflies? I did it for you."

She's going to cry. Her chin's getting all crinkly.

I need to get away, so I walk a little. I look back, and she's still standing there. Nobody's looking at her. Her grandmother and that woman are looking at the shop windows. People are passing, but they don't look. They don't really see her, not like I do. She's there, in all that noise. If some fascists came, she wouldn't know how to run away. A real revolutionary wouldn't do this. I'm sure of it. They wouldn't leave a crying girl. I go back and take her hand. We walk along to the next wall and look at the posters. She's still crying, but only because she started and now she can't stop, not yet. Soon, she's done. She sniffs.

"If only you'd seen the butterflies. It was so beautiful."

"I'm glad you saw it."

"Are all these people lost?"

"No. They're pictures of the brothers and sisters the police are look- ing for. If they find them, they'll torture them. They'll give them to the fascists. They'll hogtie them and throw their bodies in a ditch. That's why."

"But where are they? I bet I know!"

"Where?"

"They went where the swans fly!"

Maybe Ayşe's not so dumb after all.

—

Me and Ali looked at all the pictures on all the posters. Sometimes we ran back and looked at the posters again. "He's not here," Ali said. I asked him who, and he said, "Hüseyin Abi. I guess they're not looking for him."

"Nejla Hanım, let's get the kids some ice cream. They'll enjoy that. That poor boy has probably never had ice cream in his whole life."

Ali heard her. I took his hand. "She's stupid," I said. "Don't listen to her." They got us ice cream, even though Ali didn't want any.

"Nejla Hanım, I don't think you should give up on Cavit Bey. He's the right age. He's getting a divorce. He's the perfect gentleman. What is there to keep you two lovebirds apart?"

"He'd never leave his wife."

"What makes you say that? You're a funny one, you are. Maybe his wife's leaving him. It's not like men never leave their wives."

"What would you have me do?"

"Now that's more like it! A positive attitude. Just relax a little. Once you relax, things take care of themselves."

We could see Swan Park just a little way away. Ali doesn't know how to eat ice cream. It keeps running onto his hand from his cone. I show him how to lick the edges. He doesn't listen to me, though. It bothers him when he doesn't know something. As we walk into the park, Jale Hanım holds Grandma's arm even tighter.

"Let me help you, Nejla Hanım. And if you'd like, you can do me a favor in return. But only if you like."

"A favor?"

"My dress. It's impossible to find a decent seamstress these days. You're old school. You'd be meticulous and make something refined. Who could be more accomplished than a graduate of the advanced technical school for girls, like yourself. Your generation was really something else."

"My, you do go on, Jale Hanım. All you had to do was ask."

We were walking through the park with our ice creams. Jale Hanım and Grandma sat on a bench. We were going to look at the swans, but Ali ran over to a wall. He looked at the posters. Jale Hanım kept smiling and talking.

"And then, when Bülent appeared on stage, the audience started chanting—you're going to love this—chanting, 'Take it off! Take it off!' Well, the poor guy had a nervous breakdown, right there, on the spot. He left the stage in tears."

"What a shame."

"A shame? What do you mean, Nejla Hanım? Think of how much money he earns a night. And he doesn't pay any taxes. It's in all the papers."

We were looking and looking at the posters when Ali dropped his ice cream. His hand stayed in the air. We were standing in front of the wall in Swan Park.

"Hüseyin Abi! So they are looking for him!"

Jale Hanım came up behind us. "Poor dear," she said, pulling out a handkerchief and wiping Ali's hand. Ali didn't move. "You poor little boy," she said. "Don't cry. I'll get you another one. And it was your very first ice cream. I feel so sorry for you." Ali didn't even look at Jale Hanım. He looked at me. I ran up and held his hand. We went over to the swans. I was still holding my ice cream, but that was okay. The only thing that mattered was that Jale Hanım didn't see Ali crying.

—

Revolutionaries don't cry, so when Hüseyin Abi looked out at me from the poster I went over to the swans. It got crowded everywhere when a truck with SCHWEPPES on the side drove up. There were women and kids in the back of the truck. Up on top of the truck, men were throwing out these Schweppes plates. People were trying to catch them.

—

They started throwing out Frisbees from the Schweppes truck. I remembered seeing them at Jale Hanım's, in *Weekend*: "The American craze that's wholesome fun for the whole family." You throw it into the air and it spins and spins as it flies. I don't feel like watching them now, not when Ali's crying, but the Frisbees are all different colors and everyone is yelling and screaming.

—

"Throw it to me," they're all yelling. It's so loud. Nobody knows that they're looking for Hüseyin Abi. Only Ayşe knows. She's a good girl, really. She knows a lot of things. The only way I can save the swans is with her. I'm sure of that.

"Since you found some rope, I'm ready to do my jobs, too. I didn't think you'd be able to do it."

"Why not?"

"Because you don't have a Hüseyin Abi and because your mother won't ever leave you with someone else."

"You don't know that! They don't love me very much. I mean, not a whole lot. My grandmother loved me a lot but now she's sick or something."

"Maybe they'll love you more if we save the swans."

"Maybe."

—

"Here! Throw it to me!" they're all yelling. Nobody's looking at the posters. They all have their backs to the wall, so they can't see Hüseyin Abi. Maybe they'd get scared if they saw him. They make so much noise that the swans all run away to the hut in the middle of the lake. We'll save them.

"Ayşe, that's the one we'll save. See it? The little one flapping its wings."

Jale Hanım is still laughing.

"It cracks me up every time I think of it. They're all chanting, "Take it off!" like a bunch of soldiers at a strip show. But Bülent had it coming. The whole country's coming unglued, and yet he prances around with his wigs and his makeup, off in his own world. That'll teach him a lesson! He deserves far worse."

Ali started playing with his strings. He's scared we won't be able to do it. When he gets scared, he plays with his strings. I had to say something.

"When we get home, shall I show you some secret letters? The writing is green. But they're extra secret revolutionary letters. And there are some things in a big yellow envelope. My mother's secret things."

Everyone was yelling so loud Ali couldn't hear me. He's studying the swans. He's so smart!

UNIT 12

A Lie Never Lives to Be Old

Nobody Likes a Liar

When they did that, I started pushing the button on the laugh box. It was morning, and they were eating breakfast real fast, when Dad said to Mom, "Let's have a drink and a little talk tonight. Just you and me." Then, when Mom said to Dad, "Why? Is something wrong? What do you want to talk about?" and her tea glass shook in her hand, and they both went quiet, and they started jiggling their legs under the table, I went and pushed the button. The laughter stopped, so I pushed it again and again. They both yelled at me.

"Ayşe! Stop it!"

Grandma came into the kitchen. She was dressed, with red lipstick on, even. That's because Jale Hanım said to her, "Let's you and I go and visit Mr. Vanishing Cream together, this Saturday. Then you can stop brooding."

"Good morning! Let's have a good weekend, children!"

Mom and Dad shook their heads at Grandma. She crossed her arms on her belly.

"Jale Hanım and I arranged a little Saturday outing for today. I was thinking of taking Ayşe along."

"Mother, speaking of Jale Hanım, what are you doing with that fabric? She's not having you make a dress for her, is she?"

"Good morning, Sevgi! And a good morning to you, too, Aydın!"

Grandma looked a little cross when she went out into the hallway. Mom gathered up the plates and left them in the sink. She put her hands on the counter and leaned there for a bit. Dad went to touch her shoulder, but she turned around before he could. When she bumped into him, she said, "Excuse me," and left the kitchen. Dad looked at me. He lit a cigarette and was about to go out onto the balcony when Mom poked in her head.

"Aydın."

"Yes, dear?" Dad smiled.

"I was wondering . . . what was the name of Aliye Hanım's husband? Ah, it just came to me: Hasan. Could you tell Hasan Bey that I'd like to take Ali and Ayşe to the theater next week? If he'll bring Ali to Kızılay Square, we can meet there. In front of Gima."

"Okay, Sevgi."

The light went out in Dad's face. I pushed the laugh button again. "Yay!" I yelled. Dad gave me a bad look. But I cried a lot last night and said I wouldn't eat if Ali didn't come. That's why Mom said it. And because she's sorry for what she did to Auntie Aliye. Of course, Dad doesn't know that. When his face got dark, I went off to find Mom.

My mom and my grandma were hugging in the hallway. "Mother, you really should take Ayşe and go out for a while. Aydın and I need to talk," Mom said. Grandma leaned close to Mom's ear.

"Loneliness is hard, my girl. Never forget that!"

She was going to smooth Mom's hair, but Mom did this kind of shake of her head. When neither said anything, I pushed the laugh button again, but only Grandma laughed.

"Sweetie! Go on, get dressed. You and I are going on a little trip."

Mom didn't smile.

Because I was looking at Mom, not her, Grandma clapped her hands on her knees.

"I'll get Ayşe a candied apple, too. You'd like that, wouldn't you?"

Mom went into her room. I didn't feel like talking to her either. So I did it again, *hah-hah, hee-hee*, all up and down the hallway.

We stood in front of a shared taxi. All the people inside were looking at us. The driver yelled at Grandma.

"Ma'am, are you getting in or not?"

If I hadn't tugged Grandma, she wouldn't have got in. That's because when we knocked on Jale Hanım's door she said, "Oh no, it completely slipped my mind." She had those round things on her hair, the ones ladies wear on TV to make their hair curly. "If I started getting dressed this minute, it would still take ages. Oh dear. What shall we do?"

Grandma just looked at her.

"Nejla Hanım, why don't the two of you enjoy a day out and then we'll go tomorrow?"

Jale Hanım is so stupid! Grandma got all small as we were going down the stairs. She was going to wipe off her lipstick, but she didn't have her handkerchief. She curled in her lips, stopped on the stairs and said, "Ayşe, my dear, perhaps we won't go after all? I've suddenly grown weary." I yelled, "No! Let's go, Grandma." She looked up the stairwell. Mom and Dad are talking, so we can't go home, not now. She tried to wipe her lips on the inside of her hand, but it didn't work. When we stepped out onto the street she did up her top button. We'd just started walking when the shared taxi to Citadel stopped in front of us. But she said, "Good gracious. Without Jale Hanım, I . . . All alone." And then when the driver shouted, "Are you getting in or not?" I yelled, "Me and Grandma are coming."

When we got into the shared taxi, Grandma became like before in the hamam. She was sad, so I needed to tell her a story, the kind of story that makes the scary feelings go away. Some stories can make the monster under the bed go "poof" and disappear. I held Grandma's hands, the same way Jale Hanım did at the hamam. The shared taxi was jumping up and down, and it was noisy, but I told her a story anyway.

"Listen, Grandma. There was this girl. But she was a curly girl, so curly she thought about everything. You know, curly people think about mixed up, hard things. So, this girl had a friend. A boy. Grandma!"

She wasn't looking at me, so I had to yell. But then everyone turned around and looked at us.

"But I got the butterflies into Parliament, still. When will they love me more, Grandma?"

Everybody clucked like chickens. Grandma said, "Driver, please let us out as soon as it's convenient."

The Citadel is up on top of the hill, but Grandma had us get out of the shared taxi early. "What's come over you?" she asked. She leaned over. "Sweetie, what is it?" When grown-ups bend over me like that, I know it's serious. I had to say something.

"Is it true that Ali's never, ever coming to our house again?"

"You poor dear. Is that what's upset you?"

Grandma took my hand. There's a patisserie on that street with such nice things. She got me a candied apple. I love those candied apples in the beginning, but then, when I bite into it and those hard pieces of red sweetness cut into my mouth, it's not at all nice, not one bit.

"Ahhh! September's come, but the heat is still intolerable. What shall we do, Ayşe? Would you like to go to a museum?"

"Let's go to the pharmacy, Grandma. Remember? You wanted to say something to Cavit Bey."

"I did? What is it I supposedly wanted to say?"

"You're going to tell him everything."

"My stars, Ayşe. You're the drollest little thing alive."

She stopped walking and stopped laughing right at the same time.

"You know, Ayşe, I wish we *could* say everything we want to in life."

Then she laughed again. She opened her top button. We started up the hill. Grandma's hair was getting messed up, but she was laughing, so it didn't matter. She looked so beautiful right then. And her cheeks got pink. I might tell Grandma about the swans later. Maybe she'll even help us.

When we got to the pharmacy, there were two women inside. They were both as old as my grandmother and they sounded like my laugh box, except they were talking, too.

"Cavit Bey, you've heard about Bülent Ersoy flashing his new breasts, haven't you? The whole country's in shock!"

"Breasts on a man, Cavit Bey. And I thought I'd seen everything. Well, the audience certainly got their money's worth—and more."

"That fellow has finally flipped his wig, ladies. So to speak. Well, it was a long time coming."

Grandma and I stood in the doorway. We were waiting for Uncle Cavit to see us. Grandma did her button back up. We went over and pretended to look at the medicines under the glass. I mean, Grandma did, so I did it, too. We could stay there until those two ladies went away. Then Uncle Cavit noticed us.

"Oh! Look who's here. Welcome, Nejla Hanım."

"Don't let us disturb you, Cavit Bey."

"Disturb me? You honor me with your presence. The ladies and I were just—"

"Pleased to meet you."

The women gave a little bow with their heads, but didn't say anything. The shop went quiet. After a moment, one of the ladies said, "Well, we'd best be going, Cavit Bey." He went all the way to the door with them and said, "Do come again soon, ladies." Left on her own, Grandma looked at medicines, and she got a handkerchief and a bottle of cologne off the shelves to wipe my hands. "Let me welcome you, again," Cavit Bey said. "Can I get you some nice cold lemonade?" Grandma undid her top button as she sat down in a chair and said, "If it isn't too much trouble." The helper in the white coat went off to get lemonade. Grandma looked at Cavit Bey a little, then. They looked at each other and smiled. "So, how can I be of service?" Cavit Bey asked.

When Grandma started talking, I walked a little further along to look at the other medicines.

"Cavit Bey . . ."

"Your wish is my command, Madam."

"It is not my wish to command, Cavit Bey. I wish only to speak. What I am about to say might surprise, but please do me the courtesy of listening until I have finished. Perhaps you'll dismiss my words as childish or naïve, but surely one of the joys of growing old is the greater ease with which one can be frank, even if, ultimately, one makes a fool of oneself. Do you not agree?"

"Absolutely, Madam. And I know for a certainty that you would never make a fool of yourself."

"Now, if you'll permit me."

"I'm listening."

"As you know, we, the two of us, belong to another time. We could never have imagined that our country would come to this! But it has occurred to me that we may be partly to blame. I wonder, sometimes, if we failed to take enough interest in our children. Or perhaps, secure in our assumption that everyone thought exactly the same way we do, we failed to appreciate and understand what was happening under our very noses. We pursued what we assumed was a common set of ideals. Even now, at my age, I tremble with emotion during every national holiday, Cavit Bey. My breast still swells with pride every time a child of our republic enjoys success in a foreign land. Nowadays, such sentiments are regarded with amusement, or even disdain. But that is how we were brought up and those were the values instilled in us. I remember what a hardship it was to get me enrolled in middle school. Hunger was widespread in those years. You remember. I'll never forget the days when I had nothing in my lunchbox but the fish bones from yesterday's dinner. Sitting in a corner of the schoolyard, I would gnaw at what little meat remained on those bones. We believed, back then, that an education would enable us all to work harder than ever for our country, to work all together for a brighter future. We grew up scrimping and saving, and watching American movies. I remember how dumb-founded I was when the first demonstration against the American Sixth Fleet happened, back in 1969. For me, America had always meant Clark Gable and Greta Garbo. Our generation was brought up not to cherish ideas, but to chase a dream. We didn't have time to ponder. We were too busy striving to realize the dream of a modern, secular republic. We thought that if we minded our manners and respected conventions we would never end up alone. Well, as it turns out, life is a great mystery, a puzzle that pays no heed to propriety. Still, it seems to me, Cavit Bey, that while our generation has somehow preserved our youth, the later generations were born old. We, the children of the Republic, were always striving to be the most industrious in our class, to be the most methodical and disciplined. We never considered what it would mean to grow old. Nobody taught us or prepared us for that. Don't you agree, Cavit Bey?"

"Nejla Hanım—"

"I wasn't expecting an answer, Cavit Bey. That was a question straight from the heart. Please hear me out. I realize I'm meandering here."

"It wasn't my intention to interrupt. Please, continue. It's always a pleasure to listen to you."

"The long and the short of it, Cavit Bey, is that growing old apparently doesn't mean one gracefully awaits death. No, it's far more insidious than that. One becomes null and void. A banknote that's been taken out of circulation. Something with no real value that can't simply be tossed into the trash, either. Consigned to a bottom drawer or a forgotten corner. I understand now what it is to grow old and to have your feelings and desires completely disregarded, as though they don't even exist. But, at any age, one is still drawn to the breath of life. We're advised patience, told to wait, as the lovesick rose awaits the ardent song of the nightingale. That's what we were taught. But our country, our people, and even life itself, are nothing but a load of nonsense! These days, everyone prefers to 'spill their guts' and 'get things off their chest.' In our day, that was for teenagers. Blurting out one's deep-est emotions was a mark of immaturity. One didn't bare the deepest yearnings of the soul, just like that. Why, to do so is a form of suicide. One runs the risk of bleeding to death from the cut of rejection. And yet, Cavit Bey, I am prepared to take that risk, now that I've learned that you and your wife have decided to part ways. How do I put this, Cavit Bey? My feelings for you are suicidal."

"Here you go, ma'am, it's your lemonade!"

"Oh, look! He's brought your lemonade."

I'd already got the medicine and put it in my pocket. When the lemonade came, Cavit Bey jumped out of his chair so fast that Grandma was still looking at the spot where he was sitting a second earlier.

"It's a glorious day outside, Nejla Hanım, isn't it? Now that September has arrived we can all breathe a little more easily."

The glass of lemonade was getting wet on the outside with tiny, tiny drops. Grandma wiped it with the same handkerchief she'd used to clean my hands.

"Nejla Hanım, there's a woman who lives in Liberation neighborhood, a terrible gossip. Her name escapes me. But I suspect she is the source of these rumors."

Grandma picked up the glass and wiped away the water on the little plate under it.

"These rumors are baseless. My wife and I remain happily married. I'm not faulting you; others have also fallen for her idle gossip. I have no idea why that woman would say such a thing, though."

As fast as Grandma wiped the glass and plate, it kept getting wet.

"Your kind words have left me speechless and not a little humbled. I am indescribably honored to have been the object of such a heartfelt compliment, and from a true gentlewoman such as yourself, but—"

Crash!

I dropped my lemonade. Actually, I threw it on the floor, but I knew Grandma would think I dropped it. Then I ran straight outside. So Grandma would run after me and get away. She was screaming, "Ayşe! Wait for me, dear! Where are you going?" She was trying to sound mad and trying to run. I don't think she was mad, not really. I kept looking

back when she couldn't keep up with me. I ran all the way to the Eth-
nography Museum, and waited for Grandma in front. She finally came.
She was breathing hard. She looked back over her shoulder.

"Don't worry, Grandma. They can't see you here."

She looked at me. Her eyes got big. I yelled it out as loud as I could.

"Everyone's so stupid, Grandma. Jale Hanım is, and so is Cavit Bey!"

We went into the museum garden. Then something weird happened.
Grandma forgot everything, it seemed.

"We were at the pharmacy, but we didn't get anything. Is that right,
Ayşe?"

I was a little scared. But I mustn't be. I mustn't be, because me and
Ali are going to go to the theater. I pulled it out of my pocket.

"We got this, Grandma."

"What's that, dear?"

"Cough syrup, Grandma."

I held my hand over the bottle so she wouldn't see *Chloroform*. It was
written by hand, but I knew what to look for. I'd practiced at home.
Even though the letters were so small, I saw it, right there on the shelf.

The Truth Always Wins

"This is all I've got. Take it, and clear out. Don't stay in Ankara."

Without looking back, Mom held out her hand. Her hand was looking
for his, there, in the air. Nobody in the restaurant noticed, not yet. They
weren't looking at us. But if they did, and if they recognized him . . .

In the morning, right after Dad left, Mom came running up to me.

"Don't tell your father, my lamb, but we're going somewhere today.
But not a word about it. Okay? Don't tell anyone no matter what.
Okay, Ali?"

She hugged me. I shook my head "no, I won't." My head was hurting. We weren't going to go to Ayşe's ever again. I couldn't ask to go.
Mom said she wouldn't. She said it to my dad the other night.

"Hasan, find me some other work. That lady, Sevgi, seemed like a friend, but she's not."

"I saw her husband the other day. He was hiding in a shop during a protest. I didn't say anything about it to his face. I think he saw me, though. They can't be trusted. I see that now."

"We thought they were with us. . . . Oh, well."

"Let me get back from Amasya, first."

"I still don't see why you have to go. Why can't they get there on their own?"

"He left behind a wife and two daughters. How are they supposed to get to his funeral? I'll be back right away. I'm only staying for a night."

"When are you going?"

"The day after tomorrow. I've got to ask for leave at work first."

"All right then."

That night, after Dad came home from work and we were eating dinner, he laughed and shook his head. He was talking to Mom but his eyes were on me.

"You'll never guess what our boy's done now, Aliye. I found out today that he's a real heartbreaker. You know Aydın Bey's little girl. Ayşe. She's been crying her eyes out. It's Ali this, and Ali that. He's all she talks about. The little rascal! Ali, did you go and steal her heart? What do you have to say for yourself?"

I didn't say anything. Mom laughed, too.

"What's she saying about our Ali?"

"That if he doesn't come to her house she'll never eat again."

"My word!"

"That's what her dad told me. And her mother wants you to bring Ali so she can take them both to the theater."

"Oh, so now she's sorry and trying to make it up to me."

"Do it, Aliye."

"I don't know. I'll have to think about it."

They didn't say anything else about it. And that's when my head started hurting. I couldn't say, "Take me to Ayşe," not to Mom, not after what happened. She doesn't like it there. If I tell her I want to go to the theater, she'll think I'm on their side, that I've become like them. Now we can't save the swans. That's what made my head hurt, and it hasn't stopped.

Mom's holding a piece of paper. We're walking through Ulus and she keeps looking at it. She's holding my hand so tight it hurts a little, but I don't say anything. We're almost running. It's crowded, and if I don't hold her hand she might get lost.

We stop in front of a restaurant. Through the window, I can see rice and chickpeas. And three chickens. It's full of people.

"Ah, this is it," Mom says. "Now listen up, Ali. Not a word, dear. I don't want a peep out of you. Okay?"

I don't understand. Mom sits down and tells the waiter to get some rice "for the boy." We have our backs to the window, so we're looking at the wall. I start to turn around to see the food and the people coming in. "Don't turn around," Mom says. She puts her hand on my leg. "Don't move."

Right about then, he sits down behind us. He whispers.

"Hello."

I was going to yell, but Mom covers my mouth.

"Hello."

"I'm sorry about this, sister. You've had to come all this way. I'll be quick about it. They're looking for me. I came to Ankara, but I need to leave."

"If it's money you need, I haven't got any. This is all I've got. Take it, and clear out. Don't stay in Ankara."

Mom hands her wedding ring to Hüseyin Abi. Her hand looks for his hand. Nobody looks at us, but if they did, and if they recognized him . . . I can't look at Hüseyin Abi. I wonder if he looks like the photo on the "Wanted" poster. If I don't look, and if I forget Hüseyin Abi, will I always remember him from that photo? Mom still has her hand over my mouth. The things I want to shout can't get out. I wish Hüseyin Abi would say, "Get over here. Why have you got that crazy look in your eye again?" But I can't make a sound. Unless I . . . I stick my hand in my pocket. They're still talking.

"I won't take it, sister."

"Take it. What do I need a ring for?"

Click, click, click. It's too noisy. Hüseyin Abi can't hear it.

"I've got it. Thanks. You need to clear out your coal cellar. I should have told you. I'm the only one who knows. Destroy them. That's number one. And number two—"

"Go on!"

"Look after Birgül. And give her this."

Click, click. Hüseyin Abi! I'm here. I've got your lighter.

"I've got it. Unless there's something else, me and Ali better go."

The rice came.

"Come on, Ali. Eat up your rice."

I don't want any rice! Mom says it again.

"Eat up your rice."

I start eating. My mouth fills with rice. I swallow, and swallow, and swallow without chewing. I don't take a single breath. My hand's in my pocket. *Click, click* . . . I don't want to cry! Hüseyin Abi can't see me cry!

"Have her burn the letter after she reads it."

"Okay. We're going."

We get up. My mouth is so full. The tears are running, and so is snot. I can't open my mouth. Hüseyin Abi looks at me and smiles. I do it again. *Click, click.* He doesn't look like he's "Wanted" anymore. Not one bit. Hüseyin Abi has a big beard now.

We go outside. We get on a bus. Mom's shaking. She looks at me. She leans over and whispers in my ear.

"Don't tell anybody, Ali. Nobody!"

I look at her and look at her. Rice flies out of my mouth. I throw up a lot on the bus.

When the power goes off that night, Mom digs a hole in the garden. Hush, hush. Then she takes the guns out of the sack and buries them. Nobody sees, nobody sees. I see it. A sick cat sniffs at the dirt.

Get away, cat! I'll never eat rice again. *Click, click, click.* We're going to
the theater tomorrow. Because Mom's scared I'll never talk again. She's
scared that I will talk, too.

On the bus, I put my head in Mom's lap. I can see the writing in blue
ink on the back of the seat. So much writing:
    "Long live the brotherhood of the people!"
    "Son of a bitch!"
    "I love you, Ömer!"
And there are a lot hearts, too. With arrows and drops of blood.

A Half Truth Is a Whole Lie

"I don't know, Sevgi. Perhaps I believe in the power of whispering
now. When everyone else is shouting, it's one way to be heard."

"Why did you give these to me in the first place?" Mom said. She was
trying to pull the yellow envelopes out of her handbag, and she was
mad. "As if I've ever managed to keep anything safe."

Everyone is small in the train station because the roof is so high.
There are lots of villagers. A lot of kids with shaved heads. There's a girl,
and even her head is bald. She keeps looking at me. Behind her there's
what I think is a bed. It's rolled up, though, and lots of people are sitting
on it. An old man, an old woman, a young man, a big sister. The big
sister's wearing a purple dress, velvet. On it, there's silver thread. And she
has a picture of a purple rose on her chin. Her shoes are pure white. The
man's wearing black socks, but his shoes are white, too, with little heels.
They're too big for him, but he sure loves those shoes. He keeps looking
at them. And he keeps spitting on his hand, and cleaning them.

There's an uncle with a hat and he has this round red thing he holds
up and puts down. It's for the trains. He's picking his nose. When he
gets snot on his fingertips, he throws it on the floor. Sometimes it's too
wet, and it sticks to his fingers. He can only throw the drier ones. The
wet ones he wipes on his trousers.

There are three big brothers, bald. Resting on their laps are post-cards. They're all the same picture of Youth Park. But they only have one pen, so two of them are waiting. The first one writes real slow. "Is there one 'l' or two in "willing?" he asks. Then he asks the others if they have a "signature." He says, "I haven't worked on one yet. I'll do it when I get in the fucking army." A different brother says, "What good is a signature? You'll only use it when you write home or when you get married." The first one stabs the other one in the leg with the pen. They all think it's funny.

There's so much going on here, so much to look at, but Mom keeps looking inside her handbag.

"These files are so damn big."

Uncle Önder takes Mom's arm.

"Shall we sit for a while in Station Restaurant?"

Mom's shoulders must have been way up. When Uncle Önder said that, I saw them come down.

"Ayşe, would you like a cola?"

She doesn't need to get me a cola. I'm not going to tell Dad. That's because this morning, when Mom pulled her nice shoes out of the closet on the way out the door, I yelled, "I'm coming to Parliament, too!" Mom said, "I've got a lot to do today," and Dad said, "Sevgi, why do you keep wearing those shoes? They cut into your feet and give you blisters." Mom said something about her shoes being "fine" and "what blisters?" and lots of other stuff. And then Dad said, "Well, that's not what Ayşe said. The other day she said those shoes always hurt you." I looked at Mom, and then at Dad, and then back at Mom. She made big eyes and suddenly changed her mind.

"Ayşe, all right then. You're coming with me."

I was going to whisper something into Mom's ear, but she said, "Come on. Be quick about it." Grandma came up and said, "Aydın, my boy, would you mind changing the bulb in the hall light before you go? It exploded again." Dad said he'd do it when he got home, so Grandma said, "Don't forget," but real quiet. Mom didn't look at me even once. I wanted to say, "I didn't tell Dad."

When the cola came to the table, I said, "Aren't you going to put some water in it?" She lit a cigarette without looking at me.

On the way to the station, Mom said, "Ayşe, Uncle Önder's leaving today. We'll never see him again. That's why I need to meet him one last time and give him something. Listen, Ayşe . . ." She talked and talked, but she looked at the ground, not me. When she saw Uncle Önder in the train station, she took my hand. But she hadn't held my hand before.

"Stop doing that, Ayşe!"

They were sitting without talking, so I wanted to make some noise. When I blow into the bottle of cola, it gets all fizzy and almost overflows, so I stop at the last second, and then I do it again. Mom got mad.

"You're going to spill it!"

Mom put her handbag in her lap. She held her knees together. She acted like her handbag was huge, like she couldn't find the yellow envelopes, like she couldn't lift her head from her handbag. Then she slowly pulled out the envelopes.

"They were sealed, weren't they?"

"Yes, but your director must have opened them."

I blew on my cola again.

"It was Abdullah who opened them. The dirty rat!"

I made it fizz again.

"And he did do that, too?"

"Did what?"

"They're burnt. The faces are burnt. I mean, someone burned them. Sevgi, who would do that? Are they nuts?"

"What? There were photos inside? Of children? And they burned them? Who did it? It's outrageous!"

The cola fizzed all the way up to the mouth of the bottle. Then I blew real soft, just to keep the foam there.

"Whose photos are they, Önder?"

"They're childhood photos of our friends who got killed."

"Why did you ever give them to me, anyway?"

"I don't know, Sevgi. Perhaps I believe in the power of whispering now. When everyone else is shouting, it's one way to be heard. It's silly. There are so many photos of dead young men our age. I wanted them to be remembered like this, as children. Everything's being swept away and destroyed. I wanted those photos to be preserved in Parliament. Images of children reciting poetry on national holidays, playing in the park, posing for their school photograph. Stored away and on the record, right there in Parliament, in the heart of the nation. Do you understand? Never mind. Like I said, it's silly. Are you giving back the letters as well?"

"Yes. I can't risk it."

"You mean you can't risk upsetting the order, Sevgi? The order in your home, in your marriage?

Mom didn't laugh. Uncle Önder half-laughed. I stopped fizzing my cola because they didn't understand. If they had, I'd have sprayed cola everywhere.

"There's room for everything in the national archives except for these kids. So, that's how it is, huh, Sevgi?"

Mom looked straight ahead. Uncle Önder looked at a train.

"There will be a record of everything in Parliament but our kids. Okay, I get it. But why did the bastard have to scorch their faces?"

After one last fizz, I drank the whole bottle in one go. Mom lifted her head and looked at me, finally.

The whistle blew. The nose-picker shouted.

"Istanbul Express. Platform One."

Uncle Önder leaned into Mom. He was going to hug her. She took a step back and pulled me in front of her. I stood there, between the two of them. He's handsome, but he should just go now.

A Still Tongue Is Better Than a Lying One

They finally came. We were waiting in front of Gima for Ali and his mom. "They're probably not coming. Ayşe, shall we go now?" Mom said, but I pulled her by the hand.

"They'll come. You'll see."

And then I saw Ali. He was tugging his Mom's hand. Lots of people were getting in their way. I grabbed Mom's hand and pulled her toward them, past all the people. They were banging into my lunchbox.

"Hello, Aliye Hanım. Ayşe was so worried you wouldn't come."

"Hello. The whole neighborhood went off to Çubuklu Reservoir today. But when Ali insisted on going to the theater—"

"The play lasts for two hours. You can get him here when it's done. Aliye Hanım, there's something I want to say to you. You completely misunderstood me the other day."

"Sevgi Hanım, it was you who misunderstood."

"Really?"

"We won't leave our boy with you and run off. We're not that kind of people."

"Aliye Hanım, there's no need to explain. That's why I wanted to see you today. We consider Ali to be our own child. He's stayed over at our house any number of times. And we're the kind of people who don't shirk our responsibilities. Let me put it another way, Aliye Hanım. If something happened to us, would you look after Ayşe?"

"Of course! Of course I would."

"And there's one more thing. If you'd agree, and only if you really want to, it would please us greatly if you came this Thursday, as usual."

"I'll be there, Sevgi Hanım. You can count on it."

———

Ayşe's mother took my mom's hand. Mom took Ayşe's mother's hand. It was the first time they shook hands. My mom was happy. We went to the theater. The entrance to the theater is the most exciting thing in the world. Like the door to a fairy tale.

—

"The Honey That Makes You Go Prrrt!" That's what I yelled, to make Ali laugh. It's the name of the play we're going to see. Then I went, "Prrrt, prrrt, prrrt." And then, while Mom was getting the tickets, I told him, just like that.

"You'll never guess what I did."

"I saw Hüseyin Abi."

"Really?"

"He grew a beard."

"A long one?"

"Yes. I added another thing to my list."

"What?"

"Not to die before I grow a beard."

"Grow a mustache. They're nicer. Ali, I have a surprise for you."

"My head hurt so much."

"Do you know what I did?"

"And I threw up a lot."

"Hey! Ask me! Ask me what I did. Okay, I'll tell you. I got chloroform. Right from the pharmacy, too."

"You did?"

"It's in my lunchbox. I brought it because I knew you wouldn't believe me."

"Let me see."

"Look! Are you glad? Are you? I found it because I could read the little letters. I did a good job. Didn't I?"

"Yes."

"And something else happened, too."

"What?"

"They didn't understand."

"The photos?"

"Yes. Uncle Abdullah works in Parliament, and he's kind of a fascist. Mom thinks he did it."

—

I made a *click click* in my pocket. Ayşe laughed. Nobody else heard.
Only Ayşe knew why we had to burn those photos. They all look like
me. And if they make all those kids "Wanted" and they catch me,
they'll make me say "O Turkish Youth!" at the police station, and then
they'll torture me. They'll kill me and put me in a sack, like the fascists
do in Almond Stream. They could even hog-tie me.

—

I'm glad we burned the photos that day. When we got back from Swan
Park I showed Ali the place where Mom hid the yellow envelopes. They
were in the closet under the extra blankets. With the letters in green
ink. Ali was scared.

"They shouldn't have photos. Photos make it easy to find people
when they're 'Wanted.' They can't find you without photos. That's
why your mom hid them. She doesn't anyone to find them. When the
time comes, they'll all fly away to where the swans go."

"I understand," I said. Then Ali took out his Ibelo. One by one,
he held the fire close to the faces of the children. They turned black
down to the neck. "Don't burn their necks!" I said. Ali asked me why.
"'Cause they have to breathe, silly!"

—

It's noisy at the theater because everyone is happy. Nobody can hear
me and Ayşe.

"Did your mom understand that we took one of the letters?"

"No."

"Not at all?"

"She didn't look at them. They make her cry, so she doesn't look. She
gave them all back to Uncle Önder. But—"

"Shhh. Your mom's coming. Is the letter in your lunchbox?

"Yes. Here, hide it! I can't keep it at home. If Dad finds it . . . Take it!"

—

"Come on, we're going through that door." Mom found us in the middle of all the kids. She put her hand on Ali's head. "Is this your first time at the theater, Ali?" Ali didn't say anything. He just nodded his head yes. "That's nice. You'll be watching your very first play with Ayşe. It'll be a good memory. First times are always unforgettable."

—

The theater's a weird place. Up on the stage, they all have red faces and huge eyes and big mouths. They always shout. They're not like normal people. They're from another world. A nicer world. The big brothers have mustaches like Hüseyin Abi and the others. The big sisters look a lot like Birgül. But they're so happy up there, behind all those lights.

—

It was such a funny play and, best of all, we got to sing along. Ali doesn't like singing, I guess, because he covered his ears. But I loved that song. It's about honey and sharing and making all the sick people well again.

—

All the kids in the audience started singing. Ayşe made my ears hurt. While all the kids were screaming along, her mom got a mirror out of her handbag. She looked at her eyes. With her finger, she pressed the skin under her eyes and above her eyes. She pulled up her eyebrows. She looked at the little white hairs by her ear. She pinched her cheeks.

She set the mirror on the lap and looked at the stage. She never smiled. She's a nice woman. I think she's sad, though.

—

There's this old woman—in the play I mean—and she's terribly poor. And there's a rich man who has honey. The woman asks for a little honey. The man won't give it to her, so she says, "Then everyone who eats this honey will go 'prrrt, prrrt.'" And later, everyone really does go "prrrt," so much that they can't even talk right anymore. Ali keeps looking at Mom. He doesn't like plays or singing. And he didn't do his jobs. I'm doing everything. But bad things keep happening to him, so that's why.

—

Ayşe found chloroform. If Hüseyin Abi were here, he'd say, "If that don't beat all!" He'd say that when someone was really brave. He says it, I mean. All we need now is a sack and a wheelbarrow. I'll be the one to find them.

—

"They said the play was two hours long."

Mom didn't know what to do at first. "We have an hour. What shall we do?" she asked. Me and Ali yelled at the same time.

"Let's go to Swan Park."

Mom laughed.

"Well, it's agreed then. Okay, let's go."

Me and Ali pulled Mom by the hands so we'd get there faster.

"What's the hurry, kids?"

We just got to the park when an auntie yelled.

"What are you doing to that swan? You'll kill the poor thing if you're not careful."

We started running. Us and the auntie were the only ones looking. Nobody saw it but us. "Slow down, kids," Mom shouted. "What's
going on?" Ali ran faster than me. Two men were holding a swan by
the wings. The swan's neck got longer and longer, and wriggled like a
snake.

—

The only sound was the swan's wings. *Flap, flap, flap,* just like the kite.
I knew those men. They were the ones in Uncle Şeref's van. They were
yelling at each other.

"Fold down its wings. Fold them under."

"This one's like an ornery ostrich. Settle down, you bastard."

I was going up to them when I saw Uncle Şeref. He threw down his
cigarette and ran over.

"That's enough! Stop torturing it. There's a right way to do this. Let's
tell the vet to come and get it himself."

The two men smiled at Uncle Şeref just like that day.

"Şeref Abi, I guess you lefties believe in equal rights for animals,
too."

"Get going," Şeref Abi said. He didn't know me. They left the
swan. It was just escaping into the water when one of the men yelled
again.

"You're not going anywhere! I'm going to catch you if it's the last
thing I do. Nobody's going to say I can't even catch a giant chicken like
you."

—

One of the men runs and jumps on the swan. He grabs it by the tail.
The swan sticks out its head. It opens its mouth, but I can't hear anything. Ali's pulling out his hair. His mouth is open, wide. But I can't
hear anything. Mom goes up to the auntie.

"What are they trying to do?"

"I've got no idea. They've been torturing that bird for half an hour at least."

I understand now. We have to save the swan. For Ali. So he can talk. So he won't stand there with his mouth open, not talking. That's why we have to save it.

—

They took the swan to the van. I couldn't stop them. Ayşe was looking at me. But there was nothing I could do. My head started hurting again. Ayşe came up and held my hand.

—

"There's another one over there, Ali," I said. "See it? The little one. We're going to save that one. Don't cry, Ali. Come on, don't cry." Ali didn't cry.

—

Mom is waiting in front of Gima. My head hurts. When Mom saw me, she understood. "What happened?" she asked. Ayşe's mom started talking.

"Aliye Hanım, I didn't understand what they were doing, or why. They wanted to go to Swan Park. So we went there, but . . . something happened to Ali. He didn't say anything, but . . . I wonder if he's ill?"

—

"He's fine," Ali's mom said. She pulled him close and covered his face with her hands. "Let's go," she said. They walked off fast. Auntie Aliye's shoes are too big for her. Just like that man with the white shoes at the train station.

—

Everyone wanted to go to Çubuklu Reservoir, so the municipality took them in a bus, for free. Now the neighborhood's empty. It's so quiet. "It's strange like this," Mom says. "There's not a soul around." She held my hand. My head still hurts. I saw the swan's tongue. That's why. It stuck out its tongue, black and thin. But it didn't make a sound, and now my head hurts. I can't even play with my strings.

—

When we got home, Dad was in the hall. The front door was open and he was looking at something. Grandma was saying, "It must be one of Sevgi's old friends. I can't remember the name. Just throw the light bulb away. You don't have to put it in its box." When we stepped inside, Grandma squeezed her hands together and wrinkled her forehead. In a tiny voice, she said, "Look, Sevgi's home." Then she held my hand, real quick. Dad showed Mom the box. The light in the hall was burning. The old bulb was all covered with dust. "What's this, Sevgi?" Dad asked. "Whose number is it?" Mom stumbled as she was taking off her shoes.

—

Mom was still putting the key in the hole when the door opened all by itself. "Oh no! I must have left the door open. Now that's asking for trouble. Ali, you're hungry. That's why your head hurts. Once I make you some soup, you'll be—Owww!"

The man grabbed Mom by the hair. Another man grabbed my neck. They jumped out from behind the door. I could hear walkie-talkies. Mom was on her knees.

"Don't make a sound, you bitch!"

"This is my house, you bastard!" Mom yelled. He punched her in the face.

"Who are you calling a bastard, you fucking commie bitch!"

Mom banged her head on the floor. I couldn't hear anything.

The man was yelling at me. But I couldn't hear. There were three of them. When they yelled, their eyes and their mouths got close. But the only thing I heard was a *whoosh* in my ears. Mom was saying something, but I couldn't hear her, either. The man hit her every time she tried to talk to me. Dad wasn't there. They threw *Ulduz and the Crows* on the floor.

—

Mom looked at the lightbulb box. I pulled my hand out of Grandma's. I don't want to go to my room. I want to tell Mom that I didn't tell Dad anything. "Sevgi, this number belongs to the Ankara Hotel. Do you know anyone there? Perhaps the man you met at the train station?"

I clapped my hand on my mouth. To keep the sounds in. Dad looked at me.

"Ayşe, who did your mother meet at the train station?"

"What are you saying, Aydın?"

"What do you think? I'm asking who the man is that you met at the train station. What's been going on behind my back? What are you up to, Sevgi?"

Grandma took me into her room. The light was burning bright in the hall. Mom got all small. Dad got bigger and bigger. I could see them through the keyhole, but Grandma pulled me away.

—

The sounds slowly came back. "Don't be scared, Ali! Don't be scared!" Mom was saying. They threw us both onto the cushions. Mom hugged me.

"Do what you will to me. But let the boy go!"

"Do to you? Why would we bother, you dirty bitch! Who do you think you are? Where's Sinan? Tell us. Where'd he go?"

"Who's Sinan? I don't know anyone named Sinan."

They grabbed Mom's hair and banged her head against the wall. They threw her back on the cushions. The big man said, "Why bother with this peasant? Their husbands rough them up so much they don't feel anything. String up the boy from the ceiling."

Mom screamed.

"Leave him alone! I'm begging you, don't hurt my boy."

I couldn't hear anything again.

—

Dad yelled at Mom.

"Look here, Sevgi! I've had it up to here. I've never been good enough for you, but I'm no fool. I've devoted my life to making you happy, and look what I get in return. Are you having an affair, Sevgi?"

"Don't be ridiculous, Aydın."

Something fell over.

"Let go of my arm, Aydın!"

"Enough, Sevgi. Tell me what's going on. Who is he?"

Grandma turned on the radio. I could still hear them. "I've squandered my whole life on you," Dad yelled. "Stop the theatrics," Mom yelled. Something else fell over.

—

"Then tell us where Sinan is."

"I swear I don't anyone by that name."

They're hitting Mom. But I can't say it. I can't tell them Hüseyin Abi's other name is Sinan. They'll find him if I do. But they're hitting Mom, they're hitting Mom because I can't say.

"Hang that kid up by his feet."

"Wait! I'm begging you. Spare my boy."

It won't hurt. Not by the feet. I don't care.

The man holding the back of my neck turns my head so I can see him. "Where's Sinan?"

"He can't talk," Mom says.

"What do you mean? If he can't talk, we'll get him to sing. An anthem would be nice."

"I'll do anything you want, but leave the boy alone."

"I bet you know an anthem. Go on, give us a few lines."

Maybe they'll let Mom go if I do.

"Fear not, for this dawn shall not fade!"

"Fuck off, you little bastard. You see what this runt's doing? He's monkeying around with us. Now sing us one of your revolutionary anthems!"

They throw Mom on the floor again. I can't hear again. I see Mom's tongue, hanging out of her mouth. Maybe she's saying something I can't hear.

—

I looked through the keyhole again. Grandma said, "Shame on you!" I pushed her hand away, though.

"Let go of me, Önder!"

"Önder?"

"Goddamn it. Let go of me, Aydın."

"Who's Önder, Sevgi? Tell me!"

Dad had Mom by the arm and when he pushed she hit the wall. She cried even more. She ran to their bedroom and locked the door. Dad was yelling in the hall.

"Either come out and tell me everything or it's over. Sevgi, do you hear me? Sevgi!"

The doorbell rang. The door was still open, but the bell rang.

—

"Put that Alevi bastard in that sack. Look here, woman! We know you've been meeting with Sinan. Of course, you know him as Hüseyin.

I want that son of a bitch and I want him now. Tell me where he is or I'll throw this brat off the top of Almond Stream hill. You'll hear his screams from here."

Mom couldn't say anything she was crying so hard. She tried. Words came out.

"What . . . I don't know . . . my arm."

"So you're not going to talk, huh? Okay then. We've got all the time in the world. Nobody move. We'll sit here until Sinan comes."

They made me and Mom sit on the cushions. We stayed there. They got on their walkie-talkie and ordered food. None of our neighbors came. It got dark. Mom was still crying. The men smoked lots of cigarettes. They laughed a lot, too.

"So, I hear you Alevis like to fuck each other all the time. Go on, tell us about it."

Mom didn't say anything. One of the men yelled at me.

"Do you even know who your dad is?"

"Prrrt!" was all I could say.

"What?"

"Prrrt!"

"Are you nuts, kid?"

"Prrrt!"

Mom got on top of me. They hit her. And when they kept hitting her, she got heavier and heavier. "Prrrt, prrrt!" I couldn't stop.

—

Jale Hanım was at the door. She was talking a lot, and loud, too. And she was trying to look inside, past my father.

"I hope this isn't a bad time. Nejla Hanım left some fabric with my daughter Feride when I wasn't home. She said she wasn't going to make me a dress. Naturally, I was wondering why she changed her mind and thought I'd stop by to—"

"Why don't you come another time, Jale Hanım?"

"I do apologize."

"That's okay. Later."

Dad closed the door in Jale Hanım's face. Mom was crying in the bedroom. I looked at Grandma. She was covering her mouth with her hand.

—

Later, much later, Mom said, "The boy's hungry." I was hanging from my feet. It scared them when I didn't make a sound. "He's retarded," Mom said. "You won't get anything out of him." They let me down after a while. Mom rubbed my ankles. Then, later, she said I was hungry and she wanted to make some soup. They said she could. She went to the kitchen. She lit the stove and stirred flour into some water. Steam rose up and the soup bubbled and bubbled. The window got steamy. She wrote "police" on the glass. Someone yelled from the other room.

"Where's that soup? Why's it taking so long?"

Mom wiped the window with her hand. She turned off the stove.

It was almost morning. I must have fallen asleep. The noise woke me up. Mom was saying, "Let me leave the boy with a neighbor. He can't stay home alone." But the man said, "Someone will come and find him." They took Mom away.

I found a candle. I lit it with my Ibelo. While it burned, it got darker everywhere. Nobody came.

—

I slept with Grandma that night. Mom didn't come out of her room. Dad didn't come home at all. I woke up in the middle of the night and went to my room. The laugh box was there. I threw it out the window.

UNIT 13

The Tenth Anniversary Anthem

"We Wove a Web of Iron"

"I swear it, Nejla Hanım. Cross my heart and hope to die, I swear I thought it was true. Why would I lie to you, dear? Am I crazy?"

The keychain in Jale Hanım's hand is swinging back and forth. She sits in the chair, legs crossed, shaking her leg and making her slipper *slap-slap* the bottom of her foot. She's cross, ever so cross. Grandma can't look at her. It's Grandma who's embarrassed, not Jale Hanım.

"I was utterly bewildered, Jale Hanım. Words fail to convey the awkwardness of the situation. To have acted so impulsively, so rashly . . . on a false rumor, no less—and at my age!"

"Nejla Hanım, don't even try it! You can't do this to me. A false rumor? I tell you, I'm not having it! You wrong me."

Grandma got even more embarrassed. She pulled a bit of thread out of the seam of her skirt and rolled it into a ball. Then she found another loose thread. Jale Hanım won't be quiet.

"We're next-door neighbors, and yet you accuse me of . . . Who does Cavit Bey think he is, anyway? That randy old goat! How dare he try to come between us. I won't stand for it, Nejla Hanım. I won't! Are you really prepared to risk our friendship?"

I don't quite understand how it happened, but Grandma apologized a second time. Jale Hanım seemed to forgive her. She even laughed.

"Never mind, dear. Even the best of friends can have their little misunderstandings. Don't fret. Let's get back to my dress, or it'll be too late. I'm sure you'll get it done in time, though. You've got the nimblest fingers in all of Ankara. The young women have nothing on you, my dear. Ha-hah!"

Grandma tried to laugh, too. I didn't want to watch it anymore, so I walked around the house to check my things.

I found the bobby pin, still trapped under the carpet. But Mom doesn't call out to Dad with the news anymore. They don't talk about politics, even, because we don't visit Samim Abla and Ayla Abla. If we did, maybe they'd talk again. You can't be mad, not in front of other people, not when you're a guest. So, no more bobby pins dropped out of Mom's hair when she was calling out the news to Dad. That was the last one. There won't be any more.

Grandma's pulling out the fabric as far as her arms will go, left and right. "One, two, three . . . There's enough here for the skirt." Jale Hanım won't be quiet.

"They're pouring the first concrete for the metro on the ninth of September. If Prime Minister Demirel tries to stop them, a group of 'young volunteers' are apparently standing by to build the metro themselves. Our mayor's out of control. If he had his way, Ankara would become another hotbed of communism, worse even than Fatsa. We all know what he means by 'young volunteers.' It's code for 'terrorists.' Kızılay Square's going to turn into a battlefield on Tuesday, the communists versus the government. I mean, really! Who cares about trains anymore? In the end, that's what it'll be, an underground train. The communists are such a bunch of reactionaries. They don't want anyone to drive around in their own car, nice and comfy."

Dad's button is still here on the windowsill, the one from his sleeve. There won't be any more buttons, though. Dad won't say, "Come quick,

Sevgi!" They won't watch the news and get sad together. I mean, they're still getting sad, but not together. And they don't want to be "nice and comfy" in their own cars.

"Well, who did you think I was talking about? My Ferit. The bridegroom! Anyway, he made a fortune with Banker Kastelli. I'm telling you, the boy's sharp as a tack. He doesn't pay any mind to those leftists and their whining. Why, Demirel himself praised Kastelli to the skies, calling him a trailblazer in the transition to a market economy. And that's even before the government has managed to pass its reforms. And he's so generous, too. Nejla Hanım, don't breathe a word of this to anyone, but Ferit's taken a big chunk of the money he earned and gotten the most delightful wedding gift for my girl: a summer house in Bodrum! Isn't he wonderful? Such a thoughtful boy. And he's got 'vision,' which we can all agree is just what our country needs right now."

"If we drape the bodice, we won't have an inch to spare, Jale Hanım. We might run out of fabric." Grandma's working fast to make Jale Hanım go home. "You might have to do without a draped bodice."

"What? No bodice? You'll have to manage it, Nejla Hanım. I simply must have something that's both sophisticated and flashy."

The pin's still in the corner of the shelf, still tittering like fox whiskers. But Grandma's not laughing much these days. And when she does laugh, it's a Sue Ellen laugh. The house smelled happy and nice when she used to make börek. Now she hardly ever cooks. And when she does, she gets mixed up. She forgets. Her food smells wrong and tastes wrong.

"Oh, before I forget: you'll never believe the latest on Bülent Ersoy. After he flashed his boobs to the audience at the fair, the police marched him straight to the station. I can't tell you how relieved I was, Nejla Hanım. That's the end of that, finally. He'll shape up now if he knows what's good for him, and we'll get to talk about something else, for a change."

"They've come down hard on the poor girl."

"Poor? Girl? God forbid! He's got more money than he knows what to do with, which is why he went out and bought himself a pair of tits. Your fingers are nimble, Nejla Hanım, but if you think Bülent's a woman your mind's not what it what used to be. Well, you're no spring chicken, I suppose."

Grandma froze. So did I. Jale Hanım doesn't know how mad Grandma is. She doesn't see the things I do. A hard look, a lifted eyebrow, lips pressed tight. When you see those things, you're supposed to be quiet.

"Enough! Jale Hanım, I think it's time you and your fabric went home. I've had quite enough of you, your rich bridegroom, your gossip, and your Bülent Ersoy. Leave me in peace!"

Grandma kind of rolled up the fabric, but in the air, so not really. She shoved it into a bag.

"Hey, what are you getting so sore about? What did I say?"

"You've said more than enough. I won't be ridiculed, not at my age. Now off you go!"

"Are you throwing me out? Is that how you treat your guests?"

"Stop talking, Jale Hanım, and go."

"I should have known. What can you expect from a communist? That's how they treat their guests. Just wait until I tell my husband."

"Tell the whole world. Go and file a complaint with the martial law commander, for all I care."

"Look here, Nejla Hanım! I've got connections. You don't know who you're dealing with."

"Go! Get out!"

"I'll show you. And I'll show that communist daughter and son-in-law of yours, too. You'll be sorry then, but it'll be too late."

Jale Hanım yelled all the way to her house, slippers slap-slapping on every stair. Grandma slammed the door.

"Oh! What a relief! Sweetie, I felt like an ox was sitting right here, on my chest, and now it's finally got up and gone."

Grandma undid her collar button and pulled her hair up and off the back of her neck. Her face was red. She switched on the fan.

When she stood in front of the fan, it smelled like Grandma. The living room smelled like Grandma's soap. She uses a little piece of it to mark the fabric, that's why. Grandma closed her eyes. She forgot all about me. I went and looked in the drawer. The flattened box with the telephone number was gone. Dad must have taken it with him.

Eyes closed, Grandma turned her throat to the fan. Nobody talks anymore. Maybe they will if me and Ali save the swans. We'll be on the news, and Dad will say, "Sevgi, come here quick!" And Mom will say, "I don't believe it!" Grandma will come up with a pair of tongs in her hand. "Turn up the volume so I can hear it," she'll say. "I can't leave the kitchen. The börek will burn." The house will smell like it should again. They'll even go out on the balcony and call out: "Samim! Ayla! Turn on the TV. It's Ayşe and Ali!"

Grandma still hasn't opened her eyes. She's singing to herself.

> *In the cellar, wine matures through the years*
> *In my heart, your love matures through the years*
> *And now, of a sudden, I drink of them both*
> *For believe me, believe me, believe me . . .*
> *I am aflame.*

We can't save the swans without a wheelbarrow and a sack. The two things only Ali can get. Maybe he'll bring them Thursday. Maybe I'll die before then. If there's a fight, I could die. We could all die. But there are the swans, and there's Ali, so I'm not going to die. And I don't have to die so they love me more. When we save the swans, that's what they'll do, anyway. I know it.

"We Acquitted Ourselves Honorably"

When the candle went out, it was getting light. I was down under the cushions. Then I picked up the sack, the one they were going to put me in, the one I was going to die in, maybe. I got into the sack. Is this what it's like to be a silkworm in its cocoon?

Things were happening, but it's like they weren't. And because of that, I wasn't scared. I was in a cocoon. The world was outside the cocoon. And there was something else, too. I was in a book or on TV, but it wasn't the real me. And those men didn't take away my mom, not the real one. It was the mom in the book or the movie whose mouth the man covered when she begged him to let her take me to a neighbor. That's what made me go down under the cushions and play with my strings. In the morning, I could hear sounds outside, but I wasn't there, not the real me, so I couldn't come out. Even if I tried to say something, nothing would come out. That's how I felt. I heard sounds. Birgül Abla came and sat in our garden. She smoked a cigarette, because I heard a match. She drank tea, because I heard the clink of the spoon. There's another big sister with her, because I hear her reading the news to Birgül Abla.

"Our side can barely shoot straight, but five of them managed to break into a prison in Konya and free seven fascists. And I don't know if you've heard about the fascists in Akdere. They're leaving notes at all the houses saying, 'You have one day to move out, or we'll kill you.'"

"I can't believe Aliye Abla is still sleeping. I wish she'd get up."

"What do you want with her?"

"Nothing. I was going to stop in. I like her a lot. And Ali's such a cute kid."

"Birgül, what do you think about Vedat?"

"I don't know what to say."

"The neighborhood doesn't think much of him. He's a smart guy, but he's not as friendly or as practical as Hüseyin. All he thinks about is the cooperative. He's missing the big picture. We need to do something big. Don't you think so?"

"We'll have to get used to him. It's true, though, even Ali's been different since Hüseyin left. I can't believe that boy's still in bed. Poor kid."

Poor kid? Is that me? Is she saying that because all I have left of the car is the red string to pull it? There's nothing fascists won't do. They break into prisons, they take your car, they stop you from getting water. But we're going to win, that's what they all say. Mom's not sleeping. She's not here. I'm here, but if I say it, it won't come out. They won't hear me. I want to see Birgül Abla. But I can't come out, can't leave my strings. I need my strings. Maybe I'll stay under the cushions until I die. Or not talk until I die.

"Oh, come on! What's this doing in one of our newspapers?"
    "What is it?"
    "Bülent Ersoy! The revolutionaries in the left-wing press just had to cover the dramas of a singer. 'Are you a man, or a woman?' the headline asks. The article itself focuses on alleged tax evasion at the İzmir Fair. You know, as befits a 'serious' newspaper. Well, I'm not falling for it."
    "People lap that kind of thing up. They won't leave Bülent Ersoy alone until they've picked his bones clean."
    "Birgül!"
    "What is it now?"
    "What was the name of that Black Sea woman who just joined us?"
    "Do you mean Nuran?"
    "That's it. She asks why they don't take the money we raised for arms and give it to Kastelli. I can't help feeling we've lost our way."

Maybe everyone feels like I do, even Birgül Abla. Like none of this is happening. Here, under the cushions. Even Bülent Ersoy. When I wrap the silver braid from my circumcision hat around my finger, it comes apart down the middle, like it's two strings, not one. But then it becomes one again. We became men that day. We cried. We were scared. Then we were men, not kids. There's no going back. The string comes apart. I'm a man now. I have to act like a man. Or they'll pick my bones clean.

"Birgül, are we going to go to the groundbreaking for the metro? Has the municipality invited us?"

"We're going."

"Have you heard about the minister of public works? He said the metro's no different from a shanty house and that they'll tear it down. The mayor's trying to build a metro all on his own, but the government is determined to block him. What's wrong with these people?"

"I think we should check in on Aliye Abla. She's always up by this time. Did you see her yesterday? They didn't come to the reservoir with us."

"She said she was going to take Ali to the theater yesterday."

"I'm going to check. Maybe something's wrong."

I mustn't be scared, mustn't cry, mustn't make a sound. Birgül Abla doesn't know I'm here. Maybe something's wrong. Why did Samim Abi have Hüseyin Abi's Ibelo? Why was his "Wanted" photo so ugly? If I told them where he was, would they have let Mom stay home? Maybe they wouldn't find him. Does Birgül Abla know what to do? I need a wheelbarrow. For the swans. And for Mom. But I can't make a sound. I'm sorry, Birgül Abla. I can't. Will she find me? I want her to. Find me.

"The door isn't closed all the way. What's going on?"

I'm yelling to Birgül Abla but inside. I can't make a sound.

"Someone's been here! Look! Everything's scattered all over the place."

Can you hear me, Birgül Abla? *Click, click.* Don't yell. You won't hear me. *Click, click.*

"Do you hear that? What's that sound?"

"What sound, Birgül?"

"It's coming from over there. From under all those cushions. Shhh! A lighter! Ali! Ali! What are you doing in there? Are you okay? Ali, come out of there. What happened? Who put you in that sack?"

Birgül Abla asked lots of questions. So many questions. I can't open my mouth. They can't hear me. She's asking and asking and asking. And I'm telling her, but not with my mouth. I can't, I can't. And then I can, but my mouth's stuck together. It's dry and it's cracking. But the words come out, in pieces.

"Birgül Abla. A wheelbarrow. How?"

She hugs me. If she hugs me, maybe. Not now, but maybe, I can tell her. I want to come back. I want to be here, all of me. I want to talk, to tell her. She's hugging me, nice and warm. Warm and nice, but not soft like Mom. The swans. I want to save them. With Ayşe.

"15 Million Youths in Ten Years"

"How many people have died, Aydın Abi? And that's without factoring in all those who have been terrorized, alienated, enraged, and disillusioned by all the killing. If you mow down plants year after year, for ten years, right from the root, do they ever grow back? Sometimes I wonder if people are going to give up and stop having children. Aydın Abi, aren't you listening to me? Not you, too!"

Detective Nahit yelled it. Everyone looked at us. They're all policemen, but they have mustaches like Dad's, so there's nothing to be scared of. They're all from the Law Enforcement Association. That means they're good cops. Dad told me about it on the way to the meeting. It hasn't started yet, so everyone's standing. Dad's going to give them a sociology lesson. It's called the social sciences, or something, but we won't do it until fourth grade. Dad doesn't want to be here. I can tell. He's jiggling his leg.

"Detective, it must be that Mustafa Pehlivanoğlu business that's bugging you. I guess you feel sorry for him, and now . . . Just forget about it. It's not your fault."

Detective Nahit banged his fist on the table.

"It's never anyone's fault, is it? That's the problem with this country."

Two policemen came over. They've got walkie-talkies that go *khhh khhh*. They want Detective Nahit to get up. His fingers are bleeding. There's no more fingernail left for him to chew. The tall one with the bushy mustache is mad.

"Nahit, are you drunk or what?"

"He's not drunk, Chief. He's just cracking up a little."

"Take him to the bathroom. Get him to wash his face. And get him a strong cup of coffee. What's the matter with him?"

Dad talked to the chief while Detective Nahit was in the bathroom.

"Sir, I think Nahit's kind of shook up by this Mustafa Pehlivanoğlu—"

"No, that's not it. It's more than that. Nahit told me something about a friend of his. This friend asked to have his wife followed. And his neighbors, too. And the guy's supposedly a leftist, one of us. Everyone's going out of their minds these days. By the way, I didn't catch you name."

"Aydın. I'm speaking at the seminar."

"Welcome, Aydın Bey. Let me thank you on behalf of the association. Anyway, that's what's bugging Nahit. What's worse is that he saw the guy's wife with another man. And the neighbors are up to something, too. It's weird. Nahit's been totally unfazed by all the fascist massacres and the psychos he's had to deal with, but when it comes to this friend of his . . . It's different when you can't trust your own friends. At this rate, none of us are going to have friends left."

Dad lifted his eyebrows, blinked, and played with his mustache. The chief played with his mustache, too. They all did. All around me were twirled mustaches and the *khhh khhh* of the walkie talkies. Dad was right. This is no place for a child.

After lunch, Grandma had said, "Come on, we're going. I need to do something. If I don't, your mother and father are going to end it. Come on, Ayşe, put on your shoes."

We surprised Dad at his workplace.

"Is anything wrong, Nejla Hanım? What are you doing here?"

"Aydın, I wonder if I could leave Ayşe with you. I need to talk to my daughter alone. This has to stop."

"Is Sevgi expecting you?"

"No. I'm going to surprise her. I'll take her out for a beer. Ayşe has to stay here."

"Nejla Hanım, perhaps it's best you stay out of this?"

"Is that so, Aydın? You're doing such a good job, you're afraid I'll make things worse, is that it? It's not fair to the child, Aydın. Anyway, Sevgi's got issues with me, not you. Because . . . never mind! Look after Ayşe, would you? See you at home this evening."

"I've got a seminar with the police this evening, Nejla Hanım. It's no place for a child."

"Right now, your home's no place for a child, Aydın!"

They turned down the sound on their walkie-talkies, pulled up chairs, and sat down with their arms crossed. Dad got up and stood in front of them. "Sociology," he said, "is a hybrid word formed from the Latin *socius* and the Greek-derived *-logy*."

He stopped. I thought he wouldn't be able to talk anymore. Then he laughed.

"This may be one of my last lectures. With twenty or thirty people getting killed every single day, we sociologists won't have a society left to study!"

Nobody laughed. Then Dad talked to the policemen for a long time. I was bored, so I watched them. Some of them wrote things in their notebooks. All of them smoked. Only Detective Nahit slept with his chin on his chest. When noise came out of his nose, he woke up. Then he fell asleep again.

When Dad was done, he said, "I'll try to answer any questions you might have." One of the cops raised his hand, kind of, partway, but then he put it down again. They all turned up their walkie-talkies. Maybe they didn't want to talk. They wanted their walkies-talkies to talk for them.

Afterwards, Detective Nahit walked down the stairs with us. His eyes were all red. Dad put his hand on his shoulder.

"Nahit, have you been able to find anything out about Samim?"

"Aydın Abi, it's kind of complicated. Oh, screw it!"

"What are you talking about, Nahit Abi?"

"Everyone's doing what they can. That's the best way to look at it. And nothing's a crime, because nothing is anyone's fault. Think of it that way, Aydın Abi."

"I'll decide for myself what I think. But you haven't really told me anything, Nahit."

"Well, Samim and . . . now what was his wife's name? Ah, Ayla. The two of them . . . we've got everything under control. You can rest easy. We're on top of things."

"For God's sake, Nahit! Tell me what's going on."

"I will, but on one condition: Never ask me to do this again, Aydın Abi. So, here's what we learned . . ."

I don't want to hear. Dad's listening and playing with his mustache again. I don't hear a word. It's awful. It's shameful. I'm ashamed of myself. I don't want to give back Mischa the Bear. If we don't like them anymore, I'll have to, though. It would be wrong not to.

"Ayşe, hold my hand when we cross the street!"

"No! I'm going to walk alone."

"What's got into you, Ayşe?"

I'm ashamed. That's why I start flapping my arms, like a butterfly.

"I'm a butterfly now, Daddy. I don't have any hands."

"In Every Battle for Ten Years"

"Aliye!"

Dad sounds like a mosquito. Mom came through the door. Policemen hold her by the arms, because she can't step on the ground. Her feet are huge.

"Aliye, what have they done to you?"

When Dad ran over to Mom, one of the policemen punched him. He's on the floor now.

"Shut your fucking mouth. No talking. Just tell us where the guns are."

Mom threw herself on the floor and hugged the policeman's legs.

"I'm begging you. Just let me get a bowl of pickles."

"What? Pickles! This bitch is talking about pickles."

"I promised her. She's going to have a baby soon. They tortured her. She's craving pickles. I promised."

"You said you'd show us where the guns where. We didn't come all this way for your fucking pickles or for anything else. Show us. Now!"

"Don't kick me. Let me get some pickles first. They're tasty. I'll give you some, too. Don't kick me."

But they do kick Mom. Dad flies up from the floor and they kick him in the head. They're both on the floor. Am I here? Is this happening?

After I came out of the sack and Birgül found me, we waited for two days. I slept with Birgül Abla. She flops around in her sleep. I kiss her arms when she moves them around like that. She has a broken wing, that's what Mom said. I never woke her up. I kissed her soft as a bird. Dad came home two days later. They'd arrested him in Amasya because he looked like one of the "Wanted" men. Dad hugged me. He cried, but I didn't. Birgül Abla told him what happened. I couldn't.

Then Dad squatted in the garden. He lit a cigarette and stayed there like that, squatting. For five cigarettes. Birgül Abla sat on the ground next to him. I didn't move. I stayed on the cushions and watched them from the window. "We'll have to wait," Birgül Abla said to Dad. He squeezed the end of the burning cigarette between his fingers.

"They'll let her go, Hasan Abi. Don't worry."

He squeezed the fire between his fingers again. The fire got buried deep inside the cigarette and the paper got black. The cigarette choked on fire. Dad's throat was like that, too. Choked on fire.

We waited two more days. Dad smoked the butts of his cigarettes. He didn't go to work. And then it was evening and Mom came home.

They'd beat the bottoms of Mom's feet with a big stick. That's why her feet were huge. I knew they did that, from before. She can't walk. I knew we had pickles, too.

The police got tired of kicking Mom. She crawled to the kitchen. "They're tasty. I'll give you some, too."

One of the cops laughed.

"Go on, then. I love a good homemade pickle."

Blood was dripping out of Mom's nose. She got to the kitchen. Grabbed the door. Pulled herself up. I followed her. She smiled at me.

"Don't be scared, my little lamb. Never be scared."

She put pickles in two bowls. One of them, she set in front of the policemen. So slow, everything was so slow.

"Please, let me take the other bowl to that girl. Then you can do whatever you want. I don't care."

"Yeah, okay," one of the cops said. They were crunching pickles, picking them up with their hands. They took Mom by the arms again. A little juice splashed out of the bowl she was holding, crooked.

Dad stayed on the floor until nighttime. Birgül Abla came, and so did the other big sisters. We waited two more days. Then, early one morning, her salwar torn, Mom came through the door. It opened— the door—and banged against the wall. Mom was hanging on to the door. Barefoot. Dad jumped up and grabbed her. He lay her down on the cushions. She breathed and talked, breathed and talked.

"They left me somewhere in Ulus, the bastards. I didn't have any money. A taxi driver brought me home."

Mom smells like pee. She laughs.

"They punched me in the car, but I kept my promise. And she got her pickles."

Dad's laugh was snotty, because he was crying. They hugged for the first time. The first time in front of me.

Mom kissed my arm. Because it's broken. It's badly broken, though. It won't get better with a kiss. I need a new wing.

"The Breadth and Width of the Motherland"

At night, Mom got up, slowly, because of hurting so bad. To my Dad, she said, "Hasan, take me outside. I've got something to say." I watched from the window as Mom showed the place where the guns were buried. Mom and Dad stood there like they were praying beside a grave. Then they went to the coal cellar. Dad didn't want to go, but he had to, to hold up Mom. They stayed there for a moment. When they came out, Dad was holding something. They came inside the house and looked at me. "Give it to me," Mom said. She lay down on the cushions. "Come here, my little lamb," she said. "This parka was your uncle's." She pulled it out of the sack. It smelled nasty. Like coal. Dad said, "Don't, Aliye. We'll be coming straight back from the hospital. Don't act like you're going to your grave—" Mom didn't let him finish. "Hush," she said. Then she looked at me and smiled.

"Ali, me and your Dad are going to the hospital tomorrow. I want you to have this parka. It's yours now. You'll keep it."

I put on the parka. It was huge. I sat down on the edge of a cushion, next to Mom. She rolled up the sleeves. My head was buried, that's how big the parka was. I looked at the bloodstain on the collar. It was black, because it was so old. Dad lit a cigarette. He squatted in front of the door with his back to us. Because I was wearing the parka, Mom hugged me. She sniffed me. For her, there was no stink of coal. "Oh!" she said.

In the morning, when I was leaving with Birgül Abla, I had the parka in its sack. "What are you going to do with that?" she asked. "What's in it?" Mom was getting into Teslim Abi's taxi to go to the hospital. She yelled to Birgül Abla.

"Leave him be, Birgül Abla. Let him take it with him."

Me and Birgül Abla waited for the bus to take us to Kızılay Square. The men waiting for a shared taxi were talking.

"They've finally arrested Bülent Ersoy."

"You're kidding. Because of his breasts?"

"No, an inspector came to his house over a rent dispute, and he started carrying on, or something, so he got arrested."

"Where will they jail him? With the men or with the women?"

"They gave him his own private cell."

"Really?"

"And his own TV."

"Really?"

"He's been crying in his cell the whole time. That's what it says in the paper."

"Let him cry! We've been getting tortured to death while he cries in front of his TV."

The men looked at us.

"If you're waiting for the bus, don't bother. There's no more service."

"What do you mean?"

"Somebody tipped over a bus the other day. They set up a barricade and lit it on fire. They say it was the fascists from Almond Stream, but I'm not so sure. Haven't you heard about it?"

Birgül Abla gave my hand a squeeze.

"Yes, I have. I heard it was an accident, though."

"Well, the mayor's cancelled service to Rambling Gardens. He wants to teach us a lesson."

"You're kidding!"

"It's a terrible disgrace for our neighborhood. You should go and talk to the municipality. People are having trouble getting to work."

"We'll see what we can do. So, you're saying there are no buses today?"

"You'll have to walk."

Birgül Abla looked at me.

"Can you walk that far, Ali?"

I nodded my head.

"Okay. But if you get tired on the way I haven't got any money for a shared taxi. Are you sure?"

I nodded my head again.

"All right then."

I looked at her.

"Ali, do you have to carry that sack all the way? Shall we leave it at home?"

I shook my head no.

"Ali, aren't you going to talk? All you're doing is shaking your head."

"Nope! I won't talk."

Birgül Abla smiled. After we get to Kızılay, we're going to Liberation. Birgül Abla is taking me to Ayşe's. I'm going to tell her my mom's sick and can't come. Maybe I'll stay the night there "if they're willing." Dad's taking Mom to the hospital. Her belly got all swollen. And last night she was bleeding "down there." Everyone in the neighborhood is going to the metro groundbreaking today. They want to support the mayor. Nobody knows what's going to happen. It might even be like September 9th in the War of Liberation. That's the day we drove the Greeks into the sea and freed İzmir. It's the reason the mayor's holding the groundbreaking on September 9th. He says either the prime minister and the fascists are going to bury us in the excavation site, or we're going to bury them. So, everyone is going there today. Even the kids. We sent Mom and Dad to the hospital, and then we left home.

—

Grandma whispered into my ear, waking me up, pulling back the cover with her fingertips.

"Time to get up, sweetie. You and I are going out this morning."

I wasn't awake, not yet. I tried to remember.

It's morning. This isn't a nap. I went to bed last night, sad, because Mom and Dad were saying terrible things. I'm still sad. In the morning, we were going to go out. The metro. Going to the groundbreaking for the metro. There were butterflies in my dream, butterflies I couldn't catch. And swans, of course. But we couldn't save them. The dream ended too soon. Like always.

Grandma is talking with the tips of her lips, slowly lifting the cover with the tips of her fingers, coming closer with the tip of her nose. Everything is tiny, just the tip. Like a cat's nose. Grandma is wearing trousers, and that means fun. She has me wear overalls, too, the ones I love. When we both wear trousers, it's like we're both happy. If I wear a skirt and shirt, bad things can happen. But now, like this, it feels like we're going out to the countryside. Like nobody will look at us, so we don't care. Like everything's comfortable and easy.

Grandma's holding my hand inside the house. You're not supposed to hold hands at home! Why are we walking in secret? Then I hear Mom and Dad in the kitchen, whispering. Smoking a lot and making a big cloud. The smoke curls and bends, like it has a bellyache. Because they're talking about serious things. Not politics serious. No, it's the other kind of serious. That's why me and Grandma put on our shoes so quiet, so sneaky, so full of adventure. Mom saw us in the doorway of the kitchen. She didn't say anything. I was going to say, "Good morning," but I wasn't supposed to, I think. Something's going to happen. And it's serious. But they don't know what it is. Not yet.

When they came home the night before, Mom and Grandma had red eyes. They'd both been crying. They didn't ask me, or Dad, how we were. They smelled like beer. Mom put on her nightgown right away, and that made things better, that meant nobody was going anywhere. We were all home, together. So then Dad and I watched TV. Dad didn't look at Mom once. Grandma called me to her room, but I didn't go. I watched Mom and Dad. Mom sat on the edge of the armchair, looking now at the TV, now at Dad. Dad played a little with the cigarette resting in the ashtray. His eyes on the TV, he talked to Mom.

"It's best we don't see Samim and Ayla for a while."

"Why? What's happened, Aydın? Is something wrong? Is there really a reason not to see them?"

Mom was doing it again. Talking too much. But Dad kept his eyes on the TV.

"We'll talk about it later."

After that, it was different. Mom and Dad were on the same side now. They weren't like that before. Now they had new enemies, enemies they were against, together. They didn't talk, though. Dad won't talk to Mom. I watch TV, but I listen to them as they wait for me to leave.

"Aydın? Something important has happened. I'm under investigation."

"Why?"

"You know, Ayşe hid those silkworms in the archives. How she managed, I have no idea!"

"So?"

"Because of that."

"Nothing will happen."

"Well, what if it does?"

She wasn't going to tell Dad! I didn't tell him, but now Mom told him everything. But Mom's acting like a child. As if my dad is her dad, too. He nods and strokes his chin. He's a giant.

"I'll handle it. Don't worry."

Mom's getting smaller on the edge of the chair. It's not fair what she's doing. It wasn't the butterflies, it was the yellow envelopes. I got the butterflies into Parliament for her. It's not fair. It's not at all fair. Then I felt sleepy, all at once.

While Grandma was putting on her shoes, I listened to Mom and Dad again. In secret. Mom had a cigarette in one hand, and with the other hand she was slowly scraping the edges of a jam plate with a teaspoon.

"It's not just me. They're investigating Muzaffer, too."

"Who's Muzaffer?"

"That young guy who works in Microfilm. He's an Islamist, a bit unusual. He writes poetry and so on."

"If he's an Islamist, it's strange they'd investigate him."

"Perhaps he hid something in the archives, too."

"Like what? Surely not love letters! So what would he hide?"

"I didn't ask."

"I see. Perhaps it's best you don't go in to the office for a few days. I mean, best if you stay away while the investigation is under way."

"Do you think so?"

"Yes. We need to go and see my father, anyway. The incidents in Fatsa have terrified him. He can't come here. We need to see how he is."

"When shall we go?"

"I don't know. If we left Friday morning, we'd get there by evening. That detective friend of mine said I could borrow his car on Thursday. It's an old rust-bucket, but it's a Renault station wagon. There's plenty of room for Ayşe in back. We could make up a bed. Your mother would be comfortable, too . . . Sevgi, if you truly want our relationship—"

"All right. I'll speak to the director. I'll ask for one and a half days. We're leaving Friday afternoon and coming back on Monday, right?"

"That would be fine."

"And Ayşe and Mother are coming, too?

"It's up to you, Sevgi. Whatever you say."

That's when I ran into the living room. I got my things from under the carpet, on the windowsill, in the corner of the shelf. They were all dusty. I blew on the bobby pin and the button. I blew on the pin, too, and stuck it in my collar. That's what you're supposed to do when you find a pin. The button and the bobby pin I put in my pocket. I want to tell them all my secrets. If only they understood. If we leave Ankara, nobody'll save the swans!

When Grandma and I left home, we still didn't talk in normal voices. "Grandma, we're going to visit Grandpa. All the way up in Ordu. Did you hear that?" I whispered.

"Yes, sweetie. Your mom and dad need to talk a little more. May it all work out in the end."

"Are we going too, Grandma?"

"We'll wait and see. Let them decide for certain first."

We were walking down the stairs past Jale Hanım's door. Grandma whispered, "Don't touch that filthy thing," but I picked it up anyway. It was sitting on the doormat: *Weekend*. There was a big picture of Bülent Ersoy on the cover again. At first, they all loved Bülent Ersoy, but then, when he grew breasts, everybody got mad at him. Now, they rip his posters off the wall, but they laugh when they do it. Even famous people, like other singers, rip up his posters and have their photos taken with the torn pieces. People are weird.

"As though we're living in a lunatic asylum and they're looking for a witch to burn." That's what Grandma said.

"Look, Grandma!" I said. Jale Hanım used to have a welcome mat knitted out of old socks, but it's gone now. The new one says, HOME SWEET HOME. I ask Grandma what it means. "I don't know, Ayşe," she says, "but you can be sure it's common." I threw *Weekend* back down on the mat.

———

Birgül Abla isn't like Hüseyin. When she walks with me, she always looks ahead of us and around us. Birgül Abla always looks at me and where I'm walking. "Be careful!" she says. She tells me there's a hole or a rut before we get there, like I'm a child. And it makes me feel like maybe I don't want to grow up.

She wears shoes with rubber bottoms, but one of them has a hole. And the other one has a short lace that only goes halfway, so she flap-flaps when she walks. We were running across the street and the shoe almost came right off. A car nearly hit us. I reached in my pocket and pulled out the short shoelace Mom gave me. I looked at her shoe. "Thanks, Ali!" she said. She tied my lace onto hers, and it reached. She laughed. When she stood up, she smoothed my hair. She stopped smiling.

"It's better messy."

She took my hand and we walked down the hill, *clop clop*, the two of us. There's a dry cleaner's on the corner. They hung up a big Bülent Ersoy poster but with a mustache drawn on it. A Grey Wolf mustache. Birgül Abla looked at it.

"Ali, what do you think about Mustafa the Grocer?"

I didn't say anything because I was looking at Birgül Abla's shoes. Maybe she'll step on a stone or her foot will land in a hole. She kept talking, though.

"It seems we've become as heartless as our enemies. Ali, I think we were too hasty with Mustafa. We shamed him in front of the whole neighborhood, and then it turned out that some of his relatives were policemen. But when we found out . . . Nobody could come out and say he was innocent, that we'd made a mistake. That's what's wrong with this country, Ali. We stone someone in front of everyone, but then, when we apologize, we do it in secret. The women have been taking food to Mustafa for the last two days. He won't accept it. He's not talking to anyone. He won't answer his phone. He won't tell anyone when a call comes to his store for them. He's heartbroken. And he's right to be. They're doing the same thing now with Bülent Ersoy. Later, though, they'll all whisper about how they sorry they are. That's how it is, Ali. People are too ashamed even to apologize. But the people who make you most ashamed are the ones who never get ashamed themselves. Look what's going on with the CHP. We need unity on the left, they say. Everyone went to their metro event . . . but they've been leading the left all my life. Going back to the CHP makes you feel like you're going back to your parent's house. It's like admitting you failed in life, and it's embarrassing to do that. And it's not as though you get welcomed back to the party with open arms. No, they make you kneel and plead. . . . Never mind me, Ali. I've got a lot on my mind."

"I need a wheelbarrow, Birgül Abla."

"You keep saying that, but you won't say why."

"It's a surprise, for Ayşe."

"What's in that sack, Ali?"

"My dead uncle's parka. Do you want to see it?"

"No . . . No, that's okay."

"I need a wheelbarrow, Birgül Abla."

"What kind of surprise, Ali?"

"Hüseyin Abi surprised you with a sandwich wafer. Remember? It's kind of like that."

She smiled and took my hand.

"Where on earth can I find you a wheelbarrow right now?"

"We're revolutionaries, Birgül Abla. You'll think of something. Right?"

She laughed for a long time.

"You bet we are! We're revolutionaries. If we put our minds to it, we can fly through the sky. Right, Ali?"

"That's right. We'll fly."

Birgül Abla laughed so hard I decided to tell her about the swans. That they'll fly, too, I mean. That we'll all fly, and soon. But if I tell her we might come back as swans, maybe she'll say what Ayşe did: "No, we're all going to heaven."

—

We're having fun because we're both wearing pants and we're walking to Kızılay Square. It's going to be great. I've got the button and bobby pin in my pocket and the pin in my collar. We're taking big steps, and I have everything with me. It's like Ali said, that your chest gets real big, right here, when you take a breath. A giant revolutionary, that's what you become. Grandma's a giant revolutionary, too. Her shoes are dusty, and so are mine. Just like Ali's.

So many people are walking to Kızılay Square. And they're all happy to see each other. We're going there for the train, that's why. Everyone here loves trains. Grandma greets everyone. "Good morning, sir," she says and, "Hello, my boy." Grandma is "a real lady," just like Jale Hanım said that one time. But now they're not talking. Jale Hanım "took advantage," you see, and that's wrong. The walking people are talking about politics, but they're happy, so they don't get mad about it.

"That Özal . . . I wonder who dug him up? Demirel? That bastard's a true enemy of the working class."

"Özal's nothing more than an undersecretary, he's not even a civil servant. Yet there he is with an opinion on everything. Who is he to demand an end to the strikes? And have you heard the latest?"

"No, what did he say now?"

"Something about Turkey making great strides despite those who would sabotage our progress. And he's warned that there will be a terrible economic crisis unless, basically, the government gets to enact all of its reforms unopposed."

"Well, it's nice to know we're making great strides!"

"He said it, not me."

Özal doesn't like trains, and we're walking to the new train, so we don't like him. We don't like Ecevit very much, either, but we don't get so mad at him. Ecevit's going to understand one day and then we'll all join together and everything will be great. That's what they say, or something like it. Aunties my mother's age are talking, too.

"Let's say early elections were called. What difference would it make? The fascists would keep murdering all the leaders of the Republican People's Party. That's what he wants."

"Demirel, you mean?"

"Yes. Have you seen? It's in all the papers, not just *Cumhuriyet*. They're keeping a running tally of all the CHP leaders killed since Demirel took office. And it hasn't even been a year yet."

"How many have there been? Ten?"

"Worse. Twenty-nine!"

"That many!"

The more people that are walking, the closer we get to Kızılay Square. That's how it feels. Grandma's getting happier and happier.

"Sweetie, look at all these people! When you spend too much time alone, you end up thinking sad thoughts. Buses, shared taxis, trains, ferryboats . . . they're all for people. How can I put it? There's a vanity in misery, Ayşe. An arrogance. You think you're the only one who's unhappy, and you forget how to make others happy. You'll understand once you've grown up. Ferryboats and trains . . . they make everything possible. They make it possible to meet, to fall in love, even."

Grandma looks at me. She doesn't feel the heat. She feels a breeze that isn't there. I pull the pin out of my collar and hold it out. Her eyes can't see it unless I put it right under her nose.

"What's that, sweetie?"

"The fox whiskers pin."

"The fox whiskers pin?"

"The one that titters."

"Oh, you are a goose and an angel! Now give me that before you prick yourself."

Grandma sticks the pin in her collar. Pins don't get thrown away. Nothing gets thrown away. I still have the button and the bobby pin left.

—

"Hüseyin Abi's in Ankara, isn't he, Birgül Abla?"

Birgül Abla lets go of my hand, stops and looks at me.

"How do you . . ."

She goes quiet. She takes my hand, and we start walking again. She didn't answer me, so I don't tell her about the rice restaurant. I don't tell her about Hüseyin's beard, either. We're walking along when somebody shouts behind us.

"Birgül Abla! Birgül Abla!"

It's one of the big brothers in high school. The one who got out of prison.

"Hello, İsmail. What are you doing here?"

"I'm going to the square to hand out pamphlets with some class-mates."

"What kind of pamphlets, İsmail?"

"They won't let the high schoolers in prison take any of the exams. We're trying to do something about it."

"Let me see. Hmmm. Nice job. Did you write it yourself?"

"Of course, I did. Thanks, Birgül Abla."

İsmail Abi is old, at least fifteen. That's why he writes the pamphlets himself now. But he gets red when he sees Birgül Abla. And he's got more teeth than anyone I know. They all show when he smiles.

"All right then, İsmail. Off you go. Why are you standing there and grinning like that?"

"Nothing. It's just, when I see you . . ."

"Never mind, İsmail. See you later."

"Okay, then. Bye, then."

"Bye, İsmail."

Birgül Abla smiled at me when İsmail Abi left.

"He's a strange boy, Ali."

"He's in love with you, Birgül Abla."

"Oh! You don't say. Who else is in love with me?"

"All the high schoolers. And—"

"And who?"

"And Hüseyin Abi."

Birgül Abla let go of my hand again. She lifted her hair up off her neck and said, "Whew, it's hot. Sometimes I wish I didn't have so much hair."

I gave Birgül Abla another string from my pocket. When she was tying up her hair, she tossed it around, up and down, left and right, like a horse's tail. She's beautiful.

"You gave me that string in just the nick of time. Thank you, Ali."

"It's from the kite. Hüseyin Abi made it for me."

Birgül Abla took my hand and we walked for a while. She forgot me, because she was thinking of Hüseyin Abi. Then she remembered me.

"Is that sack heavy, Ali? I can carry it for you."

"No, Birgül Abla. It's not heavy at all. But my hands are too small for it."

"We should have tied it shut before we left."

I pulled out the string from the car. Birgül tied it around the mouth of the sack. My hand wasn't too small anymore.

—

"The square has been beautifully organized, Nejla Hanım. Wait until you see it. We couldn't stay, though. My granddaughter was getting all fidgety."

Grandma ran into an old friend from school. She has a granddaughter, too, but much littler than me.

"What all have they done, Özden Hanım?"

"Well, you know the picture of Atatürk looking out of a train window. They've used that image on a huge banner hanging in the square. It's a pointed message to the Demirel administration."

"Clever. Why did this little lady get so fidgety? Sweetie, didn't you like it in the square? Was it too crowded?"

Grandma patted that girl on the head. She tossed her head to get away from Grandma's hand. I talked to her a little, because I was the big sister.

"There's no need to be scared of crowds. Everyone's a revolutionary, so there's no need."

Grandma and her friend laughed at me. But not like I was being funny. I took out the bobby pin and put it in the girl's hair. Now that I'm old, I should take care of the little ones.

I gave the auntie my button. I don't know why. Maybe because her boobs were showing. She looked like the ladies who visit Uncle Cavit. The line between Grandma's boobs was showing when we went to the pharmacy, too. I didn't want the auntie to get sad like Grandma did.

"Ayşe! Are you giving everyone little gifts?"

The auntie laughed. Nobody knew, but all my things were gone. I had nothing left. Because I was all grown up now.

—

"What do you think is going happen, Ali? Over the next year or so?"

When Birgül Abla pulled up her hair, she didn't talk for a bit. Then she asked me that question in a loud voice, out of nowhere. It's like that sometimes. When people talk to themselves a lot, they can suddenly ask a question out loud. I didn't answer, so she answered herself.

"I'll tell you what I think, Ali. We'll soon take over all of Ankara. That's what'll happen, one way or another. How much is left, anyway? Just a few neighborhoods. Once Ankara is ours, the rest will be easy. General Evren just issued another statement. He said martial law should be lifted, but then he went and said that the armed forces have embraced their enforcement of martial law and will strive day and night to safeguard the peace and happiness of the people of our nation. And on and on. Which means they're going to keep torturing people. Either they break us, or we overturn them. There's no middle way. It'll all be over soon. Ali, I'm telling you this to help you understand. Yes, your mother got tortured—and that was terrible for you, too, dear—but don't let it get to you. Never be scared. Why? Because we're at war. Your mother resisted to the end, a true hero. When the time comes, we're all prepared to resist just like your mother."

"Birgül Abla, do you think we can find a wheelbarrow at the metro place?"

I don't want to hear sad things. I have a job to do. Birgül Abla's talking so I don't get sad, but she's making herself sad. I found the silver cord from my circumcision and made a ring for her. When I put it on her finger, she laughed again.

She's not wearing the ring Hüseyin Abi gave her. I wonder why?

My strings are gone now. There are no more in my pocket. Because now I have a parka. Strings are for kids.

—

"To oppose a rail system is to oppose humanity! In order to save gas and diesel, and in order to break the chains of dependency on foreign resources . . ."

An uncle up on a high place is yelling into a microphone. Everybody's clapping. We clap, too. Sometimes I yell, "Shoulder to shoulder against fascism!" But Grandma doesn't yell, of course.

I think you're only supposed to yell three times. When I do it a fourth time, I'm the only one. Then they start laughing at me, but in a nice way. Big brothers are walking around with yellow ribbons on their arms that say, "On Duty." They're the most serious. They go everywhere and look at people and keep things right. I guess they're the youth revolutionaries. When it's time to yell, they look at everyone and yell, and they lift their hands in the air. They make fists, so the veins come out on their arms.

—

When we got to the square, Birgül Abla looked around. There's a big ditch right in the middle. Everyone stands around it. I want to look inside, down into the ground, to see what's under Ankara. But everyone's yelling, and it's so noisy. Nobody's looking inside the ditch. They have their eyes on the mayor, and he's shouting. Birgül Abla sees someone she knows.

"Bahri!"

Bahri Abi isn't very tall. In Swan Park, with those other two men, he was taller. Now he seems short. Maybe because he's standing alone. Birgül Abla takes the sack from my hand.

"Ali, if you get up on Bahri Abi's shoulders, you might be able to see our neighbors. Do you want to? Is that okay, Bahri Abi?"

"Ready, Ali? When I say 'go,' jump up."

I jumped and suddenly I was high in the air. As high as Bahri Abi is when he looks out at things. I felt a little dizzy. Then I looked at the people. They gather and scatter, gather and scatter. There's a roar. I closed my eyes and took a deep breath. It smells good, like fun. And then all the people shouted together, and Kızılay Square smelled like an apple.

—

"Did you hear that, Ayşe? This uncle right here says he'll pick you up. Would you like that? Are you going to get up on his shoulders, sweetie?"

"Yes!" The uncle laughed and I climbed up onto him. Grandma and the others laughed harder. I was up high, and it was wonderful. When everyone claps, it sounds like water, like those when the water is cut, but then it comes back on and sprays into the glass, all gray and cloudy and bubbly. I closed my eyes. I could smell it, the spraying water.

—

I see Ayşe. She's up on a man's shoulders, just like me. I hold up my arms, so she'll see me.

—

Oh! It's Ali! His arms are open wide. Like he's about to fly. I laugh and open my arms, too. We both turn into swans, me and Ali.

—

Birgül Abla was talking to Bahir Abi. I didn't point to Ayşe. I can see her, and that's enough for me.

—

Grandma was talking to the uncle holding me on his shoulders. I didn't say, "Look, Grandma! Ali's over there." It's nicer when only he and I know something. It's an adventure, a secret.

—

Me and Birgül Abla got a wheelbarrow from the metro construction. She asked the workers if we could borrow it for a bit and then leave it with the municipality. The workers said, "You're from the Gardens, aren't you? Take it, sister." We walked all the way to Liberation with the wheelbarrow. Birgül pushed it, and I put my sack inside it.

"We're famous. Everyone's staring at us because of the wheelbarrow, Ali sweetie," Birgül Abla said. She called me "sweetie!" People talk like that on TV, but never in my neighborhood. I got embarrassed. But Birgül didn't.

"We spend so much time going from the neighborhood to the protests and back. We have no idea what the people living in places like this are doing. They're ordinary people. Although it's true that ordinary people don't know anything about us, either. Ali, do you think we're too angry to see them? Or do we ignore them because they ignore us? What do you think?"

I shook my head.

Birgül Abla pulled back her toe so it wouldn't show through the hole.

"They're laughing at us, Ali. In their eyes, we're naïve and gullible at best, a threat at worst. They sneer at us as though it's terribly old-fashioned to talk about things like hunger. As though this is their time, not ours. And that sneer is the most dangerous of weapons. That sneer can build and build until it smothers an entire country. If you ask me, their ridicule might defeat us, but their submachine guns never will. Ali, what if they understand everything perfectly well? We tear ourselves apart, trying to get out the word, and they gawk at us with empty eyes and blank faces. We assume they don't understand what we're saying, that we need to try harder. Perhaps there's a simpler explanation. Perhaps they don't want to understand. What do you think, Ali?"

I shake my head.

"Listen, Ali. There's something important I want to say to you about *not* speaking."

Birgül Abla let go of the wheelbarrow and put her hands on her hips, just like Ayşe.

"Speak out, Ali. Everyone's going to look at you, but don't be frightened of making a mistake. The only way to make yourself heard through all this noise is to shout it out, loud and clear. Okay, Ali sweetie?"

"Okay," I said. Birgül Abla took her hands off her hips and pinched my cheeks.

"Good for you!"

I can't push the wheelbarrow alone, but I've got Ayşe. We can do it. We're big enough now.

When we got there, Birgül Abla said, "Is this the place? Are you sure?" Then she looked over at Samim and Ayla's apartment building, shook her head, and said, "That's funny." I clicked the Ibelo. I'm not going to speak out, though. Not a word until after we rescue the swans. Then I'll tell Birgül Abla everything: Hüseyin Abi's beard, the swans . . . I'll give her the lighter, too.

UNIT 14

Neighborly Relations

Neighbors Are Dearer Than Relatives

"Why, of course he can stay with us! There's no need to explain."

Dad and Mom came home together. They were taking off their shoes when, in a tiny voice, Grandma told them about Birgül Abla and about how Ali was going to stay with us.

"Ali's mother got tortured, or so that girl said. I found her a bit rough around the edges, though. Why would they have tortured Aliye Hanım? Do you think they really did, Sevgi?"

One foot naked, the other in a shoe, Mom stopped for a moment and looked at Grandma. She didn't say anything. Sometimes, Grandma acts like my mom's child. Mom looked away as she was taking off her other shoe.

"Aydın, we could visit the hospital and find out how she is."

"We don't know which hospital she's in, Sevgi. Hasan Bey will probably call this evening and let us know."

Dad wasn't very curious. He was too mad to care. Mom was acting like Dad's child.

Grandma rubbed her hands together and talked in that tiny voice.

"Sevgi, the boy's not well, I'm afraid. He's staring blankly."

"It's okay, Mother. We'll take care of him."

Now, nobody was looking at anyone else. My finger was in my mouth. I left it there, because nobody was looking at me.

Grandma is all small right now, but when Ali's Birgül Abla came she stuck her nose in the air. Just as the door was opening, Birgül Abla said to Ali, "So this is the house your mother cleans." That's why Grandma stuck her nose in the air. And that's why she said, in her most ladylike voice, "Won't you come in, my girl?" Birgül Abla stepped inside and asked, "Can we speak in private for a moment?" Grandma folded her hands on her belly and said, "Certainly. Please follow me." Then she pointed to the welcome mat and said, "That's where we remove our shoes."

"I'll only be a moment, auntie."

Grandma led the way to the kitchen, and she shut the door so we wouldn't hear. But we heard everything! Birgül has beautiful, long hair. But she wore her shoes in the house.

Ali's holding a sack and looking at me in front of the kitchen door. A strange look, as though we've never spoken before. He's making the lighter go *click click* in his pocket. He has a lot to tell me. He looks at me, then at the sack, then back at me. I understand what he's saying. Through the frosted glass of the door, Grandma and Birgül Abla are slivered and split.

"Do you have any idea what's been going on in our neighborhood?"

"We keep abreast of current affairs in this house, too. There's no need to explain."

"You misunderstood me."

"I don't think so, young lady. I'm listening to you. Please, go on."

"I feel as though we've got off on the wrong foot. Well, it's like this, Nejla Hanım. Ali's mother, Aliye Abla . . . Goodness me. Where do I start? How can I make you understand?"

"I wasn't born yesterday. We live in the same country, after all. You can start by telling me where Aliye Hanım is."

"Hmmm . . . The same country, you say. Well, here goes. Your cleaning lady, Aliye Abla—"

"We never refer to her as our 'cleaning lady.' She's our helper."

"Your helper, Aliye Hanım, was arrested and has been badly tortured."

"What! Mercy me!"

Ali still hasn't said a word, but I understand. He's saying, "Look at the sack. I can't show you. I can't move." I take the sack from Ali. He keeps his eyes on me. He doesn't blink. There's a green coat inside the sack. I pull it out. It smells dirty, like a winter night. I hold it up to Ali.

"A coat."

"A parka."

"What's a parka?"

"A bloody coat."

"Whose blood?"

"A swan's."

Ali clicks the lighter again. Maybe it's a coat for rescuing swans in the park.

"Nejla Hanım, don't get so agitated. They let her go."

"Those scoundrels! Why would they do that to a poor cleaning— . . . torturing Aliye Hanım like that!"

"We're members of an organization, Nejla Hanım."

"An organization? Her? She's a married woman with a child."

"Please lower your voice, Nejla Hanım. It's been a terrible shock for Ali. Let's not make it worse."

"God help us! One trouble after another . . ."

"Nejla Hanım. Aliye Abla's in the hospital."

"How is she? If only we'd known."

Ali clicked his lighter again. His mother was in jail, that's what the woman said. Maybe Auntie Aliye bled and bled. All over the floor! Ali hasn't cried at all, I can tell. He's too scared to cry. He pulled his list out of his pocket. "I don't have strings anymore," Ali said, so quiet I almost couldn't hear him. "I don't need a list, either."

Ali lit the list with his lighter. All his "to do" things burned, starting at the end.

6. Save the swans (Or as many as possible. Maybe they're too big for me to save all of them. *The wingspan of a mature mute swan is typically between 79 and 94 inches.*)
5. Get the butterflies into Parliament (then Hüseyin Abi can get into Parliament, too).
4. Get Mom a whole roomful of bread (like in *Heidi*) and meat (like in *Hagar the Horrible*).
3. Get the biggest gun ever for Hüseyin Abi.
2. Wear my uncle's parka and do something important.

Only one thing was left.

1. Read the *Wonderland of Knowledge* from cover to cover.

He burned it, too, and let it fall to the floor. When Ali rubbed his foot on the carpet, the ashes melted away. I didn't tell him about my secret things, the ones I gave away because we're grown up now. Maybe he understands the things I don't say. Ali's lighter is still going *click click*. He's big now, but when you grow up, I think you can feel small. We're smaller than we were yesterday, somehow.

"We decided it would be best to leave Ali with you for a few days. I mean, that's what his father and mother decided. But only until Aliye Abla gets out of the hospital. As you know, Ali's a sensitive boy, and things are kind of mixed up in our neighborhood. There's nobody to look after him—"

"Why, of course he can stay with us! There's no need. Can you believe it? Aydın and Sevgi aren't even home."

"If you'd like, I can wait here until they come and explain it to them."

"No, no. There's no need to explain anything. It's fine, just fine. Allow me a moment to regain my composure. Oh, dear! What shall we do with the boy?"

"You don't need to do anything. All he needs is a safe, quiet place to spend a few days. Children bounce back."

"Oh dear!"

Ali took the parka from me. His neck is kind of down, and to one side. He seems smaller and his neck seems skinnier, because he's grown. Ali pulled the letter out of the pocket of the parka. The letter with the green ink Uncle Önder gave to Mom. He gave it to me. We lit it with the lighter. The words burned quickly.

> *Dearest Sevgi,*
>
> *To love is, in a sense, to live with a broken wing. Did you know, my beloved Sevgi, that they break the wings of show pigeons to prevent them from flying away? To truly love someone is to present them— freely, joyfully, fearlessly—with a piece of one's own wing bone, to let them know there's nowhere else you'd rather be. That piece of you is safe with me. And mine is safe with you. This, dear Sevgi, is the last letter I will write to you from prison. Soon, I will be released. Soon, the two of us*

The letter burned until just there. Then the rest of it burned to ashes, too. We had nothing left. There was just the two of us, with nothing. I crushed the ashes into the carpet with my foot. Now, we really were grown up.

"What's that smell? Is something burning?"

"Nejla Hanım, there's one more thing–"

"Hang on! Something *is* burning. Let me have a look. Children!"

Ali stuck his lighter in his pocket before Grandma could open the door. I stood right on the ashy spot. There was a little bit of smoke, though. We stood in the smoke, looking at Grandma and Birgül Abla. Without a word. "What have you two been up to!" Grandma said, but not really.

She looked at Ali and went quiet. Then she said, "Oh dear! Oh dear!" ever so many times. She rubbed her hands together. Birgül Abla untied her hair and gave a piece of string to Ali. She shook out her hair, and smiled.

When Birgül Abla left, Ali and I went out onto the balcony. We saw Birgül Abla going into Samim and Ayla's apartment building. "Look, Ali!" I said. "Shhh!" he said, his eyes wide.

When Mom and Dad came home and Grandma told them about Birgül Abla and Auntie Aliye, they lit cigarettes and talked for a bit. Then Dad patted Ali on the head. He didn't say anything, though. They looked at him with pity, that's all. Dad and Mom didn't say a word until the evening news. When the speaker started talking, then they talked. But Dad doesn't say "would you mind" and "please" to Mom, and she doesn't get mad at him like before. Mom's been grounded, I think.

"... *main opposition leader Bülent Ecevit emphasized that the price of basic foodstuffs has skyrocketed more than one hundred percent in the past year...*"

"Were you able to get Friday off? What happened with the investigation?"

"Aydın, let's not talk about it right now."

"Just tell me what happened, Sevgi. Have they launched it?"

"Yes."

"On what grounds?"

"Let's talk about it later."

"Just tell me!"

"Immorality."

"... *rampant tax evasion. Ecevit also criticized Prime Minister Demirel for...*"

Dad lit another cigarette. The smoke covered his face.

"What did you expect, Aydın? They weren't going to cite my political views or Ayşe's moths."

"A charge of immorality suggests that they've read those letters from Önder. Doesn't it, Sevgi?"

Mom said nothing.

". . . *nine people, four of them children, died in political clashes and terrorist incidents yesterday. We now bring you the weather* . . ."

"Ayşe, why don't you and Ali go and play in your room. Your father and I are talking."

I took Ali's hand as we went down the hallway. "Shhh!" I said. But Ali doesn't talk, anyway. I listened to Mom and Dad.

"Aydın, if you're unable to let it go . . ."

"What do you expect, Sevgi? For me to act as though nothing happened? I'm not even allowed to ask who Önder is, yet he's the reason you're under investigation."

"Aydın, I'm the kind of woman who always wears long underwear to protests in case I get arrested and tortured. They know how to hit me where it hurts. Immorality! What else? Don't come for me. Please, not you, too."

Mom said nothing. Dad said nothing. Mom had said, "Please," so Dad stopped talking.

When the weather forecast ended, Mom was ready to talk again.

"I got both Friday and Monday off. We can go to Ordu. First thing in the morning, the day after tomorrow, if that's what you want."

And that's when the phone rang.

"Ah, Hasan Bey. How are things? Your wife's fallen ill, I heard. If there's anything we can do . . . Which hospital? . . . We can come at once. I mean it. Okay. No, no. He's fine. He's playing with Ayşe right now. Don't worry, he's fine. Listen, we're ready to do whatever we can. Okay . . . Okay . . . Oh, Hasan Bey, before I forget. We're going to Ordu this Friday morning, the 12th. My father's not well. I'm sorry about that. What? . . . Okay then . . . Call me at once if there's anything we can do. And tell your wife we wish her a speedy recovery—It went dead!"

Ali ran down the hallway when he heard his father's name, and stood in front of my dad. He kept his eyes on Dad the whole time he was talking. Ali got a light in his eye. His mouth was open. The light went out, though, when Dad said, "It went dead!" Ali closed his mouth, tight, like it was locked. Dad patted him on the head again. Dad thinks Ali will talk if you pat him on the head.

"Don't worry, Ali. Your mom's fine. But she'll be staying in the hospital for a couple of days. We're leaving for Ordu on Friday and they'll get you before then. In the meantime, you and Ayşe . . . Right, Ayşe? You and your friend can spend lots of time together until then."

"Why'd you say that, Aydın?" Mom said. "You more or less told him he has to get Ali before Friday." I took Ali out onto the balcony. A light went on in the dark room in Samim and Ayla's house, and then it went off. We both saw it, but we didn't say anything. Sounds came from the police station, terrible sounds, but we didn't say anything. There were other sounds, too, like the happy song coming from Jale Hanım's apartment. And there were the big brothers and sisters racing through the street. The mulberry tree whispered, and still we didn't say anything. Finally, Ali talked.

"I saw your shoes by the door. They're dirty."

"Do you want some Şokella?"

"Birgül Abla always takes off her shoes, but she thought rich people didn't."

"She has nice hair."

Then we had some Şokella on bread. Ali didn't eat all of his, though. He left half of it, because his mom is sick and she can't have any. If my mom was sick, I'd leave half, too.

When we went to bed in my room, Ali said, "Tell me about the butterflies and how they got into Parliament." I told him everything. "They were orange," I said. I'm mad at Mom. And Dad, too. They wanted butterflies in Parliament, but then they got scared when we did it. "Did Auntie Aliye bleed," I asked, "all over the floor?" Ali was asleep, though.

—

"He's with us, watchman! Let him go!"

Ayşe begged a lot for her grandma to take us to the park. I didn't say anything when she asked if I wanted to go, so her grandma said, "All right, it'll do the boy good." I want to "scout out" the park. That's what you do before you "take action," and that's why Ayşe begged her grandma so much.

Ayşe's grandma was sitting on a bench in Swan Park, reading the newspaper with another woman and talking about Bülent Ersoy. That's all they ever talk about now.

"You can't go mincing around like that and then cry your eyes out when they throw you in jail."

"Nobody should be thrown in jail."

"Enough is enough. It's time the state flexed its muscles. Our very survival depends on it."

"And what would you have the state do?"

"They say the army's going to seize control. And I say, let them. Somebody's got to impose some order on this country. Then we'll all know where we stand."

Ayşe was sitting on a swing, and I was looking at the swans. Then those kids came to the park, the ones from the shantytowns. They were yelling and carrying on so everyone would look at them.

They climbed on top of the swing set and stood on the edge of the slide. They made the seesaw go all the way up and they crashed it to the ground with a thud. The watchman came running over, blowing his whistle. The kids were running away when the watchman caught one of them. The other kids stopped running and started cursing, so the watchman hit the one he'd grabbed. I walked over there. Slowly, right up to the watchman. He grabbed me, too. I didn't make a sound, just stood there.

"Stop disturbing the peace, you little bastards. Get the hell out of the park!"

The other kids yelled and cursed so he'd let me go. The watchman was from a shantytown, too. I could tell from his shoes. Ayşe got off the swing. She looked over at her grandma, but her grandma didn't see, didn't hear. Ayşe took a step closer to me and looked at her grandma again. The other kids didn't run away. Ayşe didn't come over to me. Finally, her grandma yelled.

"He's with us, watchman! Let him go!"

That's when Ayşe ran up to me. She held my hand and tugged. The watchman was pulling me by the scruff of the neck, and Ayşe was tugging my hand.

"Uncle Watchman! He's one of us. He's not with them. Let him go!"

The other kids went quiet and stared at me. Ayşe didn't see how they looked at me, but I did. They laughed at me, and left.

Me and Ayşe sat on the swings. The woman talking to Ayşe's grandma got up and went, so it was just the three of us. Ayşe's grandmother didn't know how to talk to me, not with my mom in the hospital. Ayşe didn't know how to talk to me, because she didn't yell at the watchman. Nobody was talking. So I did.

"I can't save the swans without you, Ayşe."

Ayşe got happy again.

"Really?"

Me and Ayşe went over and looked at the swans. You can always see their eyes, but just one of them. I can see and so can Ayşe. She took my hand. "I wish I was one of you," she said. I shook my head. No. The swans looked at us for a while with one eye, and then they turned and looked at us with the other eye. I wonder if they see the same thing with both eyes?

Ayşe was happy to talk now.

"When we save the swans, I'll be one of you, won't I?"

"Nope!"

"Why not? I won't be like Mom and Dad anymore. I'll be like you."

"It won't make any difference. But let's save the swans. In a way, everyone will be saved if the swans are."

The back of my neck burned all the way home. I was running a temperature. That's what Ayşe's grandma said. I stayed in bed until dinner, when that detective came. Ayşe sat next to me and held my hand. I didn't like it, but I let her so she wouldn't be scared. Ayşe's grandma said it three times: "Here it is, September the 10th, but this Ankara heat is still so oppressive."

Uncle Detective yelled down the stairs from our front door.

"Shut your door, ma'am. And keep it closed."

He laughed, but the angry kind of laugh.

"Is that the neighbor you were talking about, Aydın Abi? What's her problem, anyway?"

"What did she do now?"

"You won't believe this. She must have called the police. As I came up the stairs, I heard her yakking about how her upstairs neighbors were communists and so were the tenants in the next building. Anyway, I sent the officer back to the station and told her to mind her own business."

Dad turned to Grandma.

"Did you hear that, Nejla Hanım? So much for 'meaning well.' What do you think of your Jale Hanım now?

"She's taken umbrage over my refusal to make her dress. Perhaps I should go down and talk to her. What do you think, Sevgi? We have to do something. It's shameful what she's done."

"Everybody's gone crazy, Mother. How do you reason with a woman who just called the police on us?"

Uncle Detective spoke to Grandma as he was pulling off his shoe.

"I'd stay out of it, Nejla Hanım. Sevgi's right. Everybody's gone crazy. Just the other day, in Amasya, a group of fascists and revolutionaries got into a fight over a cat. Two people were killed. And they cut off the mukhtar's head."

"What next!" Dad said. Mom pointed to me.

"Not in front of . . ."

Grandma shut her open mouth.

Dad took the detective by the arm.

"Let's go to the living room, Nahit."

Uncle Detective gave Dad some keys.

"Here you go, Aydın Abi. Bring it back whenever you want. I can always use the patrol car in the meantime. I might even sell it to you if you're interested. We'll talk after you've given the clunker a test run to Ordu and back. What I was really wondering about was that investigation. Sevgi, has anything happened with that?"

"Sevgi can handle it, Detective. Don't worry about it. They've concocted some trumped-up charges—immorality, or what have you. Typical Koran thumpers. They think they can intimidate women by attacking their so-called virtue. Sevgi's laughing it off as best she can."

Even though Mom's mad at Dad, I thought I saw her smile when she walked to the kitchen. Dad poured Uncle Detective a glass of rakı in the living room.

Uncle Detective tossed some papers onto the coffee table.

"Huh? How'd I end up with that?"

"With what?"

"You remember Timur, the journalist? Well, I was trying to relax with a drink at the *meyhane* and he came up, mad as hell, and gave me an earful. Apparently, tomorrow's the anniversary of the Chilean coup, and he'd been planning to publish a transcript of Allende's last speech. At the last minute, the Istanbul office refused. Timur was furious; it was all he could talk about. Anyway, he was waving that transcript in my face and I grabbed it. Then I must have stuck it in my pocket."

"You're up to your neck in transcripts and letters, Detective."

"Excuse me?"

"Nothing. Let me see that. It's been years since I read it."

Mom made Ali rice soup. Sick soup. Bits of parsley floated in it, all green. Me and Ali were catching the lemon seeds. Ali's "traumatized," that's what Mom said, and that's why he's "running a temperature." He's better now, and he can eat. Dad gave us a happy-sad look while we were having our soup. He pounded his fist on the table so hard the seeds jumped off the spoon.

"Kids, Allende was an amazing man. He was the president of Chile, a nice country in South America. The poor people loved him, and the rich people hated him. And that's why the rich people had him killed."

When Dad said "Allende," I pictured a spoon of soft, sweet pudding. Chocolate.

Dad put little squares of cheese on a plate. Mom turned up the TV. When terrible things happen, the TV is always turned up.

"*. . . the warden allegedly opened fire on political prisoners and other inmates at Mamak Penitentiary. Democratic organizations have condemned the . . .*"

Dad began reading out loud because he wanted me and Ali to hear it, too. Ali put his hand over his ear.

"*. . .I will pay for loyalty to the people with my life. And I say to them that I am certain that the seed which we have planted in the good conscience of thousands and thousands of Chileans will not be shriveled forever. . . . History is ours, and people make history.*"

The lady on TV put down a piece of paper and picked up another one.

"*Referring to Prime Minister Süleyman Demirel's description of the state treasury as 'completely depleted,' a spokesman for the main opposition asserted that the prime minister's statement was a tacit admission that 'wild capitalism' can only be successfully implemented under a Latin American–style military dictatorship . . .*"

Dad was reading the chocolate pudding paper in the voice of a student reciting a poem on National Sovereignty and Children's Day.

"*The people must defend themselves, but they must not sacrifice themselves. The people must not let themselves be destroyed or riddled with bullets, but they cannot be humiliated either.*"

There were men with bushy beards on TV. They had big wooden prayer beads hanging from their necks.

"*Reactions continue to the 'Liberating Jerusalem' demonstration staged by the National Salvation Party in Konya. Organizers are facing charges for the event, during which protesters sat on the ground during the National Anthem and shouted Islamist slogans such as 'The Koran is our Constitution!' and 'We want Sharia!'"*

Ali put his other hand over his other ear. Now he can't hear the pudding paper or the TV. He put down his spoon.

"Go forward knowing that, sooner rather than later, the great avenues will open again where free men will walk to build a better society.... These are my last words, and I am certain that my sacrifice will not be in vain."

On TV, fat men in ties are having a nice dinner somewhere.

"Referring to the ongoing nationwide labor union strikes, Halit Narin, the chairman of the Turkish Confederation of Employer Associations, warned that production would stagnate unless State Security Courts were established . . ."

When Dad was finished, he nodded his head "yes" a couple of times. Then he turned to me.

"How much of that did you understand, Ayşe?"

I didn't answer. Ali's not talking, so I didn't answer.

"What about you, Ali?"

Ali looked at Dad. Looked like crazy, and it scared Dad and Mom and Grandma. I'm the only one who can look Ali in the eye. I didn't help him in the park today, though, so I can't really say anything. We didn't answer Dad.

Mom cleared the dinner plates.

"Okay, kids, off you go to your room." She said something to Dad, too, but real quiet, when we were in the hallway.

"Aydın, the boy's feeling overwhelmed as it is. Reading out that entire speech . . ."

Me and Ali went out onto the balcony, where it's dark and windy. The light went on again in Samim Abi's secret room. But this time there were three people in the room! I could tell, even behind the curtains. A man and two women. The light went out. "Oh!" I said. Ali said nothing. The streetlight was shining yellow on Ali's face. He smiled. He finally smiled. He pointed at Samim Abi's house and laughed.

"When we save the swans, they'll come out of there. Hüseyin Abi and Birgül Abla. Do you understand?"

"But what will happen if we go to Ordu and don't save the swans?"

"That won't happen. We'll do it."

Then we stuck our feet through the gaps in the iron rail. Ali put his mouth against the metal.

"There has to be a sacrifice!"

There was that speech by the chocolate pudding man, that's why Ali is sad. And he has a hole in his sock. Two reasons. We fell asleep.

In the evening, there was a *bang bang* on the door. I was making curlicues in the margins of my notebook. I felt bad. Ever since that phone call this morning . . .

"Aydın, run! The phone's ringing. The operator must have got through to Ordu."

"I'm coming, Nejla Hanım. There's no need to panic."

Grandma's scared of the phone, but not a lot. She thinks it's going to break, or go quiet, or that we'll miss whoever's on the other end. Mom and Dad were getting ready for work. Ali and I were in the kitchen. Ali was putting his olive pits right on the table and I was picking them up and putting them on his plate. He doesn't know it's shameful.

"Hello! Hasan Bey! Is that you? Good morning. All right, then. I can only imagine how upset you must have been when you got cut off last time. Hold on. I'm giving the phone to my son-in-law."

Ali swallowed a whole olive, pit and all, when he heard his dad's name. My dad stood in the doorway, doing a "come, come" with his hand. Ali got up, but so slow. The phone was too big for him. He couldn't get his mouth and his ear in the right places at the same time. He didn't say anything. "Say hello," Dad told him. Ali looked at Dad. Nothing. We could hear Ali's dad.

"Son! Ali! Can you hear me?"

Village people always yell on the phone. They think nobody can hear them, but then they yell so loud everyone hears them, even me and Dad.

"Son! Are you okay? We're coming to get you tomorrow. Early in the morning. Your mother's fine, son. Don't worry about her. Ali! Are you there?"

Ali shook his head. Dad yelled.

"He's here, Hasan Bey. He can hear you."

"Ah! Good. Talk to your mother, Ali. Here she is, Ali."

Auntie Aliye yelled into the phone.

"Ali!"

Ali started kicking the shoe cupboard, but soft, like a tap. People do that when they want to run away.

"Ali! My little lamb! Are you okay, my boy? Darling!"

Ali kicked the cupboard again, but harder this time. I think he was crying. He didn't say anything. Then he gave the phone to Dad and ran to the bedroom.

"Hello? Aliye Hanım? Don't worry, Ali's fine. He's feeling a little shy . . . Yes. No, really, he's fine. We'll be expecting you then. And let me say again how sorry I am about what happened. . . . Okay then. If you need anything—We got cut off again!"

I ran to the bedroom to see Ali. When I came in, he ran away to the bathroom. He closed the door. I didn't even see his face. I'm getting a little tired of chasing Ali all the time. The phone rang again.

"It must be Ordu this time. Hello? Dad? Good morning. How are you, Dad? Are you feeling better? Ah, I'm sorry to hear that. Dad, we're coming. . . .Yes, we're coming to see you. We're leaving tomorrow morning, first thing. What? Sure. We can do that. Okay then. See you tomorrow. Bye."

Dad laughed.

"Your grandfather's a funny man, Ayşe. First, he says, 'My heart, my old heart. I hope you make it here in time.' Then he adds, 'Can you pick up a melon on the way?' Sevgi, did you hear that? Hey, why are you reading the paper? We're going to be late."

Mom was wearing one shoe and looking at the newspaper while she looked for the other shoe.

"The headline caught my eye. Just when you think things couldn't get any worse. The commander really did fire on the political prisoners in Mamak Penitentiary. I thought they had to be exaggerating, but it's been confirmed. When did we become so cruel? All they care about is liberating Jerusalem and—"

"Come on, Sevgi. I'm already late."

"They broke into an apartment and killed a CHP family. MHP partisans living in the same building did it. It's madness."

"Sevgi!"

Mom never wears her nice shoes these days, just the old, ugly ones. Grandma picked up the newspaper as they were leaving.

"Let me see. Was it here, in Ankara? Neighbors killing each other . . . Oh dear!"

"What is it, Mother?"

"They gouged out the eyes of an eyewitness to a bank robbery. Oh dear, oh dear!"

"Mother, Aydın and I are coming home together again this evening. We might be earlier than usual so we can start packing. See you later."

Mom left without kissing me. Again.

I got bored then, so bored. Grandma made herself some coffee and sat by the window in the kitchen. She smoked and smoked, like a train. She looked out the window. She puffed, and she talked to herself: "I need to do something . . . talk to her." Ali stayed in the bathroom, and I went to my room. I got my box of pencils. Opening it up, I took a sniff. It smells like pencils, erasers, and my hand, but my hand last year. We'll probably come back from Ordu on Sunday. On Monday, school starts. Mom will get me new stockings, all white. And new shoes, red and shiny. On my first day, I'll wear my lace collar. Grandma will wipe my knees with cologne, and my neck, too. I'll be "fresh as a daisy." I'll wear braids, and we'll put a new white ribbon in my hair. Everyone and everything is always extra clean on the first day of school. Even the toilets. The schoolbags are new. We'll play with a rubber ball during recess. Then we'll go to the stationer's and get a whole bunch of note-books. I'll use a ruler to draw red lines in the left margins of all the pages. That's where you start writing, from the red line. Once the line's there, the notebook's not empty anymore. But the best part is the right side. The page on the right is always clean, always waiting. It's cool when you lean your arm on it. The left side pages get warm and dirty. I think maybe I'm getting sick of Ali, but just a little. He's like the left pages. Always sad. Always down. When school starts, I'll use my lunchbox every single day. In the afternoon, when it's full of mandarin peels, the whole class will smell orangey. And it will smell like hand towels, too, because of the mothers who want kids with clean hands. Kids who always smell like soap. It's nice when everyone's so clean. Ali doesn't have a lunchbox, I'm sure of it. He probably doesn't know how to draw squiggles and flowers on the left side of the red line, either. I know how to draw braids in my notebook. First, you draw three lines, top to bottom, and then you draw loops, one after another, between the line the most on the left and the one the most on the right, but around the middle line, too, and . . . now how do I do that? I'll remem-ber if I look at last year's notebook. I need to remember. I find a nice sharp pencil. I get happy when I draw braids. That's why I keep doing it. And I don't hear anything, not when I'm drawing. Everything is fine, nothing bad happening, nothing to be sad about. It's better to be one of those sparkling clean girls in white stockings with a white ribbon and notebooks that don't have the corners turned back. I draw and draw, not thinking about Ali, not getting sad. Even if I asked him to make notebook decorations with me, he wouldn't. Oh! He's coming out of the bathroom. He'll come up and say, "Let's look at the encyclopedia," or "How are we going to save the swans?" It's because we're going to save the swans together that he likes me, or acts like it, anyway. It's more fun to play with the kids at school, the ones who bring bananas during "Made in Turkey Week." I'm still bored. If I had lots of new notebooks, I'd make even more red lines.

"Ayşe, sweetie, I'm running to Jale Hanım's for a couple of minutes. You'll be good while I'm gone, won't you, dear? I'm leaving the door open. I'll be back before you know it."

I stood by the door and listened to grandma walk down the stairs. Ali finally came over, but I don't want to talk to him anymore. Always sad, always boring. And he won't visit when school starts, anyway. He won't say to his mom, "Take me to Ayşe's." He won't miss me when the swans are saved. Why would he? He doesn't really like me. I made crazy eyes and looked at him, without talking. How do you like it? He got scared. I could hear Grandma talking at Jale Hanım's door.

"Jale Hanım, good morning."

"What can I do for you, Nejla Hanım?"

"Nothing . . . About yesterday, I wanted to—"

"Nejla Hanım, I'm awfully busy right now. We're getting ready for the engagement. It's tomorrow night."

"It's shameful what you've done, Jale Hanım. We all know what you said to that policeman."

"So what."

"So what? Can't you see it's shameful? How many years have we been neighbors? These are trying times, Jale Hanım. Brother against brother, neighbor against neighbor, they're all killing each other. You know us. We're ordinary people who keep to ourselves. And we know you, too. You're good people. What quarrel do we have each other? We had a misunderstanding, but no malice was intended. Let's make peace and go back to being good neighbors."

"Look here, Nejla Hanım. Don't think I don't realize how your daughter and your son-in-law and those communist friends of theirs ridicule my family every chance they get. For all I know, they even call us fascists behind our backs."

"That's not true, Jale Hanım. How can you even think that?"

"I don't know."

"Such a word would never leave my lips, and I—"

"I don't know about that, Nejla Hanım. All I know is you dumped a bolt of fabric in my hand a week before my Feride's engagement ceremony. Fortunately, my future son-in-law arranged for the best tailor in Ankara to make me a dress in less than three days."

"I'm so happy for you."

"As it turned out, I wasn't forced to depend on communists like you and yours."

"That's enough, Jale Hanım!"

"Enough of what?"

Grandma started walking up the stairs.

"Enough of everything. You've gone too far. Why, I've never met a more ill-mannered woman in all my life."

"It's you communists who are ill-mannered!"

"Trouble, nothing but trouble . . ."

Grandma came in with a tomato-red face. She closed the door.

"That fascist harpy!"

She clapped her hand over her mouth.

"Ah! I called her a 'harpy.'"

From the kitchen came the sounds of Grandma clearing the breakfast table, beating up the dishes, clinking and clanking, yelling to herself.

"It's my mistake! Why attempt to humor her! What do you expect of a woman who would call the police? It's all my fault. Damn it to hell!"

Ali doesn't know I'm not talking to him anymore.

"Are your neighbors really fascists?"

How am I supposed to know? Fascists are for grown-ups!

"If they're fascists, do you have guns? For if they attack?"

Ali's being silly. Always thinking the worst. Always expecting terrible things to happen. I'm going to read *Heidi* tonight, and tomorrow I'm going to run through all that greenness in Ordu, and then there's school on Monday, so I'll have lots of notebooks with straight red lines.

"Where's your gun?"

"I'm not talking to you!"

I went to my room. Ali didn't come. I took out all my notebooks and made decorations, a whole lot of them, and sang songs. Happy songs. The sunlight came in through the window and those teensy things, the dust and the I don't know what, whirled around. I watched them for a long time. I wrote, "I am a Turk, honest and hardworking. . . . My existence shall be dedicated to the Turkish existence," so I'm ready if my teacher calls on me for the Student Pledge. I read the whole pledge out loud, twice. Ali didn't come into the room, even once. But I don't care. I don't want him to. Then it was time to draw braids, and flowers, and squiggles . . . and someone knocked on the door. Not a normal knock. A *bang, bang* knock. Maybe Jale Hanım's come to say "sorry"? I ran to the door. So did Ali. But we're not talking. Not one word. Grandma came, too, still yelling.

"Coming! Coming! There's no need to knock so hard. I can hear you."

It's Samim Abi! His shirt is undone. He's sweaty and red.

"Samim. What's happened, son?"

"Auntie Nejla, we've got to leave at once. Someone will come and get this package from you. Give my best to Aydın Abi and Sevgi Abla. We'll be gone for—"

"Samim! Hurry up!"

Ayla Abla was shouting up the stairs. Samim Abi was about to go, but he looked at me and Ali first.

"Ayşe! Ayşeyevich. We'll be back, kids. Ali! Your Hüseyin Abi and Birgül Abla are coming back, too. Don't be scared."

The package in Grandma's hand was shaking.

"Samim!"

Samim Abi was on the stairs when he turned and asked.

"What, Auntie Nejla?"

"Be careful, son!"

Samim Abi didn't laugh like wild horses this time. He laughed like all the horses had run away. And were gone. And then he was gone, except for the *clop clop* of his shoes on the stairs, quieter and quieter.

Music began filling the stairwell.

"... *My hair grew white before I grew old.*"

As the door to the building slammed shut, the song ended.

"*Snow white hair I feel like tearing out.*"

Jale Hanım slammed her door shut, so there was no more music. Grandma yelled down the stairwell.

"That's a sad song for such a self-satisfied woman!"

Ali and I just stood there. Grandma remembered the package in her hand.

"Whatever could this be? Who's going to pick it up? Did he say? Good gracious. It's a wonder I'm able to keep my wits. God help me."

Grandma was shaking so much she almost dropped the package. Ali took it from her and put it on the shoe cupboard. It was covered with newspaper. *Cumhuriyet.* He pulled it off. Grandma was still shaking.

"My blood pressure's gone through the roof. I think I'm about to faint. What's that in there? God have mercy!"

A gun!

I think I said it. "A gun!"

"One's a STEN and the other's a fourteen caliber. They're Hüseyin Abi's."

Then Ali turned to Grandma.

"Have you got a coal cellar? Pieces are hidden in coal cellars."

Grandma swayed and grabbed at the wall.

"I'm feeling terribly woozy, children."

Shouting came from the street, big brothers and big sisters.

"You'll pay for Mamak!"

"Death to fascism! The only path is the revolutionary path!"

We were running out onto the balcony to look down when there was a huge *boom.* "A bomb!" Ali said. He knows everything.

Grandma sort of crossed her arms, but in the air, not on her belly.

"The bogeyman's coming, Ayşe! Time to hide!"

Grandma wanted to play "Safety Drill." Ali and I just looked at her. "We have to hide the guns," Ali said. Grandma stood there, waving her arms, trying to play "Safety Drill" all by herself. I looked at Ali. It was no time for games.

—

"What's keeping them? I hope they get home safely."

For the ninth time, Ayşe's grandma was saying that. We hid the guns. I said, "If you don't have a coal cellar, hide them in a pot." Ayşe's grandma got a pot and put the guns inside it, and then we put the pot in a cupboard in the kitchen. The yelling outside didn't stop.

Dhak! Dhak! Dhak! They're spraying bullets out there. With an automatic. At each "*dhak*" Ayşe's grandma makes us sit closer together. We're on the sofa across from the TV. She's doing this weird prayer.

"I enclose the children in a dome of light and crystal, of satin and pearls. Presto. They are sealed in their dome. May God protect them!"

We watched a cartoon while she was doing that. Heidi missing the mountains, and telling Clara about them. Ayşe said, "Don't you miss your neighborhood? It's in the mountains, isn't it?" I didn't answer. What can I say? Besides, we have jobs to do. I can't think about home. My head will hurt, and I won't be able to get any jobs done. The door to the balcony is behind the TV. I can see Samim Abi's house over there. Me and Ayşe are watching *Heidi*, but we're keeping an eye on Samim's house, too.

Ayşe's grandma gets scared again when the news starts. She turns it up and sits next to us.

"*Commander of the Air Force General Tahsin Şahinkaya, who returned from the United States today . . .*"

"I wonder if Sevgi and Aydın decided to do some shopping for tomorrow. Could that be why they're late?"

Ayşe's grandma is looking at me. As if I'd know. Maybe she's asking me because I'm a man. When I don't say anything, she turns back to the TV.

"*In a statement released by the Ministry of the Interior, provocateurs and anarchists have been warned not to . . .*"

"Ah! So that's why they've taken to the streets."

Ayşe's grandma is looking at me again. Maybe because I'm a revolutionary. She thinks I know everything.

"Where could they be? I'm getting worried."

I feel like I have to say something.

"It was the Port-Said that misfires. The fourteen caliber works fine."

"What did you say, my child?"

"Samim Abi took the Port-Said."

Uncle Dürüst stares like that when he talks to himself, the way Ayşe's grandma is staring at me now. She got up and closed all the curtains. She went over to the phone, picked it up and listened.

"It's working."

She went into the kitchen and lit a cigarette. Ayşe opened the curtains back up. Because she's smart, actually. Then we watched some commercials.

"Spread it on thick! Eat it up!"

It's spreadable cheese. "I've never eaten spreadable cheese," Ayşe said. "Me neither," I said. "It must be one of those American things, like Corn Flakes," I said. "Things that make you smile." "But we're going to eat them now, aren't we?" Ayşe asked. I didn't say anything. "You spread a little at a time, right? But so it covers all the bread, even the corners?" "Of course," I said, even though I have olives with my bread. "It wouldn't taste good if you had too much," Ayşe said. "Nope," I said. We were both watching Samim Abi's house and the TV.

There was a knock on the door. Ayşe's grandma yelled from the kitchen.

"Thank God, they're home."

It was Ayşe's mom and dad. Her grandma was holding the pot when she opened the door. Ayşe ran up to them. She hugged her mom. Her mom hugged her.

"I was worried sick, Sevgi! Why are you so late?"

"Haven't you heard the gunshots, Mother? There's a firefight right on our street. We waited until it was safe, just around the corner. You're white as a sheet. What are you doing with that pot?"

"Don't ask. Don't even ask what's happened. Ayşe, take Ali to your room . . . Never mind. They've seen it all. We've got nothing to hide. Samim came by this afternoon. In a big hurry. He looked such a fright. He dropped off a package. He said someone will pick it up. This was inside the package."

Ayşe's dad cursed when her grandma opened the lid. Ayşe went in between her mom's legs. She looked at me from in there. When I looked at her, she ran over and sat next to me. She thinks everything will be okay if she holds my hand.

"Mother, did Samim say anything else? Who's going to pick it up? When?"

"I don't know."

"Nejla Hanım, concentrate. Are you certain he didn't tell you? It's important. Maybe we'd better ask the kids."

"Do you think something like that would slip my mind? He said they'd be back. What's going on, Sevgi? Or is Samim . . ."

We keep our eyes on Samim Abi and Ayla Abla's house. They keep talking. But Ayşe grandmother forgot what I told her. They're Hüseyin Abi's guns. Nobody's asking me.

"What shall we do, Aydın?"

"What can we do, Sevgi? Nothing. We'll wait. We're leaving tomorrow morning, and as long as somebody comes by then—"

"Well what if nobody comes? Should we still go to Ordu? Or should we wait?"

"Wait for what, Sevgi? Why did they go and get us mixed up in this? Think of the children!"

"Aydın, aren't you concerned about them, at least?"

"What good is your concern doing you, Sevgi?"

They looked at each other. Then they came into the living room, went out on the balcony, and looked over at Samim Abi's house. They turned their backs to me and Ayşe. On TV, a man was telling a bedtime story. Ayşe's parents and her grandma were whispering to each other, little streams of words coming out of their mouths. They'd forgotten us.

I held tight to the lighter in my pocket. Hüseyin Abi forgot all about it. When someone forgets something and you see that they forgot, and you say nothing, that thing just stays there. Like it never belonged to that person in the first place. And they suddenly leave like nothing happened and it was never theirs. That nothing doesn't make a sound. It waits there until it's remembered. Then, if someone says, "Oh, I forgot it!" and comes back, the thing kind of comes back to life and cheers up. When Hüseyin Abi comes back, his Ibelo is going to come to life. It'll be happy. For now, it's waiting in my pocket.

Ayşe's mom closed all the curtains. Tightly, without a gap. We can't see Samim Abi's house anymore. They went to their bedroom after that, whispering all the way. They didn't look over at me and Ayşe. She got scared. Her mom and dad did, too. Her grandmother was already scared, because she's old. They're scared because nothing happened. They're scared because they didn't do anything. Because they didn't yell. If they yelled, they wouldn't be so scared. Ayşe got up and opened the curtain. She sat back down next to me. A movie started. *The Mouse That Roared*. It's a funny move, I think, but me and Ayşe are watching the darkness. The balcony window is like a big TV. A broken TV that doesn't show anything.

Before they went to bed, Ayşe's mom and dad got the pot with the guns from the kitchen. They looked over where the phone is and in front of the door. They put the pot in a drawer. Then they pulled it out and took it to the kitchen. Ayşe's grandma kept walking back and forth in front of me and Ayşe.

"Are you leaving early in the morning?" I asked Ayşe. She nodded her head "yes." "Then when are we going to save the swans?" I asked. She shrugged. I didn't ask anything else, because Ayşe was scared. If she thought about the swans, she wouldn't get scared. You don't get scared when you have a job to do. Hüseyin Abi's coming back. That's what Samim Abi said. Revolutionaries never lie. If they say they're coming, they come. Ayşe's grandma was standing right in front of us, by the balcony door, with a bunch of clothespins.

"Sevgi! I did some laundry, but in all the confusion I forgot to hang it up. It's too late now, isn't it?

From the bedroom, Ayşe's mom said something.

"What did you say? I can't hear you."

That's when it happened. *Flap flap*. Like the sound of a kite. A kite flying right past your ear.

"Surrender! Surrender!"

It all happened so slowly, heavy and slow. The light in Samim Abi's house went on. Ayşe's mom and dad came into the living room. Ayşe's grandma stood in front of us with her clothespins. Samim Abi's balcony door opened. Hüseyin Abi! Birgül Abla! Hüseyin Abi's holding his Port-Said. Birgül Abla's hair is wild. They both climbed up onto the railing. They stopped. Hüseyin Abi saw me. He lifted his gun into the air. Did he smile? Birgül Abla was next to him. She was looking at Hüseyin Abi, not me. She held his hand. Then . . . *flap, flap, flap* . . . Hüseyin Abi and Birgül Abla began to fly. Over to Ayşe's balcony. Through the air. The curtain closed. The clothespin fell to the floor. Ayşe's dad yelled, "Go to the bathroom! Go to the bathroom!"

It all got faster. Ayşe's grandma was trying to gather up the clothespins.

"Mother, leave them there. Come to the bathroom!"

Ayşe started crying. But without making a sound. I was standing there. We both looked at her dad. He was yelling.

"Go to the bathroom! Go to the bathroom!"

We didn't move. I took Ayşe's hand.

"We have to save the swans tonight. Before Hüseyin Abi and Birgül Abla land."

Ayşe opened her mouth wide. She shook her head. We looked at Ayşe's dad.

"Quick! Go to the bathroom!"

I didn't let go of Ayşe's hand. We were both embarrassed. It was because of Ayşe's dad. He was doing something bad, and we were embarrassed. Revolutionaries can fly, though. Ayşe's dad doesn't know that, of course. But for them to keep flying and for them not to get shot, we have to save the swans. Nobody knows that. Not Ayşe's dad, or her mom, or her grandma. But Ayşe knows. I won't let go of her hand. She cried without making a sound, that's why.

UNIT 15

Civics

Solidarity

Soldiers go blind when they look at the light. That's why we're squatting under the glowing aquarium in the dark. Me and Ayşe, in the shadow of the light. Together, we're wearing the parka, my right arm in my uncle's right sleeve, Ayşe's left arm in his left sleeve. Uncle Sait, a tent for us both. We're inside him, and nobody can see us. From behind the wheelbarrow, we peek. *Tramp, tramp* is the sound the soldiers make as they get out of their jeeps. The fish gurgle as they swim around and around. The aquarium light *hmmms* and *hmmms*. Fish pass in front of the light, becoming shadows of themselves. A murmur and a soft clatter comes from the many windows of the many apartments. The people, like the fish, are gliding shadows. Curtains *swish!* open and *swoosh* shut. The fish press their eyes to the glass. The only sound now is the aquarium . . . *hmmm* . . . and the fish . . . *gurgle, gurgle*.

They won't do anything if they catch us; I made Ayşe put on her white socks. But it'll be terrible if they look inside Ayşe's lunchbox. I thought she was scared, so why is she smiling?

—

It's wonderful this, "the middle of the night." This is my first time. If Ali hadn't woken me up, I wouldn't have seen it. I was asleep, or something like it. When he got me up, he made me wear my white socks. And I put on my overalls, too, because I'm strong in them. Then Ali got my lunchbox. Inside it was the rope and the chloroform. We have the sack and the parka, too, for going to the park. Ali hears everything, so we can't make a peep. He listens in the hallway. "The sound of sleeping," he says. I sniff the air. The house smells like sleep. "Shhh," goes Ali when I whisper, "It smells blue." He opens the door so slowly I think we'll never go. We creep down the stairs. The wheelbarrow is waiting where Ali put it, in the entrance hall. It's heavy at first, before it gets light. Walking makes it lighter. Ali talks normal now.

"I thought your mom and dad would never sleep." He laughs, but a scary laugh. "They got scared, of course. They thought Hüseyin Abi and Birgül Abla fell to the ground. Then they couldn't sleep."

When we pass a streetlight, I see Ali's cheeks, all red. Maybe he has a fever again; maybe everything is a dream to him. "This is a shortcut. It's called Ahmetler Hill." Ali thinks he's grown-up because he knows the name of the street. He thinks Hüseyin Abi flew. Or maybe Ali thinks everything is a game. Even falling. And if you fall from the balcony, you die. That's what Grandma said this one time when Dad was handing me to Samim Abi.

"You'll end up dropping her, God forbid! One day she'll fall to her death."

But if I tell Ali that falling isn't a game, he'll get sick; his head will hurt; he won't talk. What's more, if I say that, I'll be the same as Dad. Why did Dad close the curtains? Hüseyin Abi and Birgül Abla were going to jump onto our balcony, and they wouldn't have fallen. Or does Dad think it's all a game, too? Maybe I should pretend it's a game. That's what the soldiers are doing.

—

Maybe the revolution happened. But probably it didn't, because the people in the windows are scared. They close the curtains when they see soldiers, open the windows when they don't. When they look out, they get scared. Maybe they get scared when they don't look out, too. When the fish pass in front of the light, become shadows of themselves, become dark, their colors are no more. Are they scared to go outside? Or are they scared to be inside? Ayşe leaned closer to me in the parka and whispered, "It's wintery, isn't it? Inside this parka, we're playing the wintertime game." Her voice is the wind in my ears, *whoosh whooshing*. I shiver. The soldiers *clomp, clomp* into line. Nobody talks. Nobody looks like Hüseyin Abi. No, the revolution didn't happen. They're not laughing; there are no big sisters. Something bad is happening. Something awful.

—

"Ayşe! Let's go!"

Ali stood up all at once. He got mad at the wind noises I was making in his ear, I think. He doesn't want to play that game. He wants to play real games.

"We have to go in the dark, Ayşe! A coup's happening."

There were soldiers—one, two three . . . ten of them—in front of the post office. The other ones got into a truck and left. Ten soldiers, frozen and still. Like a photo. Like everyone is watching. Like the national anthem is playing. The street is empty. Nobody's out here! It's funny, this "coup" thing, but the people in the windows aren't smiling. They aren't making a single sound. Nobody laughs at this "coup," so it isn't a funny thing. But it is exciting, I guess.

—

Since Ayşe's a girl, we go real slow. I'd go fast with the boys from the Gardens, but they wouldn't believe it, either. They'd make noise, sing anthems and things.

"Ali, if we go behind the light, they won't see us, I'm sure of it."

Ayşe's smarter than them, because she's a girl. If only I was stronger. We'd push the wheelbarrow up the hill faster then.

"Ali, we'll be back before they wake up, won't we? With the swan. Then we'll all have breakfast together. Right?"

But because she's a girl, she still thinks it's all a game. Birds start singing. The sun will come up soon. It's not possible to get the swan before that. If we get caught, Mom will be so sad.

"The littlest one, Ali, that's the swan we should save. It's worse for the little one. They haven't operated on its wing yet."

Yes, Ayşe is smart. The smartest girl of all. Two more birds start singing. They look down on us, two black shadows on top of the streetlight. Soon, it will be morning. Everyone will see the soldiers. Right now, everyone is at home, waiting for the sun. They'll yell when the light comes. Soldiers probably won't come to my neighborhood. There's nothing there, not even a bus stop.

—

Ali's not scared at all. I am, though. But only a little bit. In one window, I see a father, a mother, and a daughter. There's a radio on the windowsill, and they're standing around it. The mother's in a nightgown, blue, and the father's in pajamas. The girl's pajamas are just like mine, I think. Her mother and father are sleepy. They're both smoking, puffing white smoke into the blackness. Birds are chirping. I can't hear the radio. If I were up there, in that apartment, I'd go to sleep. I wouldn't be scared at all. If they catch us, though, they won't take us to the police station. That's what I think. They'll say, "What a pity. They're so little." I cleaned Ali's shoes before we left, so they won't do anything to him, either. That's what I think. More birds start chirping. They fly high in the sky over Ankara, so they know all there is to know. Two sparrows sit on a branch, not chirping, tiny and quiet. What a pity. They're so little. "Get down! Get down!" Ali yells.

—

Me and Ayşe get down on the ground in front of an apartment building. We need to hide. Big brothers are handcuffed. They get in a jeep.

Why don't they say anything? Then a man comes. A watchman. I think it's a place for students, a dorm. The watchman yells.

"Let them go! What have they ever done to you?"

A soldier with a flat hat gets out of the jeep. He hits the watchman with the handle of his rifle. The watchman spits. Is that blood? "Mind your fucking business!" the soldiers says, with a kick. "That'll teach you!" The big brothers aren't fighting back. Are they scared? Maybe they're not revolutionaries, not real ones. So why do they have to get into the jeep? A dog comes up to us, quiet as can be, not a sound but its breathing. It's wagging its tail. Ayşe gets scared.

—

The dog smells terrible. We'll get rabies if it bites. Stray dogs have rabies, that's what they say at school. Then you get a shot in the stomach, with a big needle. I hide in the parka. "Don't be scared," Ali says. "It's a street dog. It wants to protect us." But I say, "But what if it bites?" and Ali says, "Street dogs want to protect you." The soldiers beat that man up bad. But the big brothers didn't say or do anything. One after another, all in a line, the soldiers smack the big brothers. They do that with a ruler at school, too, smacking one hand after another, all in a row, and nobody ever says anything. I think the dog likes us, but he can't come. They'll hit it, too, if they catch us. The truck drives away fast. The wheelbarrow is light now, at the top of the hill. The sky is dark blue, such a nice color. So this is what they mean by "the wee hours."

—

"The park is at the end of this street."

We're close now, but I'm a little tired. My face is hot, too, but I think it'll pass before we get to the park. "Ali, we have to be extra careful now," Ayşe says. "We'll hide as we go, right?" More jeeps pass by, fast. If we get caught, Dad will get mad, mad that I took Ayşe along. And

Mom will get sad. The dog leaves us on the corner of Tunalı Hilmi. It barks behind us. It's not wagging its tail. "Come back," it's saying. "Don't go. I can't protect you." Street dogs want people to protect, or they get scared. I'd be scared, too, if Ayşe weren't here to protect.

—

We stop in front of shops and apartment building. Three times. We were getting ready to go again and another truck passed. So we stayed down on the ground in front of a pastry shop. There were big sisters in the truck. They were in the back, in the open, and they looked at us. They looked, but they couldn't see us. They're like a photo, too. Still, hands chained together. Hands wriggling, but not moving. They hold out their hands, but they can't hold each other. The truck jumps and they fall. Down go all the big sisters, and they can't get up again. Ali looks through the window. Maybe he wants a pastry, now, all at once. He forgets me. He doesn't turn and look at the big sisters. A bug crawls up between my feet. A big, black bug. The truck lights turn its black back to purple. The truck drives away. The big sisters are gone. Ali comes and sits next to me. He looks at the bug.

—

Big sisters are in the bed of the jeep. I didn't look, couldn't look. They're scared, maybe. I mustn't look. They'll get embarrassed. They wouldn't get so scared if they knew we were saving the swans. But now, in the truck, they don't know who they are. Like they're weak. Like they're not revolutionaries. *Vınnn* goes the fridge in the glass box in the pastry shop. The pastry is nasty, all of it. When the jeep drives away and the buzzing stops, I go up to Ayşe. There's a bug by her leg. It's crossing a crack in the sidewalk and it gets turned onto its back. Its feet wriggle and it wants help. Ayşe looks at me. She gives the bug a little push. Back on its feet, it walks away. I think Ayşe can hear it when bugs scream. Just like me.

—

When all the jeeps and all the soldiers are gone, we run to the park. The wheelbarrow tips to one side, tips to the other side. It doesn't fall over, because we're inside the park. The big arms of the parka hold it straight, keep it steady. It'll be terrible if we can't save the swans. But if we do save them, Mom won't get mad at me for running away in the middle of the night. Dad won't get mad, either. And he won't be scared. We'll laugh, and Grandma will say, "My goodness, Ayşe!" We're almost there. We see an uncle and an auntie. The uncle has a little suitcase and they're running, running straight toward us. Running away from the park. The auntie can't go very fast. She takes off her shoes. "Wait!" she says. "Run!" he says. "The car's waiting. It's our only chance." Me and Ali stand there. They're surprised, but they don't stop. "Go home," the uncle yells at us. "Children, at this time of day?" says the auntie. They look back at us, but they keep going. It's kind of funny to watch the auntie run in bare feet. They're scared, though. I don't laugh. Then, out come the butterflies. Orange!

—

Ayşe laughed when she saw the woman and the man. The woman made a high sound, like a whistle. Like she had a dead bird inside. The man coughed and coughed. They're running away. Escaping. Are they going far far away? To a place where Turkey can't get them? But if they don't get caught . . . I mean, if you're playing "catch me if you can" and you don't get caught, not even once, it feels like you never played the game, like you weren't there. If nobody chases you, you disappear, like you aren't even there. Ayşe pointed to some butterflies and went, "Orange!" But they're not orange. She thinks all butterflies are orange, because they make her happy. Then they disappear, those butterflies. We got the butterflies into Parliament, and they got caught. If nobody caught them, and nobody saw them, nobody would know they got into Parliament. It's weird.

—

Ali can't see the orange butterflies, I think. He believes Hüseyin Abi and Birgül Abla can fly, but he doesn't believe in orange butterflies. They got between the books, and the big ones got between the big books. And they made marks there. Orange ones. Later, when they look at the archive, they'll say, "Ayşe and Ali brought butterflies in here." They'll know, because when they touch the books they'll get orange dust on their hands, the dust of butterfly wings. And they'll laugh and say, "What clever kids, that Ayşe and Ali are. Nobody's as brave as them."

—

We left the wheelbarrow in the tall grass. Ayşe lay the parka inside it. "To make it nice and warm," she said. If we make noise, they'll catch us. I can see jeeps, not so far away. Up ahead. They don't see us, but they can hear us, maybe. If they do hear us, soldiers will come running and they'll yell, "What are you doing here!" Really loud. My head will hurt, and I won't be able to do a thing. Maybe Ayşe will yell, "He's with me! Let him go!" But then they'll take away Ayşe. They won't care if her socks are white. Don't be scared, Hüseyin Abi. I'm going to do it. I'm almost there.

—

Ali's going to hold the chloroform cotton to the swan's nose. Then I'll put the swan in the wheelbarrow. It's a little swan, so we can get it in there. And then we'll take the same streets home. I think it'll be easy. Ali's a hero. He's sneaking up on the sleeping swan, slowly, like a cat. Ali goes for the little swan's beak. It lifts its head. The other swans wake up. They all look at us. The little swan sways its head, back and forth. But Ali's holding its beak. And he's holding the cotton to its nose.

—

The little swan didn't make a sound. Even when we were tying its legs together. The other swans looked at us. Then they looked over at the soldiers, at the jeeps. But not a sound. These swans don't have voices, but that's not the reason they're quiet now. It's because they know who we are. They get up on their feet, but they don't walk away. They just stand there, looking. One eye on the soldiers, the other eye on us. The little swan falls asleep right away.

—

Ali opens the swan's wings. "This is the one," he says. "It has the nicest wings." I don't think they did an operation. It's still so little. And then, the swan seems to get longer and longer. Like a roll of dough. Soft and white. But it kind of stretches and falls apart when you pick it up. Long and sad. We get it in the sack. Me and Ali each hold one side of the sack, and we slip it under and around the sleeping swan. Its head goes inside, too. "Will it be able to breathe?" I ask. "Yes." Ali said. He knows everything, because he reads the encyclopedia. We open the sack and look at the swan's head. Beautiful. All white. With an orange beak and black marks around its eyes. "Snow White," I say. "These swans don't make any sounds," Ali says. "Only when they die—" *Rat tat tat!*

—

The sun's almost ready to come up. A man is running, down into the park. Holding a gun. "Freeze!" a soldier shouts. Just once. Then, *rat tat tat!* The man's on the ground. His face is looking at us. But not his eyes. He didn't have time to close his eyes. Me and Ayşe sit in the tall grass. Ants walk by our feet. They didn't hear any of it. They're still in line, walking. Some go into a hole, some come out. They walk and walk. *Clank!* goes a shop shutter. The grocer doesn't look at the man.

The grocer doesn't look at the soldiers. He looks at the key in his hand. The key goes into the hole. The door opens. Is he deaf?

—

The man looked at us when he fell. I didn't look at him. I'm mad at the ants. I step on their hill. I close their hole. "Don't," Ali says. I stop doing it. We're going home. We'll give the swan some lettuce. We'll have breakfast with the swan. Maybe Mom will spread the Şokella all the way to the edges, again.

—

People look out at us from windows. We look at them. Nobody says anything. Nobody makes a sound when they see us. I look back. Do they see something we don't? There's nothing there. Why is everyone so quiet? Smoke starts puffing out of chimneys. In the summertime? All the chimneys are smoking.

—

There are uncles in pajamas out on the street. They walk real close to the walls, hiding. Like they're playing hide-and-seek on the way to the bakery. Then they run home with their bread. It's a bread game, but a serious game. They have to get their bread as fast as they can, so they don't really look at us. The swan is sleeping, nice and quiet. We'll wrap it in a blanket when we get home. We'll give water. We turn into our street and see Mom and Dad. Mom's been crying. Dad's face is dark. They don't shout when they see us. Nobody shouts, "Ayşe!" Dad runs up to us. We were going to run to him, too, but we stop. Dad is so, so mad. Mom claps her hand over her mouth, so she doesn't make any noise. We stand between our building and Samim Abi's. They'll be happy soon, but they don't know it, not yet. There's a lot of film in front of Samim Abi's building. The film for the projector, a mountain of it. His secret film.

—

Ayşe's dad is running up to hit us. It's okay. We have the swan. The sun has come up. The colors have come back. Red is back, too, there on the ground. There, where Hüseyin Abi and Birgül Abla went flying. So, there was some blood. It's okay. It's okay. When Ayşe's dad picks her up and runs away, I push the wheelbarrow all by myself. Ayşe's mom cries when I push it inside the building. She hugs Ayşe. Nobody hugs me. It's okay. "Darling!" yells Ayşe's mom, making the doors open one by one. The doors of the neighbors all listening to the same thing on the radio.

A door opens:
"Parliament and the government . . ."
That door closes and another one opens.
". . . dissolved."
That one closes and another one opens.
"Across Turkey . . ."
It closes and another one opens.
". . . martial law . . ."
And again.
". . . declared . . ."
The last door closes. No more doors open.

UNIT 16

Cleanliness Is Next to Godliness

Let's Keep Our Environment Clean

"Ayşe! Ali! Stop it. The only reason the poor thing's scurrying around like that is because you two are. Oh dear! And there's been a coup d'état. Sit down and keep still, children!"

The swan wanted to run because it opened its wings. It ran in the hallway first. Now it's running in the living room. We're trying to catch it. Mom and Dad are smoking and listening to the news on the radio. But there's music, not news.

"It's rearing up again, oh my
The gray horse of the column leader . . ."

The more that song plays the more the swan opens its wings. Grandma's so mad at us. She's smoking a cigarette now, too.

"My dear girl, it's nearly one o'clock, time for the news to begin. The pashas will appear on the television any minute now. Ayşe! Leave that bird alone. Sevgi, do something! Why are you listening to Ottoman marching music at a time like this?"

The man on the radio has a nice, deep voice. It makes the swan want to run more and more.

". . . it looks as if

We are off to do battle!"
Mom didn't answer Grandma, but she did turn on the TV.
"Aydın, could you turn off the radio, dear? The generals are about to take center stage."
Mom called Dad "dear"!

—

Ayşe's mom and dad are still in pajamas, in the middle of the day. They stayed by the little radio the whole time. Over by the window. The radio keeps talking about what's happening out in the streets, but they never look out the window. They only look at the radio. Even when it plays folk songs. Like they're waiting for the radio to tell them what to do. The swan sat in the hallway at first. It didn't move. Then it started running all over. Me and Ayşe gave it some lettuce before it walked and walked. Grandma said to shut it in the bathroom, but they couldn't because Ayşe was going to cry. Then it ran round and round the coffee table in the middle. When Ayşe's mom turned on the TV, the swan got in front of it. Ayşe's mom and dad are watching TV. We're behind them. There's a general, holding pieces of paper. He's reading, not talking. You're not supposed to do that. Nobody listens when you read from the paper. And he doesn't say "the people." He says "citizens." That's wrong, too!

"*. . . as we have all witnessed in recent months, the Republic of Turkey, which was entrusted to us by the Great Atatürk, and which is a nation whose state and citizens are united, has been subjected to treacherous attacks— both mental and physical—at the instigation of foreign and domestic ene- mies that target its existence, its regime, and its independence . . .*"

—

When Dad opened the sack this morning and saw the swan, he said, "What the hell have you done?"—but he wasn't that mad, I think, because they were scared we were dead—and that's when Ali whispered in my ear, "You tell them." I looked at Mom. She was crying hard. Dad had red eyes. Grandma had muslin wrapped around her head and was sleeping on the sofa because her "blood pressure spiked." I said, "We saved the swan to make you happy." I said it in a tiny voice, so maybe they didn't hear. Dad yelled, "What?" I said it again.

"We saved the swan so that we win and you're happy."

That's when that song started playing.

Off on campaign we go, oh my

Oh, from campaign to campaign!

"We saved the swan so that we win and you're happy."

That's when the swan first got to its feet. It walked and walked. The song played again and again, and it kept walking. But now the news is on and the swan has finally stopped. It went in front of Mom and Dad, though. When it opens its wings, all you can see is the general's hat. He's the chief of staff, the one we saw at the concert. The one who wanted to hurt the swans! But the swan's in front of him now, so only his hat is talking. And the swan can see him, but he can't see it. Now that's funny!

"*. . . in order to protect national integrity, unity and solidarity; prevent a probable civil war pitting brother against brother; restore the authority and the functionality of the state . . .*"

—

Ayşe's laughing, but why? The general doesn't say anything about swans. If he knows we saved one, that's why he doesn't say anything. He's mad. We saved the swan, so it didn't happen exactly like he wanted. The swan spreads its wings with a *flap flap flap*, making that kite sound. The swan knows, too, that the general's a bad man. That's why it's making fun of him. The swan's a lion!

"*Parliament and the government have been dissolved. The legislative immunity of members of Parliament has been removed. Martial law has gone into effect across the country. Travel to destinations outside of Turkey has been banned . . .*"

—

The swan starts flapping its wings even more. Mom and Dad are trying to see the general. They stick their heads to one side, then to the other side. But they can't see a thing.

"Aydın, could you grab that swan!"

"Why do I have to grab it? Why don't you?

"How am I supposed to grab it? It's huge."

"I'm not doing it."

I laughed at that. Mom and Dad are being funny. They looked at me. The general was still talking, but we could hardly hear him over the sound of the swan's wings.

"A nationwide curfew has been declared."

Mom and Dad laughed a lot. They forgot to smoke their cigarettes, their ashes got long and they kept fake fighting like kids.

"Oh, come on. I can't. You do it."

"Go on. Give it a try."

Grandma kept saying, "Goodness gracious!" again and again. Then she started laughing, too. I'm glad we saved the swan. Home smells like börek again.

—

Ayşe and her family were all laughing when the general got off the TV. Then we heard something like the call to prayer. Her grandma stopped and listened. As she listened, it got quieter everywhere. I could even hear the samovar boiling in the kitchen. It was rattling, and the man was shouting, going quiet, shouting, going quiet. Ayşe's grandma made her eyes big, like the bogeyman was really coming this time.

"He's reciting the *sala*. Someone must have died."

She stopped, and got sad.

"To die on a day like this. All alone. What a pity."

Ayşe's mom and dad looked at her. Her grandma held up her hands.

"There's a curfew. That's why I said that."

—

Mom and Dad are laughing because they can't help it. Because they haven't talked since morning, they can't stop laughing once they start. They're laughing to themselves, in secret. "My nerves are shot," Mom said. Dad went over to the window.

"Sevgi, come and see this. Jale Hanım's hanging a flag on the balcony. She's as cheery as a child on the last day of school."

The phone rang. Dad was rushing to it when the swan ran in front of him.

"Stay right there, sonny. Or missy. Or whatever you are. I can't believe this! But it is kind of funny, waddling around like that. Hello? Hello? They hung up."

—

We're all in a row looking at Ayşe's dad. Even the swan. "Hello? Hello? They hung up." When Ayşe's dad hung up the phone, the swan opened its wings. Ayşe yelled.

"Dad, let's call Uncle Selahattin. Tell him me and Ali saved a swan."

When Ayşe yelled, they got quiet. They looked at us both. They looked at the swan. Ayşe's mom sounded a little mad, but she was pretending.

"We'll discuss the swan later, Ayşe."

The swan ran ahead, and me and Ayşe followed it. We stopped in the hallway. The swan is used to us now. I think it likes Ayşe more. Only because she's a girl, though.

Ayşe's mom and dad are talking in the living room.

"Sevgi, what are we going to do with that bird?"

"How do I know? Shall we ask Selahattin Abi about it? He does have a bird shop. He'll probably know what to do."

"Today of all days, just after a coup happened?"

"There's something far more urgent. . . . Have you noticed all the smoke? The whole neighborhood's been lighting their water heaters. What shall we do?"

"We'll have to light ours, too."

"And the guns?"

"How do I know, Sevgi? I'm thinking."

"Okay, dear."

—

That's the second time Mom called Dad "dear." I heard her. They've turned into the mothers and fathers on TV. It's because they have a different enemy now. The generals came, that's why. And because they're scared. It makes me happy. But Ali is sad. He heard Mom and Dad, too.

"Sevgi, this boy's turned out to be a bit of a bother. We don't even know which hospital Aliye Hanım is at."

"They won't be able to come now. And if they don't come tomorrow—"

"He probably doesn't have any other relatives in Ankara."

"That's why they left him with us."

—

If Mom and Dad came, I'd say, "It was us who saved the swan." And I'd say, "Don't be sad, Mom. Hüseyin Abi and Birgül Abla flew away." Ayşe's dad saw us and came up. He patted my head.

"Your parents won't be able to come today, Ali. They'll come tomorrow. Right, Sevgi?"

—

Mom came up and cuddled Ali's head. "Ali! You have a fever again. When did that happen? Aydın, we'd better put him to bed. He's burning up."

The phone rang.

"Hello? Dad? The hospital! When? Who took you? You're not alone, then? We're fine, Dad. No, tomorrow at the earliest. How can we?

There's been a coup. There's a curfew. A coup, Dad! Please, Dad. Don't. Okay, we'll be there tomorrow."

Dad hung up and turned to Mom. "He says he's dying and we have to come at once. What shall we do?" One of Mom's hands is on Ali's forehead and the other is on my forehead. She's pushing back my hair. She doesn't know she's doing it, but I wish she would always do it. If I say, "Keep doing that, Mom," she'll say, "Doing what?" and take her hand away. But if I don't say anything, she'll forget to do it again.

"Aydın, we'll have to wait until tomorrow morning. There's no helping it."

"You're right. Is Ali's fever really that bad?"

—

I need to sleep. When my head hurts and I'm burning up, I need to sleep. A lot. If I don't sleep, it all gets mixed up. Real things and dream things. If I don't sleep, it all becomes a dream. But will Ayşe's parents throw out the swan while I'm sleeping?

"Sevgi, we've got to figure out what to do with this swan."

"Leave it alone for now. We'll come up with something later."

"We could always wring its neck. Then we could make some swan soup. What do you say, Miss Ayşe? Master Ali?"

"Aydın, please. Don't tease them like that."

I fell. Right on the ground. Just flowed to the ground like water. My eyes closed. The last thing I saw was Ayşe.

—

Ali fainted like those ladies in movies. The swan flapped its wings. Grandma made some vinegar water for Ali. We stayed by his bed. When the towel soaked with vinegar water slid off his feet, I put it back. The swan stayed, too. It didn't flap its wings when Ali was asleep. The phone rang again. Dad put his hands on his hips while Mom was talking. When she hung up, he asked lots of questions.

"Who was that?"

"Önder."

"What did he say?"

"Nothing important."

"Just tell me what he said, Sevgi."

"He's coming to Ankara in two days."

"And?"

"And we'll be gone. So, what we are going to do with the swan when we go? What about leaving it with Jale Hanım? We could hide the guns under its wings. What do you say, Aydın Bey?"

Dad laughed a little, then. Mom put her hand on his arm. I'm glad we saved the swan.

Mom and Dad went to the bathroom. They're going to light the fire in the water heater. They're not going to cook the swan. I asked them. Three times. They're going to burn some things. Ali's sleeping. If they do anything to the swan while he's sleeping, I'll die. I stayed next to Ali. Lots of time passed. Evening came, even. Grandma won't stop watching TV, and Mom got mad.

"Mother, you're not watching *World of Faith*, are you? Oh, I give up!"

Grandma turned up the sound all the way. She's acting funny. When I was sitting next to Ali, the window of Samim Abi's secret room was swinging back and forth. They left the window open. Sometimes, Ali opens his eyes. It smells like vinegar everywhere. It was nasty at first. Now I like it.

—

When I open my eyes, I see Samim Abi's locked room. The window is wobbling. The streetlamps are burning. In the light, there are shapes. Ayşe's dipping towels in vinegar and pressing them to my feet, my head, my hands. Vinegar dribbles onto the bed. Warm, like I wet the bed. It's nice. It flows from my forehead to my ears to the pillow. Slowly, *drip drop*. The shapes on the window look like yellow birds, like orange butterflies. Things are whirling on the window. I see Hüseyin Abi in the street, yelling. Birgül Abla, reaching out her hand to him. When the window moves, their hands come apart. They're hanging a banner in Kızılay Square. Then they're running. Hüseyin Abi runs slowly, so Birgül Abla can catch up. Yellow birds fly up from the places they pass. They go into Samim Abi's house. Hüseyin Abi holds Birgül Abla's face in his hands. Yellow butterflies fly up from her hair. They're locking the door to the room. Hüseyin Abi's thinking about me. About the kite, about Turgay Abi, about the neighborhood, about a ship, about a plane, about a car. He sticks his hands in Birgül's hair. Her yellow hair, growing longer and longer, flying and flying. There's knocking on the door, the police. Hüseyin Abi gets his gun. He kisses Birgül Abla. She's trembling on the window pane. Kites, yellow ones, lots of them, go *flap flap flap*. The police are coming inside and they're going out onto the balcony. Hüseyin Abi's gun goes *click click*, not *bang bang*. And then they turn into birds, both of them. Yellow swans on the balcony. Laughing. Flying. There are no more drip-drops when the towel gets warm.

—

Ali closed his eyes again. I can hear the man on TV, his voice terrible and black.

"*. . . to believe in Allah, may His name be exalted, is to embrace His will and to accept that all outcomes are fortuitous for the true believer. Nothing will happen to us except what Allah has decreed for us . . .*"

As the man spoke, yellow monsters showed on Samim Abi's window, their wings torn. They flew and circled over all the houses. And when they landed on apartment buildings, all the houses went dark and smoke started pouring out of the chimneys. They put all the children to sleep. The sleep of afternoon naps, always. The children they touched became like Ali when he was sick, never talking. Mothers are crying. Fathers are yelling. Children can't wake up. The yellow monsters are terrible. Children need to hide. I see Ali in the window, all yellow. Holding the *Wonderland of Knowledge*. The one with the swans. He's running away from the torn-winged monsters. He needs to hide it. I'm there, too, holding a stack of books. My favorites. If I don't hide them, the torn-winged monsters will see us, too. I'm going to cry. Because Ali seems dead. When the torn-winged monsters, all yellow like that . . .

I get up. If Ali weren't asleep, we'd do it together, but I have to do it now. I get them and take them to the bathroom. Dad's burning books. I hand him my books.

"And this one, too!"

Mom and Dad's faces are red from the fire. They look at each other. Mom pulls her hair back from her face

"Ayşe, we don't need to burn any of the *Wonderland of Knowledge* set. And what's that? *1001 Peaches*. Take them back to your room. There's no need, really."

"I said to burn them. It's the encyclopedia with the swans. Or the monsters will come . . . Mom! Burn them!"

Mom hugged me. I cried a little, my cheek on her belly. Mom has a nice belly. She looked at me and held my face between her hands. "You're a heroic little girl, Ayşe!" she said. That's exactly what she said. Mom's face is close to mine. Her breath is sweet. I want to stay there, just like that, but Jale Hanım is yelling somewhere.

"One floor up! The apartment directly above ours. You can't miss it."

Mom looked at Grandma and shouted, "Mother! Ayşe! The swan!" Grandma put her hands on her head. We ran to Grandma's room with the swan.

UNIT 17

Our Natural Riches

Let's See the Sights

The soldiers are stopping a lot of cars. We're going real slow. Nobody's talking. Mom turned the radio way down. With no noise, the inside of the car smells only of soap. We all have wet hair. Little drops of water fall, slowly, one at a time, from Ali's hair to his shoulders. When a drop of water grows big on the tip of his hair, inside them you can see the things from the window: apartment buildings, soldiers, cars. There are men lined up along the road, their backs to us. The drops are full of them. Not a sound. We all smell the same now. Ali smells of our soap, too.

—

It's so noisy. The car lights, red triangles, go on and off, *tick tock*, like a clock. Walkie-talkies crackle. Ayşe's mom is folding and unfolding a pack of cigarettes, *chussy chussy*. Her grandma prays, *psss psss*, and plays with a button on her purse, *tuckurt tuckurt*. Ayşe's dad keeps going "hmmm . . . hmmm." A general's talking on the radio. We can see Ankara from Çankaya, and in the air, there's a *nnn*. The sound of smoke. Everyone's taking baths. Soon, maybe, they'll take us all to prison. In the end, they'll catch us, take the swan, cut its wings.

—

When Dad stopped the car, he said, "Don't say anything." But we're already not talking. It's a station wagon, so they put cushions in the back for us. It's huge back here. The swan's in a sack next to us. It's sleeping, because of the chloroform. And me and Ali are sick!

—

Ayşe's dad keeps playing with the stick shift, *gurch gurch*. Ayşe's mom puts her hand on top of his. The sound stops. The car stops. He opens the window and talks fast.

"Good morning. I'm taking the family to Ordu. My father's in the hospital. He's got a heart condition. The kids are ill, and sleeping in the back. We're on our way to Ordu. That's right. My father lives there. Yes."

The soldier went quiet. He poked his head into the car. I could hear him breathing. With nobody talking, you can hear everyone breathing. The soldier pulled his head back and yelled.

"ID cards!"

—

"ID cards!"

When the police came into our house, the big tall one said it to Dad.

"Your ID cards! Get them now."

Mom was getting dressed in the bedroom. She came out, one hand pulling up her hair, one hand holding ID cards. I was watching from the bathroom door. The short policeman was smiling, sort of, but not the tall one, not one bit. Grandma said, "Stay right there, Ayşe," in a small voice. She went to my room and came straight back. But I went out before she got back. When the policemen saw me, Grandma yelled, "Ayşe, get back here." Mom said, "It's okay, Mother." The short one said, "Good morning, little miss." The tall one said, "We're going to look around." When nobody said anything, the short policeman said, "We're investigating yesterday's incident at the apartment building next door." The tall one didn't take off his shoes. The short one did. "We've learned that you knew them," he said. "Naturally, we have some questions." Mom said, "We weren't close. And we'd never met the ones on the balcony. Perhaps Samim and Ayla didn't know them, either." The short one nodded and smiled. The tall one said, "They were trying to jump onto your balcony. That's what your neighbor told us." Then he turned to Dad and asked, "What's your name?" As if Dad were a child. "Aydın," Mom said. Dad gave Mom an angry look, then lifted his eyebrows as he looked at the policeman.

"You have questions?"

"Do you know where Samim and his wife are?"

"No. I have no idea."

"Your downstairs neighbors said they visited you before they left."

"She's lying. There's some bad blood between us."

"How do I know she's the one who's lying?"

"Sir, my wife and I are both civil servants. I work for the State Planning Bureau. My wife is employed in the archives—"

"That's not what I asked."

The short one said, "Enver Abi, let me handle this." The tall one started walking around the house. Mom went with him. Me and Dad stayed with the smiley policeman. He said it extra fast.

"Aydın Abi, my name's Osman. We met at the seminar. I was about to ask you a question afterwards. Anyway, this is serious. I don't want to get you involved in this, but . . . If there's anything you're hiding in your apartment, you can tell me."

Dad didn't talk, but he sweated a lot.

"Detective Nahit is like a big brother to me. Don't worry. Is there anything here? Did they leave anything?"

Dad still didn't talk.

"Keep calm. You can tell me."

"We burned everything. No."

The policeman went quiet. They looked at each other, he and Dad. We could hear Mom.

"The bedroom's messy right now. If you'll just give me a moment to straighten things up."

A minute later.

"That's personal. You can't open that."

A minute later.

"Officer, those are my daughter's coloring books. I mean, really!"

The policeman yelled at Mom.

"Lady! The army's taken over. You don't get it, do you? Get out of my way!"

Dad and the short policeman were still looking at each other. Like in cowboy movies. The tall one walked down the hallway and opened the bathroom door. We heard Mom again.

"Mother!"

The tall policeman yelled too.

"What's going on here?"

Me and Dad and the short policeman ran to the bathroom.

"What's the matter, Sevgi, my girl? Why are you shouting? Welcome, officer."

Grandma was sitting on the floor. The swan's head was squeezed under her arm and she was poking at its bottom.

"They sent us a nice goose from the village. Once I get it plucked, we can smoke it in the water heater. Sevgi, could you bring me a big tray?"

The tall policeman, us, everyone, just stared. I was the only one who saw the chloroform cotton behind Grandma. Dad got a sweaty forehead again. The tall policeman was talking to himself.

"I thought I'd seen it all, but this beats everything."

He walked out, but the short one stayed behind.

"Aydın Abi, I'd make myself scarce for a few days if I were you. It's a serious investigation. This guy, Samim, is suspected of supplying arms to an illegal organization. His place will be crawling with police for the next few days. They'll probably come over and question you again. As for the dead student . . ."

The other one yelled from the front door.

"Osman, are you coming?"

"I'll be right there! The dead student was your neighbor's brother. He and that woman were seen trying to jump over to your balcony. If you get caught up in this, it could get ugly. Stay away if you can. And remember, my name's Osman."

The tall policeman came back.

"I need to use your phone," he said. When nobody said anything, he went over to it.

"Hello? Nazime, it's me. Me, your husband! The bakery's open in Liberation. Do we need any bread? We do? Okay, I'll get a couple loaves. Bye."

He hung up. They both left.

The door closed. Nobody talked. From somewhere inside, Grandma yelled, "Are they gone?" Nobody answered. Ali was standing in the doorway of my bedroom.

"Somebody answer me. Are they gone?"

Ali pulled up his shirt and showed his belly. It was the first time I heard him yell.

"I'm dying, probably!"

Dad didn't move. Mom ran over and looked at Ali's belly.

"That's all we need right now."

Grandma came up with a feather in her hand.

"I was so terrified I pulled out a feather. Ali? Ahhh! What's happened to you?"

Grandma looked at Ali's belly, too.

"You've got the measles."

Mom patted Ali's head.

"You're not going to die, Ali. Lots of children get measles and it's not dangerous. But . . ."

Mom and Dad both looked at me.

"But it is highly contagious. Ayşe must have it, too. Come here, let me have a look.

Mom put her hands on her hips. She said it three times.

"That's all we need right now."

Ali got red spots all over his belly because he heard that Hüseyin Abi died, and that he was Samim Abi's brother. Mom put her hand on my forehead.

"She's getting feverish. Aydın, now what are we going to do?"

Dad didn't make a sound. His eyes got big and he didn't blink at all. "Aydın? Aydın?" Mom said. Dad didn't say anything, just kept looking at Mom with big unblinking eyes. "Aydın, are you okay, sweetie?" Mom said. She called Dad "sweetie"! Grandma said, "Come along, children. Let me put you both to bed. You'll get better soon. Sevgi, I think Aydın needs you. He's looking rather odd. Has he gone into shock, or what? Oh, it's one thing after another!" Mom took Dad's arm and asked, "Aydın, what is it?" Dad said, "Huh?" Mom shook his arm and asked again, "Aydın! Say something. What is it?" Dad said, "Is this really happening, Sevgi?" Mom let go of Dad. "Oooph," she said, as she came over to us.

"Mother, what do we do for measles?"

"Nothing. They need lots of rest. I'll make some soup. It will do them good."

We slept. I mean, I did. Ali slept, too. We're so tired. More tired than ever.

———

Me and Ayşe slept and slept. My dreams got all mixed up. I think my dad called. I think he said he couldn't get me and he asked Ayşe's dad to take me to Ordu. Then we were in Ordu, and it was all muddy. In the mud, there were footprints, and they were too big for my feet. When I woke up, Ayşe's grandma put some soup in my mouth. I couldn't eat it. It spilled on the bed. They did something, and the sheet got cool. When I woke up again, I could hear the news. Someone put a hand on my forehead. "I think the fever's falling," a voice said. I woke up and saw Ayşe's foot in my face. But then I saw Ayşe's hair in my face. I didn't fall asleep. Or I never woke up.

—

It turned out to be Ali's neck. I thought it was my mom. I thought she'd got into bed with me, and I was happy. But now I'm awake and I'm not happy. Then maybe I wet the bed and woke up. Maybe it was Ali who wet the bed. It's warm and wet. In my dream, it's summer and we're at the sea, and we're walking with the swan. I think the swan came when I opened my eyes, and then I saw Grandma holding a feather and going, "Hssst! Hssst!" But it could have been a dream. I slept a hundred times. I saw Ali's feet in my dream. Then his face. He has red spots on his face. It's so funny. I laughed, in my dream, I guess. I had the funniest dreams. I saw so many peaches, a thousand or more. They're cold, and when I bite them juice runs down my chin. Ali's eating, too. And we're feeding them to the swan. The swan's laughing. That was my dream.

—

When we woke up, everyone was running around. Me and Ayşe were looking at each other's faces. Because she has red spots on her face. And so do I. They itch. We're both a little cross, the two of us. "Sevgi, they've woken up!" Ayşe's grandma said. And then she was gone. I could hear Ayşe's mom.

"Mother, what are we going to do with all that soup? Who takes soup on a car ride?"

"I know what I'm doing."

Ayşe's mom and dad stood in the doorway, whispering.

"Aydın, I'm going to bathe the kids. We've got all this hot water. They slept all day yesterday. A bath will do them good."

"There's no need, Sevgi. They're both sick."

"I know what I'm doing."

"Sevgi, what about the guns?"

"Don't ask me, Aydın. You'll have to think of something."

———

When Mom and Dad were talking, I didn't want to open my eyes. Because while they're talking, the smell of toast is coming to come, the smell of sausages. That means we slept yesterday. Is that all we did? Did yesterday just get away? Did Ali sleep, too? Maybe we had the same dreams. About swans, and peaches. Where is the swan? My tummy itches. Mom takes my hand.

"Don't scratch it, honey. Come on, get up. Let's get you a nice bath. You'll feel better."

Mom yelled at Grandma in the kitchen when she was taking me to the bathroom.

"Mother, please don't make soup just as we're about to leave."

"I know what I'm doing!"

It's like everybody wants to play a different game. I closed my eyes and when I opened them, we were in the bathroom. It smells like fire.

———

When Ayşe left, I sat up in bed. Ayşe's dad came. "Lie down a little longer," he said. "Until Ayşe's had a bath." He covered me. Dads can't cover like moms. Your foot's out in the open or the blanket gets in your mouth. "Your dad called. He wants you to go with us. He said it'll only be for a couple of days and you'll have a chance to see some sights. Okay, my boy?" Now Ayşe's dad is calling me "my boy." Is everything that terrible? I wish Mom was here. But if I think about it, my head will hurt. "Uncle Aydın, where's the swan?" He laughed. "Get up," he said, "and we'll go have a look at it." We went to the bathroom. He held my hand, like I couldn't go there alone. Ayşe had her eyes closed. Her mom was undressing her. She's got red dots everywhere. But the swan's there. "See, Ali. We put the swan in the bathtub. A coup happened, but we were about to cook a goose. That's how silly things got. Come on, let me take you back to bed." I let go of his hand and went to the living room. I sat down on the sofa across from the balcony. The door and the window are closed now. They're not swinging anymore. Ayşe ran in from the bathroom and sat down next to me.

—

Mom and Dad changed everything while we were sleeping. The books are gone. Grandma's lace is where the books were. And on the lace, they put cups. The ones that were in the cupboard. We have a vase, too, a red one. They never put flowers in it. Now it's on the shelf. And there's a lamp, a colorful one, they put there, too. While we were sleeping, our house turned into Jale Hanım's house. It's different. I uncovered my tummy. Then I uncovered Ali's. "Look, Ali," I said. "We both have belly buttons." Then we both had a bath. Mom kept yelling out to Grandma.

"Mother, why are you making so much soup?"

—

Ayşe's mom forgot to dry our heads. We went out in the street with wet hair. Me and Ayşe sat on cushions in the very back of the car. Her grandma put the swan to sleep and then they put it in a sack. "Look, Ali. The swan's bill is right here in the sack," Ayşe's grandma said. "Are you listening, Ayşe? When the swan wakes up, I'll give you a bit of cotton. Hold it right here. Do you understand?" We nodded our heads "yes." "Good for you, children," Ayşe's grandma said.

—

Grandma filled two pots with soup while we were having breakfast. She was running all around, so Mom said, "Okay, Mother. I give up. There's no talking sense to you." Grandma was laughing. Mom stuck pieces of honey-covered toast in our mouths, and so did Dad. Grandma kept laughing. When Mom and Dad went to the hall to put on their shoes, Grandma looked at us. Then she turned to the stove. We heard it, twice: *plop plop*.

Dad said to Mom, "We'll just have to leave the guns here. We'll take our chances." Then he yelled, "Our IDs! Sevgi, did you get our ID cards? Okay, good." Holding the two pots, one on top of the other, Grandma said to us, "Okay, children. Go on out to the car." We went down the stairs, me and Ali, like we were sleeping, but we were waking up, too, sometimes. It was all mixed up. We got in the car.

—

Ayşe's dad asked.

"What's keeping your mother, Sevgi?"

"She's coming. She's a little slow on the stairs."

"Sevgi, it's seven o'clock. We have to get going."

"Keep your voice down. You'll wake up the neighbors."

Ayşe's grandma came. She was holding her bag over her belly. "Oh!" she said, getting in the car. She laughed.

"What's taking you so long? Floor it, Captain!"

Ayşe's mom and dad looked at each other. The car started. Ayşe's grandma opened the window.

"Oh! Nice and cool!" she said. She laughed again. Then she put one hand on Ayşe's mom's shoulder and one hand on her dad's.

"Children, I left two pots of soup in front of Jale Hanim's door. And inside the soup are two parting gifts. Ha Ha! Let them explain that to the police!"

Ayşe's mom and dad looked at each other. They looked back at us. They looked through the side window and laughed.

"What a day!" Grandma said. "You'll never forget it."

—

"ID cards!" said the soldier. Mom handed them over.

"There are only four cards. There are five of you."

Grandma spoke in her nice, old lady voice.

"The little boy is our cleaning lady's son. We're going to drop him off on the way. The poor kids have come down with measles. Oh, such a botheration, my dear boy."

Grandma's laughing, and everyone's looking at her. Nobody else is talking. The soldier looks at the ID cards. For a long time. He pokes his head inside the car again. He looks around. He looks at Dad. None of us are breathing.

"Continue!"

We all let our breath go. It was so exciting. We drove along, nobody talking, until we reached the sign with the red "X" over Ankara. That means we're not in Ankara anymore. Dad turned on the radio. Children were singing.

> *How lovely you'll find it*
> *If you travel through Anatolia*
> *Leaving your cares behind*
> *As you travel through Anatolia*
> *There are crystal streams . . .*

Dad pointed to a little house, far up on a hilltop.

"Do you see that, Ayşe? You could have been born up there in that house. If you had, perhaps you wouldn't go to school. You'd have had ten brothers and sisters to look after. You'd lead your herd of goats along mountain paths and never have any books."

"Look, children!" Grandma yelled. "Seagulls, here, in the middle of the steppe."

"Mother, they follow the trucks transporting fish to Ankara from the Black Sea. Then some of them lose their way. What else would a seagull be doing out here?"

Nobody spoke. The children kept singing on the radio.

There are wonderful places
If you travel through Anatolia.

Mom started crying, suddenly. Quietly at first. Then real loud. Dad stopped the car. He threw down his cigarette. They both got out. There wasn't a sound out on the road.

—

We stopped by the poplars. Ayşe's mom's hair got messed up by the wind. The poplars all leaned to the same side, away from the wind. Ayşe's mom and dad stopped in front of the poplars. He gave her a cigarette. He looked for his lighter. They stood there with cigarettes in their mouths. The one in her mouth was shaking. Her lips were crying, so she couldn't close her mouth, not all the way. Ayşe's dad squatted on the ground. When someone dies, they squat in front of the house. That's how he squatted. He held his head in his hands. I climbed from the back of the station wagon into the second seat. I opened the door and went outside. I went up and looked at them. They were so scared. It was sad! Like they'd had a bad dream. I pulled it out of my pocket and held it in front of Ayşe's dad's nose. He lifted his head. He looked at me. He looked at my hand. He looked at me again. He held out his hand.

"Samim's lighter . . ."

Ayşe's mom was facing us, her dad the poplars. He threw his cigarette on the ground. He put the lighter in his pocket.

UNIT 18

The Master of the Nation Is the Villager

The People of Anatolia Are Forgiving

"Following the imposition of martial law, life has returned to normal throughout the nation. This morning, at Samsun Penitentiary, left- and right-wing inmates emerged from their respective prison wards and embraced each other in a gesture of reconciliation. The inmates declared that from now on they will happily share the same ward. . . . In response to calls for their surrender, the leaders of the Confederation of Progressive Trade Unions lined up in front of the Selimiye Army Barracks today. Asserting that they have done nothing indefensible, the labor union officials stood in line awaiting their turn. They were sent home and told to return to the barracks tomorrow. . . . The generals seated on the National Security Council . . ."

Ayşe's mom turned off the radio and rolled down the window. She stuck her hand outside, thumb pressed against her four fingers. She kept sticking her hand into the wind and pulling it out again. Sticking her hand into the wind and then—whee!—pulling it out, again and again. Fields passed by under her hand. Electric poles passed by. Her hand sometimes went up to the sky, with the birds, then down to the earth, floating over the yellow grasses. When it dove down, her hand was a dolphin; when it flew up, a swan. She turned around and looked at us with red eyes.

"Kids, why did you kidnap the swan from the park?"

It went quiet inside the car, the hush of waiting. Ayşe was waiting for me to say it.

"We didn't kidnap it. We saved it."

"Okay, then, you saved it! But why, Ali?"

We didn't say a word. Ayşe's mom smiled at us and asked, "Aren't you going to tell me?" Ayşe got a little mad.

"What's there not to understand! Goodness gracious!"

—

Mom and Dad laughed to themselves. Mom lit a cigarette. Then she squashed the packet in the palm of her hand. "Good for you, children!" Grandma said. "Well done! Bravo! Right, Sevgi?"

"What can I say? Bravo!"

"Children, that bird will be needing some water. Aydın, shall we stop at a fountain? Son?"

"Dad, it woke up! The swan's awake."

We stopped. When we opened the sack, the swan's head came out, and out, and out. "How are we going to manage this?" Mom and Dad said. They didn't do anything. It was Grandma who brought the swan some water cupped in her hand. We let it drink all it wanted. "Pet it like this, Ayşe," Ali said. We pet it for a while. Mom and Dad didn't even touch it. Mom sat over by the water, on the concrete. Dad sat down, too. While we were sitting with the swan, something rolled up to Mom's foot. An apple! Then I saw a lot of apples. They must have rolled there. Ali got out of the car and picked up an apple. He hit it on a rock, and put the pieces in front of the swan.

—

When Ayşe's grandma sat next to the swan, her mom called us over. She was smoking. Her eyes were still red. She put her hand on our foreheads. Then she looked at our bellies and our faces, up close. She looked at our red spots and laughed when Ayşe asked, "Mom, can swans get measles, too?" She hugged Ayşe. Then she saw me and hugged me, too. We sat next to the water. Me and Ayşe were so tired.

—

Dad went up ahead and peed. Mom stroked our foreheads as she talked.

"Ayşe . . . Ali . . . There's something I want to tell you. It's important. There are times . . . now, how do I put this? For instance, imagine a rare animal suddenly appears one day. Let's say a seal comes ashore in a seaside town. Or a dolphin peeks out from the water. There could be a bird nobody's ever seen before, or a tiger. When these rare creatures show up, people can sometimes be cruel. They instinctively seek to capture, to cage. But not always. Sometimes, it's different; sometimes, it's better. Ayşe, before you were born, before I'd even met your father, a pelican arrived out of the blue one day. It happened in Ankara, in a place called Öveçler. An old granny got the pelican and kept it with her chickens. Winter was coming, so she knit the pelican a pair of booties. It was such a strange and alien thing to her, this pelican far from its nest, all alone. Weird . . . But this strange pelican didn't want to wear booties. Worried its feet would get cold, the granny kept struggling to get those booties on the pelican. She kept that pelican with her all the time, as though it were a pet dog. It was our pelican in booties, and me and my revolutionary friends loved it a lot. . . ."

—

Ayşe's mom's eyes are red from crying, but she's laughing now. She's imitating the old granny, moving her arms and making funny faces.

Ayşe's laughing. When those two laugh together, they're so beautiful. Ayşe's mom strokes both our faces.

"Kids . . . on the radio and on the TV, they're going to say that all the revolutionary big brothers and sisters were deceived, were fooled. That's what they always do, and maybe they even believe it. . . . But now the kind of people who capture tigers and seals, pelicans and swans, are in charge. The ones who'd make fun of the granny knitting booties for a pelican. The ones who'd look at a seal and say, "I wonder where I can sell it? How much money would I get?" The ones who want everyone and everything to be exactly the same, even the birds and the fish and the horses. Do you understand, kids?"

Ayşe's mom washed both our faces, and splashed water on the backs of our necks and on our ears. Her hand feels different now. It feels like my mom's hand.

—

Dad yelled to us. He was standing alone under a tree.

"Sevgi! Look at all these apples. They're falling from the tree."

Mom took us by the hand and we walked over to the apple tree. She held out her skirt to make a big lap.

"Go on, kids. Gather them up."

We laughed while we picked up the apples. Because they're yellow, and little, and like bouncy puppies. Mom said to Dad, "Not everything's rotten." Dad said, "They'd have rotted if we hadn't stopped." After a little bit, Mom said something.

"Surely, someone would have stopped."

Grandma came up, too, and made an apple lap with her skirt. Me and Ali filled it up. We laughed a lot. So much that Dad went to the car and got his camera.

"Wait, let me take a photo."

Mom and Grandma showed the camera the apples in their skirts. We all turned into apples for the camera, and it was funny. Dad put the camera on the wall of the fountain. While it was going *beep beep*, faster and faster, he ran over and put his arm around Mom. "Run, Aydın, run!" Grandma was saying as he ran up to us, all happy, to get in the photo he was taking. We were waiting for the *clack* when noise came from the road. A whole line of trucks, army trucks. Mom's hand shook. An apple fell from her skirt. Slowly, Mom and Dad weren't laughing anymore. Ali wasn't laughing, either. The *clack* came. The apple that fell from Mom's skirt rolled over to the fountain.

—

I got the fallen apple from the fountain. I put it in front of the swan. We fell asleep in the back seat.

—

The car woke me and Ali up, *chick chack*. I had my head in Grandma's lap. Ali was sleeping on my rear end. Mom's voice seemed far away.

"Kids, wake up. We're going to stop for lunch and I'll give you some aspirin. Then we'll—"

"Sevgi, the car's making a strange noise. And it doesn't accelerate like it should. I'd better get it checked at the next gas station."

"Sevgi, my girl, I need to get some mints and cologne. I'm getting carsick."

—

Ayşe's grandma went to the restroom. There was this old man when me and Ayşe were getting out of the car. He had one of those hats for praying on his head. There was a fountain, and he was behind it, praying. When he was done, he rubbed his hands on his face and yelled.

"Praise be to God! They kept talking about a revolution. But what did they want to overthrow? Huh? May God watch over our army."

There were lots of soldiers in jeeps. They laughed at the old man. One of them said, "That's enough, hadji. Get back to work." The old man kept yelling. "Tell me, what were they revolting against?" Another soldier said, "Okay, calm down, uncle. Bless you."

Ali's mouth stayed open when he was looking at the old man. I was looking at the soldiers. They were holding loaves of bread. The cheese in the bread was so little. They were showing each other the cheese, not even enough to fill a roll. One of them looked at me. He smiled. Then he looked at the others to check if they'd seen.

—

Ayşe's mom took us inside. There were lots of things in there. Little things. Plastic dolls with eyes painted blue, but the paint leaking outside the eyes. Their terrible eyes. There were skeleton keychains. And lighters saying "Turkey." There were little rugs for doing prayers, and on them, compasses showing Mecca. There were wooden things showing the Turkish flag, to put on a table or hang on the wall. There were three books: *Peace of Mind Is in Islam, 100 Reasons to Take Pride in Turkishness*, and *Dishes of Anatolia*. There were bags and bags of candy. Shiny mints. Sweets shaped like white stones in boxes saying MEVLANA CANDY and COME, WHOEVER YOU ARE. Eggs made of marble. Lots of them. Pencils made of wood, but too big to get your hand around. Wooden sugar bowls, all splintery. Giant prayer beads, one after another, made of wood. A bunch of toy guns, in different colors. Houses made of matchsticks, glue dripping down. Colorful lamps with the Kaaba inside. On the floor, little statues of cats and dogs, but nothing else. They all had messy paint. Everything was ugly, very ugly.

—

The old man came inside and went behind the counter. It was his shop, and it smelled like roasted chickpeas. He started yelling again.

"If only they'd just come out and said it. What they were revolting against?"

The man seemed to be asking Mom, but she didn't answer. He asked another question.

"Peace be upon you, sister. What can I get you?"

"Cigarettes."

"I can't get my head around it. What about the, you know, state? Let's say, you know, they had brought down the state? Well, then what? Right, sister? I mean, if they, you know, knew what they wanted and then they did it, well then, maybe I could understand. But it was nothing like that, and the state hits right back with a heavy hand, you know. Serves them right!"

Mom whispered.

"The voice of the people. In all its tongue-tied glory."

"What's that, sister?" the man asked. "And some—you know— mints," Mom said. But he didn't hear her, because he was yelling.

"Let's say they did get their revolution. What then? You can't live off the fat of the land and then turn on your own state. Now, can you?"

—

Maybe because I was looking at the man too much, Ayşe pulled my pinkie. But it was the poster in the window I was looking at. The one the man had stuck there.

"Spreadable cheese! Spread it on thick! Eat it up!"

There was this boy in the poster, with cheese all over his mouth, smiling, but a nasty smile. The man wasn't done yelling.

"They don't know their own people! But the real people of this country know who's, you know, looking out for them. Those anarchists don't know nothing!"

The man was yelling, but he was scared, I think. He was afraid of the revolution, but now he's yelling because he's not afraid anymore. I let out a kick. A kick at the ugly dog and cat statues. The man didn't see. One of them fell over. Ayşe's mom saw, but she didn't say anything. "Come on, kids," she said. "Let's go."

—

"The gas station man said we'll be able to make it as far as Çorum, but we'll need to have it looked at as soon as we get there. What else can I do, Sevgi?"

Mom got mad when Dad said we should spend the night in Çorum. She let her spoon fall into her soup, *plop*. Grandma patted her on the arm.

"Sevgi, my girl. Is Çorum so very dangerous?"

"Oh no, not at all. Right, Aydın? What possible danger could there be in a place like Çorum? Kids! Finish up your soup."

Me and Ali didn't feel like eating. Grandma held a spoonful of soup in front of Ali's mouth, then mine. The soup was ugly. The bread was cut into big chunks. There were no napkins, and the glasses were wrapped in pink paper. But the paper went to pieces when you wiped your mouth on it. The spoons were too big. And the plates were plastic, with big brown flowers on them, like they were dirty. And my legs stuck to the chairs, because they were plastic, too. Me and Ali leaned our heads on our hands. The red spots made our heads heavy.

—

"I'll give Father a call," Ayşe's dad said. We can't stay in Çorum. I should say it, "No," but I'm sick, so I can't. The inside of my head itches, like it's full of red spots, too. The insides of my eyes itch. And the inside of my mouth. I can't say anything. "They gouge out people's eyes there," I should say. "Hüseyin Abi went there once, and then he couldn't sleep," I should say. But I can't. Maybe, because I'm with Ayşe and her family, it'll be different. The police didn't beat anyone up when they came to Ayşe's house. Maybe nobody will try to gouge out our eyes in Çorum. My eyes are closing. Ayşe's grandma put a pill in my mouth, and then she held a glass of water to my mouth.

"Okay, you've eaten enough. Go sleep in the back of the car now, the two of you."

Ayşe's grandma pulled a little bag out of her handbag and put a little salad in it. She winked at me.

"It's for our friend in back, sweetie."

She called me "sweetie," like I'm Ayşe. I don't remember anything else. I think me and Ayşe fell asleep in the back seat. Ayşe's grandma got in the very back, with the swan, I think. Her voice came from far away, the bottom of a well.

"I'm perfectly comfortable back here. It's nice to stretch out my legs. My knees were aching from all that sitting. The bird and I are just fine. Aren't we, my pet? Ha-hah!"

—

Me and Ali were sleeping in the back seat. I could hear Grandma.

"Sevgi, it's so well-behaved. As docile as a child. Aren't you, my pet? Look! Up in the sky!"

Grandma was showing the swan the birds flying in the sky. I looked at the birds. It suddenly smelled like winter. The sky turned gray. Were these migrating birds taking the summer with them to a faraway place? If our swan flew with them, maybe summer would end. It would finally rain. Then I think I fell asleep.

We were in a strange room. I woke up as Mom was putting me on a bed. The white light hurt my eyes. Dad put Ali on the bed next to me. They were trying not to talk, so I wouldn't wake up. But when I opened my eyes, I saw everything. Grandma was spreading a sheet on the couch.

"This sheet smells a little odd, but there's nothing doing. We'll have to manage for the night. Sevgi, use your blouses as cases for the children's pillows. We don't want them to get germs on their mouths. It's not at all clean here, is it? I've never seen a filthier hotel. Are you awake now, sweetie? Come on, let's wash your hands and face. She's not running a temperature anymore, Sevgi. She'll be well in no time."

Grandma took me to the bathroom. There were dead mosquitoes in the light above the mirror. Nobody had saved them.

"Grandma, where's the swan?"

"It's sleeping, sweetie. Now let's give your hands and face a good wash."

There were slippers on the floor, big and green. Nobody will wear them. They're ugly. And they're for men. There aren't any girl slippers. There's not much soap left, and it's stuck to the wall with a magnet. Grandma rubbed and rubbed the piece of soap under the water to get all the dirt off. The light went *bzzz* the whole time. This place bothers me. I think it's Çorum, and I don't like the fake flowers in the vase by the bed, either. Grandma opens the closet and says, "Look, there's no coverlet." The only thing in there is a broken hanger. And a little rug, for praying. There's gold writing about God. It's hung on the wall like a picture, but way up by the ceiling. And there's a picture of a big tower next to it. "Is that tower in Istanbul?" I asked Mom.

"No, it's in Paris, Ayşe. Come here and lie down. Let's get to sleep right away so morning comes quickly."

One of the pillows smells. I can smell Mom on her blouse, but at the end of the pillow there's another smell, a bad one. Like Jale Hanım's husband. It smells like curtains and ashtrays, all down the bed.

—

My eyes are open, but nobody sees me, because I don't make a sound. I keep quiet. Maybe Ayşe's mom would do this if she came to our house. Touch everything with her fingertip. Sniff everything without getting too close. Say, "Ugh, I can't sleep under this, Aydın. Even the blankets are filthy."

"May that be the least of your worries, Sevgi."

"How are things outside? Is anything happening?"

"There are soldiers everywhere. Everyone's talking about the match. Everything's 'back to normal,' just like they said."

Ayşe's grandma starts going *tss tss*. Her mom and dad are smoking by the window.

"How's your father? I forgot to ask."

"He's fine. He's out of the hospital."

"I can't sleep, Aydın."

"Me neither. Dad asked me to get a melon again. 'Be sure to pick one up on the way,' he said. Him and his melon."

Ayşe's talking in her sleep, real quiet: "Mommy." I miss my mom. A lot. When I see her, I'm going to say "Mommy" too. When I talk like the kids in books, she'll be so surprised.

—

When Mom and Dad were standing in front of the window, I could see their faces in the glass. They were looking at themselves in the window. Then Mom looked at Dad and Dad looked at Mom in the window. They suddenly closed the curtain. I understand why Dad closed the curtain the night Hüseyin Abi and Birgül Abla fell. You can see yourself in the window when it's dark. People see themselves in the dark. And it's kind of scary.

"You'll like it now, sweetie. Look, I've spread some jam on top. You need to eat something."

Grandma's trying to make me eat that stinky cheese. I don't want to. Mom's not eating it. Neither is Dad. They didn't eat anything. Dad's shaking his leg under the table. There's jam in little boxes, but it doesn't smell good. It doesn't smell like anything. Nobody's here but us in the hotel restaurant. The waiter and another man are hanging up a big flag on the wall.

"Pull it harder! We need to stretch it," the waiter says.

"It'll rip if I pull it any harder. It's worn out."

"You heard me! It needs to be pulled tight."

"Ayşe, please eat your breakfast so we can get out of here," Dad says. He's not mad at me. He's just in a bad mood.

"Come on, Ayşe. Make your mother happy. Then I'll give you your medicine and we can go. Ali ate his. Ah! Ayşe, Ali! You'll never believe what I just saw in the newspaper."

Me and Ali looked at Mom.

"Ayşe, I'll tell you when you've finished your breakfast. It's wonderful news. You'll love it, just love it."

I looked at Dad.

"It's the *Voice of Çorum* newspaper."

I started eating. If you swallow without chewing, maybe it's not so stinky. Mom started reading out loud.

"*The swans, which have stopped in Ordu for the first time anyone can remember, are thought to have arrived from Siberia. The mayor of Perşembe said that the swans were expected to resume their migration after resting for a few days. Meanwhile, locals have begun flocking to Perşembe to see the swans.* . . . Did you hear that? Did you hear that? Some swans have come to Ordu! Now finish your breakfast, Ayşe. Come on, open your mouth."

I was about to laugh and Ali was about to take the newspaper from Mom when the big brother and sister came in. They sat down at a table right away. The big sister tried to cover her head with a scarf. The big brother spoke fast to the waiter.

"Two teas!"

"Hang on, brother. Let me finish with this flag."

The big brother and sister looked out the window. They both lit cigarettes. Their faces were red, like they'd been running. Two men passed outside the window. They were holding their arms out to the side and looking mean. On their waists, they had walkie-talkies, just like Uncle Detective. They were scary. The man who hung up the flag got down and looked up at it. "It looks good!" he said. He went outside with the waiter. The big brother and sister put out their cigarettes. He held her hand on the table. Then they both put their hands under the table. They looked at each other. We looked at them. Ali got up. Mom saw the two men. "Ali, sit down," she said. Ali didn't even hear her. He started walking. The two scary men came inside and looked at everyone. Ali was walking over to the big brother and sister. He sat down at their table. The scary men were going over to that table when Ali yelled.

"Mommy! Mommy! I want some cheese, a matchbox of cheese!"

I saw the big sister's face. Her eyes got big. She swallowed. Then she yelled.

"Okay, darling. We'll tell the uncle to bring you some. You'll have to wait for a little bit, though."

"Ahmet! That's no way to talk to your mother!" the big brother said. The big sister put Ali on her lap and kissed him.

"He's a good little boy. He just forgot to say 'please.'"

The scary men nodded to the big brother and sister. Then they went outside. The big sister hugged Ali.

"Thank you, my boy. Thank you."

The big brother and sister were just leaving when the National Anthem started playing. One of the men who hung up the flag was coming in as the big brother and sister were running out. One of the men shouted.

"Show some respect!"

The other man came in, too. They both stood at attention. They looked over at us.

"The national anthem's playing. Show some respect!"

Dad went dark. He was real mad, I think. Mom put her cigarette in the ashtray. They looked at each other. They didn't say anything, but they were talking to each other. Grandma whispered.

"Get up, children. We don't want any trouble."

Grandma made me and Ali stand up. The National Anthem kept playing, longer than ever before. Dad looked at Ali. He kept his eyes on Ali the whole time. Dad seemed small. Ali seemed big. Mom put her hand on Ali's shoulder.

"You're a hero and a clever boy, Ali!" she said. She was looking at Dad. When the National Anthem finished, Dad picked me up.

"Come on. Let's get out of here."

We got in the car. Grandma had tied the swan's feet together. She undid the knot and said she was sorry.

"It's okay, my pet. It's all better now. Look, I brought you some tomato wedges."

This time Grandma sat in the back seat and we sat on the cushions in the very back. Grandma wiped her face with a handkerchief.

"It's so hot this early in the morning. Aydın, let's not forget that melon. Remember what your father said."

"I'm not getting a melon!" Dad said. He turned around, and I saw his black face. Dark as can be.

"And we're not going to Ordu!"

Grandma and Mom froze.

"We're not going to Ordu. Because . . . we're going to Perşembe, damn it. I'm going to show the kids the swans. That's where we're going! Is everyone ready for a last-minute tour?"

—

Ayşe's dad cursed like Hüseyin Abi. He lit his cigarette with Hüseyin Abi's lighter. Ayşe's mom put her hand on his, on top of the stick shift. She turned her face to the window. I think she was smiling.

UNIT 19

What Did You Do on Your Summer Vacation?

There's a Village Far Away

"Read it again, Mom!"

"Ayşe, how many times have I read it to you? That's enough. Now sit down. You know better than to jump up and down when the car's moving."

"This is the first time the swans came? For real? You're not making it up?"

"For real. Now sit down!"

I sat back down next to Ali.

"I think they found out we saved the swan. What about you? I think they came to get our swan so they can all fly off together. What about you?"

Ali nodded his head "yes." He's got measles, so he's not so clever now. He keeps falling asleep. But I want to talk about it. I need to.

"Do you think it'll be like *The Little Black Fish*? If our swan goes far, far away, it'll turn around and look at its friends in Ankara and say, 'There's a huge sky in other lands far away,' and they'll all say, 'Hooray!' And then—"

"That's not how it ended."

"Remember how the little black fish and all the other fish got saved from the pelican's pouch, and then it went home, and told all those stories and stuff? That's how it ended."

"No, it didn't. You got it wrong."

Dad said, "Kids! Look out the window. Look how green it's getting the closer we get to the Black Sea."

—

"The little black fish never comes back from the big sea," I said. "Nobody ever saw the little black fish again." Because that's what happened. The poor baby fish was saved from the pelican's belly, but then it died, right there. It never went home to its mother. Granny Fish tells the story of the little black fish to her grandchildren. When they ask, "What happened to the little black fish?" she always says, "I'll tell you tomorrow." The book never tells us what happened, though. And there's this one kid—who's a lot like the little black fish—and when the story ends, he can't sleep and all he can do is think about the big sea.

—

"It never comes back from the big sea," Ali said. "It dies in the pelican's stomach. You read it wrong."

Well, I didn't read it. Mom read it to me. Before I knew how to read. Then I never read it, because Mom had read it to me. But at the end of the story the little black fish comes home, and everybody is happy, and it tells everybody about its adventures. Mom wouldn't lie to me. Would she? Grandma pretends everything's a game, but not Mom. Right? Or are they both doing it?

"Kids, we'll be in Perşembe by lunchtime," Dad said. "They say the swans are landing on one of the restaurant's balconies. What was the name of that restaurant, Sevgi?"

"Dallas."

"Dallas?"

Mom and Dad laughed. I don't think it's funny, not one bit.

"Ali, does that mean our swan will never come back, either?"

"It doesn't matter."

"Why not? It does so!"

"No, it doesn't. When we were saving our swan, the other swans saw. That's what matters."

Ali's talking nonsense. He's not smart anymore because of the measles.

"It's going on eleven, Sevgi. Let's listen to the news."

"*. . . as we come to the end of this week's program featuring the folk songs of the Black Sea region, we conclude with a beloved folk song from the highlands of Pokut as performed by the state choir here at TRT Ankara.*"

> *In this false world every creature seeks a mate*
> *A stone has no heart, but the moss embraces it still . . .*

—

Me and Ayşe keep looking at the back. Ayşe's got her arms crossed and she's not talking to me. She's mad because the little black fish died. I turn around and face the front. When the folk song starts, it's a song full of hurt, and the sign on the road says it's forty kilometers to Fatsa. I feel, all at once, like I can look up at the sky and see Hüseyin Abi and Birgül Abla. Like they can fly and fly and land on the mountains up ahead. When I look at the sky, I want to cry. The song is sad, and maybe that's why.

> *Don't step in the mud, my darling*
> *They'll find our tracks*
> *Oh, woe is me*
> *They'll find our tracks*
> *Let's mingle with the mist*
> *May they think us dead*

Oh, woe is me
May they think us dead

I wonder where Uncle Dürüst is? Someone probably led him away when the coup happened. "Come along, Uncle Dürüst," they said. Birgül Abla wasn't there, but someone took him away. The big brothers and sisters protected the neighborhood, of course they did. Gökhan and Hamit and the others all sang anthems. The soldiers couldn't put anyone from our neighborhood in their jeeps. Auntie Seher yelled and grabbed her rolling pin and chased all the soldiers away. Everybody asked, "Where's Ali?" "Haven't you heard?" Gökhan said. "He went off to save Hüseyin Abi and Birgül Abla." I wish they said that. And if Mom heard, and felt happy and got better . . . And if Dad laughed and said, "That's my little lion!"

—

The red lights came on. I'm not talking to Ali anymore, but he's not looking at me! He thinks I'm stupid. I didn't even tell him Hüseyin Abi and Birgül Abla fell. I didn't want him to get sad. But what would happen if I did tell him? Well, then we'd see who's stupid!

—

The car pulled over, hard, pushing me and Ayşe to the window.

—

Our faces are side-by-side now, mine and Ali's, by the window. "You know, Hüseyin Abi and Birgül Abla . . ." I was going to say, but then we saw the dog. The muezzin was singing out the call to prayer and the dog was barking at the minaret. Its eyes closed, it was howling. Like the song on the radio, sad and hurt.

In this false world every creature seeks a mate
Oh, woe is me
Every creature seeks a mate
A stone has no heart, but the moss embraces it still
Oh, woe is me
But the moss embraces it still

Two uncles came out of the mosque. And they beat the dog.

"Shut up, you cursed dog!" they yelled, so loud we could hear them, even in the car.

—

The two men beat the dog for howling at the call to prayer. But the dog doesn't know it's the call to prayer, and the men don't know the dog doesn't know. So, in a way, the dog knows more than they do.

"Infidel of a dog, howling at the holy adhan!"

If Uncle Dürüst died, I wonder if he'd come back to the world as a street dog?

Ayşe took my hand. The folk song kept playing.

Your love took my mind
Leaving only my soul
Oh, woe is me
Leaving only my soul

It started raining. The car windows slowly bled.

When the rain started, the two bad men ran into the mosque. The dog had blood on its face. But it still barked again. It barked like it hadn't been beaten. Like it was laughing, even, all bloody.

"Sevgi, let's have a cigarette before we go any further," Dad said. "There are bound to be road checks as we approach Fatsa."

Grandma is sucking on a mint and praying to herself, *psss psss*. She made the magic dome over me and Ali. When the rain came down harder, the swan went *tuh! tuh! tuh!* to keep away the evil eye.

—

The soldier waved his hand for us to pass, and Ayşe held my hand the whole time. Everybody else looked straight ahead as we slowly passed. Nobody looked outside. But I did. Big brothers and sisters were lying by the side of the road, face down. The news was playing on the radio.

"*. . . truckloads of letters pouring in from across Turkey as citizen informants respond to . . .*"

They were on the ground, getting wet. They wanted to lift their heads, but the soldiers were yelling at them. The radio sounded more terrible now.

"*The National Security Council announced that all prisoners and detainees will be required to memorize the teachings of Atatürk. . . .*"

—

"Switch it off," Ayşe's grandma said. "Let's listen to the rain." Now everyone got quiet. Rain was *plip plip plopping* on the roof. It hurt, that feeling inside and in my throat, warm and wet. "Sevgi, light me another cigarette," Ayşe's dad said.

—

The soldiers were getting smaller and smaller as I looked at the mountains. Birds can fly when it rains a lot, too.

—

"Welcome. Take any table you like."

The waiter stood there with his hands full of newspapers.

"We're covering the tables with newspaper. I hope you don't mind. Our tablecloths are all in the laundry, because of the, you know."

"The military intervention, or the coup?"

"The coup, brother. The coup."

The waiter laughed, and so did my dad. They didn't look at each other, but they laughed together. Like they knew each other.

—

Ayşe's dad and the waiter knew each other. The waiter calls it a coup, too. They can be friends. But you can't be friends with people who call the "Çorum Massacre" the "Çorum Incident." You just can't.

—

"What can I get you, brother?"

"Put a salad big enough for everyone in the middle of the table. And bring us whichever fish is freshest."

"All right."

"We didn't really come here to eat, though."

"Oh?"

"We heard about the swans. I read in the paper that they come here, right onto the balcony. I don't know if it's true, though."

"It's true. The country's going through hell, but it's like a carnival here. They say the swans came from, you know, that cold place up in the Soviet Union."

"Siberia!"

Ali knew. Everyone laughed.

"That's it. From Siberia. None of the old-timers have seen anything like it. This is the first time swans have come to Ordu. And they picked the day of the coup to do it. It's strange, isn't it?"

"Everything's strange these days."

Dad played with the salt shaker and the napkins. The waiter put forks on the edges of the newspaper. When it was all spread out, Ali started reading. I looked at what he was reading. So did Grandma.

"Ah! Sevgi, look at this. Look what Bülent Ersoy said: 'I would like to express my gratitude to all the officers and enlisted men of the army, but in particular to General Kenan Evren. I am prepared, as an artist, to shoulder any duties that may be required of me.'"

Grandma poured a little cologne onto her handkerchief and wiped my hands and Ali's.

"It's just what Jale Hanım always wanted. Bülent Ersoy has been brought to heel, too. Bravo!"

Grandma didn't laugh. I thought she would, but she didn't. "Don't say that, Sevgi. The poor girl's suffered more than anyone. The real freaks are the ones who appear the most normal." She made her handkerchief into a little ball and put it in her handbag. She smelled her hands.

"Oh! And to think I'd been using Cavit Bey's nasty tobacco-scented cologne for all those years."

—

Right by Ayşe's hand there's a "joint statement" from famous singers and actors: "May God bless the generals!"

They're all dressed like teachers. Everyone is serious now. They look like they're going to school tomorrow and none of them are smiling.

—

"Aydın, let's order some rakı, too. What do you say? A double for each of us?"

Dad laughed.

"Mother Nejla, would you like a single?"

"I suppose so, seeing as you two are having a drink."

Mom and Dad laughed.

The waiter came.

"I've brought you a bottle of rakı, just in case."

"Bless you!"

"You did say you came for the swans, brother. I figured you'd want a drink while you were waiting. They should be coming in an hour or so. They always come at the same time. Sister, do you want ice in your rakı?"

The waiter always comes running up and when he's walking away he taps his fingers on the back of his big tray. He's so jolly. When the waiter's gone, Mom says, "People still don't realize what's hit them."

———

I leaned close to Ayşe's ear.

"They were waiting for us. The swans, I mean. Waiting to take away the swan we saved. Do you understand? They came here every day to check. I wonder how they knew we'd come?"

"They know!" Because she has red spots on her face, Ayşe is beautiful when she opens her eyes big like that. Funny and beautiful. Ayşe's mother has her hand on her glass of rakı. Sometimes, the sun comes out and the edge of the glass shines and you can't see her hand. Then a cloud comes, and it's just her mother's hand on the glass. Maybe Ayşe's mother doesn't know that only when the sun comes out does she tap her ring on the glass, *click click*. But then she stopped doing it. "Ah!" she said.

———

The fish came. "Brother, would you like to debone it or should I give it to the missus?" the waiter asked. "Let me do it for once," Dad said. Then he looked at Mom. "What is it, Sevgi?" he said. "Nothing," Mom said. They listened to the music a little, their eyes on us. The restaurant was playing grandma music.

"*You're gone, and you don't know . . .*"

"Sevgi, I'm only asking because you said, 'Ah!'"

"It's nothing, Aydın. For a moment, I . . . Well, here we are! Anyway . . . are you serving the fish? I'd like you to do it."

Dad cut the fish's belly, but it fell apart. Then he cut the tail, a little. He couldn't do it right. The fish got smaller and smaller. It made me laugh. "What's so funny, Ayşe? You think your clumsy dad's funny, don't you? Not you too, Ali. Don't laugh at me. This fish won't get the better of me, I can promise you that. Woah! There we go!" We all laughed a lot, but Mom didn't make a sound. The music was nice.

—

Ayşe's mom is looking at Uncle Aydın. She's leaning back and looking at him like she's somewhere else. Ayşe's dad knows, and he's trying to be funny. The more Ayşe laughs, the more her mom's eyes fill with tears. She turns her head and looks at the sea. She bends over and looks at her foot. She has a bandage on her heel. She pulls it off. She scrunches up the bandage and she scrunches up her mouth, too, until they're both tiny. Then, when we started eating our fish, she reached over and took Ayşe's dad's hand.

"You did a great job with the fish, Aydın."

Ayşe's dad squinted as he looked at her. He didn't understand. Then he picked up his rakı glass with the two fingers that were still clean.

—

"Mmm, this is delicious. The fish is so fresh," Dad said. "It really is," Mom said. "Are these salad greens clean?" Grandma asked, twice. Mom laughed. "Don't worry about it, Mother. Just for today."

When Grandma finished her rakı first, Dad laughed.

"Mother Nejla, shall I order you another one?"

When they clinked glasses again, Grandma got like she did with her liqueur. She turned to Mom with wet eyes.

"Sevgi, I've been meaning to ask this for years, but somehow the time was never right. That scar on your cheek. When did it happen, my girl? I can't remember."

Mom put her hand on her cheek. Her smile was gone. Dad leaned over his fish. He lit a cigarette. Her hand on her cheek, Mom looked at Grandma. She opened her eyes wide. "Mother?" she said, like a child. "Are you saying you never . . . ?" Dad blew out a big cloud of smoke.

"Mother Nejla, that's not a scar! On the day she was born, Ayşe gave her mother such a big kiss that it left a mark."

Mom looked at Dad. She closed her eyes and smiled. Grandma laughed.

"Good heavens, Aydın!"

Dad kept his eyes on Mom. They touched their glasses, softly, without making a sound.

—

Ayşe's smiled as she looked at her mom and dad. Then she turned to me.

"It's good we saved the swan, right, Ali? I'm glad we did!"

As I looked at Ayşe's face, I saw the long shadows of wings behind her. They were coming from far away. Moving their wings, *flap flap*. It was raining a little, but still they flew.

—

"Uncle Aydın!"

Ali called my dad "Uncle Aydın"! He yelled it out so loud that Dad jumped out of his chair. He was holding a glass of rakı and a cigarette, but he stood up.

"What is it, son?"

"Uncle Aydın! We should get the swan out of the car."

Ali was acting like a big brother. He moved his eyebrows closer together and stared up at the sky.

He pointed and showed me. "The swans!" I yelled. Everyone got up. Grandma yelled, too.

"Oh my! They're coming, children!"

Mom asked, "What are you going to do with the swan, Ali?" He put his hand on his hip.

"We're going to let it fly," he said.

"All right then, little captain!"

Dad laughed when he said that, but Ali gave him a serious look. The sound of the swans' wings was coming closer: *flap, flap, flap.*

Then Ali said it in a low voice Mom and Dad didn't hear.

"Do that much, at least!"

———

Ayşe's mom and dad left their rakı on the table and went to the car. They brought the sack back with them. "Wait a minute," I said. They're listening to me. Because . . . because I'm not thinking about if they'll listen or not.

———

Ali stopped Mom and Dad. He's so handsome right now! The swans flew and flew and came right up in front of the balcony where our table was. They walked on the water to stop themselves. With their big feet, they walked, their long necks held high. As if the swans don't know what it is to stop.

"What's that string for, little captain?" Dad asked. Ali didn't answer at first. Then Mom asked.

"Ali, dear, what are you going to do with that string?"

Ali looked at me. I went over to him, because I understood.

"We're going to tie it to the swan's foot," I said.

"And why is that, little miss?" Grandma asked.

It got a little quiet. The swans weren't even flying. Ali finally said it.

"This is from the string for the kite. It's so Hüseyin Abi and Birgül Abla know which swan is ours. They flew from Samim Abi's balcony, you know. And turned into swans when they flew. Well, this bit of string is for them."

Mom closed her mouth and turned around. Dad went black. Grandma whispered to herself, "Oh God, please give us strength of mind." Ali had already tied on the string, quick as can be.

—

Ayşe's dad put the swan on the edge of the balcony. So that the other swans would see it first. They were out on the sea. All of them were looking at us. The waiter came up and laughed.

"Brother! Is that swan really yours, like a pet?"

"Shhh!" went Ayşe's dad. The swan stayed there on the edge of the balcony. The swans on the sea stayed there. The air filled with mist. It was about to rain. "Fly! Fly!" I said to myself. "Go to Hüseyin Abi."

—

The swan opened it wings. It turned and looked at me and Ali. I know it looked at us. "Thank you! You're both heroes," said the swan. Then it waved its wings. It waved them, again and again. And then . . . it fell!

"Oh no!" we all said. We looked down from the balcony. The swan was flying. It walked across the water so it could land in the sea, but it walked like it would fall. The waiter stood there with us.

"Damn! They're such beautiful animals!" he said.

We all fell quiet.

"It's done," Ali said. He sat down. He started eating his fish. The rest of us were standing. The waiter stuck his hands in his pockets and was walking away. Then he turned around.

"Brother, shall I open up another bottle?" he said.

He didn't wait for an answer.

"It's on me!"

—

I've never eaten fish before. How do you swallow those sharp things that get stuck in your throat? Ayşe's dad called out to the waiter.

"Hey, buddy! Could you bring us a couple of plates of melon?"

Glossary

1001 Peaches: *1001 Peaches* (sometimes translated as *One Peach and 1000 Peaches*), *Ulduz and the Crows*, and *The Little Black Fish* are children's books by the Azeri-Iranian author Samad Behrangi.

Ajda Pekkan: glamorous, apolitical singer known as Turkey's first "superstar" in the seventies and eighties

Alaaddin: a local ultra-nationalist leader

Alevi: a Muslim sect marginalized in the Ottoman Empire and associated in Republican Turkey with secular, left-wing values

Ankara Sarması: a sponge cake spread with a soft filling and rolled up into a spiral

ayran: a cold beverage made of diluted yoghurt and salt

Bahçelievler Bloodbath: the murder on October 1978 of seven left-wing university students by ultranationalists in the Istanbul district of Bahçelievler

Bairam: one of the two Muslim festivals falling after Ramadan

Balgat Bloodbath: a series of attacks in August 1978 in the Ankara district of Balgat. Ultranationalists opened fire on four coffeehouses, killing five and wounding scores

börek: pastry filled or layered with cheese and/or vegetables

Bülent Ecevit: served as prime minister three times in the 1970s as the leader of the CHP. Was the leader of the main opposition at the time of the 1980 coup and was jailed and banned from politics along with the leaders of the other main political parties.

Bülent Ersoy: a gender-fluid actor and singer whose performances, along with those of other transsexual and transgender people, were banned after the 1980 coup in Turkey. Ersoy had sex reassignment surgery in London in 1981 and was legally recognized as female in Turkey in 1988.

Cem Karaca: Leftwing rock star stripped of his Turkish citizenship after the coup

CHP party: The Republican People's Party is the oldest political party in Turkey and describes itself as "a modern social democratic party, faithful to the founding principles and values of the Republic of Turkey."

Citadel: the hilltop ruins of a castle in central Ankara

Çorum: a landlocked city in the Black Sea region of Turkey

Çorum Massacre/Çorum Incident: the massacre in Çorum in 1980 of at least fifty-seven Alevis by radical Sunni Muslims. Hundreds were injured and thousands fled for their lives.

Cumhuriyet: oldest upmarket daily newspaper in Turkey; center-left, secular

Decisions of January 24: roadmap for liberal market reforms prepared by the Turkish government and announced to the public on January 24, 1980

dede: spiritual leader in the Alevi sect

Deniz Gezmiş: a Marxist-Leninist revolutionary executed in 1972 at the age of twenty-five who became an inspirational Che Guevara–like figure for later generations; often depicted in a green parka

DİSK: Turkish acronym for Confederation of Progressive Trade Unions

Diyarbakır: largest city in Turkey's predominantly Kurdish southeast

Edip Cansever: a leading member of the "second new" generation of Turkish poets

Ernő Nemecsek: one of the main characters from the *Paul Street Boys*

Fetullah Gülen: a former preacher with millions of followers and an international business and education empire. Gülen, a former ally of President Recep Tayyip Erdogan, has been accused by the Turkish government of masterminding the 2016 coup from his exile in Pennsylvania.

Füsun Önal: actress and singer popular from the 1970s onwards

gobit: an onion, bread, and egg sandwich

Gong: magazine specializing in celebrity news

Gırgır magazine: a humor magazine published from 1972 to 1994; *gırgır* means "fun" in English.

Grey Wolves: an ultranationalist organization

Gün Sazak: a politician and former minister from the ultra-right Nationalist Action Party (MHP), Sazak was respected across the board for stamping out corruption and smuggling during his stint as minister of Customs and Monopolies. Members of the Revolutionary Left claimed credit for gunning Sazak down in front of his home. Members of the MHP responded to Sazak's assassination by attacking Alevis in Çorum and leftists across Turkey.

hamam: a Turkish bath

harmandalı: a folk dance for men associated with honor and courage

hodja: teacher

Hû! Ya Ali!: *Hû* is a name Alevis and Sufis use for God, and *Ali* is a shout-out to Muhammed's son-in-law, Ali, who was the successor to the Prophet and the one true caliphate, according to Alevis and other Shias.

Hürriyet: a mainstream newspaper founded in 1948

iftar: the fast-breaking meal held at sundown during the month of Ramadan

İnciraltı Massacre: the killing of at least six students by military police at a university dormitory in the İnciraltı district of İzmir in June 1980

Kemal Türkler: the founder and leader of the Confederation of Revolutionary/Progressive Trade Unions (DİSK), Türkler was assassinated by Grey Wolf militants in front of his home in Istanbul in July 1980.

kokoreç: grilled lamb intestines

Kurtuluş: a neighborhood in Ankara; means "Liberation"

Laz: an ethnic group living along the Black Sea in Turkey and Georgia

Liberation Park: Kurtuluş Park

Mahir Çayan: a Marxist-Leninist political activist and leader of the People's Liberation Party of Turkey. He and nine of his comrades were killed by soldiers in 1972 in the Black Sea village of Kızıldere.

Maraş Massacre: the weeklong slaughter of more than a hundred unarmed Alevi men, women, and children by Grey Wolves in the city of Maraş in 1978 after a percussion bomb was tossed into a movie theater popular with ultranationalists

meyhane: a traditional tavern serving alcoholic beverages and communal plates of hot and cold food similar to tapas

MHP: the Turkish acronym for Nationalist Action Party, a far-right political organization affiliated with the Grey Wolves

MLSP: the Turkish acronym for Marxist Leninist Socialist Party

mukabele: an informal home gathering in which the Koran is recited as guests follow along; said to be one of the ways Fethullah Gülen organized a following

Mustafa Pehlivanoğlu: sentenced to death for his role in the Balgat Bloodbath

Nationalist Action Party: a right-wing party affiliated with the ultra-nationalist Grey Wolves

Nazım Hikmet: Turkey's best known poet, translated into more than fifty languages. A communist and a pacifist, Hikmet was repeatedly imprisoned for his political views before he escaped to Romania and then spent the rest of his life in exile in the Soviet Union.

Nesrin Sipahi: a singer of classical Turkish music

Nihat Erim: the prime minister of Turkey for fourteen months after the 1971 coup, Erim was assassinated in Istanbul in 1980

Okey: a game similar in some ways to gin rummy, but played with tiles rather than cards

pasha: a traditional title used for Turkish military officers

The Paul Street Boys: a youth novel by Hungarian author Ferenc Molna, first published in 1906

Rambling Gardens: the shantytown on the outskirts of Ankara where Ali and his family live.

Republican People's Party: *see* CHP

"SaBuHa": a popular song and early example of "arabesque," an oriental style of music particular popular with the working classes and with the rural folk migrating to the cities; comparable in sociological terms to early American blues

sahur: the Ramadan meal eaten just before sunrise

Sakarya: a fashionable street in Ankara full of bistros and pubs

Seyyal Taner: a singer, dancer, and actress

shalvar: traditional baggy trousers generally favored by village men and women

slipper backwards on the floor: the superstitious believe it brings bad luck.

Şokella: a Turkish hazelnut chocolate spread similar to Nutella

Sugar Bairam: the festival held to mark the end of Ramadan

Sugar Feast (Eid): Secular Turks used to exchange sweets on Eid, the festival that ends Ramadan, and serve their guests liqueur, an approach similar to emphasizing Christmas trees and Easter bunnies on Christian holidays.

Tercüman: a center-right newspaper

TRT: the state-run Turkish Radio and Television, which had a monopoly on all programming until the 1990s

Turgut Özal: the undersecretary responsible for preparing the liberalization program known as the Decisions of January 24. In the first free elections held after the 1980 coup, Özal's newly founded party won a parliamentary majority. He went on to become the prime minister and then the president of Turkey.

Turgut Uyar: a "second new" movement poet

Ulduz and the Crows: see *1001 Peaches*

wafer sandwich: http://www.cizmecitime.com/content/uploads/2016/08/gofrette-sutlu.jpg

Weekend: weekly entertainment supplement

Ya Allah bismillah Allahu ekber!: *In the name of God; God is Great!*
Originally a Janissary rallying cry, was later adopted by Grey Wolves
who chant it as they prepare to attack.

Yeni Karamürsel: first Turkish department store

Zeki Müren: flamboyant singer with costumes similar to Liberace's
and a "wink-wink" approach to his sexuality